WHO MADE THE LAMB

LANAYRE LIGGERA

Who Made The Lamb

Copyright © 2024 by Lanayre Liggera. All rights reserved.

No part of this publication may be reproduced, stored in a retrieval system or transmitted in any way by any means, electronic, mechanical, photocopy, recording or otherwise without the prior permission of the author except as provided by USA copyright law. Every effort has been made to ensure that credits accurately comply with information supplied. We apologize for any inaccuracies that may have occurred and will resolve inaccurate or missing information in a subsequent reprinting of the book.

Additional Copies:

www.amazon.com
www.barnesandnoble.com

Published in the United States of America

ISBN paperback: 9781956895629

WHO MADE THE LAMB

CHAPTER 1

It was one of those beautiful sunny days everyone always remembers in the summer when the war began. Black was the fashionable color for women. Heads of state like Kaiser Wilhem of Germany were vacationing, as July lazily unrolled itself in London like a flowery carpet, while yachts tugged at their moorings on the Isle of Wight.

We were staying at Brown's Hotel, the only place for anybody that was Anybody from New York City, New York stayed, the place where Theodore Roosevelt held his wedding reception.

"Amanda, come look at this!" commanded my cousin Becky, with excitement in her voice. 'Auditions will be held today for *The Lady of High Street,* the latest production in the *oeuvr*e of the Hon. Brandon Whitefield, elder son of Rodger Viscount Stroplea and Viscountess Huldah Stroplea, at the Apollo Theatre at one o'clock this afternoon.'

"Wouldn't it be fascinating to meet such a fellow!" I knew what she meant. For the peerage, theatre was declasée.

We were traveling with our newly-widowed aunt, Becky's mother, which effectively cut her off from anything "frivolous" until the mourning period was over, which my poor cousin likened to the Second Coming.

"Anna!" she cried to my aunt's maid. "Please bring out our hats! We are going to take a walk in the park." At the last moment she charged into her mother's room to change her gloves.

We two were allowed to stroll in nearby Green Park, unaccompanied as we were, under the eye of watchman of the door at the Ritz. Our furthest border in the opposite direction was Buckingham Palace.

"I'm going to ask the doorman at the Ritz for a taxi!" she said, once we were on the pavement.

"But we haven't any money!"

"Oh, I pinched some Mum's cash drawer. I want to do Something Fun before we leave."

Becky grabbed my elbow, propelling me over to the Ritz. The doorman, an imposing figure in his top hat and uniformed tail coat, stepped into the street, whistling us up a cab.

"Drive us around the theatre district!" commanded Becky. We had never attended a theatrical production our elders had not selected as "appropriate: some Shakespear, The Passing of the Third Floor Back, Peter Pan. Now we were surrounded by marquees which our elders would have considered putting us on the 'slippery path to Hell.'

I looked very carefully out my window at the people who were walking up and down the streets of the West End. They did not look like people about to plunge through the pavement into hell, like Don Juan. Nor did I see anyone lurking about who looked like a white slave trader ready to whisk away any young woman who had succumbed to the deterioration of the female character a British drama critic named Clement Scott had declared would be the predestined fate of any woman following a career on the stage.

As a matter of fact, as we passed Aldwych, my cousin received an impression never imparted to us by our elders. We passed the Gaiety stage door with its crowd of stage door johnnies hanging around for Gaiety girls to arrive for the matinee.

"Amanda, she said turning to me seriously. "I'm beginning to wonder what is the use of being a good girl waiting for Prince Charming. They're right here, looking for a showgirl!"

I had no ready answer.

Finally the taxi pulled up at the corner of Shaftesbury Avenue and Rupert Street. There stood the Apollo, one of London's smaller 'playhouse for hearers,' pennons flying from its peak. There was no one in the box office, or in the lobby to stop us. It was a few minutes after one o'clock, so Becky opened the door to the theatre just a crack. Peaking inside, then, she gestured to me to follow, opening the door only wide enough to slip through.

In front of us, in the first row of the dress circle, which curved around the orchestra pit, we saw the backs of the group of women who had gathered for the audition. They stood out all the more sharply because, to our surprise, they were mainly wearing black, which was 'all the rage' and which stood out against the theatre, which was draped completely in white covers.

My eye lifted to the stage. It was bare except for a battered grand piano. The fire curtain had been raised. To the rear was a threadbare curtain, and ropes hanging down from somewhere on high, all of which provided a lackluster backdrop. To each side of the top of the stage were golden half-women with bare breasts. We quickly lowered our eyes!

As we stood wondering what to do, a man who had been standing near the proscenium under the shadow of the draping hanging from a box started toward us with a fast, annoyed stride. He was coming to inform us this audition was not open to the public.

"I am sorry, ladies, this is private." The man stopped in front of us, neat as a cat, with brown hair brushed back, completely dressed to the angle of handkerchief showing in his sleeve.

"But my cousin has come to try out!" Becky said quick as a flash. He looked at us with a sardonic twist of his mouth.

"Yes, indeed?" he drawled. "Then what is your name? And who has recommended you?"

As if she were Aaron to my Moses, Becky retorted, "Miss Amanda Ten Eyck from New York City, America—and Daniel Frohman recommended her." Becky drew herself up in her finest society stare. "And who are you, may I ask?"

"Gerald Murdoch, Mr. Whitefield's stage manager." He obviously didn't believe a word, but the fact Becky had cleverly picked the less well known of the Frohman brothers stopped him just long enough for the other man who'd stepped out of the shade of a box to come forward.

"Prov, she claims Daniel Frohman recommended her." Mr. Murdoch spoke as plaintively to the other man as if this were the last straw in a day which was already putting upon him.

We suspected that the way he appealed to the other man for a decision meant he was the Mr. Whitefield who had so sparked out curiosity. Then Murdoch asked my cousin, "Where Frohman does have his office?" A trick question meant to weed us out.

"The Empire, of course—but the neatest thing is he has an apartment right above the stage with a large glass window so he can watch the play while he is eating."

"Frohman has been known to pick some talent," Mr. Whitfield said.

I appreciated what I had long despised, Becky's habit of only reading the entertainment sections of the paper, as well as (surreptitiously) 'The Theatre' magazine –it was she that was making all the pieces fall together.

As he came towards us, I had thought him tall. As he came closer, I had realized I had that impression was because he was wiry. He was dark-haired, with fine pale English porcelain skin, not that brick red visage thought to be the product of the beef and claret consumed by the real men of those days, the sort in the song "The Roast Beef of Old England," described in a song my Uncle Benjamen had taught me. An angular cheek and a sharp jaw gave him a hawk like expression. He was not a handsome man nor an ugly man, yet his intensity lent him an unforgettable presence.

"Are you from America, then?" he asked us.

"We are!" Becky replied.

"I would like to hear an American sing one of my songs. Which of you would do it?"

"Oh, Mandra will!" said Becky, indicating me.

He turned to look me over. He did it in a thorough manner which was, however, professional, rather than offensive, as if I were a public package whose size, shape, and color he had a perfect right to assess. I was supposed to undergo his gaze with the same professional acceptance.

"Is that what they're wearing in New York just now?" he asked me.

"No, it's not up to the minute. We've been in Europe over a year."

"I thought it owed to Paris," he remarked, in the same business-like tone. And, as society often took its fashion cues from those it saw on its favorite actresses on the stage, and these Paris fashions often appeared in real drawing rooms, it was not a ridiculous speculation.

So he fancied himself able to detect *le doigté francais*, the French touch. I was always prickly toward Europeans who managed to intimate they were just naturally more cultured than we were. So I replied, *"Nous descendions la quelque mois plus tôt cette anneé."* Let's see if he knew I'd just told him we'd stayed in Paris for several months earlier the year.

Without turning a hair, he replied *"Paris je connais. Mais je voudrais bien savoir qu'on porte et qu'on fasse a' New York. Ça m'interesse vraiment. Je ne suis pas un des ceux qui pense que vous soyez les apaches, mademoiselle."* So he was not one of those who thought we were a bunch of apaches.

"I'm glad to hear you think we are not a nation of cowboys," I said.

"Take down their names, would you, Gerald." Becky leaned forward to help with the spelling, which, as usual was defeating this Englishman, as did anything that was not British.

We stood, looking at each other. He affected a formality of dress that set him entirely apart from the blazer, straw hat, and striped sock set. He wore a smart suit with a double breasted waistcoat, a shirt with a high, stiff collar, and an elaborate cravat secured with a moonstone tie stud. I thought it must be calculated to reflect the color of his unusual and unsettling gray eyes.

Suddenly I realized I had been looking at him too long and that this small caesura was growing awkward. I dropped my gaze to the spring of lily of the valley in his lapel. I thought he wore all of it as if it were a parody of his own real arrogance.

"I'm not an actress." I said in a low voice.

"I've gathered that, Miss Ten Eycke. Still I'd like to hear an American sing my song for me—after the auditions, if you like."

"Why?"

"Come sit down and listen—let us see if you can figure the answer for yourself!" he said, giving me a riddle of the Sphinx smile.

"Thank you! We would love to stay!" my cousin interjected. We entered the door inside the theatre, and saw the stage, with the curtain and fire curtain lifted.

He indicated we should sit at the end of the second row of petitioners seated on the aisle, behind the first row of women. One young woman who had running along a bit late, made a gesture which asked, 'could you move over one seat so I can sit down?'

Becky and I glanced around circumspectly. We were taken aback to find the women around us were dressed as well as we were, and far more up-to-date. We had never seen the theatrical advertisements which read 'dresses well on and off.'

"I think he took to you, "whispered my cousin.

"Who?" I asked with a faint flush.

"Mr. Whitefield, silly! Face it. Mandra. You draw the Serious Sort just like a magnet."

This only seemed a compliment if you did not know 'Serious' was one of the worst pejoratives in my cousin's vocabulary. It was the opposite of 'Fun.'

To her, Martin Vandemler, the man everyone always thought little Amanda would marry one day, was definitely a Serious Sort. So I realized she was a bit disappointed in this Mr. Whitefield she thought would cut such a dash. And no wonder. He spoke French. Becky found languages other than her own Boring. Despite all the efforts of our French governess, she had a minimum knowledge of that language. She wasn't exactly an Asset to my cultural campaign. Yet she wished to stay. She must have had some Fun in her little spelling interlude with Mr. Murdoch.

It was half past one, Mr. Murdoch stepped in front of us and ran through the drill. He wanted all the sheet music all back. God help the person who tried to spirit one out of the Apollo Theater. He came down the line, and the contestants drew numbers out of his hat. He did not extend it to me. No one noticed except the young woman sitting next to me.

The first young woman mounted the stage. "All right," Murdoch yelled up from the floor. "Twice through, first time a warm-up!" (This would test whether the candidates could read music). He turned around. "Put the limes down, you imbecile!" he called to the limes. "Put on the spot."

He and Mr. Whitefield stood in the aisle in the darkness slightly behind us, listening. Half way through the rendition after her warm-up, Mr. Whitefield said, just loud enough for us to hear, though the woman on state mercifully could not, "My dear Gerald, she's just frightful! Get her off the stage, that's a good chap!"

Murdoch dutifully climbed the stairs and stopped her. She handed her music back with lowered eyes which doubtless hid tears. There was a moment's embarrassed silence. Then the lights came up.

"Goodness," I breathed to the young woman next to me. "Are they always like that?"

"Oh, the fire-the-first-five, next-next-next trick?" she replied, snapping her fingers on each 'next.' "I expect you've never seen him act in quite this way before?" She deduced we were acquaintances from the fact I'd been excluded from the lottery.

"I've never met the man," I said. "We—well, we sneaked in. He's let us stay. I'm not sure why."

"Probably liked your nerve," she replied. She offered me her hand. "Felicity Westcote. Tree's academy and the Liverpool Rep. Blackmore's sent me round".

"Amanda Ten Eycke. This is my cousin, Becky."

"I think you're from the same kind of social set he is, and he wants to see how a lady sees his lady."

"It seems to have something to do with being an American," I said.

"I've no idea on that one, luv. But I will show you how to handle the business he's set out." She pulled a paper called *The Era* from her pocket book, opening it out in front of her, flipping the pages over deliberately, held it just high enough as to ostensibly read it, but it was just high enough so that the title appeared over the top of the seats and heads in front of her.

She was scanning the theatrical trade paper for news of other auditions. When the lights went on again, she whispered "You can tell me what you make of his Lady."

The next contestant was clearly nervous, she none the less passed the audition. While Mr. Murdoch was on stage talking to her. Miss Westcote asked, *sotto voce*, "Do you like the Lady?"

"Actually, I don't like her."

"Really? Why?"

"I don't suppose you've heard of Edith Wharton, the American writer?"

Miss Westcote shook her head no.

"She's from the New York social set. She's considered terrifically advanced for a woman. But all she writes about is her social set. Apparently everyone wants to know what we eat for dinner, so it's not really so advanced—it's really commercial."

"What's wrong with commercial?" And what's wrong wanting to know how the tone lives? You came out to see how we do things in the theater."

"You wouldn't feel your privacy has been violated?"

"Heavens. No. An actress hasn't got much privacy. And maybe a toff writing about the same set he belongs to is like the Wharton woman. It's madly good for sales—but that's exactly why I want this part. What do you think 'advanced' is?"

"Well, to me, advanced means doing something for a cause, selflessly, not for profit—rather like your Pankhurst sisters and the other suffragettes who are force fed—and probably not getting your name in the newspaper."

I stopped.

"What is it?" asked Miss Westcote. She could smell the wood burning.

"I was going to go on and tell you what I don't like is that the Lady wants people to find her profound and to admire her for it, and they let her think she is profound, and people let her think that because she is young, reasonably attractive, and has plenty of money," I said.

"Phew!" exclaimed Miss Westcote. "Are you saying she's the sort that talks about democracy but would take a fit if you asked her to do washing up?"

"Yes."

"I can grasp that. The other bit, about her, or yourself or whatever, you have said that she lacks conviction."

"I guess I am."

"Is *that* the same as you, or different?" she asked.

"I'm afraid my people think I've got far too much conviction. I wouldn't have a coming out because I felt it was like a cattle call—or even slavery auctions."

"There must have been a ruckus about that."

"There was."

"If you've the conviction this Wharton person is commercial, what about him?" She jerked her head toward Mr. Whitefield.

"I don't know anything about him. So I don't know why he's doing this."

"Why should that make any difference?"

"Because I don't know what his intentions are."

"You've lost me, "said Miss Westcote.

"Why does he write what he writes? To help, to hurt, to profit, to improve ...that sort of thing."

"When he first came down from Cambridge, he started out at the Court Theater with something called 'The Rites of Discount.' It set off a terrific row in the press which gave him marvelous publicity, because his father is a big banking nabob in the City. And he didn't do anything which would let you cry off thinking he was writing about his family: he called the older characters Lord and Lady Wealthy, as if he was imitating an eighteenth -century farce. But everyone felt they knew better, of course."

"It sounds almost like revenge."

"Can't say I would have done it. But he seems to live with it quite well," she said with a casual shrug

But Mr. Whitefield's uneasy turn of the head in our direction to gauge how we, his social equals, were judging his *mode d'emploi* and his behavior made me suspect it wasn't so amusing to be a maverick as Miss Westcote assumed it was.

Our conversation had been an interrupted one, punctuated by auditions. Now it was Miss Westcote's turn. She withdrew from conversation and by some intense act of inner concentration, began her transformation formula. It was fascinating. I almost could imagine a familiar spirit coming over her. The vivid, penetrating personality which had been communicating with mine disappeared entirely, as if it had died, its energy taken into Miss Westcote, where it was becoming some new entity like a naked newborn babe, but which would soon burst its chrysalis and in a blur of foreshortened maturation appear full grown.

I awaited the metamorphous with interest and an eerie discomfort. Whatever would come forth, would in some way reflect me back onto myself, for she was good, and I knew it, though I didn't know exactly how.

"Break a leg," Becky hissed. She'd read it was the thing one said in the theater. I doubt Miss Westcote even heard her. She stood up and moved out into the aisle. As she moved toward the stage, I watched her spine take on the carriage of a young woman who was told at every turn, 'sit up straight, dear' and whose posture was later emphasized by being laced up in a contraption with stays that would stick her should she slump even slightly. She moved in a languid, unhurried way which proclaimed that neither work nor life had any vulgar claims upon her time: life would not rush her. There were people who took care of such things. How amazing she could catch the entire being of a young woman born to carriages at eleven and become her within a few moments.

Messrs. Murdoch and Whitefield were standing to either side of the stairs to the stage. I watched them each take an inadvertent step backward to acknowledge the coming Lady, who, like the Queen, must not be touched. With the genius of inspiration, Miss Westcote extended her hand weakly, limply, to be taken care of by a gentleman, to Mr. Murdoch, who instantly bent over it. It was a daring gesture although she did not quite dare to extend it to Mr. Whitefield.

Mr. Murdoch introduced her to the accompanist. Her face had sharp planes which took the spotlight well, and which I thought was indelible, yet somehow her face softened into a plump complacence which had never had to yield to the common need to create attraction with the help of paint and powder. She sang the first lines. Immediately we leaned forward. We were aware we were listening to what critics call 'a consummate musical instrument.' It was a soaring soprano which lofted right of to the ceiling with deceptive delicacy, for when its force hit the back wall it was like a home run by the New York Highlanders.

When she finished there was one of those little silences that indicate that the listeners are slightly stunned. We had heard something head and shoulders above anything we had expected. Then Messrs .Murdoch and Whitefield crowded up, wanting to make sure Miss Westcote would read the next day: clearly, they didn't wish to lose her.

"Oh, we must congratulate her!" I said aloud. I jabbed Becky in the ribs then I stood up. I didn't tell her I was feeling panicky and I was maneuvering to make a run for it.

In the lobby, Miss Westcote was drawing on her gloves. "Thanks so much," she said when we told her she was marvelous. I could see she had grown used to such glowing reactions to her talent and had become professional about it. "Awfully nice to meet you both—I'm sorry, I must run off. I'm playing in a one-act opener in Islington and I'll just make it!" She shot out the door, leaving us staring at the wake of a tornado.

Before I had a chance to say anything to Becky, the door from the auditorium shot open. Mr. Whitefield came through, grey eyes blazing, and blocked our path. "Come now Miss Ten Eycke, I hope you are not running out on your word?" The words were controlled. The anger underneath them was not.

"Oh, Mr. Whitefield , I'm ashamed to sing after hearing that," I blurted out.

All the angles of his face were drawn hard as if the skeleton might pop through. His fingers tightened into a fist around his fountain pen. At my confession, his face relaxed. I saw that the maverick had felt we might be taking our sport with him, with no compunction for his sensibilities, which deserved no consideration because he had betrayed our class. I was shocked. I realized I'd almost inflicted real emotion damage on a fellow-human being who'd taken the chance of believing my sincerity.

"I shall take that as a commentary on Miss Westcote's talent, which appears to have scared you off. But why should you be ashamed? You made it clear you were not a professional."

"I know. But—then I think something's off with the rhythm."

"Yes, it is and its name is Harry Cockburn."

"Then why let him play?"

"He comes with the theatre."

"What is it supposed to be like, then?"

He handed me a music sheet which I scanned. "It's the same timing as *Alexander's Ragtime Band.* I was wondering if an American could hear it," he said.

"But how can I sing it if he's murdering it?"

"It will be an interesting set-to," he said with a smile. He caught the change of my expression as I discovered he liked the music of my homeland and I was surprised he knew such a popular melody.

"What's happened to the audition?" Becky asked demanded nervously, as she sensed a pull between us.

"It will wait on me. That is one of the few advantages of being what you Americans call 'the boss.'"

We followed him back inside. The last audition had finished.

As she handed her sheet music back to Mr. Murdoch, Mr. Whitefield stepped over and offered me his arm. I took it. My knees were shaking.

The accompanist gave me an unfriendly smile, baring the gap in his tobacco-stained teeth. "I don't think you have quite got the rhythm, Mr. Cockburn," I said.

"For Heaven's sake, I'll play for her, Cockburn."

"It's in me contract to play for each and every."

Suddenly I felt my Uncle Ben's presence, right on cue.

Cockburn seemed to take a brutish pleasure in thwarting Mr. Whitefield.

"I don't—" Mr. Whitefield began to say.

"It's all right," I repeated. I let go of his arm uncurling the fingers of my left hand, which I automatically always kept hidden because the tips were calloused from playing the violin. My mother had always groaned that her brother-in-law had caused me to ruin my hands. In those days, it was a Problem.

I reached up. Slowly, very deliberately I removed the long hat pin from my Watteau hat. I took the hat off, and set it close to the piano lid. Then I placed the hat pin beside it.Mr. Cockburn stirred uneasily on the bench. He couldn't make me out. He couldn't rule out the possibility I was a madwoman of sufficient temper to run him through. I had absolutely no objection to his wondering about it.

Beside me someone—was it Uncle Ben or Mr. Whitefield? gave an inward laugh. Mr. Cockburn bent to his task, first giving me one last distrustful glance. He played the introductory bars with the loud pedal fully depressed, giving notice that whatever might come to him, he would play as he had always played, the way it was always played for King and Empire. "Oh, Lord make speed to save us," I muttered. I always prayed the Psalms when I was in a jam.

I came in on my own beat, keeping time with my foot. We proceeded along, the discrepancy obvious, like the one blind man trying to get the other one out of a ditch.

Then, as I sang, beyond the almost perceptible aura of my uncle's presence, I sensed another presence in the rim of the spotlight, calling to me. My inner spirit went to him and was filled instantly with the insight I was living out a great part of my life in these few moments. Then all the presences faded. Mr. Whitefield stared, as it was not usual for an auditioner to have her mind illumined on stage.

Cockburn slammed the lid shut, making me jump. "See Mr. Murdoch for your cheque," said Mr. Whitefield. This was said brusquely. Harry slouched away.

"Have a go at it with me, Miss Ten Eycke." He sat down at the piano bench. He leaned over the keys with the slightly restrained movements of a man in bespoke English tailoring would make, for it was cut high in the arm hole. He played in a flowing pleasing fashion, almost catching the emphasis of the syncopation.

"How is it?" he asked, having finished a run through for me.

"Dangerously close."

"Dangerously close indeed," he said softly, his eyes catching mine again. I became weak in the knees again, but for a different reason. Remember, I told myself, the most foolish illusion for a young woman is that of love at first sight. It's different for men! There is no drawback to them creating the illusion they are smitten.

"I am in your debt," he said, sure of my attention. "I have never known anyone to put the wind up Harry Cockburn. I don't know whether to kiss you, or hire you to conduct my orchestra!"

From this remark I had no doubt of his admiration, which was far too strong for my tastes and mores.

I said, "I am sure Mr. Whitefield, that the notion of kissing anyone you have just met could occur only in a realm like the theater."

"Ah," he said, and took my hint. His tone grew more formal. "Shall we try it together, Miss Ten Eycke?" He played the introduction then I began the lyrics.

'I'm tired of curtseying, curtseying , curtseying curtseying to God and King/

And society is just a silly thing that bores me,/

France had Madame Guillote and Americans are keen,/

On democratic vistas,/

but for me,/

The gown by Worth that I'm entitled to by birth/

I'd like to say, *je m'en fichce* à,

But I sit and I repine 'cause I must invite to dine/,
Some vestigial earl or viscount,/
Whose virtue is he can recount his lineage,
All the way to Domesday/
Oh, *J'en suis tout si fatigue!*

Chorus
'I'd love a love that's free/
Of this dread hypocrisy/
But I'll be,/
Wed not to a man but a whole damn social plan/
Society's proprieties agreed on/
Voudrais dire a tout va-t-en! (I'd like to say just go away)

I'd been listening to the score for a while, and felt the weak point was the line society's proprieties agreed on: so I had elided the first two words with a Z sound between them.

"Jolly good!" he said.

But I'd only dealt a momentary cease-fire to the lurking intimacy hovering between us, ready to pull us together the moment my guard was let down. Music can't be brushed away the way words can. It penetrates far deeper inside one's being. Here I was, singing Mr. Whitefield's melody and lyrics, accompanied by him. It created a strong emanation of his being which seemed to rush through mine like the wind, carrying my voice along out of myself, and merged into the empty void in front of us. When I sang, "I'd love a love that's free of this dread hypocrisy," I might have blushed just a bit—it certainly didn't match my upbringing.—

Mr. Whitefield gave me a most encouraging smile—the rat!

For an instant we were both embarrassed, not sure if I was seconding the execution of dread hypocrisy, or trying to exorcise the pull between us, and what note to strike as we emerged from our cloud of Togetherness overshadowed by unseen wings.

"Mandra!" Becky cried, fortunately intervening again. "Come on! Look at the time! We're already late!"

"Oh, drat," I exclaimed. I grabbed my hat and hatpin in a panic and in my haste, and managed to prick my scalp on the first try.

"Are you all right?"

"Oh—my aunt doesn't know we've gone out further than we are supposed to be!" No further explanation was necessary. He knew the restrictive world of young women like us.

"Let me help you down!" The spot had just been turned off and the house lights came up. He was anxious that my eyes had not yet refocused and I might make a misstep on the stairs. He jumped in front of me. I stopped. He went down a few stairs, and reached his arm up. I took his hand. He brought me down.

Disconcerted by the warm clasp of his hand, I made the archetypal gesture of a woman in a long skirt, raising it slightly so I wouldn't slip. I did not catch my petticoat up with it. As Mr. Whitefield reached floor level he turned sideways and saw the host of animals I'd embroidered on my lingerie brushed by him at eye level.

"What's this—a trip to the zoo?"

"It's a design after Hicks called the peaceful kingdom." I saw his knowledge of our culture did not extend that far, however. I'd come down to the floor but he was still holding my hand.

"Won't you come for the readings tomorrow and see if your Miss Westcote gets the part?"

"Oh—I don't think we could get away again after this!" His face fell. Had I given him the impression I did not want to see him? Then I added, "But then...one never knows about tomorrows, does one?"

"No, one doesn't." Still he held my hand. "I've an idea. If you cannot attend us, let me send my script round. I'd value your assessment—you are very clever. Where are you stopping?"

"Amanda, hurry up!" called Becky, scooping up our parasols and dusters. Should I give my address...there wasn't time to figure it out.

"We're at Brown's," I blurted in a whisper.

"Fancy that! You're just the other side of the Academy of Art from my flat at the Albany. I could drive you—it would be faster—"

"No, you couldn't." He knew full well the trouble it would cause were we to arrive at our hotel in motorcar driven by a strange man.

"I shall flag you a cab, then."

For the last time we followed him up the aisle of the theater on that memorable afternoon.

CHAPTER 2

"I don't know what got into you. We were about to call Scotland Yard."

If only our cab could have rocketed back to Brown's like Elijah's chariot carrying him to Heaven. But after crawling through the early evening traffic we arrived at our hotel to find my aunt, and the concierge, anxiously huddled in the lobby.

My aunt shot me a Dirty Look. Whatever the situation was her daughter, Rebecca, could not have done it. The story was forced out of us in front of everyone: the point was made we were not to go anywhere without a chaperone until the year 2000. Then we were marched upstairs to our suite.

"It was my idea!" Becky exclaimed rebelliously, not shrinking from the role of fallen angel, one to which, I suspected, her mother had assigned to her on this occasion. But I was different. I had never given her a moment's doubt of my predestined election. I was a model of biddable outward behavior. If I had stumbled, we both knew she should administer punishment as hard as she could, lest I stumble and go on something worse.

My aunt had fallen silent. She was swinging her folded lorgnette, which was suspended by a chain around her neck back and forth with her index finger. That was always a bad sign.

She believed in election. I believed in election. We were Dutch Reformed. An act like this shook my aunt's conviction about my possible salvation. My outward evidence of good behavior had always been taken as equal to the fear of the Lord. Any indication someone might have stumbled and fallen from one's predestined path to Heaven was The Fearful Thing in our lexicon. She was searching for a penance so indelible it would leave a permanent mark on my soul.

"We will return to this theatre tomorrow and apologize to them for inconveniencing them." she commanded. "We will express our remorse for having disturbed them." In other words, we would return to the scene of the crime to underline its unsuitability.

Why not Becky?

She's given up on her. We my foot. I will have to parrot my designated lines. It would be me who would appear before Mr. Whitefield as an errant child, and have the humiliation of watching the delicate web of feeling between us torn to shreds. I didn't sleep all night.

Next morning I could not eat a bite. I sipped tea and endured admonitions of setting forth for the day on an empty stomach. Becky, elated by this so-called penance which to her was another adventure, put away a breakfast worthy of an athlete. With the aura of a headache coming on, I endured being goaded without reply. It would only be construed as 'sassing' Aunt Bea.

I sat before the mirror, watching Anna yank my hair into place. The pulling on my scalp made me paler still. "Please don't pull so hard!" I asked.

"It won't stay otherwise. Pinch your cheeks: you haven't got a drop of color."

As we stood on the curb, waiting for the doorman to call for the automobile and driver Aunt Bea used in town, my aunt was resplendent, almost imperial, in a white suit with a long jacket, a white blouse with a high lace collar which covered her aging neck, a pearl choker and several strand of pearls, not to mention most of the items of her daytime jewelry. Lest it was not perfectly obvious from her outfit Mr. Whitefield and company they were dealing with Somebody, her head was crowned by a gigantic feathered mythic bird, whose feathers had not been curled and tightened in the last few weeks and which waved madly. I thought if we were in America, we would have been accosted by the Audubon Society.

It was only when we pulled up in front of the Apollo and spotted Mr. Murdoch lounging on the steps, smoking a cigarette, that Becky came to life and shot forward on her seat, calling a "Hulloo!" despite her mother's slap on the wrist, which she didn't even notice.

Mr. Murdoch leapt down and opened the door for us. Becky chatted with him animatedly while my aunt had to occupy herself with arranging her exit from the car and placing her hat on, which had been too large to wear in the back seat.

Once on the sidewalk, she swung around, ready to confront this bold young person to whom she had not even been Presented.

"Mummy, this is Mr. Murdoch. Mr. Murdoch, this is Mrs. Ten Eycke, my mother."

"Charmed!" he said with a peppy bow.

Aunt Bea nodded her head to Mr. Murdoch which meant she had not met someone in a standard way: my aunt had been introduced but not Presented, which would have meant an introduction by an intermediary of our social class. Everything was obvious about our background as my aunt inclined her head to indicate he was not as yet of any particular consequence in her constellation. She asked him to take us to Mr. Whitefield.

Mr. Murdoch surveyed the phalanx of respectability drawn up in front of him with a smile. "Follow me," he said.

We walked up the aisle single file and through a pass door into the gritty passageway backstage through which everything channeled onto the magic circle onstage. In the half-light ropes reached up to nowhere and the impedimenta used for 'noises off' were to one side. Becky impulsively seized a padded hammer and hit a cymbal used to simulate rolling thunder. It was the precise translation of the pathetic fallacy. The storm within my breast had been echoed by an instrument of artificial nature.

"Deuce take it! Cut that out!" cried a voice behind the door of the star dressing room (which was always at stage level though I didn't know that then). The voice was Mr. Whitefield's.

"Ladies to see you, Prov," said Mr. Murdoch loudly.

The door opened Mr. Whitefield stood there looking us over. My aunt returned his quizzing-glass stare with her own. I myself was shocked by his appearance from the day before. He wore slightly dirty white flannels, a pullover jumper (sweater) a soft-collared shirt and a knitted tie jerked open at the neck. A smudge of something oily and black clung to his left temple. His hair was windblown and uncombed. He was holding a half-eaten sandwich and he hastily swallowed what he had been chewing. I noticed an odd odor hanging about his clothes I would come to learn it was castor oil.

"I rang your man," said Mr. Murdoch. "He's en route."

"Beg pardon. I took my aeroplane out from Hendon this morning and broke a piston rod, and hadn't time after arranging for repairs to pass by my flat for a change and wash-up."

"My daughter, Rebecca," my aunt said. "and my niece Amanda. We have come to apologize for disturbing you yesterday. My card."

Mr. Whitefield took the proffered wedge of paper and pondered it momentarily. I waited for her to start our apology. However, my aunt's careful plan was immediately thrown considerably into disarray when he spoke first, asking, "You are not by chance connected to the banking house near Baring & Co. on Wall Street?" I knew he knew darned well he knew we were—he had investigated us!

Startled, my aunt blurted, "What would you know about that, young man?"

"Only that my father, Rodger, Viscount Stroplea, has had Ten Eycke endorse bills for him in America."

"Good Heavens!' my aunt answered in raised tones. Becky and I immediately realized the signs she was now aware she was speaking to a representative of a Big Fish who dealt in large transactions. The realization she was unexpectedly dealing with someone of Consequence had apparently shocked my aunt as if a comet had burst into her universe from another galaxy.

"Why don't you come in." Aunt Bea stood uncertainly in the doorway with Becky and I each peering over one of her shoulders, the pressure of our curiosity almost pushing her forward. We breathed in the scent of grease paint and sweaty costumes in the room, and stared at the dressing table with its mirror set with lights enough to show up the slightest flaw in makeup.

Meanwhile, Mr. Whitefield had turned and plunged behind a screen and brought out three stage gilt thrones for us. Finally, my aunt gave in to the inevitable and settled herself in a chair, fussing with her gloves, purse, and umbrella like a dog licking itself, which was her way of Giving One Time to Think. She needed a hiatus to figure out how to behave. The famous Ten Eycke Family Dictum for unpleasant interviews, i.e., Get In, Get It Done, and Get Out, would obviously no longer Do. She had a Situation on her hands.

Meanwhile, Mr. Whitefield shot me a strange half-smile. Suddenly my headache lifted. Fascinated, I noticed the eerie quality of those gray eyes of his I'd only partially noticed yesterday. They were cloud-like. They were fixed at once and the same time on you, and on someplace far off beyond the horizon that you could not see. As I watched the two perspectives came together like a range finder on a camera.

I knew somehow he wasn't like this with most people, because the new focus shut us both inside a door like a door that had been closed behind us.

"I was afraid you might think our errand peculiar," quoth my aunt. "However I have confidence that a son of Viscount Stroplea will understand how imperative it is for certain standards of behavior to be maintained."

"Indeed I do, Madame," he said with such a smooth politeness she shifted uncomfortably in her seat. "However, if your niece apologizes, the standards you have just invoked would make such an apology impossible."

"I beg pardon!"

"I think your standards do not encourage you to offer insult. If your niece apologizes it implies my occupation is such, a young woman is sullied by simple exposure to it. By extension it calls my character, breeding, and morals into question. I hardly think you would wish to offer such an affront to a member of the Whitefield family."

My aunt grew slightly pale. Behind her back Becky and I exchanged incredulously triumphant glances, as if our horse had come from behind to win the Derby.

"I think our two countries think differently about the theatre, young man, if you will accept that as an apology." My aunt's expression that our two countries must also think very differently about Speaking Up to One's Elders played across her face.

"You need not make it a matter of nations, Madame. We have our Purity crusaders and disapproving non -conformists here, too. In fact, I am descended from a family which contained a reformer who preached a crusade against the theater."

"Good Lord!" my aunt said, the light dawning.

"Not George Whitefield," I said.

"You are familiar with him?" he asked us all.

"He's like Jesus Christ in our house!" Becky burst out.

"Do I take it you have no respect for him?"

"Because of my occupation? Hardly, Madame. Whitefield lived in a very different, very decadent age of the theater. And all sorts have expropriated George into their works—Milton, Blake, now Shaw. I confess I thought someone in the line should have a crack at him rather than leaving him to Milton, Swedenborg, or Don Juan and the devil."

"You refer to Shaw's *Man and Superman?*"

"Have you seen it?"

"I have not! Nor is it appropriate reading for my daughter."

"I see," he said.

"I found no mention of George Whitefield in it," she replied.

"No, it is Miss *Ann* Whitefield who is the high priestess of the life force John Tanner preaches but, in the end, does not practice. I have it on authority of a friend that in the early drafts Shaw called Tanner's parents Mr. and Mrs. George Whitefield Tennario, to indicate they are founders of a new religion called 'the life force.'"

"Good Heavens! I was not aware he planned to give such calculated offense!"

"One must always consider whether or not one is being manipulated by calculated offense," said Mr. Whitefield. "I am not sure he means to do that at all. My friend in fact contends that Shaw is not the great radical he is set out to be, but, as a dramatist, presents a seemingly radical person with seemingly radical ideas, who, however, succeeds, in the plot, at play's end, in returning back to that comfortable value, the world of the English drawing room. In other words, he sends his audience home: they have been forward enough to hear the new and advanced ideas they may have heard of, but in the end, everyone one is brought round to the status quo: it is a very, very clever formula."

"Why—I believe you are right, young man! Should you give out trade secrets just like that?" Aunt Bea said with a smile and a snap of her fingers. "Do you intend to manipulate your audience, young man?" my aunt asked in a flash. Mr. Whitefield's face said 'oho'! He had spotted my aunt's predilection for intellectual conversation. Conversation—not music. That was Uncle Ben's purview.

"I operate within the current mores, Madame, which include our up-and- coming suffragists, and those who are would-be suffragists."

My aunt leaned forward, both hands on the top of the handle of her umbrella. "Then you must have a singularly clear conscience?"

"An interesting reply, Madam, and I suspect it says more about you than about me." My aunt flushed.

"I beg pardon?

"I only elicit that because you will read things you will not go to see, Madame. Is that not only exhibiting half- a-conscience?"

"Not exactly, my dear sir. One reads to see what is fit for our younger people as part of one's duty. We read a great deal aloud at home. Provincial stuff next to your tastes, I am sure." She smiled, and added, "my niece took her nickname Mandra from the exception she took to Donne's assertion there is a woman nowhere true— "

"Or fair!" he finished. "Hardly provincial, as I am sure you are aware. Donne was scarcely read before your countryman Mr. Eliot brought him back to public attention."

"You are familiar with his work?"

"Both the sermons and the poems, Madame. He was my tutorial at Cambridge."

There was a tap at the door. "Yes," Mr. Whitefield called. Entered what could only could be called a gentleman's gentleman, with a small luggage case.

Mr. Whitefield consulted his wrist watch. My aunt frowned. In her lexicon, a man among Men should have kept his watch in his waistcoat pocket.

"Dash it all, Briggs, you're late! Have I any oil on my face?" His man nodded and took out a handerkerchief. Mr. Whitefield was a head taller than Briggs, so he bent forward slightly so his man could wipe the dark spot near his temple. There was another tap at the door, and Mr. Murdoch stepped inside without a by-your-leave. "We've got all our auditioners here, Prov." He had a bunch of sides in the crook of his arm.

"Give one to Mrs. Ten Eycke," he said, as his man handed him a comb. He had his back half to us as he bent toward the dressing room mirror to run it through his hair.

"Whatever is this for?"

"I would like to invite you all to be our guests for the audition, Madame, especially after our little talk about Shaw. I was up all night making revisions and I should be most grateful for your opinions. I thought the lady actually wanted to change her life. But I have realized yesterday she only thinks she wants to change her life—she would have to change her opinion if she encountered any consequence of her ideology. Am I right?" He asked me directly.

"That is my impression," I said. "Change involves sacrifice."

"You do not conceive her as evil, do you?"

"Oh, no. She need not be that—all she needs if the ordinary dose of human nature."

"Original sin."

He sounded sure of himself, but we could see his reflection in the mirror, while my aunt could not. His reflection shot an imploring look back to us as if to say, 'could you do something?'

Becky was always quicker than I and she burst out, "Oh, Mama, let us stay. We have no engagements today!" It was a brilliant maneuver. To cry off an invitation with no excuse would have had no possible social interpretation but cutting a proffered acquaintance. It was not Done in these circumstances: so my aunt asked if she might quickly vet the script.

"Please do, Madame, that is why I have secured one for you. I thought the Lady I had drawn really wanted to change, until yesterday when I saw your niece trying to get inside the Lady's character." He turned to me with the full force of his gray eyes, his energetic personality. "Then I observed that you feel she only thinks she wants to change—am I right?"

"Yes," I said faintly.

"I know you gave Miss Westcote the benefit of your observations— would you share them with me?"

"All I said was that the Lady was in such a position in society she is always indulged because she is rich and pretty so she never had to really think about what she thinks, so she assumes she really thinks what she thinks."

"Do you like Miss Westcote?"

"She does have a wonderful voice, but I haven't seen her act. I don't know how well she takes direction, or whether she can make constructive suggestions. This means she doesn't put them in the form of a tantrum telling me I am an idiot."

"Do they do that?" I asked incredulously.

"Despite my exalted social status? Indeed they do. I started a new song very much along those lines," he said to me. "I'd like to see what your niece makes of it."

"Prov," asked Mr. Murdoch, "what dialogue do you want to use for this?"

"The sunflower business. You take Charlie, will you?" Seeing the object of his ministrations standing still, Briggs stepped over and skillfully wiggled the knot of his necktie back up into the correct position.

"If you'd take off your jumper (sweater) and put on this suit jacket, it would be an improvement, sir," said his man.

Mr. Murdoch began to speed read the improvisation. "I don't see it," he said.

"Try it. I can always go back through and change it." Whatever this meant, they understood one another perfectly. I felt jealous of Mr. Murdoch's presence in the creative process.

By now, my aunt had succumbed to that curious sense of involvement emitted from being included in the magic circle. She was coming to feel herself part of the company even as we had done the day before, however impolitic it may have been.

"Well," Mr. Whitefield said, to Murdoch, raising his right hand and crossing his index and middle finger in some obvious ritual. "Here we go." Murdoch made the gesture back at him. "Ladies!" he said, and bowed us out the door into the passageway.

We trouped hurriedly along, Murdoch in the lead, Mr. Whitefield just behind me, my vigilant aunt in position between Becky and me. I felt his hand on my elbow stopping me just a minute. "Mandra who things invisible does see—would you tell me exactly why you came yesterday?"

Of course it was very risqué that he not only used my Christian name, but my nickname!

"From what I thought the Lady felt at first —a sense of limitation."

"Thank you."

Still holding my arm he bent closer. Frightened at his intensity, I wrenched away blurting, "Mustn't you get the auditioned started?"

I was stunned by how forward he was, given the mores of the day. But then, Mr. Whitefield knew things that I didn't.

He bowed me through the pass door to a seat on the dress circle. I saw Miss Westcote in the same seat as the day before, nervously describing circles with the toe of her foot. She jumped up and gave me her hand, exclaiming "Ever so!" Mr. Murdoch handed her a script and I sat down with my aunt and cousin with some relief.

Next to me, my aunt was holding the script out in front of her with one hand, and her lorgnette to her eyes with her other hand. I leaned over and began to read it also, as well as I could; I discovered that the Lady's ideological efforts were directed toward Yarrell (Charlie) Harris, a wet-behind-the-ears, newly-minted university graduate just arrived in London aspiring to be a knute of the first order. He is transfixed by the Lady and installs her as his mentor. She mildly mocks his desire to have her amend his undergraduate views of life by implying that, as a woman with a lack of education imposed on her, she could not possibly be his teacher. In the speech Mr. Whitefield had indicated the auditioners to read, she is berating Charlie for having asked her about aesthetic theory.

"I am not a sunflower, Mr. Harris! Nor have I ever worshipped one, nor burned incense, nor sat beside the Cherwell, as you have, to imbibe the pearls of Mr. Walter Pater. I have never burnt with a hard, gemlike flame. These experiences are all denied to the members of my sex. So how can I in any way be considered to hold a valuable aesthetic opinion?"

"Blimey!' I heard Miss Westcote mutter under her breath. She was finding it heavy going. I sensed she was not so confident of her acting abilities as she was of her own musical genius. She knew she was close to her big break. She didn't want to wreck it.

Just then, Mr. Whitefield stood next to me (my seat was the one on the edge of the aisle, courtesy the activity of my cousin, who had jumped into a seat furthest in so Aunt Bea would be between us).) He asked, "What do you think?"

"It sounds like a practiced sophistry. I think she's used it before. It sounds almost"— I said and stopped. I think he knew that my last word would have been 'autobiographical'.

"You do see things invisible."

Suddenly I was aware of Miss Westcote, in front of us, catching our dialogue, and it had given her some good direction. She half turned and flashed me a smile.

"Miss Westcote." She had been last yesterday but was first today. She got up, and mounted the stairs. As she walked toward him, she tripped slightly and we all heard her mutter, "Blast." She had torn her hem.

"I've got some pins," I said, standing up.

"Amanda, dear, you are not a lady's maid." My aunt was snapping at me, holding my wrist.

"But I *can* sew." She withdrew her hand.

On the proscenium, I knelt at her feet. Opening my purse, I lunged for the pincushion with several threaded needles stuck in it which I always carried so I could embroider if I had time on my hands.

"This isn't the strongest thread," I told her." It's for embroidery, but it will hold for a while."

It was only because I had knelt at her feet that I became aware that her knees were trembling slightly.

Mr. Whitefield came over and helped me up, and did not waste time—he asked my aunt if I could play the melody line, and before she could reply, he handed me a piece of tattered paper on which a melody line and chords were marked. "Can you make it out?" he asked me. From my singing yesterday, he had deduced that I knew music.

"I've got no pianist today," he said to my aunt. "If your niece can oblige with just a simple melody, you shall hear the whole of last night's labors." Despite her appearance, Aunt Bea had a weakness for intellectual curiosity—or she would not have been reading John Donne.

"Stand here," said Mr. Whitefield to Miss Westcote, placing her behind me. "Let her play the tune. Here's a copy of the lyrics." Miss Westcote took it dumbly. I could hear her exhale as she read it.

Being nearsighted, I bent toward to read his tiny scrawl. The melody was in three quarter time, and was exquisitely simple. I played it over once: the next time I added the chords. Next time I played it, I heard Miss Westcote try the words from behind me.

Pretending that you love me, pretending that you'll always be
Faithful and true, no matter what I do,

Has let me see you're pretending
That you're the girl for me,
I've pretended you could be
But your love is not for me
But for some other self you see
As loving you....

I looked up at Mr. Whitefield, who was listening carefully. It was useless to try to fight the flow of dialogue which passed wordlessly between us.

"Let's have you try it. Have you got it, Gerald? (For it was Gerald playing the part of Charlie). "Try coming up from left rear," he said to Miss Westcote. "Step by step, pausing when you hear him singing."

"I can't walk so slowly on a bare stage without something to fix my eyes on," she said apologetically. Gerald placed a chair on stage.

"Gerald..." he pointed right front. "Try it from there."

"Deuce take it, Prov, I can't just come out with something like that."

"I expect some temperament from my actors, but not my stage manager." Gerald paled slightly.

"Sorry," said Gerald, and moved upstage right.

. "Now, Miss Westcote, you are overhearing him along with the audience, with this difference: you are the object of his words. They will be watching for your reaction, save your part must be mimetic, telling her her spell is at an end."

"Am I sorry my efforts have come to an end, or sorry I've lost Charlie?"

"You think it must be one or the other, not both?"

"I—I may be wrong, but I think she is too singular to feel both at the same time."

That scored a point, I thought.

"Very good, that's how I wrote her." Miss Westcote immediately brightened up." He rocked back on one foot, lost in thought. "Come forward toward him on the diagonal and stop center to take in what you are hearing."

"Could you give me a mark?" Murdoch pulled piece of chalk out of his pocket and moved around center stage. "There," said Mr. Whitefield, and Gerald marked the spot with a X.

"Ready?" he asked. "Ready?" he asked me. I nervously attacked the first notes into a waiting space. Mr. Murdoch came in a bit late and caught up. Miss Westcote started briskly toward him, late for an appointed meeting. She stopped as she heard him. She registered shock. Then, in a bold stroke, she indicated by a vicious shake of her umbrella the annoyance of a cat who sees its prey elude it. Then, she turned on her heel. Let the ingrate wonder what had happened to her!

"Now let me hear the sunflower dialogue." Holding the script in her hand, when she got to the last lines about having no aesthetic opinion worth the name, she put the script down on the piano, and brought her palms together in front of her lower face in a gesture of mock Oriental wisdom.

"Very Zuleika, very nice." The rest of the auditioners read the dialogue. As the auditions went on, Murdoch took them over more and more, as more and more he became familiar with the routine.

"What did you think of Miss Westcote's improvisation?"

"She cut him dead, just as any lady would have the right to do." As he looked down, I could see the nervousness in his eyes. He might be a peer's son, but this was his first crack at the West End, and he had to make a decision. The fact he'd been up all night was beginning to show. He asked Briggs to bring him a cup of tea, and "pour in the sugar." Would you stop Miss Westcote for me?" he asked, *sotto voce*. But then, he called on one of the auditioners. I was deeply disappointed. Had he decided not to use Miss Westcote? He threw me a brief smile.

Instantly the disappointment that had seized me lifted. He was only being tactful. He had decided: the aspirants would get courteous rejections. I shot up the aisle, calling her name. "I didn't want you to leave without having an opportunity to say goodbye." Then I whispered, "He's asked you to wait." Her face lit up.

As soon as the front doors had closed Murdoch opened the stage door. There was a commotion as a straggle of men burdened with cameras, tripods and photographic plates with flash powder platforms struggled in. I saw Becky turn in her chair and bounce with excitement. Then my aunt called, "Amanda, come here at once!" Only then was I conscious I'd been operating for the last half hour at least without any concern for what she might be thinking, or even that she existed, for the first time in my life.

Mr. Whitefield swung around toward me and put a hand to his brow in a short gesture of distress. All had been going so smoothly, our world melting imperceptibly in his, he'd forgotten the dictums of our world completely. One of the foremost caveats was: a lady only appears in the papers four times in her life, birth, coming out, marriage and death. My aunt was already picking up her umbrella and putting on her gloves. She wasn't taking any chances.

"Gentlemen!" said Mr. Whitefield, springing forward to shield my scurry for my seat in the dress circle. "I would like you to meet the actress I've selected for the lead role in The Lady of High Street, Miss Felicity Westcote."

The reporters lined up like a bunch of greedy sharks.

"How is it you haven't used Lillah Compton? Wasn't she available?" asked one reporter with an emphasis on the name I didn't understand.

"Neither. I thought she was unsuitable for the part." His interlocutor nudged his elbow into the next reporter and snickered.

"And who have we here?" another reporter asked. Turning toward me, he answered "Some ladies of my acquaintance," he said, stressing we were not members of the theatrical profession.

"Oo, ladies, 'ave we?" Before anyone could stop him he walked over to us, opened his notebook and asked Becky, "Oo are you, darlin' and where do you come from?"

"Rebecca!" said my aunt, seizing her arm.

"How about a photograph? "Another reporter asked. Fortunately a photograph was still a complicated affair and one which required the subject's cooperation.

"I should say Not!' said my aunt, and opened her umbrella in front of her as if to shoo away a recalcitrant bird or insect. "Get your things! "She snapped.

Murdoch was on the reporter the next instant. "Take your photographs of our ingénue, and leave these ladies be, or I'll throw you out of the theater."

"Oo, don't get your dander up." answered the reporter. "Don't blame me for trying to do my job." Truth told, no matter what Mr. Murdoch could have done—or did do—this was a tidbit of human interest, even without names or pictures.

"Gentlemen, gentlemen. Take your pictures of Miss Westcote and take down her story and my production schedule." He pointed toward the private box door to the street with just a click of his index finger, but Mr. Murdoch got the cue. "Follow me, "he said.

"So sorry!" Mr. Whitefield said

"Please quench this story or I will have to swim back to America," I concluded.

CHAPTER 3

It was Early Morning. This meant that Aunt Bea was still asleep with a silk mask over her eyes, and that Anna had tiptoed into her bedroom to close her window (Aunt Bea always demanded in a very aggrieved voice, that one thing she would quiz of God should she get to Heaven was why He made birds go Cheep so early in the morning). Aunt Bea also complained about motor car 'hooting' at night, too, but then so did everyone else in London.

Becky was still getting her beauty sleep, so I got into my clothes as silently as possible, with Anna lacing me up, and I, the Early Riser, walked in my stocking feet to the door of our suite. Anna handed me my shoes and my violin.

Brown's was a classy hotel in a country dedicated to preserve eccentricity, so my request to practice my music in the ladies' retiring room below the ground floor had been indulged, provided I use a mute. I paced up and down between two lines of washing basins as that way, there was more room for bowing. I was right in the middle of a soulful version of "Aura Lee" when a chamber maid popped in, saying, "Something for you, Miss!" holding a package. I dropped the expensive bow Uncle Ben had bought for me so hurriedly into the case that he would have cringed.

My dear Miss Ten Eycke, I promised you a script and here it is. Don't feel you need to be restricted to the drama, I would welcome your comments on anything. I can be reached via these channels as well as at the Albany—(here he listed his clubs—Royal Aero, Green Room, Athenaeum and his R.T.A, Registered telegraphic address—Whitsend, London). *I also include a Paris address, as most unfortunately from my point of view I am off for Paris Saturday to attend a portion of the Caillaux trial, which involves—how to put it delicately—two people who were keeping company with each other, despite the fact they were both were married to someone else, which has proved a temptation to the fourth estate, especially as it will impact Caillaux's political career.*

The publication Figaro, with Gaston Calmette as editor, kept threatening to reveal love letters from Caillaux to Henriette, who was to become the second Mme Caillaux. On March 14, Henriette shot Calmette, the editor, dead.

No one regrets the incursion of the men of the fourth estate more than I do, and I have written your aunt to ask if I may host you all for tea this afternoon, and mend any broken fences.

Good Lord, is there a chance I might see him again this afternoon?

Having read his letter, I smuggled the script to our quarters by concealing it in the daily newspaper. Hearing the door open and close, my aunt called, "Bring the papers, Amanda." She was sitting up in her peignoir, leaning against three sturdy pillow bursting with goosefeather stuffing. There was a tray across her lap, but she had already finished her breakfast. She wiped her lips then motioned Anna to take the tray away with the gesture one would use to shoo a fly. Her hair, now hanging loose over her shoulders, was far grayer than when it had been arranged. She slipped into the robe which was automatically there (the sign of a good ladies' maid). Anna waited until my aunt had slipped into her armchair. Then she placed my aunt's Bible and the newspapers on the table beside her, and was handed the lorgnette, already open. We would have to wait.

My aunt, since we had been in London, had been attending some peculiar sounding religious meetings, which were supposed to be led by the Holy Ghost, just like on the day of Pentecost. Ever the dutiful Calvinist lady, she felt it her duty to reprimand such goings on. She had come back 'convicted.' She told us groups in various parts of the world were receiving prophecies. A group in Armenia had received words of a coming holocaust, and had moved bag and baggage to California!

Poor Becky groaned with each 'revelation,' for it added to her assessment that her mother was the most restrictive mother on the planet—and now she was going Dotty to boot. "If only she'd take up something fashionable, like séances!" Becky moaned. She's been reading about the Souls, a very smart set that included Arthur Balfour and Lady Desborough.

Now she appeared more riveted by the newspaper than the Bible. One day in late June, she had read out to us: 'Vienna, June 28: the Austro-Hungarian Heir Presumptive, the Archduke Francis Ferdinand, and his wife, the Duchess of Honeburg, were assassinated yesterday morning at Sarajevo, the capital of Bosnia.'

"Wherever *that* is!" Becky said with a toss of her head.

Anna appeared, bearing the silver tray with correspondence on it which had been handwritten. My aunt tore it open as I recognized the stationery. She raised her lorgnette. Did anyone ever take so much time reading a short note? Then she said, "Mr. Whitefield would like to take tea with us this afternoon." To our surprise she dispatched Anna to ring his man, to indicate this would be agreeable.

This, predictably, led to Fight #3 between Becky and her mother. Fight #1 was Becky's behavior, Fight #2 was restrictions to be followed by young ladies, and Fight #3 was not having anything fashionable to wear.

If only she could have visited more up to date modistes than the conservative modistes on Bond Street. She did not know that some milliners allowed men in to watch fittings—(which led to young ladies in a state of undress and whatever might follow). But Aunt Bea knew.

After the bickering ceased and we dressed for tea, descended, and arranged ourselves at the back of the tea room in a sort of rectangular alcove under a stained glass window. Aunt Bea followed proper procedure: our acquaintance with Mr. Whitefield was not intimate enough to invite him to our suite. At four promptly, Mr. Whitefield stepped into the lobby wearing a white suit with gray lines and a Panama hat with a gray hat band—no straw boater for him. We waited for Aunt Bea to start our conversation, as was also proper.

"Gratify our curiosity as to how you came to a career in theatre."

"I suppose it may have been started by my father. When we were young, he took us to things like the panto, 'The Prisoner of Zenda', or 'The Three Musketeers.'

"He enjoys the theatre?"

"He was frightfully keen when he was younger. One of his favorite anecdotes was attending Irving's "Romeo and Juliet" with Ned Baring—Lord Revelstoke,—who punctuated the play by continually snorting, "Remove that man from the stage!"

"By the time I was packed off to college, mother wanted to send me to Eton, but I made a dreadful ruckus about being so far from London, that they settled on Harrow instead.

"I met Gerald, and between us, we tried schoolboy versions of Craig's architectronics, Irving's lighting, Elsie Fogarty's elocution, Barker's ideas of working with a company."

The tea arrived. I poured. He loaded in sugar.

"When I moved on to Cambridge what was positively most annoying was a drumfire of questions 'what has our author intended here?' I found I was *not* an archivist and one fine day I thought to myself, 'There is one author I can jolly well be certain of'-myself.' So I dashed off my first play."

"When was that?" Aunt Bea was a fishing for his age.

"Midway in my second year—that would have been '05." So he would have graduated in '08 or '09.

"But when did the music come in?"

"I have no answer for that, Madame, it simply presented itself."

"Have you ever thought to write something about Reverend Whitefield?"

"It would be exceedingly difficult. I cannot imagine not being able to have him utter his favorite line, 'O, earth, earth earth, hear the word of the Lord.'"

"But why should you not?"

"You do not know that we have a Theater Act?" He could see we did not. "It had been law since 1843. It forbids portraying Biblical characters or quoting scripture. I could hardly write Whitefield without his favorite quote, 'Oh, earth, earth, earth, hear the word of the Lord.' David Garrick was an admirer of Whitefield, and was quoted saying, "O, to say O like Mr. Whitefield, but he could hardly turn down good business such as Samuel Foote's 'The Minor,' a satire on Reverend Whitefield."

"*What* was that?" my aunt asked.

"A satire on Reverend Whitefield."

"Good Heavens! "My aunt exclaimed. She was truly shocked.

"The Act was put in place so there would be no repetitions."

"Then how is it something like 'Everyman"'is still played?"

"As it was written before the ban, Madame. But there are a few ways around it: by inference, as in Jerome's "The Passing of the Third Floor Back," or the use of prayer, as by a little known playwright, Harold Chapin."

"Well, then," said my aunt with a burst of impish wit, "There is no help for it. You will have to put it on in America!"

"Are you offering to be such a backer, Madame?"

"I would have to read the script first."

"Are you the sort of backer who wants a say in exactly how it is written?"

"No doubt, young man! And I cannot see the music in it."

"Then you are short sighted, Madame. Whitefield wrote both lyrics and music for hymns himself. Its use as mnemonic device helps graft the subject onto the audiences' minds. As to its effectiveness, I believe Gilbert and Sullivan are credited with sparking the naval reform."

"You do not think the British Navy was up to date?"

"The Navy?" said Mr. Whitefield, picking out an egg salad and watercress tea sandwich. "I manage not to think about it too much. I let mother worry about it. She takes this three- keels- to -every -two very seriously."

"Your mother is English, is she not?""

"Madame, she is a Prussian. I was raised on von Tirpirtz and the German naval program." Aunt Bea absorbed this fact slowly.

Aunt Bea also perceived that this line of conversation had run out. She switched topics. "What might you know about the assassination of the Archduke?"

"It has definitely, alas, lit some fires, Madame. Actually, it happened when their driver took a wrong turn. One would hate to have to think a war could be based on a wrong turn. But his assassin is a hero in Serbia, of course."

"And what are your mother's thoughts on our current situation, if you don't mind me asking?"

"Mother is very well informed, but her analysis is shared by herself and my father in confidentiality."

"Would you say she is one of those coming-war-types?"

"Again, Madame, I must demur. We do not wish any of her opinions to go out on the rialto. It is a subject which we must handle carefully. As far as coming-war types, if the war you seem to foresee occurs, Madame, young men and some women will march off to fight a war for reasons their elders have agreed upon. How many of us will die, do you think, Madame?" He looked her right in the eye.

There was a silence.

Then he added, "I cannot say I feel any fervor except the ignoble desire to have all these ultimatums die down so I can produce my show before we get closed down by some catastrophe. But like everyone else, I read Doyle's "Danger, England's Peril" in the Strand. I am not unaware of Lord Robert's National Service League, which has been preparing for war with Germany since 1910, or of the air reserve. I have a friend who belongs to both.

"An air reserve? I am afraid I can't see anything which would lead me to believe aeroplanes would be of any use in an upcoming conflict."

"Then you are not *au courant* madame. The aeroplane can now use wireless-I think you call it telegraphing—to the ground below—which will render the role of the cavalry for scouting outdated.

"I plan to go out to Hendon Aerodrome tomorrow to see if repairs are complete on my machine. I think you will see something which surprises your assumptions, Madame, if you will accompany me. I will send over a book which I think will be a bit more illumining."

This offer was a bit too tempting for my aunt to veto. She always prized herself on being up to date. However, she did have a matter of concern which she broached which surprised us all. She was used to being blunt on occasion.

"Before we accept, young man, and we continue hand in glove, I think it is my duty to inform you of something which may possibly change your enthusiasm for dashing about with us." Before I could even complete a feeling of impending disaster, she added, "I think I should inform you, young man, that my niece has an —understanding with a young man in America, Martin van Demler."

I dropped my teacup. The liquid was running over the table toward me, and he stood up and hurled his napkin in its path. I moved to the one vacant seat.

"And just what is understood, Miss Ten Eycke?" he said, ignoring my aunt, and speaking to me directly.

Speaking in a very low voice, with my eyes down on the table, I replied, "It is an understanding shared by everyone except myself."

"Amanda, that is ridiculous!' my aunt exclaimed.

"It's true, Ma," said Becky, much to everyone's surprise, especially mine. She gave us both a look which indicated We will Sort This Out later. I sent Becky a thankful glance, and hoped it would not go too badly with her mother.

It will kill tomorrow.

But she could not let it drop. "What led you to this conclusion, Missy?"

"It was Grunewald's triptych, Aunt Bea."

Seeing there was more to this than first met her eye—and that it was Religious—Aunt Bea, to our surprise, subsided. I began to think better of this new group to which she was connected.

"Madame," said Mr. Whitefield boldly, "the assumption you make about your niece, whatever her problems may be, will not be solved by marrying this fellow, Martin. I believe her problem is that she is simply not in the pattern with the rest of you."

"What leads you to say that?"

"Observation, Madame. Recall that I am a dramatist—that is, one who studies character." How neatly he avoided her.

My aunt pondered this non-answer answer. Mr. Whitefield smiled.

"Come, Madame, did not your visit to my theatre give me the right to insert myself into your drama?" (He was defusing the situation). "You cannot blame a dramatist for giving what he thinks is an honest observation. Really, it is a fascinating situation we find ourselves in, don't you agree?"

It was so true, Aunt Bea could not duck it. Having cleverly built his case, he awaited Aunt Bea's reaction.

"Sir, may I ponder this for an hour or two—I will have Anna ring you with our answer."

"Quite agreeable, Madame." Tea came to an end and we were bound to thank him for having been our host. The situation lightened slightly.

A half hour later, the desk rang. "A gentleman has left a book for you. One of the maids will bring it up to you."

The book was H.G. Wells "War in the Air"—autographed—my aunt opened to the marked page, and there before us lay an illustration of New York City, burning after an attack by a German airship—with one lone aero- plane attempting to stop it.

Aunt Bea had had enough food for thought as to render the proffered trip worthwhile. Anna rang to say we would accept. He would come for us and ten o'clock tomorrow.

CHAPTER 4

And now we shift our scene to London's aerodrome broad and green, as the Bard might have marked it. Promptly next morning, Mr. Whitefield did arrive to shepherd us to Hendon. Aunt Bea had had Anna dig out everything we would need to ride in a motor car—gloves, hats, veils— but Mr. Whitefield had made such gear unnecessary by hiring a London taxicab.

"Good heavens, I hope this does not cause you undue expense!"

"Tosh, Madame, it is only six and a half miles from Marble Arch," he replied, not bothering to add he had hired it for the day. As we rode along, Mr. Whitefield regaled us with the story of how Hendon Aerodrome came into being. It was the brainchild of one Claude Grahame-White, who had married a woman of substance from New York City, then decided that a couple of hundred acres at Hendon Hill were his *Darien,* where White had wasted no time converting it into an aviation center, and wasted no time setting up Offices at 1 Abemarle Street, not so very far from Brown's.

"One can take one's 'ticket' there on biplanes or monoplanes for seventy-five guineas, which is precisely what I did in 1912." Mr. Whitefield explained that the aerodrome was packed with motor cars and spectators on Thursdays, Fridays, and Sundays, when —as advertised—there were races and 'looping' attempts—looping being the very latest dare-devil maneuver.

Grahame-White had learned to fly from Blériot, having caught the 'microbe' at the famous aviation meet at Reims in 1909. He then enticed M. Blériot into business partnership with him.

"Blériot is the one who flew the Channel?"

"Indeed he was."

"Wasn't Hammel lost over the Channel with some woman?"

"Yes, Miss Trehawk-Davis owned the aeroplane."

"I wonder your mother does not worry over your undertaking something so dangerous!" interjected my aunt, usurping the conversation back from my cousin.

"Tut, Madame," he said, raising an eyebrow. "My mother is the garden variety of come –back-with-your-shield-or-on-it Prussian mother. She would worry if I showed no signs of spunk. Today is Wednesday, so all you will see is the behind-the-scene type of activity." That was fine with Aunt Bea. By the time he had finished with Hendon's short history, we were already crossing the tracks of the Midland Railroad embankment onto Aerodrome Road. We saw a series of workshops and hangars with logos like Blériot, Farman, Avro, Grahame-White.

Mr. Whitefield handed us down from the taxi one by one, being careful not to pay me special attention with a wry smile; then he directed the taxi where to park to await us. He seated us under a red and white striped awning of a tea tent.

Excusing himself to see his aeroplane, he handed me a pair of binoculars, informing me that someone was going to try to have a go, pointing to the racecourse a mile and a half around. "You can see it more closely if you watch the pylons," he said. "It is a Farman Longhorn pusher—he looks to be practicing his racing banking." He handed them to me with a little bow.

"Let me have a look!" said Becky, holding out her hand.

"No, move over here—I have got the sight set right on the aeroplane." I stood up, Becky moved into my chair, and we carefully tried to keep the binoculars steady. We were so involved watching through them at the completely open machine in which one could see the pilot sitting amidst a tangle of spars and wires, with a whirling engine behind his head, curving around Hendon's famous pylons, we hardly noticed he was gone.

Our attention was caught by a group of men bringing a machine out of a shed of the Flying School. The crew was moving it in a strange, choreographed lock step. We did not know that one stumble, one misstep, could break a spar or knock the rigging out of true, or crack the varnished surface of a wing. Gingerly they brought their burden to a halt. It seemed to stand with its tail only lightly resting on the ground, because of some kind of sleigh runner that ran under the front, along with a set of wheels on either side of it. At the center of the group was a man with a suit and cap set backwards on his head. Another man was vigorously pointing to the various parts of the machine, and explaining things emphatically. This must be a Flying Student.

"Is he learning to fly?" Becky asked Mr. Whitefield, who had just returned to us.

"Yes, would you like to come a bit closer and watch?" We were upstanding in a flash.

We came up just behind the gaggle of men, hanging back a little. Most were in overalls and shirt sleeves. Few (if any) looked the sort who would ask a lady's permission before they fired up one of the cigarettes which seemed to ingeniously stick to their bottom lips, and which they threw away only when the instructor reminded them they were too near to smoke when they were so close to petrol.

Mr. Whitefield, whom they all seemed to know, remarked as they turned to him, "Gentlemen I've some ladies here from America on their first visit to an aerodrome."

"I hope they aren't checking on the Wright brothers patent!" someone said and the others all laughed loudly. Several men obligingly stood aside so we could look through at the machine. It was all pieces of long, thin wood, joined together, and a nest of wires. In front it came together in an extension that jutted out far in front of the wheels, and ended in a flapping rectangle which was covered with fabric.

"What is that?" Becky demanded, (Pointing, which ladies never do) taking the liberty to do it because this was obviously not a hot bed of well-bred manners.

"That is the outrigger, with the elevator at the end. It is part of your vertical controls which make your airplane go up or down." Now the student was climbing up into a seat on the lower wing, which looked like a washbasin cut in half, sitting on a board. Some levers stood up beside the seat, and there were the metal blades of the propellor behind his head.

"I'd be afraid it would take my head off," Becky said.

"Miss Ten Eycke, in the event of a crash, a pilot might have the same apprehension." We watched as some blocks were put underneath the wheels.

Now one of the men in overalls stepped up and began to slowly revolve the propeller blades. "He is bringing up fuel into the engine," Mr. Whitefield informed us. The man stopped and looked at the student. They began to call a rubric back and forth to each other which began 'Switch off' and ended 'Contact.' The man in overalls spun the blades hard. Nothing happened. The process was repeated three more times. Then the engine roared to life. Belching smoke and spewing oil, the gusts from the engine blew the grass down flat.

Becky grabbed for her hat. Too late! It blew onto the airfield and she automatically started after it. Mr. Whitefield grabbed her elbow unceremoniously and signaled the men holding the biplane not to let go. As he crossed the field in front of the machine, his suit was blown back flat against him, and his hair whipped loose.

"Mademoiselle," he said as he returned her hat. The crew was pulling boards out from under the wheels, and grabbing a wing to help steer the aircraft. The machine lurched forward, air beginning to fill out its form. Getting up more speed, it steadied. As more air filled it out it began to look majestic. Finally everyone let go. It headed for the other side of the field as the crew jogged along behind.

"Oh, will he take off?" Becky demanded.

"No, he is only doing straights. He is practicing steering and taxying, that is to say the machine has clipped wings, in case he had ideas of going up. Don't fret, you will see another take-off." Quick as a flash, he jogged back toward the hangars.

In a few minutes, he strolled back towards us. Another man, obviously an acquaintance he had just run into, walked beside him, talking energetically.

We turned. Another air crew was being pulled out a machine of a completely different sort. It only had one set of wings and the body was complete enclosed, and the engine was in front of it. The propeller was thrust through by a band of metal I would later learn to call the cowling. A couple of posts stuck up from the top of the machine beside the hole the pilot would sit in, and wires radiated out from these posts to different portions of the wings, and wires also came up from the bottom to serve the same purpose. Again, I would learn later that the post and wire constructions were called the *cabane.* Many terms, I would come to learn, were *toujours française* because the French were such aviation pioneers.

Mr. Whitefield came back to us with his acquaintance, whom he introduced as Mr. Jones. Something about him seemed familiar, but in shirtsleeves, a cap turned backward, grease stains and large spectacles, I didn't place him immediately. More exciting was the machine, which turned out to be Mr. Whitefield's.

"Why does it only have one wing?" Becky demanded critically as if it had suffered some sort of disability.

"It is a monoplane, Miss Ten Eycke—it is another form of design."

"How does it get to be made like that?" I inquired.

"They wind strips of wood in cross directions to form several layers which then get glued together," he responded.

"And the –middle?" I asked steering away from the word "body" like a good Victorian girl.

"The fuselage is a *monocoque* structure."

Just then a man came up and leaned a ladder against its side.

"Do you need that to get in?"

"I don't, but I thought perhaps you ladies might like to inside, at the cockpit."

"Yes, we would," said Becky definitively, before her mother could open her mouth. She sprang over to the bottom of the ladder and planted a white-booted foot on the bottom rung. I noted it was already stained with the green of the grass, which is why Anna tried change them for another footwear.

Mr. Whitefield sprang over and lifted up his leg almost like a man about to mount a horse, and put the toe of his boot into a little crevice, which I (once again) learned was called the stirrup, gave a spring off with his other foot, leapt up, and seated himself on the rim of the cockpit facing towards us. He propped one foot on the top of the ladder to steady it.

"Come along, Miss Ten Eycke," he said, reaching his hand down to help Becky. As Becky reached the top, he swung the other leg inside the cockpit so he was sitting astride, so he could bend down from the waist and point things out to my cousin. Becky peered over the rim into the interior of the machine. My aunt, meanwhile stood guard at the bottom of the ladder like a bulldog, lest anyone approach too closely and catch a glimpse of Ankle or Worse.

They were leaning so close together I felt a twinge. Certainly not the sentiment of a Well-Bred girl. Finally, Becky had apparently seen everything there was to see, and clambered back down reluctantly. Now it was my turn. When I got near the top, I took his extended hand.

"Would you like to sit inside?"

"Sure!"

He pushed himself off, down into the cockpit, and popped up on the other side. "Just sit on that back of the cockpit, put your knees together and swing them over flat. I shall look the other way." I was an athletic young woman and it was an easy maneuver. "Now, put your feet down and stand on the seat, and let yourself down."

Suddenly I was inside an airplane. It was a cocoon of wood with the sparkle of metal instruments on the dash in front of me, with a steering wheel coming up from the floor, where it attached to pedals, instead of a joy stick. All I could recognize immediately were a clock and a compass. Bending closer, I deduced another was a fuel gauge. "That one tells you your height in the air," he said, as I moved my finger across the panel. "Put your feet on the rudder bars...slide your feet under the straps. Now, push down on the right side and look over your shoulder." I could just see the tail section move behind me. "Put your hands on the control wheel." I did not know it was an anomaly of the Depredussin –for such it was—that it had a steering wheel instead of a control stick. He bent down inside the cockpit as if to show me more of how it works,

"Miss Ten Eycke, are you going to write to me? I was awaiting some commentary on my script."

"Oh—I didn't know what to do. You write so well."

"Deuce take it, all of my writing you have seen has been revised time and again. As a letter writer, I misspell, cross words out, use the awkward turn of phrase, just like ordinary mortals. Your aunt is everywhere—it is our only avenue. I can have a man from my father's brokerage bring letters straight across every day for you while I am in Paris, and you can write to me via the same courier."

"All right, but I do have two questions."

"Fire away."

"I don't know anything about the theatre."

"You feel you might not fit in."

"Yes. And just one other thing. I am not sure how the theater would square with my religion."

"If you get to know me better, Miss Ten Eycke, you will find out I share your apprehensions, but I pray you do not divulge it." He didn't want it getting around that this aristo had a contemplative side. "Aren't you going to add flying?"

"I haven't gotten that far."

"Give me your first impression."

"I think I'd insist you take me with you when you fly. It must be nice to be so fearless."

"Don't confuse the fact that I have been half in love with easeful death with being fearless." It appeared there was a good deal to learn about Mr. Whitefield. "Would you like to have us get to know one another further, or am I wasting my time? Will you use the ruddy courier?"

"I will." I knew we were running out of time; my aunt's tones wafted upward to us calling my name—"Aman—duh!"

"We have almost finished, Madame. If she asks what took so much time, tell her I was showing you the fuel pump and the *manettes*. Have you got that? Sometimes petrol isn't getting to your engine properly and you have to pump it." He reached over and gave the pump handle a short push.

As I stood up and leapt to sit on the back rim of the cockpit, we were so close, I felt an attraction between us that certainly not the reaction of a Well-Bred young lady. I was no expert in these matters, but it seemed to affect him in the same way. He put his hand on my shoulder to seat me as I swung around, and the touch almost melted me down into a puddle instead of a descending aviatrix.

He swung across the cockpit and jumped down.

"Just one minute, young man, grant me a look also, so I can be—*au courant.*"

"*Touché,* Madame," he said with a little bow. Behind us, Mr. Jones had a rather delighted lock on his face.

"Do not worry, I am not too old to climb a ladder." She handed Becky her parasol. Mr. Whitefield sprung back into position, jamming the ladder firmly with one leg again. Becky and I held our breath. Aunt Bea began to mount at a slow, stately pace. She made it to the top, and when she leaned over, all we could see of the S-curve of her corset was the bottom of the S, where it ended in a 'shaped' *derièrre.*

"What was going on up there?"

"Nothing much."

"All right, Miss Tight Lip."

Above we could hear my aunt barking questions in her usual tones, the one which enunciated the most clearly having to do with the cost of such extravagant machinery. We strained our ears, and made out it was not a strict matter of pound, shillings and pence, but his older machine being traded at an auspicious moment, a very auspicious moment indeed, just as Deperedussin had been bought out by Blériot. At last, she started down again. We all suffered in suspense again. When she was safely on terra firma, I happened to glance up at Mr. Whitefield, who grinned, and, to my surprise and astonishment, humorously made the sign of the Cross. Then he jumped back down.

"Ready to test her out, Guv?" asked the head of his crew.

"Ready in a second." Mr. Jones came over to him. "Brandy, I wouldn't wear that white suit jacket—it will become all stained."

"Righto." Mr. Whitefield stripped off his suit jacket (for suits and ties were usually worn to fly in those days) and Jones helped him into a smelly leather jacket. He reached into his right hand pocket, took out some kind of rag, and threaded it carefully through a top button hole. Mr. Jones handed him his helmet. Then Jones looked about him for a place to toss the jacket.

"I'll take it," I said. Folding it carefully, I laid it over my left arm.

Once in the cockpit, Mr. Whitefield put on his helmet and pulled down its goggles. A mechanic with an oil began to squirt the contents into the machine's innards. "Switch off!" They echoed each other. "Petrol on! Suck in!" Mr. Whitefield bent to flip various switches as petrol flowed into the crankshaft. The mechanic swung the blades slowly to bring it up to the engine. A liquid began run out of the engine and down onto the grass. I sniffed vigorously. It was a familiar smell—castor oil—the spring tonic.

"Contact!" they called, as he flipped the magneto switch. The mechanic braced himself to give a hard swing. We were seasoned veterans. We did not expect it to catch on at the first try. But it did. With a road and a fog of vaporizing fuel it came to life so loudly we put our hands over our ears. Then, we grabbed our skirts and held them down. As Mr. Whitefield ran the engine up, air whipped about us. After a bit the terrible commotion moderated in to a steady rotation.

Mr. Whitefield extended an arm and pointed slightly to the left. The crew shifted the aeroplane slightly. "He's turning into the wind," remarked Mr. Jones. "Can you see the windsock over there?" An inflated piece of cloth shaped like a sock without the bend at the ankle blew in the direction of the aeroplane's nose was attached atop a pole. Mr. Whitefield's arm went up. The boards in front of the wheels were yanked with ropes. The machine moved forward gathering incremental gulps of speed as it ate up the slightly uneven ground. The crew at the tail and wings had to let go. The tail came right up, along with the stick-like apparatus at the back that dug into the dirt. The machine was fairly skimming over the grass now; the nose lifted and –it was air borne.

"Oh, my stars!" Aunt Bea gasped. Becky gave an excited yelp. I realized I was pressing Mr. Whitefield's jacket against me so hard that if I had been in my right mind I would have been extremely concerned over the wrinkles I was making. Our heads went back little by little as he went higher and higher. Aunt Bea opened her parasol.

"Oh, will he loop the loop?" Becky gasped.

"He does like to fly those French machines that bite you the moment you don't fly them."

After about a half of an hour of rising, I curiously asked one of the bystanders, "How high do you think he is?"

"Around two thousand feet."

Quite without warning, the machine rolled over, then righted itself. Now his machine seemed to be planeing through the air sideways. "That's a side slip," said my informant. Then the machine zoomed down at a scary rate, he cut the engine, soared up until it lost some of its velocity, and flipped the nose over, flying down again, motor restarting.

"That's the fastest thing in the air." *(Of course, it would be!).*

My aunt smiled. She was becoming *au courant* at a dizzying pace. I thought it was the first moment she actually realized she was no longer in New York, with its rituals of coming and going, and that she was enjoying herself. If she wanted to visit an aerodrome, there was no one to 'tut tut.'"

The Deperdussin described a figure eight above us for all the world like a gambling porpoise of the sky. Then he began to circle lower.

"He's coming in," remarked our friendly informant.

As he came toward us, suddenly, the engine shut off. "My God, he's crashing!" Becky exclaimed.

"No, he is only blipping his engine to slow down." We heard the reassuring roar of an engine again. "He can only blip for a few seconds without flooding the engine."

Without realizing it I began to slowly trail along behind the air crew who were rushing out to grab the wings as the little wooden piece at the back began to dig into the ground. He cut the engine after landing neatly and rolled towards us. The machine came to rest about thirty yards from us. Before he swung himself down, I had come up to the machine, vaguely realizing that my aunt and cousin were somewhere behind me. I saw him lift of his helmet and goggles, waving to me. But....why was he running toward me all of a sudden? Next thing I knew he grabbed me by the waist and was holding me. I felt someone ease me down onto some kind of trolley they used to wheel the back end of the aeroplane.

Oh God, I had fainted.

I was completely mortified. This was the sort of thing that would happen after Uncle Bejamen died. The front of my dress was spotted with oil. Mr. Whitefield was kneeling on the grass right in front of me. "Put your head down," he was saying. "Put your hands on my shoulders..." As I reached out, his jacket, which I still was clutching, fell into my lap. My aunt bustled up with her smelling salts.

"Let her be," Mr. Whitefield said to her. "People can faint from fear. Get her a glass of water."

The tea pavilion was not in full cry, as it would have been were it an exhibition day, so Mr. Whitefield suggested stopping at a genteel 'local' that had big pitchers of lemonade. Aunt Bea, who was now firmly back in command on the quarterdeck of the U.S.S. Propriety, agreed, realizing she had now spent three very interesting days. We stopped, descended from the taxicab and were shown into a small semiprivate back room. The owner himself, with a cheery florid face and a clean white apron which covered him from neck to knees, took our orders, Mr. Whitefield opting for a bottle of ale.

"Well, thank you, young man, that was interesting enough, but am afraid I still do not see a use for this machine in the event of a war. Does your government share your views?"

"Grahame -White sponsored a Parliamentary Air Defense Committee demonstration in 1911, Madame. All the right people were there, and it left some of them pushing for the further development, chief among them Mr. Churchill, who is already buying machines from private contractors.

"Many uses will be made of aircraft. First is spotting the enemy and directing artillery fire. They can send bracketing signals by three different colored flags to the ground. There is bombing. The Channel and the adjoining sea will be mined and have destroyers on it, while we have seaplanes that can launch from ships, and a few Curtiss flying boats. The enemy will use whatever means possible to attack England and we need aeroplanes to ward that off...but I go on. Perhaps the rest can wait until Miss Ten Eycke recovers."

"She always does. Tell me who of your family in your generation has gone into the brokerage? Have you an elder brother?"

"I am the eldest, Madame."

My aunt's face expressed Surprise. She had thought since there was not a 'Sir' in front of his name, someone else was eldest. "My parents very wisely have discarded the rite of primogenitor. My brother has the talent for business."

"Shall we leave for home soon, Mr. Whitefield?"

"Immediately, Madame."

"I wish to thank you for a most interesting day."

"Indeed, I hope to resume our friendship when I return from Paris. A friend has procured entrance to the Caillaux trial."

"And you are leaving—"

"Tomorrow, alas, Madame."

"Oh! We shall miss you, my dear sir." My aunt was becoming less formal.

I was glad he had already informed me so I would not appear too distressed. My cousin was dampened for a few moments, but brightened considerably when she realized she had something to write about to her friends in New York which would turn them green!

CHAPTER 5

*I did contemplate giving up this little jaunt on which I am embarked this morning since the day I met you, dear Miss Ten Eycke, for reasons we both know but are not yet appropriate or proper to refer to (*although I was glad he had*) yet which form the basis of my reluctance. But my friend Robert had gotten admittance to the trial, and as well, set up a meeting for me with Henry Bernstein, the French playwright. It would be grossly impolite to cry off at the last moment.*

I know I have been more forward than I ought to, but time is running down on me. (And I thought he was referring to his play).

Thus began a very long letter from Mr. Whitefield, obviously written the night before his departure, when he left us at Browns, his swinging walk carrying him down Piccadilly to his flat.

'My dear' was formal in Britain, not intimate, as it would have been in America—' Dear' Miss Ten Eycke, therefore, was more intimate.

He spoke at length of the family he would be staying with, the Desperniers, his hosts of many a childhood summer. The reason given was to improve his French; the actual reason was it was not a good idea for him and his mother to stay under one roof for several months. This, he would explain later. They owned a *hotel particulaire* in Paris, where M. Desperniers was engaged in a business which was a counterpart to his father. They owned a country house in Brie, further north.

He had always been attached to Mme. Desperniers, to the point he nicknamed her 'Xiema,' short for *duexième Mamman,* and he still addressed her in the same manner. As a child he was so greedy for her sole attention he would go to Mass with her (so that's where he learned to cross himself*). He had no competition for her affections at that time—she complained she had raised pack of heathens. Sometimes she would read to him the reflections of a young nun, Térèse of Liseux, whom she greatly fancied.

Robert and he were contemporaries and had passed through the vagaries of youth together (pardon him if he did not elaborate). She did not harass him about the religious phase he went through at one time, as his own mother did.

As for Bernstein, last year he presented a play entitled 'Aprés Moi', which created such scandal, there was rioting in the streets and finally the mounted police had to be called out to disperse the protests. He had to withdraw the play, and 'repented.' I will meet him tomorrow night, and will recount to you what happened.

(I must tell you that when I read Aprés Moi, it made me smile--it centered on financial doings). It opens with a chap in sole charge of a sugar-beet refinery corporation with his dead partner's son as ward and no one to look over his shoulder at the books. He falls in with a scheme to set up an oil cartel to buy up crude and create a monopoly which can set prices. The other partners quarrel with him and do not buy in as necessary so he diverts funds from his business and falsifies the books to cover the oil purchases. The inevitable discovery plunges his own sugar beet stocks down lower 'than hell'. Meanwhile during this discovery, the chap has a houseful of weekend guests hard at bridge and billiards, along with an occasional female who takes in in her head to be risqué enough to ask every guest what is the one thing a woman can lose without remedy? After lights off the guests creak about in the usual French amorous escapades which I shall not detail to you…

With sincere affection, B.W.

My dear Mr. Whitefield, I replied: Time has resumed it stately and rather tedious pace since you have left us. You certainly have made our lives lively the last few days. I can readily understand what you say about your stays with your friends. I was always uncomfortable at home, and comfortable at Uncle Benjamen's. Luckily they lived across the street from us. He had a great enthusiasm for collecting and playing folk music, and it was this enthusiasm which got me to fiddling (as distinct from playing the violin), probably a parallel to your 'Xiema.

My poor aunt was always distressed by his pursuit of such a 'low' art, and to unburden herself, I suspect, of some guilt when he died, has set out on the pilgrimage which has had such unusual results. Yesterday, I saw her smile and enjoy herself which she has not for some time, and I thank you for that. I also suspect she is grappling with a new-found freedom ,in which she is slowly accepting ,and discarding, customs which are irrelevant to her any longer.

The Caillaux trial was not considered fit reading for young people, so my aunt would tear pieces out of the newspaper which contained such information. Becky was again her antic self, and retrieved the cuttings from the wastebasket when Anna was not looking. The plays of Bernstein posed me a dilemma. I would like to read them (in French) despite Aunt Bea's censorship. But she could not read French, so how could she form a 'correct' opinion barring me from reading them. What if I simply ordered these plays? Unlike the canon set against self-slaughter of Hamlet, there was no canon set against reading Bernstein! This meant I would have to decide for myself. I had the uncomfortable feeling that Duplicity was not the black and white matter of my youth.

I met Bernstein ahead of schedule, when he unexpectedly burst into the courtroom, demanding to testify. He is a big man, taller by far than most of the people around him, and a thoroughgoing dandy with dark hair, with spit curls to one side of his forehead. Judge Albanel found himself temporarily pulled into the whirlwind. Bernstein then dramatically declared 'I don't know where Caillaux will be if war breaks out, but if I do any killing I shall do it myself, and not send a woman to do it for me!' Bernstein continued, full throttle, 'M. Caillaux stands on a coffin and makes a pedestal of it!'

Then, the judge, showing more artistic discernment than I had previously credited the judiciary with, restored order by unexpectedly exclaiming 'But this is literature!" This apt description knocked the wind out of Bernstein's sails. I was introduced to him outside. He recalled I was to meet him at his digs on Rue Haussman next evening.

I wrote, *I was amazed when Becky told me that Mme Caillaux had been acquitted of shooting someone! As to the author of these plays L'Assault and Aprés Moi, I decided to order them, and the concierge has promised to sequester my package for me.*

He replied, *We sat in his study, a very heavily carpeted place silent enough for thinking. There were pencils everywhere; in mid conversation he stopped several times to jot down an idea. He told me I had the makings of a fine playwright 'But you need more force majeur, mon vieux'.*

I told him that English sensibilities could not hold up the sweep of sentiment admired on the Continent. 'Bah!' he said. 'Consider Shakespeare, old boy.' He did not even mention the music as he probably feared being too critical of its usage.

Then on July 29 I received a cable and a letter, both of which upset my tidy little world.

'Mandra, Please do excuse my familiarity, but I hope you will see what prompted it. I did tell you my time is running out: because war is coming, and I have no idea what it will do to my theatre career, perhaps my life.

Your good aunt asked about my mother's analysis but I did not answer, but I know it well. She told my father when the Germans moved their gold reserves to Spandau that the' unavoidable war' was coming. Of course, she did not base her opinion on this alone: she is good friends with Ambassador (Prince)Lichnowsky and his wife. She feels Lichnowsky has given the German government the incorrect impression that in the case of a war, England would stay neutral. However, we have a treaty with France which compels us to act if they are attacked. And I ruddy well doubt whether our government would like it if Germany attained all the Channel ports of France and the deep water ports of Belgium. All this I ask you to keep to yourself until the situation makes such secrecy irrelevant, but in the meantime, I ask for your silence.

You can imagine that such a war would impact my family badly; although mother is a British citizen now, still, her background will put them and the business under surveillance, as will be the case with all such persons.

On the other hand, father had a leg up financially, due to her analysis: perhaps yet another reason for them to be viewed with suspicion. The idea is to bring my brother Vessey to be more and more the head of our bank.

My friend Bob, the actor Robert Loraine, who prefers to keep his stage and flying careers separate from one another, has already written the Navy and the Army, volunteering his services as a pilot. I fear he is not premature.

M. Desperniers was in the war of 1870, and already has his hackles up. He is talking of moving to Brie to burn the crops so the Germans will not have the benefit of them, as well as removing any valuables. This, you can imagine, will be a major amount of labor, and though no one has come out and said it, they are hoping I will come and help them. In the event of a mobilization, their sons will be called up.

I know this is asking a good deal of you to be able to send me a telegraph to the French address, and here is the one for Brie, in the event I should be needed.

A bell hop carried my missive to the post office and sent by telegraph, 'Go with friends. We're Ok and will pray for you.'

Back came a short note, '*Have gone to Brie.*'

A bit longer message arrived. *It's an odd thing to feel innocent again, but Bernstein's ending of Aprés Moi made me feel this was too much artistically, and one loses sympathy for the lot of them, they are such unpleasant characters, and I find I wished the husband would take up his revolver and put all of them out of their misery instead of just himself. This sentiment made me realize that I still have a bit of me that has been uncorrupted.*

After that there was only one note from the courier, who told us he had great difficulty getting out of Paris himself, as all the telephone lines, trains, postal service and wireless were getting tied up, because, it seemed plain, they were being reserved for use in the event of a mobilization. He was sorry, nothing from Brie had been able to reach him. Having our communication lines depart I was—of course—upset.

But life was sweeping me along with it. The countries of Europe were mobilizing like a snowball growing larger and larger as the debacle rolled downhill. In England, emergency Cabinet meetings were being held every five minutes and Sir Edward Grey was darkly declaring that 'the lights had gone out all over Europe.' That weekend was a Bank Holiday and a run on gold was reported. Cables flew back and forth to the family in New York; then the cable to Germany was cut.

Then came the deadline night of August 3-4. Aunt Bea did not want to accede to our requests to go outside to join the crowd in the streets, because she could hear unruly yells from our open windows. But finally she agreed to sally forth with Anna as our Readguard. Outside, some rakes were climbing lamp posts or jumping on the hoods of taxis. Many were intoxicated. My aunt let us go to the edge of Green Park where we could look toward Buckingham Palace. Of course we couldn't see anything, but we knew that their majesties must have appeared on the balcony when the huge crowd began to sing 'God Save the King.' As the song swelled up, up, past the tops of the trees, and we were caught up in an emotion pierced with the realization a monumental event was happening which would prevent life from being just the same. Midnight struck. England was at war.

As we finally went to bed, we knew that somewhere in the dark the British Expeditionary Force—B.E.F.—Kaiser Bill's 'contemptible little army'—was moving toward its appointed transport at the Channel.

CHAPTER 6

The next morning I was in the lobby early as usual, and hopeful. A man was at the desk, talking to the concierge, with his back toward me. Somehow I knew they were talking about us even before the concierge inadvertently glanced at me. The other man half-turned. There was something so familiar about him; I even took a half-step toward him, then stopped, profoundly embarrassed. Our eyes met. He touched his hat to me, then stepped out into the sunlight, where I could see a motor car hood that glistened like silver. Silver? Could the whole thing have been an illusion?

"Who was that man?" I asked.

"He didn't give his name, Miss," and we both knew it was because he didn't have to.

Now the Bank of England and the Royal Exchange announced they would stay closed after the Bank holiday. As my aunt was always trying to interest us in the news of the World, I therefore considered it permissible to open a London newspaper. One item jumped out at me. *It is regrettable that one of the Hon. Brandon Whitefield's greatest supporters, the Princess Lichnowsky, will not be in London for the opening of his play."* The Lichnowskys had been unceremoniously whisked out of England. The Prince, when the news was delivered to his London residence that he must turn in his passport and leave the country, burst into tears. The messenger found him prostrated in his pajamas in bed. He and his wife left England sobbing.

Aunt Bea and Anna were ringing around to inquire about booking a passage home. I sat, too depressed to stir, thinking I would never see Mr.

Whitefield again. Why hadn't I paid more attention to his statement his time was running down?

But it became obvious as the day wore on that my aunt was having Big Trouble. The glut of tourists-cum-refugees had produced was so overwhelming demands for passage could end one up in Steerage Class, of all things! Persons of Consequence who were used to traveling first class were now of No Consequence now. Becky gave me a nudge with her elbow and started pitching a fit about submarines. Aunt Bea got out her smelling salts. It seemed we were going to stay in England a little while longer. By the time the logic of Becky's fake outburst was solidified in September by the sinking of the Aboudkir, Hogue, and Cressy by submarines, events were already keeping us in London for more than 'just' a while.

Then, after what seemed an eternity, another letter, scribbled on brown wrapping in pencil arrived.

I am jolting toward Paris in a farm cart. M. Despeniers decided to burn the crops instead of trying to find thrashers to flail, although he did find some for two fields, and I ended up working behind them. I can still hear the flails whistling through air and hitting stalks with an indescribable WHACK. I tried to help, but developed a hearty respect for the strength of men who ply this trade. I've never been so stiff, so sore, so exhausted or so hungry in my whole life. I was so tired when Robert and his brothers bade farewell to go to their mobilization points it seemed unreal as a dream. The whole countryside emptied of men of a certain age.

As I stood watching, gendarmes came around to take the horses. There was one old timer I'd known for years and the thought of what lay ahead for him seemed unacceptable. I bribed the official to leave him behind. Silly and sentimental: yet the old horse came to our rescue as we hitched him to a cart, and set off for Paris; we found many stranded motor cars blocking the roads, but we walked around them. We even picked up the Desperniers!

Several days later the phone range in our suite. Anna answered it as usual but motioned my aunt to come and take the receiver. It was Mr. Whitefield.

He was fresh off the train and with no news of us, he had stopped at the hotel desk. He would go to his flat and clean up, then return.

Aunt Bea insisted he come up.

Indeed, he did look a bit disheveled, as if he had been sleeping in a field.

"Let me order some tea sandwiches," said Aunt Bea. She realized he must be famished. "What happened in France?"

"I was with friends at Brie and the church bells began to toll. At this sound everyone of mobilization age dropped their tools and ran to the Mayor's office to find out where to mobilize.

"And Paris? How did you find Paris??"

"In a frightful state over the assassination of Jaurès, Madame. All the newspapers were bordered in black. I have some in my luggage which unfortunately is still in Paris."

"It was very kind of you to write your father on our behalf, "said my aunt. "I have a very nice note from him offering to stand guarantor for any financial debts we might incur while the banks are closed."

Said Mr. Whitefield, tackling a sandwich, "Morgan-Harjes was the only bank in Paris still cashing cheques. A fine example of America flexing its financial muscles."

"Anna, bring Mr. Whitefield some cognac. Bring in my blue suit." Anna returned with a glass of amber liquid. "I understand England is only honoring English gold right now?" My aunt asked. She picked up a pair of scissors from the desk and dramatically tore open the seam of the skirt, stitch by stitch, each new opening releasing a sovereign with Queen Victoria or King Edward engraved on them.

"Bully show!" He said, downing his cognac.

"Anna, bring them out." Other costumes appeared. American Quarter Eagles, Swiss twenty franc pieces, French gold angels and (just for good measure) Venetian ducats spilled across the floor.

"Perhaps we should open a bank, "said Mr. Whitefield, somewhat awed by this master plan for a Dire Emergency.

"I plan to ask Ambassador Page what we can do to help. My church group feels man more refugees will be arriving in England. My church group"—we'd never heard her say that before. Then it struck us—we were staying. Becky and I exchanged excited glances. I looked shyly over at Mr. Whitefield; he smiled a very tired smile. As he considered the pile of gold coins on the floor, he turned to my aunt and asked, "You are quite sure these people are trustworthy, Madame?"

"Come and see tomorrow. After I have seen our ambassador I have invited Mr. and Mrs. Seddon round. Now get some sleep."

"I shall be here at four, Madame—with my cheque book."

CHAPTER 7

Very Early next morning (for Aunt Bea) we were on our way to the American Chancery at 4 Grosvenor Gardens. Anna had ascertained that Ambassador Page had resumed his (interrupted) custom of seeing people there in his office for two hours daily. Aunt Bea had been acting as if she expected an invitation on a silver tray from the ambassador ever since he was quoted as referring to 'The Big Smash' (the outbreak of the war). She had not met him before, as she Absolutely Refused to enter that Disgraceful Hole at 123 Victoria Street which heretofore served as our nation's Chancery (Embassy). The Embassy, where the Pages lived, was at 6 Grosvenor Place.

We looked over the new Chancery as we got down from our car. It was a narrow building, only three windows wide, like all its fellows which lined the street. It was white, and had concrete fencing bordering the second story balcony which jutted forward over the entrance. The ground floor was likewise fenced up to the portico which sported a red marble pillar set at each side of the door. The building faced a small, triangular park.

Our ambassador had also acquired as his responsibility the German and Austrian embassies, as their ambassadors had been handed over their passports and had left the country. Our American organization, as we would learn, now sprawled over into the Consul-General's office, rooms at the Savoy hotel, and the American Society in London. No one showed any signs of having been sitting around waiting for Aunt Bea. She finally began to catch that signal. We discovered that we were an hour early. The doors did not open until 11 o'clock. Such lassitude drew a 'tut-tut' from Aunt Bea, even though she was never up and around at that hour. So my aunt decreed a stroll down Ebury Street. We were back at the Consulate promptly at 11o'clock. The flag had now been set out on a pole from the balcony railing above the portico. Passing through the doors, we turned into a large room on our right, with a plain marble mantel over the fireplace and a wooden arch at its back wall. My aunt presented her card and asked to see Ambassador Page.

"It will be a wait, Mrs. Ten Eycke," said the man behind the desk. "I cannot predict how long unfortunately."

We would have Left Immediately. But Aunt Bea's back straightened to indicate her determination. She did not want to face tea empty handed. We took a turn around the ground floor. The large reception room across the entry hall was high ceilinged and graced with a large center plaster medallion. It was full of people in various stages of dress and undress. To my aunt's obvious shock, a very well-dressed woman had actually lain down in one corner so fatigued was she was unable to Comport Herself with Dignity.

At the end of the hallways was a door to a smaller reception room, likewise full of people. To our right, a graceful staircase arched gently around the dumbwaiter which ran from the basement all the way to the fourth floor offices, emitting cooking smells which caused some of the refugees, the ones who were obviously hungry, to cast savage glances in its direction. I was sure my aunt would give up and leave. But for the moment she indicated we should take a seat. With a sigh, I rummaged in my purse, and pulled out my embroidery hoop. I wondered why I had been told to come with her. *Ours is not to question why...&etc.* as Uncle Ben used to say.

After about an hour and a half, her name was finally called. We followed the embassy page up the flight of stairs. Though the ascent was gentle, Aunt Bea climbed more and more slowly, resting at the landings. She was used to elevators. We passed a second floor like the first. The third floor was cut up into smaller rooms used for offices. Ambassador Page's was toward the back of the building, ringed around a cluster of offices more junior functionaries whose jobs were to divert all traffic save that which needed to be funneled to him directly.

We were shown into Mr. Page's office. He half rose from his chair and extended his hand to my aunt. "Mr. Ambassador," she said, giving him hers. He sat back down and indicated chairs for us with a movement of his hand. My aunt automatically looked behind hers for someone to settle her chair under her, but there was no one.

Mr. Page was not a physically impressive man. I suppose he knew it. Some years later I saw a photograph of him he had given to Col. House. And it was inscribed, 'Here I come without one plea except the thing does look like me.' He was one of the Ohio appointees who were scattered across Europe: Whitlock in Belgium (which he thought was going to be a 'quiet post') Herrick in Paris, Gerard in Germany. Mr. Page's ears stood out and he wore spectacles which rested on a large nose set above a bristly mustache. He was rapidly balding. He had a furtive, somewhat rodent-like mien, all of which made me think of a raccoon. My aunt settled herself impressively. She did not look reassured.

"Mr. Ambassador. I am thinking of staying in London." Mr. Page tilted his head slightly, without a word, waiting to see what might this portentous opening meant. Annoyed, as if the Import of this should be Obvious, my aunt added," I should very much like to know what sort of charitable works are being organized." Mr. Page sighed so feelingly that my aunt stiffened. He noticed her reaction.

"Not to offend, Mrs. Ten Eycke, it is only that I have been accosted hourly by ladies in pearls, all with demands and suggestions. One of them even went on a hunger strike when she found she'd have to voyage in steerage." He smiled; unfortunately it struck too close to home for my aunt to find it funny!

The interview was obviously off on the wrong foot, but, stuck with it, Mr. Page sighed again. He was already obviously weary. He would grow much wearier still in the next four years, sleeping only a few hours a night, wrapped in a blanket, sitting in his chair. He died shortly after the Armistice, having given his Last Full Measure of Devotion.

My aunt sniffed significantly. He could see she expected that he knew exactly who she was and thus out to be taken Seriously.

"In reply, Mrs. Ten Eycke, the immediate need is to the American traveler. Fred Kent of Banker's Trust has put together an Americans Citizens' Committee.

"He and I have buried Washington with cables. We've finally got the U.S. TENNESSEE en route out of New York three days now, with enough gold on board so that the London banks will give substantial advances on it. Herbert Hoover, who is an American mining engineer with broad international interests, has set up an office in the consulate. He is lending small amounts from his own personal capital. (From the glance he gave my aunt, I could see he was not prepared to take any one seriously who wasn't willing to throw in a couple of quid). "Mr. Hoover has set up a committee to deal with the unaccompanied women at the Savoy. Hoover has also put together a Residence Committee. He asking for contributions from *all* Americans living here in London."

"I shall ring him immediately. We also possess some gold."

"Really?"

"Yes—and I am also part of a church group in London which would like to aid with refugees we assume will soon be arriving on these shores from the Continent."

"You will need a translator."

"My niece speaks fluent French." So that's why I was here!

"I hope you realize that she will be hearing some dreadful terrible stories."

My aunt frowned. She had not considered this.

"I wish you well on that venture. Keep me *au courant.*" He rose from his chair. She followed suit. She managed to thank him gracefully. My aunt was not used to being Dismissed. We would not have much time until the Seddons arrived! I should have been curious about meeting the famous Mr. Seddon, head of my aunt's mysterious church group, who Becky and I had both decided, must have the charisma of Rasputin. But obviously all I could think of was Mr. Whitefield.

We certainly had no time for lunch, and by the time Anna opened to the tap at our door at four, I was looking forward to tea. Mr. and Mrs.

Seddon stepped over the threshold, diffident as church mice, confused as Anna took their coats. Everything about Mr. Seddon was gray—his receding hair, his complexion, his wire-rim spectacles, his neatly brushed but inexpensive suit. Mrs. Seddon's hair was gray, too, and tucked under her hat. She also wore spectacles. They were obviously uncomfortable in such swank surroundings.

"Pray, my dears, do come in," said my aunt, swarming up to them, very warmly, seeing that each of them were seated comfortably. "Rebecca, Amanda, Mr. and Mrs. Seddon." We all nodded gravely to each other. Everyone had their hands clasped on their laps.

Another tap at the door. A familiar voice made my heart leap, and then seemed to stop. Mr. Whitefield breezed in, freshly shaven, hair trimmed, and dressed to the nines. He was every bit the quizzing aristo (even though he had brought his cheque book). When he bowed to Mr. Seddon, I could read the signals passing between then. Mr. Whitefield was indicating that no unaccompanied foreign women were going to be taken advantage of by an English religious confidence man (should such prove to be the case) as long as *he* was around. Mr. Seddon mounted no defenses. He was open to being investigated.

"I trust that you are recovered from your ordeal?"

"Oh, quite!" he replied cheerfully. My aunt briefly recounted Mr. Whitefield's movements to Mr. and Mrs. Seddon, who listened intently. "I hear you are set on getting up some charitable endeavor?" He shot at Mr. Seddon.

Mr. Seddon got up. He handed Mr. Whitefield his card (he was a verger in an unexceptionable church in an unfashionable—in fact poor— part of London.)

"I am sure if you ring the bishop he will vouch for me. Since you have been in France, sir, perhaps you can answer to our inclination whether the refugees will be arriving soon."

"Sooner than anyone thinks and more of them."

"There will be differences in language, of course," said Mr. Seddon.

"I speak French. My mother is German, I fancy I could cobble some of the dialects together, and there will be dialects," said Mr. Whitefield.

"I mentioned to Ambassador Page that Amanda also speaks French. He did however warn me...."

"Not appropriate unless you have a very strong stomach."

"Quite!" Mr. Seddon and he exchanged a man-to-man glance.

"I understand Mrs. Ten Eycke has promised to help underwrite your effort."

"I have not had time to discuss it with her, in fact, I had thought more along the lines of most charitable endeavors in our parish which somehow manage to make ends meet, one never knowing exactly where the relief will come from. We are, sir, not a wealthy group."

"I think this may be more costly than things you have taken up before, sir. I may be incorrect of course. I should be pleased to also contribute." He took out his cheque book and pen. When he handed Mr. Seddon the cheque, the latter was obviously flustered by the amount. "How very generous! Thank you, sir."

"You are quite welcome," said Mr. Whitefield, having achieved the goal of becoming more and more ingratiated with us and our affairs.

"I have heard from a fellow verger they will house refugees at Alexandra Palace. He will ring the moment he hears news."

"Why—yes. Have you heard anything in France you can divulge to us?"

"Only that the French have mobilized, and that our army and air service are on the move—backwards, unfortunately."

"Oh, will you join up?" my cousin asked.

"Just be quiet!" I burst out. Everyone was. I hadn't expected I would say that, but I was remembering our great uncle's tales of doctoring at Bull Run.

"I had thought of joining the Air Reserve at one time, but the theater side -tracked me."

"What do you think, Mr. Seddon?" My irrepressible cousin asked.

With all eyes on him, Mr. Seddon flushed. "I have heard that Cosmo Lang, the Archbishop of York, will call war the bankruptcy of Christian principle in his sermon tomorrow."

"That won't last long."

"Indeed, sir, I believe you are correct. Soon everyone will be claiming God is on their side."

"Yes, indeed," Mr. Whitefield agreed firmly.

Tea arrived and the conversation became more casual. When the Seddons left, Mr. Whitefield, who no longer had any pretext to stay, began to depart as well.

But my aunt intervened. "Please do stay, sir, I will order supper right away as we have had no lunch." The evening ended agreeably.

CHAPTER 8

'My aunt would go to church in the morning. As I did not wish to accompany her to this strange new venture, but would have preferred to attend Whitefield's Tabernacle (but Becky refused) my aunt had to leave us both at the hotel in charge of Anna. It was the one morning my aunt was up and about and out at a relatively early hour. I was sitting in the reading room, trying to read the newspapers, waiting for the boots to bring a letter when he saw that the coast was clear. Instead, I saw Mr. Whitefield. In the Flesh. "Oh!" I started, as if I'd seen a ghost.

"Miss Ten Eycke, he said with a little bow and sat down. "Forgive the intrusion. I knew you would be up at this hour. I have several problems on which I would value your opinion," said this grey-eyed stranger. "If you shan't mind, the concierge has offered us a bit more private spot." As if mesmerized, I followed his instructions as I walked in front of him—properly, of course. He had all the clout of a member of the upper class.

"Whatever could I be of any help to you?" I asked, when we were seated in a small back room behind the front desk.

"First off, as you may guess if you do not know, this is all of a sudden not the time to launch a play. Many stage mangers have already asked their casts to take salary cuts or sworn off production altogether. I can't see my way clear to do that. I have engaged these people and they are dependent on me for their temporary livelihood, and I am not in circumstances of necessity as they are. I shall take a loss if I go on with it now instead of waiting a few months. But I feel I should do it. And I have had some good advice from old Dot Boucicault, to wit, — 'after a short stop, *the theatre always does good business during wars—the Civil War, the Boer War, why not this one?'* Do you think I am being bull headed if I try to put it on two months later than as planned? Dot seemed to think that was a proper time space."

"No, not bullheaded—just a bit of a gamble—just like merchant banking!" Then I added, "My uncle left me a small legacy."

"I don't follow."

"He said I would know what to do with it. I don't need it to live on at the moment. You must let me pledge to underwrite your losses with you!"

"Miss Ten Eycke-"

"Now, Mr. Whitefield, perhaps it is time for *you* to expand your limitations!"

"Touché."

"I would wish to underwrite Miss Westcote particularly."

"Ah, she is certainly worthy."

"Perhaps more so than a horse?"

"You drive a hard deal, Miss Ten Eycke."

"Where shall I send the cheque?"

It was my first experience with holy boldness. It certainly wasn't 'I' who said it. It was sufficient to inform Mr. Whitefield that I returned his interest.

He held out a hand so we could shake on the arrangement. It was more of a lover's pledge than a bargain for insolvency, and we were looking into each other's eyes in the rather silly way people do when they suddenly realize they are head over heels.

"Is there anything else?" I blurted awkwardly, finally removing my hand from his.

"Yes, in fact. Amanda, there is. I went to Mass with 'Xiema one day, and she handed me a piece of paper. It read 'One man rendeth, another mendeth.'Mind you—she doesn't know a word of English." He gave me the little piece of paper.

"Keep it for me," he added.

CHAPTER 9

Mr. Whitefield decided to follow the advice of the old trooper Dot Boucicault, who told him that plays were frequently avoided in the first days of a war, but that, given a month or two, business would be booming as people sought diversion from the grimness of the time. He was right. By October, theatre going had recommenced.

He decided to open in November instead of September. In the interim, many happenings took place.

Aunt Bea had decided to change our place of residence. The West End, she had decided, was going to be too busy (read: too full of men) to stay in for the Duration, for recruits that had jammed Scotland Yard so much that recruiters had to sleep under their desks, and who were now beginning to drill in the park, were scaring unwary citizen Half to Death. She wanted a hotel 'somewhere out of the hubbub.'

"Claridge's, "said Mr. Whitefield. "Brook Street."

"You are sure it is quiet?"

"When D'Oyly Carte rebuilt it, Madame, it was on the Duke of Westminster's proviso that it would not be 'anything like a replication of the Savoy.'" (The Duke owned most of property of London, and so businesses were only allowed a 99 year lease).

"What sort of neighborhood is it?"

"Well," said Mr. Whitefield with a grimace, "My parents live nearby. So did Revelstoke until the Gaucho Bond bust. Father keeps a running tab at Claridge's so as to entertain customers he does not wish to entertain at home. (In other words, the not-quite-big-enough-fish level of clientele.).

"I see," said my aunt thoughtfully.

"It is also frequented by diplomatic personnel. Princess Alice of Monaco holds a weekly salon there. I should be happy to introduce you."

Despite the fact the Princess was originally a Jewess from New Orleans, and as such a somewhat questionable personage, her salons proved the irresistible last straw. The management rolled out the red carpet when we came up to the brick and wrought-iron balconied façade. It helped Aunt Bea survive the shock of finding out the manager was an Eye-talian, as well as the cooks of the kitchen.

"I' m sure you realize, Madame, that cultures other than ours cook better food," said Mr. Whitefield, and Aunt Bea swallowed but wanted, nonetheless, to be *au courant*. After a lot of bowing and scraping, she declared she Could be Satisfied with a suite of three bedrooms and a sitting room, with the W.C. and washbasin *en suite,* and the communal bathtub down the hall.

Anna spent days stuffing our clothing with tissue so they wouldn't wrinkle in this great move of a mile or so. Everything went into a flotilla of trunks (which were actually portable closets).

My aunt (who had Rung Up the Mr. Hoover mentioned by Ambassador Page) was at some American luncheon at the Savoy, and could not help but admire the food there, cooked by Eye-talians. Becky was watching our trunks loaded into several taxis with Anna. She would accompany the fleet to Claridge's with Anna while I 'held the fort' at Brown's lest Anything come Up. I settled in the reading room.

"I say the will head up through the gap of Belfort!" one rather choleric gentleman said to another.

"Nonsense, old boy! The Black Forest would slow them down too much! They'll go up the Manheim and west of the Vosges!" (All this presupposed a guess the Germans would rally to the east to keep Alsace Lorraine). Then they saw me. They automatically lowered their voices. Young women weren't supposed to worry their Pretty Little Heads about such matters as the progress of a war. I had hated the fact we'd be further away from Mr. Whitefield until he reminded me that his parents lived nearby, and writing back and forth would be considerably easier.

Just then, Aunt Bea charged into the library, calling for me in a stentorian voice, telling me to get my gloves, hat, and coat, announcing we were off for a meeting with Mr. Hoover at his office at 1, London Wall. "I told him I could help raising funds. I am giving him a list of people in financial circles I feel I could contact. I have promised that our meeting will take no longer than a quarter of an hour. He is a very busy man—and he has pledged his entire personal fortune to providing food for those who will be in need of it."

A taxi cab pulled up just as I came out the entrance. Aunt Bea was already on the pavement. I had never seen her move so fast in my life. When we arrived, the secretary apologized. Mr. Hoover has asked if we might meet him at number 3, next door, the Relief Offices. We were shown in immediately to see Mr. Hoover. I was shocked. He seemed so young! In fact, he was only forty, and I was used to grey hair. Mr. Hoover was a clean-shaven man, neat in a stiff collar, and his gaze was very direct if he looked at you, but mostly he averted his eyes, as if to veil his thoughts. His was a face of such determined contours, he had earned the nickname **The Jaw**.

"I've made the list, "said my aunt. "These are all, persons known to me personally." Looking at it upside down, I could make out 'Jack Morgan, Wall Hall,' at the top, and noted that Mr. Hoover seemed suitably impressed. He leaned back jingling some change is his trousers pocket.

"I have been expecting this crisis since July," said my aunt.

"Oh? When did it first strike you that there would be a Smash?"

"When the money reserves were moved from Belgrade to Kragonyevatz." She pronounced the latter word correctly. I could see her answer had interested him; I could see she was not talking in terms of sentiment but of fact. "And again when Sir Edward Grey called the Austrian ultimatum 'the most formidable one State has ever addressed to another.'"

"Yes," said Hoover agreeably. "If you want to get onto these people, you will need facts. We need money, lots of it. It will take at least five million a month. And we must get assurance the Germans won't requisition our supplies. Otherwise the British and the French will not play ball. We are going to ship entirely under American auspices—from the U.S. to the embassy in London to the legation in Belgium. Talk to William Goods here and Ben Allen at A. P. London. Write Will Irwin in New York. My secretary will give you particulars. See Señor Don Alfonso Merry del Val. Here's my card to present to him. Let me see what you are going to say before you start. I see everything. OK?" We nodded. "Excellent. Glad of your assistance," he said, opening the door out of the office for us. Outside, my aunt slumped as if she had just been dropped out of a whirlwind.

But that very night, she was at the desk of our new suite, as Anna dodged and whirled around her as she was scribbling, building up wads of paper she was not happy with and firing them into the wastebasket. What we would later term **The Speech** began emerging. (Becky could imitate her mother exactly. She would raise and arms and announce dramatically, 'Bread must not fall below two hundred grams *per diem!')* And I would giggle. I couldn't help it. We were just two young girls who knew very little about any real kind of suffering.

Just before we left Brown's I was awakened one night by Becky and her mother, having the Armageddon of all arguments. Becky had been up, listening to Irving Berlin's "Watch Your Step" on the electrophone.

Apparently her mother had interrupted her with another motherly admonition. Voices began to be raised.

Wide awake, I heard Becky clearly. "You are ruining my life!" she yelled "It's quite all right for Amanda, to hang about, meeting no one, there is always good-old-Martin! But I would rather be Cast Adrift in an open boat back to America if I am not sunk by a submarine than to hang about and hang about with your mourning, and your religious—(I could tell she was searching for a word) "claptrap that makes other people miserable and all your Booooring ideas about what I shouldn't do, when you aren't even doing what a Mother is supposed to do and bring me around so I don't die an Old Maid! And you mope about and mope about, as if you are the only one who is upset, and I have lost my father, and he wouldn't neglect to let me have some fun, or get out!" Becky, I realized, was semi-hysterical. She had really been pushed beyond her limit. I heard something crash.

Nothing like this had ever happened before I was hanging on to the edge of my mattress, listening very hard!

Even my aunt must have been frightened. If she wasn't frightened for her daughter—or even of her daughter—she was at least frightened of that most terrible of all gaffes, making a scene, one that could be heard all the way down to Piccadilly. For she did not yell back. She tried to be conciliatory. And when she finally got Becky calmed down, and sent her off to bed, I actually heard her pick up the telephone, ring Mr. Seddon, and actually apologize for waking him up.

Mr. Seddon must have had far more worldly sense than either Becky or I would ever have imagined. The upshot the next day was this. Becky would be allowed to order a new wardrobe from a suitable dressmaker, and she would be allowed to walk out with wounded officers who were recovering in a very toney hospital made out of a house owned by a lady on Park Lane, whom Aunt Bea had recently met at one of the charitable meetings which were beginning to bedeck her daily calendar.

Becky did not mention it to me. Nor did she include me in her plan to outfit herself, and her "walk outs." She had obviously concluded, somehow, she must look out for number one.

We began to ready items for refugees, and wonder when they would start to arrive, and what would they be like. Richard Harding Davis, the dean of American war correspondents, had described his first view of refugees who proceeded the wave of von Moltke's army, the rich in *...'taxicabs, racing cars, limousines, ...white-faced with the dust of the road, with weariness and fear'*...and the peasants whose carts blocked the side streets. *Into these,* he wrote, *they had thrown mattresses, or bundles of grain, and heaped upon them were families of three generations. Old men in blue smocks, white-haired and bent, old women in caps, and daughters dressed in their one best frock and hat, and clasping in their hands all that was left to them, all they could stuff into a pillow-case or flour sack. The tears rolled down their brown, tanned faces.*

One morning, the call came. My aunt received news that a group of refugees had arrived at Alexandra Palace. My aunt called to me. "Will you please call Mr. Whitefield? His number is in my address book."

Why was this? The other two were busy, so, not having Anna to make the call, which would have been proper, she only had me. My finger that dialed the phone shook. Briggs answered. I asked for his master. I heard him call to Mr. Whitefield that it was a Miss Ten Eycke, and then the rush of feet to the phone. "Mr. Whitefield," I said, "they have arrived at Alexandra Palace. Would you be able to help us?"

"Of course. Where shall I meet you?" This meant a yell to Aunt Bea. Yes, he could meet all of us at Kings Cross station, where we would take the underground north. Aunt Bea said not one word of protest at this mention of the use of the transport method of the *hoi polloi*. It was here, as we were standing in a line for tokens at Harringay, that a woman approached him. We had no idea what was happening. Quickly, she stuck a white feather in his breast pocket. Then, in a very loud, attention-getting voice, she began to berate him. "You, sir, should be ashamed of yourself! A healthy, strong young man like you! Why are you not in uniform sir! It is clear you are no patriot!"

Just then, with amazing presence of mind, Aunt Bea stepped up to her. "I think that is quite enough, miss!" she uttered firmly. "You should be ashamed of yourself." Hearing my aunt's American accent, and as Mr. Whitefield had not spoken, the woman, in some confusion, retreated, under the impression she had accosted a foreigner and confused him for a national. He folded the feather in half and returned it to his pocket. We were all so embarrassed no one could think of anything to say. Our little group clustered together on the station platform, separated from the other passengers by this encounter and the stares it drew.

Once on the train, he recovered his composure. He entertained our party with an account of how the first Alexandria Palace had burned down two weeks after it had opened, how Thomas More had used a cottage nearby, and about Highgate Cemetery, where the author of *Dracula* was buried. Once off the train, we advanced on foot toward this northern version of the Crystal Palace, my aunt tackling this walk like a pilgrim doing the Spanish Steps on her knees. At the door, Mr. Seddon presented his card. We waited, and finally followed someone in a makeshift uniform down a hallway to large room.

Before us sat a group of people with the sadly bowed heads and sagging postures of a Pietà. They had been given means to wash and groom themselves, as we could see pitchers of water on the tables, but from the overpowering stench it appeared they had not had the heart to do so. I took as step backward and even felt a bit queasy. This won't do, I told myself. Despite the fact the picture was a bit obscene—ourselves, neat, fed, secure, as we stared at that naked misery, we were here. One by one, our eyes turned to Mr. Whitefield, we knew he knew their language and could take a stab at dialects. Somehow a group consensus unconsciously developed that he must be the best one to make our first approach to them. He, in turn, took me by the arm, and we moved up toward a woman who seemed most in possession of herself. It was clear to me I was with him for moral support.

He told her in French how he had been in France when the war began, that we were a church group, and we desired to be of whatever assistance we could. He knew the war was going rather badly at the moment —a fact concealed from the British public; however, he had just had a letter from a friend in France, to the effect his brother had been wounded so severely they thought he would die. Why hadn't he told me? Suddenly, the Grunewald tryptic I had seen at Colmar of a crucified Christ already beginning to rot rose before me. It was on a tour last summer I had seen it with Martin, and had noticed he did not appear to realize I was even having such a horrible reaction to it, nattering on about perhaps it was time to become engaged? I just ignored what he said, entranced by the painting, and he just assumed I agreed with him by my silence.

Today was the day. Today it was going to happen, and I was afraid. But Mr. Whitefield held my arm more tightly. *I am here, Amanda. Madame, si vous ne nous voudriez racontere ce qu'est arrivez, nous comprenons.* If she did not wish to tell us what had happened, we would understand. She began her tale in French, but as her native language was Flemish, her language was only somewhat comprehensible to Mr. Whitefield who plugged some German words to bridge the gap. *"Mais non! Il faut que le monde en sait!"* The world should know about it—even if they did not find it believable. It would take years before it was a proven fact that what they said was true. In the meantime, it led countries to doubt tales of a Holocaust taking place in the Second World War as overdone, despite the reports of Cardinal Mercier. She began a tale told simply, unfolding as starkly and terribly as a Greek drama.

"We are citizen of Vise, in Belgium, a border town to Germany. On August 3, in marched the Germans. We had destroyed the bridge over the Meuse to delay them and of course this made them very angry because they had to stop to build pontoons. When they entered the town they were even angrier. They took my husband, they took some other men, and shot them just like that in the town square, and then they burned our houses, and took other men as prisoners back to Germany to work for them. We were told we had to leave by four o'clock. By that evening, we had reached Holland, standing in the very clothes in which you see us now, Monsieur." Somewhere during the account, her hand had crept into his, and with his other, he kept patting her hand in his. The woman did not cry. I think she was too deeply shocked. I did feel the odd tear trickling down my cheek, but I did not stop to wipe them.

"Do you think they will come here?" she asked, frightened, turning her head to look behind her, as if troops were still at her heels, or would materialize behind her if she did not keep a watch out. "Do you think they will cross the Channel? Have they taken Paris?"

"What are they saying?" Aunt Bea asked in a loud whisper.

"You must wait, Mrs. Ten Eycke," said Mr. Seddon. It was the first time in her life knowing a different language appeared of some value to her.

"No, Madame," Mr. Whitefield replied. "You must assure the others that although the news is not the best, I have had word through friends I shall not mention, that our combined armies have stopped the German army a little distance from Paris, and now the war is entering a different phase, and I suspect soon our letters will have to undergo censorship. But you are safe here."

And now, rapport having been struck up with the women (for the group was composed of women and children and two elderly men) as Mr. Whitefield translated to our group what Madame had told us created an immediate rapport of sympathy. We guessed the women would have more confidence conveying some of their needs to me. All of a sudden, all the rest of them were talking to me at once.

Mrs. Seddon opened a very large bag she was carrying and produced some toys and children's games. Not much language was needed for the children to begin examining them. Other women produced tape measures, safety pins, needles and threads, and toothbrushes, (which were largely unused). Mr. Seddon's group had brought things they thought would be the most useful, and soon measurements were being taken, for everyone had lost weight on their march, and conversation took place by hand gesture and asking me what was the word for shoe, dress.

By the time we got back to the hotel, I was completely devastated and sat as if stunned on my bed for several hours, while events were spinning onward.

Aunt Bea told me Mr. Whitefield had asked if we might address each other by our first names, as in situations like that of the day, it was far faster. So pragmatic was the request, she agreed.

CHAPTER 10

"My family calls me Brand," he said

I was collecting myself to attend a run-through before going on tour. He had invited all of us, but Aunt Bea had been invited to an affair at the American Embassy which included 'young people,' for Ambassador Page's daughter Kitty was living in London with them. My aunt decided to take Becky with her, and leave Anna to accompany me to the theatre.

I had not yet met the male lead, Philip Frye. My eyes were drawn to him immediately. He seemed to exude a sort of charming pull I would later learn was a good thing in a leading man, because it was known as sex appeal. Miss Westcote, however, did not seem to be charmed. She was in fact throwing a mild tantrum.

"No one could be such an absolute twit as to take that sunflower speech right off the spoon like honey, Philip! At least show you are waking up to me, —just a hint! You aren't giving me a thing to play off, and you know it." She pointed a condemning finger at him.

"Well, Philip?" asked Brand.

"I've no notion what she's carrying on about."

"You do—and I was waiting for her to call it. She's a new ingénue and you are trying to trip her up as much as possible to focus attention on you. –Miss Westcote, try this. Don't forget there are other undergraduates in the room. Turn forty-five degrees and let them listen to the song, too —and to the audience."

"Oh, righto!" she exclaimed. She poured on more intensity. The undergraduates at the upper left registered their admiration, and sure enough, Mr. Frye, not wanting to simply stand by, suddenly thought of a different reaction.

"That does for it very nicely, Miss Westcote," said Brand. "A very nice piece of interpretation." Frye cleared his throat.

"Let's try it again," said Frye. When I finally left, Brand was encouraging the two of them to stop, to not exhaust themselves, but they rehearsed on and on as if possessed by some creative *daemon.*

"This scene has hardly been alive as yet," he said to me. "Your horse is beginning to run a race!"

Now, there as one thing I found I really didn't like about putting on a London show. That was they usually had trial runs out of town. Brand prepared to take the cast to Manchester; the Manchester Rep had always been lucky for him; he thought the world of Miss Horniman, its proprietress. However, she had decided her theatre would be closed for the duration; 'The Lady' would be the last play to tread the boards before its closing, with nothing oncoming to rush him. "I asked her if she's attending this last performance of her rep." She said of course she would be there. 'Every corpse must attend it's own funeral!'

Aunt Bea and Becky were busy, busy. I sat alone at Claridge's staring out the window onto Brook Street. What could I do with myself? There is one thing I can do to which Uncle Ben had introduced me: the headquarters of the Association for the Revival Practice of Folk Music. Uncle Ben had a long acquaintance with its president, the Earl of Lytton, the only peer eccentric enough to have taken up folk music. They met at Craven House. I had to ask the doorman how to get to Kingsway via autobus, for, as usual, we had been only doled out a few shillings and clearly the doorman felt he ought to summon a taxi.

He told me to get down at Aldwych. Once having boarded the 'omni,' I found one was allowed to climb up outside stairs in the back of the bus, to its open top deck. This was rather thrilling, as was having my ticket punched by a young woman. I smiled to myself at this version of the American Millionairess! She strode through 'Punch' cartoons, always sorry she had already bought out Bond Street before other millionairesses beat her to it. (Of course, with five dollars to make a pound at this time, this kind of million was far cheaper than the English version).

"Kingsway up that way, Miss," said the conductor as I jumped down. It was a street perpendicular to the curve of Aldwych, where Aunt Bea had told me Mr. Hoover's organization, the Committee for the Relief of Belgium, had set up a warehouse. I was careful to leap the detritus at the curb, a mix of petrol, mud, and horse dung.

At Craven House, I entered a large room, with people straggling about, and went up to a small desk, and announced myself for the first time in my life. As I did so, an older gentleman literally sprang out of a corner.

"Did I hear you correctly? Are you really Amanda Ten Eycke? How you've grown! I am so sorry about your uncle! What a terrible loss. I had many wonderful conversations with him."

Of course, I did not remember him clearly. He was one of those blur of faces who were 'friends of Uncle Ben's.' I would hang around—Becky was right, we did a lot of hanging around being seen but not heard—listening at first, and then playing.

"We were just about to call a song circle!" Said Mr. Herbert Chesterton (for such was my new friend's name).

This was a tradition. One need not quail as one might have at an audition—just ask me—if you did not have the voice of a lark: here, the song was the thing, we were just its humble transmitters. A woman began with something from the Elf Knight cycle. Then a man sang a chantey from Grimsby Next was my turn so I sang a newly minted ballad about Jesse James, which everyone seemed to enjoy a lot, I was very pleased to note. Then the man next to me began something in a sweet Irish tenor, which lulled me, as if I were listening to something poetic, lyric, beautiful…He sang, 'I'll pray for Mother England…' by the time he finished with these words, 'I'll pray that Mother England dies and drowning she may drown, And if she ever tries to lift her head, I'll be there to push her down!'

I stiffened. So did everyone else. Several people were so enraged they got up and left, effectively breaking up our circle. "And after all that hard work the Earl did in Lords for Ireland," exclaimed the Elf Knight lady loudly.

"Didn't the Earl say no matter what kind of bill they drafted, no one would be happy with it?" I asked, and thanked my lucky stars for Aunt Bea reading the paper to us.

"Oooo, now do we get that from the Earl himself?" asked the Irish balladeer, who had a tweed cap crushed down over his eyebrows.

"She may well have," said Mr. Chesterton softly "Her family was invited to Knebworth, sir!"

"Hmmph!" said the Elf Knight lady, with the superior kind of smile that implied an American who knew anything about British affairs was a rare as Dr. Johnson's dog walking on its hind legs.

"Anyone could have read it in the Times, "I replied.

"And did you read in the Times that the first casualty of this war has been Irish Home Rule, then?" The balladeer asked me.

Just then a youngish man stood up. He was holding a banjo-mandolin. He had thinnish strands of hair combed back over an already-balding scalp; his skin was pale underneath a patina which spoke of spending time outdoors, but not the Great Outdoors; his skin did not have that healthy kind of look. "I would not exactly call that making a newcomer welcome," said he.

"Quite right, Max!" seconded Mr. Chesterton.

"Oooo and what do you suggest, Maxie?"

"I suggest you shove off and only return when you are in a better frame of mind, one in which you can adhere to the Association's rule to stick to music instead of arguing about politics."

The balladeer stood up. For an instant I thought there might be blows struck, until the balladeer realized he was greatly outnumbered. Max stood easily, with some sort of authority which did not emanate from being confrontational.

"And I'd save the gin until after your next visit," Max added quietly. With another hostile glance of two the balladeer finally turned on his heel, angrily swinging out the door.

"Miss Ten Eycke," he asked, noting my fiddle case, "would you care to play something with me?" I was glad I had kept up my morning practiced sessions, for he exuded an accomplished aura. After the usual do-you-knows, we settled on a brace of hornpipes, beginning with the Liverpool hornpipe; he was pretty good, I noticed approving nods. Sure enough, after we finished, the doctor was asking me how I'd like to play some hospitals with him.

"We would have to practice and I am living in a hotel," I replied, anticipating all the prohibitions that would make this impossible—first off, not knowing this man from Adam.

"We live off Chester Square," said Mr. Chesterton. He knew the drill for young ladies. "Many members practice there. I shall have my wife ring up your aunt." I was astounded. Once again I muttered, 'thank you, Uncle Ben'.

"This time of day is capital for me," said Dr. Ainley, who, I was beginning to discover Everyone, by some strange Universal, and Communal principle, called 'Max.' "I have night rounds."

"That sounds awful!" I said, unaware that soon I would adhere to the same schedule.

"The lot of a fledgling specialist." I thought he was waiting for me to ask him in what, but the body was Delicate Turf to girls of my day. I simply blushed.

Back on the omnibus, I looked at my watch. Good! I had actually not thought about Brand for three whole hours. It may have been a pitiful feat, but a feat nonetheless; and I felt better, for I suspected he wasn't thinking of me all the time, with a play on tour.

And there was plenty to think about. Just before he departed for Manchester, he paid me another early morning visit. This time, the concierge, having been elegantly bribed, let us sit again in the small room behind the desk, where no one would spot us.

"I realize that for some reason I always seem to be departing on you, even if I wish to stay nearby. I regret that." He cleared his throat. What was he going to say?

"We both know there is a cure for our dilemma. I understand you must take your own time to consider what is problematic to you about my life. I have no similar reservations. You could be with me wherever I go in short order, three weeks to post the banns."

My God, he had just asked me to marry him.

"Let me know if you want the whole nine yards, getting down on my knees, that sort of thing!" He added with a smile.

"No. I don't wish anyone to lower themselves for me."

After that, I would awake in the middle of the night and slowly become conscious that Brand had asked me to marry him. And that secret made me feel as if I would burst with joy, even if I did not know what to do about it.

CHAPTER 11

Arriving at Claridge's for our first night on the premises, I was told at the desk that my aunt and cousin were already in the restaurant dining room, so I crossed the lobby and cut across the coffee room under the archway to join them for dinner. They were full of their various doings of the day, and it just showed how much our world had changed, that they made no big scene about my going out alone.

Once in our suite, Mrs. Chesterton rang up. Apparently the fact they had known Uncle Ben, coupled with the fact she and my aunt had crossed paths in relief circles, and a very nice address behind Buckingham Palace sat well with my aunt, who accepted an invitation for tea the following afternoon. Their house turned out to be on the end of Chester Square nearest Eubury Street, set behind a stone church, somewhat off the regimented march of uniform but elegant white houses.

Next afternoon, a footman passed us to the butler. A shortage of servants had not yet set in. We were announced. That was the last traditional thing that happened to us.

Mr. Chesterton burst in, holding a concertina. "I've things all set up, Miss Ten Eycke." My aunt wafted away toward Mrs. Chesterton's domain. Then my eyes beheld the ballroom, a big open space denuded of everything but a few chairs. It brought to mind Brand's latest letter: *I am having trouble getting across the rhythm of Fatiguée which comes so easily to you. I am counting on your help when we get to London.* I would ask Mr. Chesterton if we could rehearse it here! There was nothing to lose.

Dr. Ainley was sitting in one of the three chairs drawn into a circle. Beside his banjo-mandolin, he had a lute with him. "Do you know

John Dowland?" He asked me. That was a yes. We played 'Flow Softly My Tears,' and then one written by the Countess of Pembroke, 'If Ever Hapless Woman.'

"Shouldn't we be playing things to cheer the patients up?" I asked.

"No. It still holds true to weep with those who weep."

"I know one along those lines. It's so sad that officers of both the North and the South forbade their soldiers to sing it." I played the melody of 'When This Cruel War is Over' until Max and Mr. Chesterton caught the melody. Then I sang the lyrics, 'Dearest love, do you remember...' and when I reached the chorus, "Weeping, sad and lonely, Hopes and fears how vain! When this cruel war is over, Praying that we meet again," I teared up.

"That's a winner," said Max. "It's far better to be real than to be artificially cheerful. Otherwise you will put a burden on the patients."

We settled down to work. I began to learn the songs Max knew and vice versa.

"What do you specialize in, may I ask?"

"I'm studying at Bethlehem Hospital, Lambeth."

"You mean—"

"Yes, the infamous Bedlam. However, a good fifty per cent of our patients are rather mundane and middle class."

"You should be off, Max," said Mr. C., who apparently was completely aware of Max's schedule. We came at his heels to look for the ladies. At the door of a sitting room, the maid handed Mrs. Chesterton a sandwich. She handed it to Max. He gave her a kiss on the cheek. Off he went, leaving his instruments lying on the chair. It seemed that any house eventually became Max's house.

"A dear boy, "said Mrs. C., apparently very fond of him.

"A bit unusual," said my aunt.

"Yes, Max is very unaffected, I don't know it has something to do with St. Francis."

Good god, Max was a papist! My aunt's eyebrows shot up. I surreptitiously glanced to make sure horns were not growing out of his head.

I practiced every morning –yet again—this time in the smoking room on the ground story, below the lobby. It was had a medieval fireplace big enough to roast an ox, wood wainscotting, red leather sofas, long heavy curtains, and no customers early in the morning. The odor of cigar nearly gassed me, but practice space was practice space.

I asked Mr. C. if we might use the ballroom, and when I explained why, he was—as usual—enthusiastic.

By now, *the Lady* had played in Manchester and was headed for Edinburgh. '*While we are definitely not dead on our feet, certainly reception could be warmer. Oh well it is Scotland.*'

The reception, although modest was still remarkable, for September had been the worst ever period for the British theater, as many former theater goers now considered amusing themselves bad taste—the king and queen included. *Gerald has laid on a charity matinee each week and made wide publicity about how the matinee receipts would go to war charities. Tree put on 'The Armada' for charity in London and it was well received.*

Meanwhile Mr. C. had dropped out declaring he couldn't keep pace with the two of us, but would come with us to make it proper in terms of Aunt Bea. We were developing the easy confidence common to musical partners

Meanwhile, Brand was taking in my letters, which were now filled with news, rather than mundane rounds of our past sort of activities. I sensed he was somewhat uneasy about this new Max fellow, who I seemed to spend a good amount of time with—just as, equally, I thought, he spent time with the women of his cast.

One day I asked Max, "Do you treat people who are crazy?"

"In one form or another, hopefully, for I am studying to be an alienist. Why do you ask?"

A silence fell. Twilight was slanting diagonally across the highly polished wooden floors. Its rays illumined a pattern of light slightly in front of us.

"When my uncle died..." I began. He put his lute on his thigh, holding the top of it with his right hand. "You see, I'd always gone all sorts of places with him and met all kinds of people. All of a sudden I wasn't the person I had been, as if I were a prisoner. I felt I couldn't go anywhere, so I vowed if I couldn't go anywhere, I just wouldn't go anywhere and if I had to leave the house, I'd get faint and return again. My family felt I had gotten peculiar. I guess I've recovered balance again, but they still think that I am—odd."

"If it's any consolation, I hadn't noticed a thing."

Oh, what a relief that was! Max certainly noticed but held his tongue.

On tour, now Edinburgh had been conquered *(at least it didn't conquer us)* and they were on the last lap home. That evening several letters came which asked me to meet him at Mr. C.'s the next afternoon! When I arrived, my hands were sweaty, I was so keyed up, and Mr. C. was absolutely bursting with the news that Brand, Miss Westcote, and several members of the orchestra awaited me.

"You have met Dr. Ainley?" I asked Brand.

"Indeed," he uttered guardedly. "Bedlam. Does everyone ask that?"

"About fifty-fifty, "said Max.

"Let me show you," I said to Miss Westcote. "Put your arm around my waist." I showed her the slight hesitation step used by choirs of colored people. That was all it took. The instruments were far harder. But Max picked up the tune in double stops on his fiddle, putting emphasis correctly on things like 'Curt- seying.' When an hour later Miss Westcote and the members of the orchestra hit it, she felt triumphant. She went off to powder her nose. I sat down to rest, leaving Brand and Max in a private conversation.

"What happens to doctors now?' Brand asked.

"I'm interning at the moment and it seems useful to finish that before I start out trying to treat soldiers."

"But it's going to be a *short* war," said Brand ironically.

"Unless you listen to Kitchner. What happens to playwrights?"

Brand slowly reflected on what to say, then, "Quite curiously, I found today, my publicity agent has let out when this play wraps up I shall probably be joining the Flying Corps. He believes in the short war, and he seems he felt it would make the play go. I don't know how to tell her."

"There doesn't seem to be any way beyond it. And she may see it in the papers—better if it comes from you, Whitefield. Let me bring her over to you."

Upon hearing this news, I demanded, "How could he do that to you?"

"Do you paper the hall?" asked Max.

"I'll see that you get a ticket."

"Many thanks I must be off." Even if he didn't have to, he felt the rest was for the two of us.

"There isn't any way you can head it off getting in the papers?"

"I think not. I wanted you to know before you read it. Whether or not it is an action that has thrown me to the wolves would not really have entered Gerald's sphere of concern. He thinks only of the show. I should have anticipated something like this. To Gerald the theatre is the world; he has no other."

"But what about you? Hasn't he any loyalty?"

"He considers it a loyalty to make the show go any way he can. His ethics do not extend beyond it."

A copy of "Punch" I had been looking at in the reading room had a cartoon of of a girl walking her dachshund. Dogs of German breeds had fallen into disfavor with the public, and some were reported as having been kicked. But this woman had taped a Union Jack to her dog's tail. The caption read: "Taking No risks."

CHAPTER 12

And then –it was opening night!

We could hardly breathe, we were so excited. We arrived early; Brand had reserved a box for us, where Max joined us. I actually began to feel a trifle faint just before the orchestra struck up the prelude. "Stop breathing so fast," Max commanded. The audience rustled programs, greeted friends and settled in as the prelude started playing. Then the lights went down and the curtain went up. And...there she was....

Enter Felicity, the lady!

She moved downstage (as I was learning to call it) toward the audience, and, with an intuitive new piece of business, put one foot forward, and made them a bow. She had captured them. To all our surprise, they burst out in applause, for this was not yet the time when applause would be limited to after each scene or act.

Then she began to sing her opener. Mr. Frye entered. Audience attention continued high. At intermission, Brand raced up to our box. He looked pale. I did not know that opening nights he was so nervous sometimes he vomited. He was perfectly dressed, with an admirably embroidered white waistcoat. He had asked us to join him the next night for dinner before the play, as tonight, he would be too distracted.

It was not until the very last second that Mr. Frye got his very own piece of real business and upstaged the lady. With a raise of his eyebrow he indicated he knew she knew that she had overheard him. He stepped downstage, communicating to the audience, 'perhaps I've had a narrow escape!'

There was a split -second pause. Then a ripple of laughter ran through the house, then came waves of applause. Then he and Miss Westcote took a curtain call, and a second one which included other members of the cast. And a few more.

Then there were calls for 'Author.'

I held my breath as Brand stepped out in front of his cast.

He took a slight bow, then raised both hands for silence.

"Ladies and gentlemen, I thank you. Doubtless many of you recall the famous story of Mr. Bernard Shaw's curtain call, wherein one boo was heard from the gallery amidst a sea of acclamation and Mr. Shaw retorted, "I agree, sir, but what can two do against so many?" There were laughs and smiles. "I am pleased to have avoided a similar fate, and I thank you for your very, very kind reception. I wish to thank my brilliant cast. Thank you and goodnight."

Max had already dashed out to snag cab, for we were invited to the cast party. Max—who was used to being up all night anyway—was in fine fettle, more than ready to escort us.

I was never quite sure of the establishment which hosted the cast party, for I was far too excited, too over the moon, as my host country would have put it. But there were tables and chairs and food and drink, and a small band for dancing. Most of the cast came in bit by bit, out of makeup for they had not been in the last scene. But Miss Westcote and Philp Frye were in such high spirits they came in costume and makeup. A bit had rubbed off Miss Westcote's chin and I could see the white base beneath it.

There was champagne being passed around and trays of food. My aunt even formally allowed Becky and me to have a glass. Becky got hold of Max and took him onto the dance floor vowing to teach him how to 'cut a rug,' but they spent more time laughing at Max's two left feet than dancing. Aunt Bea was talking to an older gentleman in the cast and from the serous expressions I knew they were discussing the war.

Brand sat down beside me. He looked a trifle mentally worn out. The waiter presented him with a menu labeled American cocktails. "What intriguing choices. Shall I have—a Manhattan or a Corpse Reviver?"

"A Manhattan!" I exclaimed, with geographical loyalty. Except that he seemed to have the endurance of a Clydesdale, I half expected him to collapse after he tossed it off.

Here came my aunt. What could she want? I wondered a bit foggily. She wanted him to sign her program! Boy, that was pretty gauche, even for her. He got out his fountain pen and seemed to be writing forever. What was taking so long, anyway? Aunt Bea read it, smiled, and was very pleased, and handed it to me to read. '*Every creature is the stage, the medium, the glass in which we may see God. John Donne*'. Then his Signature and the date. That seemed pretty cogent for someone who seemed a little bit—wait a minute, it was I who was a bit tipsy. No wonder; I'd had two glasses of champagne.

Now here came Murdoch, what could he want? He handed Brand twenty pounds. "You win."

"What is that about?"

"A wager. He was sure I was committing artistic suicide to use Miss Westcote. 'You have a perfect ingénue,' he kept telling me."

"Artistic differences," I said, quoting Brand.

Murdoch was pausing just a bit too long, keeping his expression just a bit too expressionless. Maybe I was imagining things.

"May I have this dance?" Brand asked when they played a waltz. We spun away—at least he did. "Have you never drunk champagne before?" He asked solicitously.

"No, I never really have." His hand tightened on my waist to give me a bit more guidance and the band swung into 'Champagne Charlie is My Name.'

Miss Westcote and Gerald Murdoch swung by smartly, Felicity singing along—beautifully, of course—"Champagne Charlie is my name, drinking champagne is my name, there's no sound like fizz, fizz, fizz, I'll drink every drop here is, is, is... All round town it is the same, I pop, pop, pop, my way to fame, 'I'm the idol of the barmaids, and Champagne Charlie is My Name!'"

"She's asking me to change some lines already," Murdoch called. "The real leading lady syndrome."

And on top of this, he was taking us to dinner tomorrow evening to celebrate! It was almost Too Much.

Max cut in. When we were in the clear, Max said, "Tell your friend not to worry on my account, I'm about to enter a Franciscan novitiate. They've cut me the slack to continue my medical practice."

"What's that?"

"A monastery."

"Do you think I ought to tell him about my—peculiarity? I did faint once."

"I would wait just a little while. "

We slept late the next morning, but by supper time, we were dressed to the nines yet again.

CHAPTER 13

"There he is!" Becky whispered to me. We had taken the elevator down to the first floor, then walked down the hallway to the staircase, which had a between stairs turn of ninety degrees into the last half-flight down to the lobby on the ground floor. We could see yet not be seen. He had rung up to say he was waiting. He stood, nervously smoothing the white tie of his evening kit in an absent -minded gesture. Some of the people who passed him made a small turn back, the kind people made when they say to themselves, "I've seen that phizz in the dailies!"

For, as his friend had predicted, after the first fall off of an audience, theater attendance had come back again.

I am very much afraid, my dear Mandra, we may not succeed in our noble attempt to produce a deficit, he had written to me that morning. The floor was made in a black and white diamond pattern, and he seemed like the pawn in some gigantic chess game. I shook myself and shivered.

Now my aunt joined us. She was in full panoply, with a pearl and diamond Alexandra dog collar and a lace caplet over her gown. And Becky! She had finally succeeded in being up to the mode, and drew admiring glances in a feathered head dress and a gown with a sea green cut velvet underdress with a pale yellow tunic over it, which flared out into a stiffened minaret skirt. It set off her brown hair, and this was the day of the brunette— the Gibson girl!—she emphasized it with a walnut rinse.

Brand greeted us with just with a little bow. He had a white silk scarf around his neck and his black silk Herbert Johnson topper in his hand. He told my aunt that he had booked us into his father's favorite restaurant.

She looked pleased. Doubtless it was a conservative sort of place that served two kinds of potatoes.

Indeed, when we arrived, we trooped by vast expanses of the kind of dark mahogany which produced the sort of gloom I always labelled Black Forest Décor. My aunt's necklace threw glints of refracted sparkles off the walls.

As the maître d' led us along the private to the private dining room he had booked, we passed close by a table that was obviously habituated by two octogenarian gentlemen who were used to conversing with one another in the very loud tones of the Ear Trumpet set.

"I say—isn't that Stroplea's boy? "One bellowed to the other.

"Righto by Jove and it seems he's got his hands full, I should say!"

Never one to pass a cue, Brand bounded over to their table (They had obviously Known him Since He was a child) and said, loudly enough that they might hear, "Gentlemen, you should be so fortunate as to have your hands so full!"

"Sherry, sir?" Said the waiter as he placed our napkins across our laps.

"No, champagne." When it arrived we toasted Success. The soup (mock turtle) and fish (turbot) courses were consumed discussing the reviews. They had been read last night, of course, but this was a more temperate atmosphere in which to discuss the reaction in the press.

"I particularly like what the Telegraph fellow wrote," I said. I quoted, "As Pascal said, when you see a natural style you are surprised, because you wait to see an author, but you see a man, and every man who takes up a pen, fancies he can write that way, but most cannot." He knew I had memorized it.

"Complimentary, indeed," he said, smiling at me.

"Was your family pleased by your success? I did not miss their attendance, did I?"

"Madame, I expect my mother felt it might not have been terribly politic," Brand said. He stopped. We got it. Spy mania. The walls have ears. Waiters who changed from Otto to Giotto. Germans spreading rumors about omnibuses. Waterworks guarded so Germans would not pour poison into them. A German taking a shot of at the Prince of Wales, which bounced off the handle of his cane. We said no more. The meat arrived: beef wellington.

Soon enough, Becky asked a question: "What is this Air Reserve thing?"

"Rebecca!" Her daughter had not waited until her mother had finished her remarks.

"It began with balloon and dirigibles, property of the Royal Engineers," he explained. "Then a few aeroplane fanatics like Basil Barrington-Kennett crept in. An Air Battalion was formed in 1911. It became the Flying Corps in 1912. There was a Central Flying School at Farnborough, and new squadrons would occasionally break off, but at the beginning of the war, there were only five of them, with immediate need for many more. Reserve Squadrons are being scattered round the countryside. Each one will have its own instruction and come up to scratch as a unit. Civilians who join will hold temporary rank. All civilian aircraft in England have been impounded, but many of them have been rejected as of no use to the R.F.C."

"They can't just take your aeroplane!" Becky said forcefully.

"They can and they will—I don't know if mine has been rejected or not as yet."

"This is what Mr. Murdoch implied you might join?"

"I doubt that Gerald can make such distinctions as the R.F.C. or the Royal Naval Service. Madame. Let me ask you something in return. I know you are familiar with Reverend Whitefield, and, I assume, his concept of the new birth. Does your Mr. Seddon take a position on such a thing?"

My aunt blinked her eyes suddenly, as if she were seeing something she had never expected. Finally she mustered "Indeed he does."

Just then the Stilton arrived and although I felt I might never eat again, I did, as well as a traditional desert called apple hat.

"Why don't you join us in our rooms for brandy and we can discuss this further," my aunt managed to interject.

"I would be most appreciative of such an opportunity, Madame."

Then we set out for Claridge's. The taxicab fumbled through the dimmed-out streets of London. The city itself emitted a vibration, an air, a waiting for something darker than the semi-darkness to manifest itself, as if civilization trembled on the brink of being sucked back through the centuries, back through the Great Fire, back to its Roman foundations, back to some Druidic past rising up to claim its own from our present and pull the present down into some unknown underneath us on which London rested.

Once we arrived, my aunt declared, "Rebecca, you may retire, as the subject of religion always taxes you." In this way she closed off any interruption. Becky sulked, but left.

"You have read Reverend Whitefield, I take it?"

"Very particularly, Madame, all in one summer."

"May I ask what became of it?"

"A great hue and cry; it was the one summer I could not go to France, so, when my mother observed me retreat with a pile of religious books, she insisted on sending me round to a *modern* curate whose views she felt would correct my own. He was full of the Vienna school and analyzed that my interest was a kind of guilty reaction to the stirring of puberty."

"Good Heavens!" said my aunt.

"On my side, Madame, I had the uneasy feeling this chap was a bit too interested in adolescent concupiscence, like the occasional master one gets the buzz on to avoid at school. I refused to continue meeting with him. My punishment was to have all my books taken from me."

"Oh, who was it that created such a nasty chastisement?"

"O, my Mother, of course, Madame. I believe I conveyed all was not well between us."

"What happened to your interest?"

"As it happens, Madame, I began to have a series of horrible dreams, which are rather giving me a bit of a rattle even now."

"Let me read this to you, sir!" My aunt said, with great excitement. "I was reading this just this morning." She extracted a book from the pile on the desk and read: *You are an odd person, one that could not be written down on any list. You are a peculiar sinner with constitutional tendencies all your own. God says, "I will put my spirit within you, That means your heart, Yes, even yours. You have long been seeking salvation but who have not known the power of the Spirit, this is what you need.*

"You believe this is the missing piece of my puzzle?"

"Definitely."

"How does one get it, if that is not to crude or outright a question?"

"One makes a sincere commitment to Christ, then says aloud the sinners' prayer."

"Which is...?"

My aunt repeated it for him.

"Have you ever said this?" he asked me.

"Actually—no, I haven't heard about it."

"What do you say, then, that we pledge it together?"

I paused a moment to think.

"You will not regret it, Mandra," said my aunt.

Then the three of us joined hands, and Aunt Bea led us in the prayer.

"Please repeat after me:' Lord Jesus Christ, I know I am a sinner. I repent. I ask you to forgive me, be my Savior, and grant me this petition by the power of your Holy Spirit, who I ask you to send into my life.'"

As for me, I felt a rush of incredible, intense, and singular devotion to this one man, all quite unbidden. A longing came, a longing for something beyond our grasp, a desire to be one in the secret world we sometimes shared while in the presence of others, but with no one in it this time but us.

I did not sleep that night. Instead I was in ecstasy.

CHAPTER 14

"I take comfort that in this frightening cataclysm that has become our world, we, my dear Mandra, you and I, stepped spiritually together into the realm of a peace the world cannot see. I grew up believing in Progress, the survival of the 'fittest' leading to a perfectibility via evolution, and the impossibility of another futile European war. As if we could eradicate original sin! To confess I am a sinner in need of grace took a great pressure off my being. Justifying one's faults takes more and more of one's vital energy and integrity, until, perhaps, the voice of conscience can be still heard but the power lost to obey it.'

This was also the morning that I was "blooded," for Max took me to play at my first hospital. He knew and greatly respected Dr. James Purves-Stewart, whose specialty—neurology—was part of Max's training. Dr. Stewart had been placed in charge of Aldford Hospital, formerly the private home of Mrs. Freddie Guest, on Park Lane (famous for its blue silk pyjamas for junior officers, and *pink* for the more senior ranks!). Dr. Stewart, Max told me, also consulted at another hospital at Palace Green, which specialized in treating war-neurosis in officers.

Aldford had a very impressive facade, a series of curved stonework, with two curves set below and within each of them. As it was the private home of the Guests, the inside was elegant with marble. Dr. Purves-Stewart, a straightforward Scotsman with dark round glasses and his hair parted severely in the middle, had, Max told me, already served in the Boer War, and as an avocation was a considerable linguist.

Max had told me he would pick out a gentle ward for us to begin. Nonetheless the strong smells of medicine—disinfectant, heated oils for fomentations, the saline used to bathe wounds and prevent sepsis, the blood which clung to the dressings which were forever being packed and unpacked into the patients—arrested me, as did the military row of beds, each white sheet and blanket concealing beneath something the worse for knowing little about what it might be under it, or how one might react if one *did* know what it was! Women in white head dresses and aprons, and varying colors of uniforms, bustled about, some doing more menial chores (these were the untrained V.A.D.'s,) the nurses professionally moving from cot to cot.

This ward, Max told me, was simply one for men recovering from the cold and damp effects of the holes the Armies were now digging into the ground, and living in, which could get quite wet in Flanders. Some had an inelegant condition labelled "trench foot," others a generic complaint called "P.U.O.," and others rheumatic or respiratory complaints, like bronchitis (which was treated with hot linseed oil compresses).

"All right chaps, we've a bit of a treat," Dr. Stewart said by way of introduction. "Here's Dr. Ainley, a lot of you lads have met him, and Miss Ten Eycke, who is staying in England, but from New York City." The latter item I could see produced some curiosity. All the faces turned toward us were cheerful. The men were enjoying a stretch of what later would come to be called the coveted Blighty Wound.

"Here we are to play for you, gentlemen," said Max, "and a bit later on, we shall have a surprise for you!" (For the ever-surprising Miss Westcote, hearing about our expedition, had promised to trot along for a number or two, and join us in about three quarters of an hour). I could see that Max was, as I was, opening our file of Cheerful Songs.

"What about something about cowboys, dearie?" one of the lads called out.

So we launched into the ever-popular 'Jessie James'.

Max got them singing 'Auld Lang Syne'.

When Miss Westcote breezed in you could have heard a pin drop. I learned the true meaning of the phrase, ***Star Pull!*** "Hello, there, lads, how are you All, you dears??" she said, sweeping between the rows of beds, shaking a hand here, another there (while I still hung back shyly, at the end of the room). "What can I sing for you lot of heroes?" The lads cheered!

"Tipperary!"

"Champagne Charlie!"

"Soldiers of the Queen!" (There were no lack of suggestions).

Max was walking me along, from the Presentable to Wounds, from Wounds to Amputations, and Worse (Worse, to his way of thinking, being men who had lost portions of their faces).

But it would be some time before we reached the far end of the spectrum, and our next stop was a Chic Hospital on the Lane, the one where Becky played cards, chatted, flirted, wrote letters, and strolled with some of the officer-patients. She was very Superior, very much the Old Salt, when we arrived! She introduced everyone to her "little cousin." (Becky was becoming very 'sophisticated' and modern.

Then our conversation took a different turn, as Brand came by to meet us.

He had, he told us, just paid a visit to his father, at the church where his father served on the vestry, St. Edmund the King, on Lombard Street (right in the City of London, where as the joke went, God met Mammon— and Mammon won). Apparently, the Viscount took in the noonday service several days a week, days which never varied.

"Things are in rather a state for my parents," he said. "As you may know, German nationals and even 'neutrals' are being interned at the Crystal Palace, the Isle of Mann, ships in the Thames, and other scattered sites. As well, persons with German last names have been kicked off the floor of the Royal Exchange, and you have heard about Battenburg. My mother has become a British citizen, nonetheless, could be under surveillance. Dining with my parents is especially impolitic now— a days."

"Mother has long been an advocate of German naval expansion, and a close friend of Ambassador Lichnowsky's. It would be a very high-profile matter if they were to intern her, but I suppose it could happen, even though she is a British citizen. They have gone into mufti, so as to offer no provocation, and they are holding their breaths. It has affected business slightly. But that really is not the worst of it; father tells me it appears to have effected Mother's mental equilibrium. It's rather hard to imagine, she has always had such a quiver-full of intellectual arrows. Father said he thought it would be the most difficult on Christmas day.

"Usually the groaning board is set round, but my sister, Maddy, has made a brilliant match, and has a young child she feels may be 'frightened' by mother's behavior, which is a way of saying they are steering clear. Other relatives have expressed 'regrets'".

"I began to feeling rather sad about it, and I mentioned to Father I have some American friends far from home this Christmas season. I know it is an imposition. You *are* neutrals and it won't harm you, yet I would not wish to compromise your aunt's work with Mr. Hoover."

To our surprise, however, when he explained the situation to my aunt, she replied, "We accept, young man."

"Thank you!" he exclaimed.

CHAPTER 15

It was a bracing winter day shortly before Christmas. I was strolling along Actors' Mile on the arm of Brandon Whitefield. I cannot recall ever feeling so sophisticated in my life. When we paused for an introduction to an impeccable gentleman with a lady on his arm who wore a hat topped by an amazing bird of paradise, I was overwhelmed. I had just met George and Florence Alexander, the proprietors of the St. James Theatre, Alexander's high society 'little parish.'

Aunt Bea had actually allowed me out unchaperoned because we were meeting Max at Gatti's. From there we were to play carols at a Catholic hospital where Max was well-known. I, of course, carrying my violin, despite Brand's trying to take it from me in his most gentlemanly fashion. I told him I had always regretted letting someone else carry my violin: they either dropped it, placed it upside down, or wanted to feel the hair on the bow.

Alexander asked Brand about Robert Loraine, who had been wounded.

Said Brand. "It was a nasty bit of Archie, that. Came right out his shoulder blade. Stewart has sent him on a six- week cruise."

Said Alexander, "Pray remember him to me."

His wife added, "I shall never forget him in that underwater scene in 'The Great Ruby'!"

Once we had ordered lunch at Gatti's Max said, "Don't stuff yourself, you have to sing!"

By the time we got to the hospital, the combination of excitements of the day were making me feel *peculiar*—a bit swoony—and I was worried.

The nursing sisters made me even more uneasy. They glided around silently in black habits, and their head dresses were not mere wrappings to make the head sanitary, but regular works of art of millinery, as starched and steeply shaped as Alpine ski slope.

"They *don't* sing do they?" I whispered to Max.

"Not *Protestant* Christmas carols! "Max replied. He whispered back., "Nonethless they do have a Christmas present for you, if you will oblige Sister Mary Catherine by going with her for a minute."

"What?"

"Remember I asked you to wait a bit before speaking about your peculiarity?" Max said.

Sister Mary held out an arm to me. Hesitantly I trotted along behind her. She certainly was not long on conversation, I reflected. (Later I learned theirs was an order that preserved silence unless speech was necessary).

She opened a door into a little cell—her own, most probably. It was small, immaculate, and furnished in the sparest fashion, with a crucifix the only decoration.

"Please sit down," she said, gesturing to the only chair. She continued to stand, her hands plunged into the sleeves of her habit on the opposite arms.

"Dr. Ainley has asked me to ask you if you have ever heard of a disease called chlorosis," she said.

"No," I said.

"It is sometimes called 'green disease'?"

"No," I said.

"It is a form of anemia women develop from being laced up too tightly," she said. "The doctor is quite sure you have a form of it, Miss Ten Eycke, and that sometimes it makes you faint."

"I see!" I said.

"He has suggested we let out your stays and let out your waistband a bit," she said. "You will see if it affects you positively when you try to sing."

Try indeed, I thought. Well, why not. I rather shyly unbuttoned my blouse in front of this very formidable looking apparition, who in turn, unlaced and re- did my bodice very gently, very much unlike Anna (who jerked *everything*—not just one's hair!). As she undid the waistband with surgical scissors and restitched my waist, and air seemed to flood into me, all of a sudden I seemed to rise and fly with the thought: I have *never* been crazy! *This* was what was wrong with me! *I* am all right!

Although she spoke not another word after these few sentences, I was not uncomfortable any more with her. As we walked back to the ward, I breathed in air—air! I felt the "fuzziness" produced by getting more oxygen!

Max was sitting by a bed (as usual). It was a Jock, I could tell by the thick burr.

"Did you hear what the King said on his visit to France, Doctor? My cousin Willie thinks he's going to win this war, but he's not!'"

"Pity about Lord Roberts!" said Max. (Lord Roberts had died recently).

"Aye, a rum one," said his conversation partner.

Brand was in the corner, making a wrestling acquaintance with an old piano which seemed to be only half in tune. He was, in fact, working on the worst of it with a pair of pliers. It did not appear likely he would be ready to start up for some little while, judging by the fire in his eye, as he cleaned up the most egregious tonal problems in his adversary. "It's quite all right, Sister—no itinerant pianist travels without a set of these," he was saying. "Mandra, would you be so good as to sound me an A note. Have the two of you got something that will serve whilst I am tangling with this?"

We had a set of jigs and reels we called our "Wake them Up" routine. Not only were they cheery, but Max started slowly down one side of a row of beds, while I paced in time with him, down the other side. Every once in a while, we would turn to face one another and play over someone's bed.

We ended at the side of Max's Scottish friend. "Can ye play Lord Lovat's Lament?" he asked us.

"Aye," said Max, with a grin.

Then I sat down for a moment on a chair beside a bed. I had learned by now that my accent would produce the remark, "from America, are we?" and I would turn that back as quickly as I could, and out would come the name of hometowns, and the inevitable photos of children, wives, parents, inevitably well-worn, obviously treasured, the link between the soldier and what and who he loved. As this was not an officer's ward, but NCO's and other ranks, I was struck by the obvious signs of poverty in some of the photographs of children; ragged clothes, the small stature of undernourishment, the teeth, victims of neglect and too many sweets. Yet these soldiers fought as bravely as anyone for 'home.'

But now Brand sat down at the keyboard and looked over at me. It was a look that always turned me to jelly, a cross between, "Isn't she the cutest little thing on two feet?" and "Just *what* is going to happen now, my dear?"

"What Child is This?" I asked. He nodded and flipped open the book of carols he had brought.

Oh, what was it that seemed to be singing through me? Phrases flew to my mind expansively and I could tell that this emphasis came out in the sung phrases—'the silent Word is keeping, nails, nails, shall pierce Him through the Cross Be Borne for me, for you.'

It was certainly different from the setting for Christmas the next day!

CHAPTER 16

Our taxi pulled up at the Viscount's home at half past noon. (Families tried to eat early, to give servants time to clear away, and then have the time for their own celebration on the 26th, which was known as "Boxing Day.") The butler swung the door open. As we stepped inside, we realized that the rather conventional size of the house as we had judged it from the outside, was a sort of *trompe d'oeil* of a preserved facade, for inside the house had been extended into another house adjoining it. We were relieved of impedimenta and proceeded up the staircase to the drawing room. The butler was in the foyer at the top of the stairs. I could see into the room behind him. It was not exactly *le gout Rothschild* but it was definitely what the French would call *haute francaise,* refined, defined, and filled with French furniture which obviously got is due by being polished every day. It also had the marks of being keepsakes. Brand stepped out to join the butler. Then a man strolled up behind him. He had the same wiry physique as Brand, slightly lighter hair, flecked with grey. It was the man I had seen at Brown's that morning who would not give his name! It was Brand's father.

His glance of recognition at me was less appraising than it had been that morning at Brown's.

"Let's have those on," he said to the butler who pressed a switch for two *torchières* at the sides of the top of the staircase.

"What do you think?" he asked, waving a hand toward them. "They are my son's acquisitions for one of his plays, 'MacBeth,' perhaps. *Il est notre brin William Morris."* It was their little bit of William Morris. He was watching to see if I followed him. I gave him no clue.

Then his mother came towards us. No mistaking where Brand got those grey eyes. His mother was very tall. Her carriage was erect and confident, and she swept along in the stately fashion of the Julia Nielsons of the Victorian stage, who sometimes topped six feet. Her striking dress—for these were the days when a dress was a dress, and almost an architectural statement—in no way sought to diminish her height but emphasized it with lace scarves depending from the elbows. A thousand cargoes arriving and departing from the Pool of London had financed the diamond combs which held up her still-blonde hair, and diamonds and pearls, but in the middle of all these jewels, hung a singular item— a black iron cross!

Before we were even introduced, she said roughly (for she was following the line of my gaze), "I see you are interested! This is Berlin iron. It is from the time of the war against Napoleon, from the time when Germany and England were allies. We Prussians fought with Wellington! Look, here on the back!" (She turned it over). *Unvergeislick!* Lest we forget! *Ich gab gold für Eisen!* I gave gold for iron!" Her voice was so agitated, so loud, we all glanced at the Viscount, to see what we ought to do. "My dear," he said, "This is Miss Ten Eycke. I fear you have not greeted her." His voice was firm.

"How do you do," I said, putting out my hand.

"How do you do," said the Viscountess. "Pray pardon my lecture on European history."

"My dear," he said, reaching for her arm, "Why do we not save such substantive matters for after dinner." Her eyes blazed. For an instant I think we were all afraid she would lash out at him somehow. But, as he held her arm, and looked at her gently, slowly, like a great ship coming into the wind, she righted herself and came around.

"I hope you do not mind, we sit down straightaway, it is the custom Christmas day," she said to us. She took the Viscount's arm and the rest of us fell in behind, with Becky on a cousin's arm, and Aunt Bea (to her surprise) was extended the arm of an elderly relative with a campaign ribbon in his lapel, walking painfully with a cane.

I took Brand's arm. With a bit of embarrassment, I suddenly suspected it had been arranged that way.

When we entered the dining room, I took in a breath. It was done up in the most unusual wallpaper we had ever seen. Its background color was a slightly lighter than the blue Scandinavians painted their furniture, and on it were trees with black, brown, or grey branches, dark green leaves, and white blossoms in Japanese style. There were birds and butterflies with bright colors.

The table was overhung with a George III chandelier, there were Faberge place card holders, red japanned George II chairs. The effect was further lightened with Delft and export blue and white porcelain vases scattered throughout, bursting with flowers, the Limoges China, and the silver and crystal, which crowded the table with all the implements relevant to a full formal dinner. There were even footmen.

"Fantastic! "I whispered. Brand smiled.

Across the table from me, I saw Aunt Bea (who did not believe in Show) girding up for this dinner with all the stops out, *a la Russe.* (At home we ate in the Old French style with all the dishes on the table).

Brand's father rose, glass in hand. Behind him a blaze of poinsettias in a great *èperegne* defined the black of his coat and the white of his linen. It was clear he wished to offer a toast.

"To my son. To our American guests," he said and drained his glass off. We either followed suit, or took a dainty sip.

The protocol was formal, with our half of the table turning toward the Viscount for conversation, and the other half, with Becky and the cousin down from Oxford, and a gentleman in naval uniform, toward the Viscountess.

"I am not *au courant* on how you met my son," said the Viscount to my aunt.

Aunt Bea cleared her throat. "My niece and my daughter, I am sorry to say, took it into their heads to cut a dash and audition for his play," my aunt said.

"Really?" said the Viscount. "Are you doing that sort of thing in the States now-adays?"

"No, my Lord, we most emphatically are not!" My aunt said.

The Viscount discerned he ought to drop that line of inquiry.

"And I, sir, am curious as to whether it is now the done thing in England not to introduce all of one's guests to one another, as I am lacking the name of the gentleman at the other end of the table!"

"I do beg your pardon! That is Sir Henry Porter, Madame."

Champagne was poured and we started out on consommé. Next came *solettes de Dover.*

"This is one of my absolute favorite dishes," Brand said to me.

We did not speak much, although we could have, but ate, and listened. Under the tablecloth he had reached over and was holding my hand.

Brand's father remarked to Aunt Bea that when his son had recalled my family to him, he remembered meeting her husband several times, once quite some years ago, when he and the Viscountess had been in New York. "In fact we took our younger son Vessey's name from a street sign my wife fancied," he said.

"Good Heavens!" Said my aunt. It was a familiar frame of reference!

A roast beef was brought in and the business of carving began. To my aunt's side, the Elderly Relative slumped ever so circumspectly and fell asleep. My aunt and the Viscount exchanged amused smiles. "He rarely lasts past fish anymore," said Brand's father.

Soon enough they were chatting away, covering Charles Schwab's visit to London on behalf of Bethlehem Steel, the ambiance of the men's bar at the Waldorf (New York's most recent Coal Hole, where deals got made on the spot), and the legendary appetite of Diamond Jim Brady, who ate until his stomach touched the table. My aunt described one of his marathon meals at Delmonico's for the Viscount (who ate very sparingly, I noticed).

"What do you know of this Bernard Baruch chap?" he asked her.

"He is fast becoming a confidante of Mr. Wilson's," my aunt said. "He put up several millions to start a run on cotton. Paul Warburg of Kuhn,

Loeb, said that if he would buy some too, then Jacob Schiff would want
some, and the sales would rocket. And they did."

"Ah, yes, Paul Warburg!" said the Viscount with a sigh. "Quite a
position, that Federal Reserve Board seat of his."

"Some say he *is* the Federal Reserve. We always said you have to get up
very early in the morning to get ahead of the Hamburg Five," said my aunt
(using the nickname of the Warburg dynasty). But then he is, of course,
or was, a partner with McAdoo— who is now Secretary of Treasury, of
course, as we all know—and Mr. Wilson's son-in-law. Kuhn Loeb certainly
will be walking a tightrope—Germany or America."

Then his mother's very loud tones at the other end of the table
drowned the rest of us out. "Nonsense, Sir Henry! Britain has gone to war
to keep the deep-water ports of Belgium neutral! That is the realpolitik
of this situation! You have no love for the French, nor is the diplomatic
language so constructed that a way could not be found around this 'pledge
'of Belgian neutrality!"

"Ah, yes, just a scrap of paper.Realpolitik, Milady, part *schweinpolitik*
of a greater Germany?" Sir Henry shot back, utilizing the German term
for the Austrian tariff on Serbian pork, which would change arbitrarily
to demonstrate Austrian pleasure or displeasure with Serbian political
policies. Despite the fact they were obviously old verbal adversaries
and he was obviously well-used to slashing and parrying with her, the
Viscountess's Teutonic accents hung over the table in an eerie, still-heard
descant. My head began to swim.

"Are you well, Miss Ten Eycke?" said the Viscount.

"*Seulemente un brin degouté milord,*" I said, leaving him to decipher
whether *degouté* in this case meant that I was a little bit sick, or a little bit
disgusted!

"I expect you could use a bit of air," said Brand, pushing back his chair.

"Jolly good idea, I shall have dessert and coffee set for you in the
library," said his father. He looked at my aunt meaningfully, conveying to
her that he understood his wife's outbursts were not anything I was used
to, and that he knew it had upset me. Brand had suggested I could use

a breath of fresh air. His father concurred. The Viscount was a man to rectify things as swiftly as was possible. My aunt inclined her head—what else could she do—under the circumstances.

Once out of the room, Brand said, "Shall we take a walk? No one will miss us for a spot," he said. "Johnson, if anyone asks, we are in the library."

"Very good, sir."

He helped me into my coat. The butler helped him into his. Outside, there was a middling fog, cut now and again by very wet snowflakes. Only a solitary pedestrian passed us, everyone being inside celebrating Christmas. It was as if we were wrapped in our own cloud of unknowing. It was enough to be moving along together, with my arm through his, his pulling me over tightly against him, alone. We reached Grosvenor Square. The park was deserted. At the middle of the park, the fog obliterated all the house fronts facing onto it (and all the windows, which would have otherwise observed us like too many all-seeing eyes!). Brand reached in his pocket and brought out a package. "Merry Christmas," he said. My heart sunk. I hoped it wasn't expensive—but I knew it was! There was a protocol about accepting such things: they could make one *compromised!*

I pulled off the paper with tremulous fingers. There was a box inside. *Asprey's.* Oh, me. It was a beautifully made bracelet of platinum, gold, and mother of pearl, all worked together.

"Look inside," he said. There were inscribed the words, 'Set me as a seal upon thine arm.' We both knew the rest of the words, 'for love is strong as death.'

Some strange intuition told me not to make a fuss.

There he was, a living, breathing human being, about to be snatched from me by the jaws of war. A grief materialized from the air around me: all the mothers, the fathers, the lovers, the children, of the world, crying, crying, caught in a great tidal wave of grief, sweeping across the face of all the nations like a Biblical plague. It seized me, it penetrated me, in an instant. No day when I awoke would ever be the same. A sob welled up. No, no day when I awoke would ever be the same. I would wake, think all was well for a moment, and then remember.

"Oh, Brand!" With a cry of heartbreak, I threw my arms around him. My tears beaded the wool of his overcoat. I could hear his heart beating under my ear, and his breath above me like another sob. He rocked me, rocked me, like his child.

"Oh, my dearest, no one's ever cried for me," his voice said softly in my ear.

Back home millions on millions of my countrymen slept soundly.

We trudged back to the house (the way seems long when you do not want to go), and into the library, which had a scattering of Northern masters, wood paneling and rolling ladders. We sat at a round table by a window which had been set for us. Sir Henry and the Viscount were at the other end, smoking, far enough away, yet not far enough we could not pick up parts a soft conversation, although Sir Henry managed to subdue his voice to a dull roar.

Just then we heard the Viscount's soft voice, which he had raised slightly. "If this war continues, Henry, and America won't bankroll us, we shan't be able to carry it through ourselves. You'd best adjust that naval thinking of yours; it will be a different world at the end of this, mark my words."

The Viscount asked Sir Henry about Zeppelins (such was concern about these behemoths of the air, Ambassador Page had considered insuring the Embassy against damage from them).

"Those damned Zepps are overrated by the public on both sides, Rodger! That's why we bombed the sheds at Cologne and Dusseldorf in September and Friedrichshafen in November! Those ships are vulnerable! Hiram Maxim calls 'em the jellyfish of the air! That raid four days ago—all it did was rattle some windows on High Street in Dover, and alarm every old lady from there to Grimsby!" He pulled out his watch. "I think I can tell you *now,* that the R.N.A.S. sent off some seaplanes to bomb the sheds at Cuxhaven today!"

The Viscount must have remonstrated feebly, because Sir Henry continued in the same quarterdeck voice, "Willie didn't rest today either I can tell you! German seaplanes flew up the Thames as far as Erith, before our chaps at Eastchurch drove them off!"

"Since things are out in the open now, tell me how he" —and I indicated Sir Henry with a movement of my head, "knows all the things he is telling your father?"

"He is one of Blinker Hall's men, he is in Naval Intelligence. The curious question is, Amanda, why he is trumpeting things out in this particular house, where, of all places, he ought to adopt the caution that the walls have ears."

"Why is he here?"

"To grant the impression we have nothing to hide!"

"But—"

"As well he is an old family friend. Put Henry and mother together and you have a debate society!" he said with a smile.

We listened a bit more carefully. "There's a spot for a broker such as yourself to be of service, Rodger," Sir Henry was saying. "Our air industry is in a mess. We have no magnetos. Germans make 'em, doncha know. All we have is drawings one of our chaps named Jones pinched from 'em. The Flying Corps are sending blueprints for their machines to a bunch of ruddy piano makers. Then there's this bloomin' foreign patents and manufacturing licenses business which I think we should deep six but which Those in Higher Places think we need to procure."

"Ah, yes, what did the Wrights charge for the use of their patent? Fifteen thousand dollars?"

"I don't remember: I know the Wrights sued Tommy Sopwith for copyright infringement. We aren't concerned with that anymore—we are past wing warping."

"Father cannot cry off, or it will not appear he is not ratifying in the interests of the Allies," Brand said.

A few moments later, a movement began for our departure. The Viscount's automobile would take us back to Claridge's, and, with our coats on, we moved out onto the pavement to ensconce ourselves in the back seat. Becky was still talking with the Oxford cousin flirtatiously, and my aunt was tendering the proper formulas of thanks for hospitality. Brand and I silently looked at each other until he smiled. I smiled back as I ducked into the back seat.

CHAPTER 17

Just after New Year, Brand asked me if I could see my way clear to do something special. His father would like to have a chat, as he did not feel he knew me very well. He would like me to meet him at the House of Lords.

I took another autobus to the seats of Parliament, climbed into the visitor's seats, and noted the absence of anyone of the fourth estate in the press box. Apparently this was not an open debate. Staring at Lord Ripon on the woolsack and the members on red leather benches, suddenly I was aware the Viscount had slipped out of the room; so I hastened downstairs- -down the hallway to a rotunda which was 75 feet high, with equally gargantuan sculptures of St. George and St. David. He was telling a page to call for his automobile.

After a short drive, he asked if I would mind walking for a bit. Of course not! We walked along, talking, evading the main topic, which was, why was I here?

"You see, Amanda, I realize the intelligence crowd feel they have maneuvered me between a rock and a hard place, however, I am signaling we will not go down with whatever their ship. I went to a deuce of a lot of trouble to have you sitting alone in the visitors' gallery during a closed session. You have been an unwilling pawn, for which I deeply apologize.

"As you may not know, they have begun to intern German neutrals in our country. Now my wife is a British citizen, yet in a war, it is hard to tell what they will introduce in the name of security. Having an American pop up unexpectedly intrudes on their plans, and the fact you are well-connected here does not hurt a bit. You've heard snatches of debate. And have the means to spread it. We are always angling to persuade the States to enter the war—on our side, of course. You need realize that if you consort with the Whitefield clan, this is the sort of thing you might encounter."

"I am not afraid to do my bit—whatever that is!"

"I think I understand my son has proposed to you?"

"In a utilitarian sort of way," I said, as lightheartedly as possible.

"I beg pardon?"

"He said he was always disappearing on me, but if I married him, I could go along."

"I see! "

"However, I realize this would not just be a personal matter—it would involve our families—and—"

"I completely understand. We shall keep it *sub rosa*."

I was grown-up enough by now to know I did not any longer have to act as through adults' opinions were not fully blown from their brains like Athena from the head of Zeus, so I could ask a question.

"I've always been curious as to how you met your wife," I said.

"How charming. We met at Baden-Baden."

"Oh?"

"Mother took the waters annually and I would accompany her there, then come home, then go back to escort her. My wife's mother did the same, and my wife happened to be with her. I spotted her immediately; one could scarce miss her, as she was nearly six feet tall—tall enough to look me in the eye. I decided then and there I absolutely agreed with George du Maurier, men ought to worship height in women. Providentially, she was learning English, for I know very little German. I shouldn't not say learning; actually she was trying to pick up current slang. Usually I would bring one suitcase full of books, and the mothers thought it would be a fine idea if I could help her. The first day we sat on lawn chairs, watched a footman so ferocious- looking one might wonder if he ate wild boar meat raw. The mothers toddled off to Freidrichsbad for a two-hour soak in the waters.

"One morning we were commiserating about the unappetizing food of the cleansing diet, when I had a brilliant idea. I sent my man down to the local Café Koenig to buy a good amount of pastry. At eleven, he brought them out instead of the traditional cups of vegetable *bouillon.* He brought it out with a napkin over it, on a silver tray. I must say she was delighted. She ate all the eclairs. There was enough left over for her to take some back with her to finish later. She was far from the dainty demoiselle who pretends to eat like a bird.

"As we became more familiar, I asked if I might walk with her to the river Oos. It was the perfect spot; they could see us but not hear us. We fed the ducks, then I took her to the casino to see the gold and silver chips. She asked if I would read something in her diary in which she could not decide if she was using a word correctly or not. I was deeply flattered. It certainly might have been considered something too intimate to show to someone else—especially a man—but she did not appear to have that *caveat.*

"She had written 'Oh God, if there is a God, grant me a life that calls for mettle, not the vapories of feminine malingering 'Is that correct, vapories?' She wanted to know. Of course it was not, yet it was a word which clearly demonstrated what she wished to convey.

"Our visit was coming to an end. I had to take some action. Certainly one could take the path of least resistance and write for a year or two until her family deemed she was being treated properly. But that could have just as easily have run out on her end because of family disapproval."

We walked out over the bridge to feed the ducks next morning, I asked her ,"Why don't you really complete learning English?"

"How could I ever do that?"

"Marry an Englishman."

"Have you got one that would make do?"

"He is standing right beside you."

"Neither of our families were wild about the whole thing, but hers were relieved someone wanted to marry her. They were hemming and hawing about a dowry, of course."

Now we were nearing his home, and his footsteps picked up speed; he touched his hat to a young Nanny pushing a baby carriage. At the door, his wife was directly behind Staines.

"Why don't you ladies sit in my wife's small drawing room. I fancy I'd like to change from this so formal attire?"

I followed her saying several urgent prayers.

She was not a woman for small talk. She asked me if I would give her a reply to what she had been thinking of lately.

"If I am able, Madamoselle."

"The other night we were sitting reading, and I noticed Rodger had fallen asleep. I did not wish to disturb him, he is so tired lately. I went to ring for some cocoa, and when I returned, he was so still for a moment I feared he might be dead, and I watched him to see if he was breathing. I saw that he was, and I was so relieved, tears came to my eyes. It made me think. What if he is right? What if there is a God, a judgement, a heaven and hell? If so, I, whose only wish is to be with him, would be separated from him for eternity. I would instead be with the people who were so cruel to me. They will have won, not Rodger. If this faith is not true, what will I lose by believing it, if it would make my husband happy? If it *is* true, so much the better. Is this not called Pascal's wager?"

"It is, Madame. You have stated it very clearly. Your husband told me how you met, and a piece you read to him from your diary. Look at it as a prayer that has been answered, and what do you find? He said you do not go to church with him because they only tell you you are unworthy—isn't this just what your family told you despite the fact grace was extended to you so you didn't have to live with them anymore? Your husband really needs your help now. A house divided against itself cannot stand.'"

Phew. Thank you, Holy Spirit.

"Ah, " she said, her eyes lighting up. We could hear the Viscount's steps in the hallway. "Bear with me!" She said.

"And how are you ladies?"

"We have just been discussing something momentous. Would you mind if Staines brushed your hat on Sunday morning?

He's in for a surprise.

His face fell.

"I shall be too busy myself, getting ready to accompany you. "

He did say she had a sly sense of humor.

St. Edmund the King was not a large church. Nor was a church in the financial district populous on Sunday. Two more worshippers would have been noticed, and the Viscount had a lady on each arm, for they had invited me to come with them. The Vicar's face lit up. One of his favorite parishioners who always came alone now was blessed with an embarrassment of riches. "My lady! How wonderful to see you!"

"Thank you." She had taken to answering with as few words as possible, so that her accent would go unnoticed.

At the last moment, Brand came through the door. "I had the notion you might be here," he said to me. We sat, four square in our pew. Swift as an arrow came the reading from Luke…'for though he knew his duty, he refused to do it.'

After the service, Brand said to me, "I've been looking at this problem of me volunteering from my own personal perspective. It just dawned on me I am one of the fully trained pilots in England. Few, if any, of the pre-war aviators volunteered for the R.F.C. I am going to volunteer."

His parents were shocked by this announcement and so was I. I was unaccountably angry with him for three days, during which time he was sworn in.

We opened our door to a stranger, looking, in uniform, not his usual self—another meaning of uniform! Somehow, the khaki seemed so different. It made everyone the same. We gazed at his shiny new Sam Browne belt and boots, the high step collar, the rather unique side buttoning R.F.C. coat informally dubbed 'the Maternity Jacket,' with the wings sewn on its breast.

"Have you got a rank?" asked Becky.

"Second Loot, temporary gentleman."

He turned to me and added, "I missed you the other day." His swearing in! How could I have been so callous!

"I couldn 't," I said, and began to cry.

Later we realized if I had come, it would have made our relationship public. Brand had been sent for his training to Brooklands, an auto race track near London. I was most happy he would still be nearby, with access to London. His C.O. was an enthusiast of the theatre, so Brand could go in and out of London to keep an eye on his production. Like everyone else, he received two free days over the weekend.

CHAPTER 18

Life was, indeed, as Becky had put it, too, too difficult.

Gerald had a nice idea. It was a party for Our Departing Hero, in case the run of 'The Lady' was still on the boards when he was ordered to the Front (for orders came quickly, and men disappeared the day after they had received them, everyone knew!). It was on a Sunday, for Sunday was the one day theatres were closed.

He'd written to me late Christmas night. *Please excuse the outright messiness of this particular missive. I am seated in a hangar with my pocket torch, dressed in my pyjamas and my overcoat, with paper and my service pencil, so as not to wake any of my hut mates. I've returned to hear the rumor some of us may be sent to France as replacements to various squadrons who have suffered sufficient losses to be under roster. I wished to communicate this to you as soon as possible.*

Of course Becky was thrilled about the party, especially as she rang Gerald and asked if she could bring 'a lad or two' from her hospital. Suddenly she was so extremely popular she claimed two officers had even proposed to her, as she told us with a toss of her head, for she knew Full Well *every* red- blooded young blade wanted to meet the new toast of the West End, Miss Felicity Westcote—and wonder of wonders, Miss Ten Eycke knew her!

The door to Murdoch's flat opened into a burst of gaiety, accents raised into the sharply articulated punctuations of the voices of the stage. Champagne and sandwiches were being passed.

"Ah, here we have him, ladies and gentlemen!" Gerald called. The furor died down. "Spit and polish, how absolutely ripping, that wasn't turned out in twenty- four hours by Gamage's!"

A little ripple of laughter. Gerald raised his glass.

"Ladies and gentleman, to Brand Whitefield—the repudiation of Palmer's theory that good words and good music couldn't be combined together!"

"Hear, hear," sounded, and everyone drained their glasses.

"I say, Brand," said a man I had never seen before, "I hear you were giving one of my Tabloids absolute hell the other day!"

"Tommy!" said Brand, wringing his hand. "I couldn't believe the baragraph! What a rate of climb!" He turned to me. "Miss Ten Eyck, Mr. Sopwith."

"Charmed," he said. "Only just passed by, must be back to the works, I hear Bob has gone cruising for his health. Give him regards if you see him before I do."

"Quite, he is positive Salmond will get posted him back to a squadron in France," said Brand.

"Isn't that Gerald du Maurier?" my aunt asked Gerald.

"Let me introduce you, "said Murdoch, giving her his arm. As he moved away, he said over his shoulder, "By the way your erstwhile Stella rang. She demanded to be invited. I couldn't fob her off."

Brand said something under his breath.

Maybe this isn't so bad, I thought, looking around the room at the babble of good cheer and high spirits, Becky with her two officers in blue invalided uniforms, Miss Westcote chatting with Max (who had also 'just dropped by' but had to run).

And, just as if on that cue, the door opened. There was a flurry of activity. Glances went around the room as if in anticipation of heightened dramatics. Gerald was helping a striking woman out of her fur coat. The woman extended her hand to Felicity in congratulations. Miss Westcote's face was a mask and her voice was 'brilliant,' as she thanked her.

Everyone knows what's going on here, but I don't. I thought.

Brand's face was drained of color. The woman started straight for us. He took hold the very outside of my elbow as if I were his only ally in the room.

Her hair was light brown, mixed with touches of blonde and red, puffed around an archetypally English peaches-and-cream complexion. Ninety-nine women in a hundred would have contrasted her coloring with a vivid gown. But she wore *peau de soile* russet, the better to set off an unusual piece of jewelry, a cat's eye and canary diamond brooch. I had an uneasy feeling I knew that taste.

She smiled slightly, put her hand to the brooch, and cocked her head in an artful gesture.

"Hello, darling," she said. "No little greeting for an old friend? Well— at least you can offer me a cigarette." He offered her his case unwillingly. She reached out for it languidly, making him step closer. She bent forward a bit so he could light it for her. I'd never seen a woman smoke before!

Then she murmured something I couldn't hear, but was obviously an invitation. My stomach turned. I heard him say, "I think not."

She contemplated the two of us, side by side, with a quizzing gaze, a raise of her eyebrow, taking several beats to take our measure, knowing everyone was watching. She exhaled deliberately.

"Since there's no help for it, you might as well present me," she said.

"Mrs. Lillah Compton, Miss Ten Eyck." Why aren't you using Lillah Compton this time--artistic suicide.... yes, I remembered those half lights of revelation. Then he added, "*Ingenue extraordinaire et perpetuale.*"

"Darling, I see you haven't lost your tongue!" she said with delight as if she had won a triumph.

"Nor you your charm," he said straightfaced.

"I expect Brunhuldah must be beside herself with joy to find you in the company of a proper young lady!" she said. Good Heavens! That was Brand's mother! The color came into her cheeks, as if she had just lured him into a familiar exchange somewhat akin to an artillery barrage.

But, with an effort, he cleared his throat. He did not reply. She had nothing to play off of.

Confused, she blurted, "Then I suppose I must simply wish you well!"

"Thank you," he said.

"*Au 'voir,* " she said, moving off, and blowing him a music hall kiss as she turned sharply on her heel. She moved off across the room, and began to talk animatedly to someone in the corner.

I excused myself. I fled into the spot set aside for the "ladies powder room." I sat down, and began to fuss distractedly with my hair. Then I heard the rustle of silk skirts behind me.

It couldn't be. It was. She stood behind me, looking at our two faces in the mirror.

"How lovely, "she said, touching my hair. "Untouched by man's hand, no doubt?"

I said nothing.

"No doubt he hasn't mentioned me?"

"I don't believe he has," I replied.

"I shouldn't wonder," she said with satisfied-cat smile. "Here he is following in Daddy's footsteps taking up with a foreign woman. I 've always wondered what it must be like to make love to a Prussian. What do you think? Do they do it in march time?"

"I have no idea," I said. Nor did I, even about what she was talking about!

"Then let me tell you about me. Yes, that dreadful lady, who latches onto youthful undergraduates wet behind the ears, who've been milling about for years with fervent little crushes on each other, tossing off under the sheets and afraid they'll go mad or go to hell for it. It's a vintage to tap, I'll tell you. There's nothing quite as inspired as a young man who's just thrown over all that kind of poppycock! Quite like him though, to make his lady only a seducer of the mind on stage!"

She hummed a minute, poking at her hair. "You know, you can't erase our past, Brand's and mine," she said. I looked at her in incomprehension. "Oh, why does virginity make women so stupid!" she exclaimed and flounced out.

When I got back to the main room, someone was helping her with her coat. People in the room were still standing divided into a path she'd cut through the group, like the wake of a departing ship.

Brand was in the middle of the room, back to her, obviously embarrassed, trying to carry on a conversation with someone. Aunt Bea was still talking to Mr. du Maurier: Becky was still talking to her patients. None of them had heard these exchanges. Brand hustled over to me and took my elbow.

Gerald rushed over.

"I'm sorry, Prov," he said. "Really, really, old boy, I didn't think it would do any harm!"

"The hell you didn't," said Brand grimly.

"Come on, Prov, it's a party," said Gerald.

"Gerald," said Brand, "The best I can think of you is that you didn't think." He handed him his glass. Holding onto me firmly he turned, and sat us down in a corner together.

"Mandra, I am more sorry than you can ever imagine that you had to see that," he said.

"You and she were together before?"

"Yes."

"Is this what they mean when they say young men sow their wild oats?"

"Yes, I suppose it is."

I flushed to the roots of my hair.

"You must think I am some kind of fool to think after that you could settle down with someone like me!"

"Just one moment. I protected you from decisions in my life. That was one of them. A poor one, an immoral one, a very unfortunate and painful one for me to have you see. One for which I must simply ask you to forgive me, and trust in your capability for mercy, Mandra."

"It's too painful! I'm so upset I can't think!"

"It is painful indeed. I can read your mind. You are sure I will make you an unfaithful husband, and I can't blame you. So let me lay the case before you to think about when you can think. She was gone from my life a good while before I met you. I met her when I was casting my first London play. People will tell you I had all the advantages on my side, Mandra; breeding, education, position, wealth. Nonetheless it was she who had power over me. We always fought like dogs over a bone, and she always gave it out that she made my reputation. I woke up one morning, Amanda, to find a young man in way over his head. I don't mind telling you it was a fearful thing to set out and find out if she was right or not and I could not pull an audience on my own, but I had to take charge of my own house, public and personal. My nerves were deteriorating daily from lack of peace of mind. And I had begun to have the dream again."

"Dream?" I said, befuddled, and humiliated, too, because it was it was clear people were steering clear of us as if it were obvious Whitefield had some Explaining To Do about his former lover.

"I first had it the summer I was reading Whitefield. I was in a crowd of people all milling about. Bit by bit I began to feel them pressing in on me, as if some ritual were taking place they all understood but me. At first I was startled, then afraid, only to find I could not escape, and the life was being slowly pressed out of me. By that time I was so scared I woke myself up.

"It stopped when I returned to school and grew busy with other matters. After the second episode, when I bid her adieu it stopped. But then, just before the play opened, it began a third time. The panic started. But this time I looked and saw I was in a city that had walls. Outside was a hill with a man standing on it. I knew he wanted me to come to him. But a path opened. When I got close I knew who He was. He was in tears. 'Why are you weeping?' I asked him. 'I am weeping for Jerusalem,' He said. I asked why. He said, 'Because, Brandon, you are Jerusalem, in ruins.' When I prayed with your aunt and with you, the dream stopped and I knew it would never come again. You may not believe me, Mandra, but if I had ever known—ever even *imagined*—I would ever meet you, I would have made different choices. It is all the worse for me to stand before the cutting power of your innocence."

"Don't think so highly of innocence! It scarcely tells you what to do in a case like this!"

"Perhaps we should follow the pathway."

"What?"

"The pathway that opened to Him in my dream," he said. "Let us go to one of your aunt's infamous prayer meetings, and lift the matter up, instead of arguing, or depending on our own intelligence."

Well, I thought sulkily, that had to be an inspired idea.

"Are you sure you want to do that?" I asked uneasily.

"'Lean not on thine own understanding,'" he quoted. "Perhaps I am *not* the chap for you. I could accept that, Mandra, but only, only, if I were to understand it would be for your own good." He looked barely able to cover how miserable he felt with the thinnest veil of dignity. So I agreed.

At Mr. Seddon's church a few nights later, a number of people greeted my aunt. Some of the refugees we had met the first day at Alexandra Palace were there, too, puzzled, perhaps, but now part of the community, and grateful to their English hosts. Mr. and Mrs. Seddon hurried over and greeted us. Brand's uniform made him the center of attention.

We all settled into unyielding wooden pews. After a few minutes of creaking and shuffling and settling, with me rather stiff next to Brand, Aunt Bea on his other side, Mr. Seddon stepped before us.

"Our passage for this evening's meeting is this, "he said, "'We know we have passed from death to life, because we love the brethren. He that loveth not his brother, abideth in death.'"

He closed his Bible.

"When we are first regenerated," he said, "we are like newborn babies. It is just us and Him, a baby's world, and we cling to it. We expect Him to attend our every need, heed us the moment that we cry. We are angry when we are called to relinquish this personal paradise. We want to feel he supports our behavior, our point of view, and to chastise those who disagree with us. We want Him to have *our* standards for the human race. Thus we resist the work of the Holy Spirit in our lives. It demands. It makes us extend ourselves, grow up, put others first, and it demands mature habits. Mercy, kindness, long-suffering, humility and self-control—they are just the opposite of a childish demeanor."

"What these habits demand is this: that we see what we cannot bear to see, that is, that Christ accepts others exactly as He accepts us. We are offended—or we certainly would be if it happened here, today—that He extends his love to a woman who has had five husbands. He demolishes our fastidiousness, because it is sin. We wound other souls who are also seeking Christ's acceptance, just as we are, if we call their sincerity hypocrisy. There is no merit to having been granted God's grace, and we cannot call it our own virtue. Remember that no one is good but God alone: and that no one is perfected in a day, but that we all struggle to become perfected in his law and by his grace."

Then—Mr. Seddon sat down and closed his eyes! After a time, people began to pray aloud. One person even spoke in a kind of gibberish Aunt Bea had told me was speaking in tongues.

Then a mysterious thing happened. It was as though I was lifted up out of the room, my body remaining there behind me. I was looking down from somewhere very peaceful. I saw the woman sitting beside Brand. She was bitter! Hurt! Angry! Condemning! Then as I watched, I saw that self turn into a black cutout silhouette. And as I watched some more, the edges of this figure ignited and began to burn inward, the paper rolling into curls of grey ashes as it burned, until it had consumed to the very center, and I was gone.

I turned to him. I took his elbow and he bent down. I cupped my hand to whisper in his ear. "She said some terrible things to me, which have made me doubt that I could make you happy."

In turn he whispered to me, "I know she gave it her best effort!"

I felt reconciled enough to him, to join the group afterwards for a 'collation' of some tea and cookies, and, once again we were in high demand to communicate between our hosts and some of their new guests, for apparently, everyone did not enjoy the gifts displayed on the day of Pentecost, and on each side, people were longing to ask and answer questions!

CHAPTER 19

He wrote about his activities at Brooklands. He had been learning the rudiments of marching 'square bashing'—or standing in formation—and to throw a cursory salute, albeit in the dandy fashion favored by the Flying Corps as an expression of itself as a home for free spirits— individualists, eccentrics, misfits, and madmen— a dash fitted the Flying Corps, which would entitle a C.O. to one salute a day. Naturally, his inner playwright reveled in acquiring such new arrows for his quiver.

Yet there was a good deal to learn. Map reading, wireless, flying in different sorts of weather, the different sort of clouds; on low ceiling days, flying down low, he was bumped by updrafts, especially heavy ones occurring over the banks of rivers, plowed fields or woodlands. Thatched roofs were made, he wrote, for a flyer to enjoy. Then there was working with the infantry and artillery; of course, many of the students were busy just learning to fly, but several of them, Brand included, were more advanced.

It transpired that a good deal of his time was being consumed by the rather mundane task of learning Morse code. "At night chaps send the absolute in bawdy via signals with Aldis lamps," he added. "It's expanded my vocabulary considerably. Morale is good. The other issue of moment is I shall probably have to grow a mustache to fit in with everyone else."

They had suffered only one or two training accidents which were lethal—and which shook up the other students badly, although Brand had witnessed it before. Via other accidents they were left with some machines that had flipped over on their noses, awaiting a large general bonfire. It was generally discovered that more students were killed in training accidents than in the war, and Brand kept tally of accidents for his father, who tallied the loss in pounds, shillings and pence, for his own information.

'Brooklands is an old racetrack, which provides good landing space on its circular wrap around track, which is smooth. I am now getting used to more country noises, rather than the pulse of the city. Less traffic, less noise of motors,

Altogether a quieter atmosphere, which, of course, it was not on race days!

It is an adjustment I have always had to make when the family moved out to Sous Saules, our country house. Here there is true quiet. All you can hear is a stray midnight moo from the few cows and goats mother has brought up nearer the house for the cook's convenience, as there is no longer anyone to go out to milk them. Ma Mère holds that goat's milk is better than cow's milk, as it cannot readily pick up diseases.

Beyond the park of the house, ground has been plowed up where it has never been before, to provide sustenance if food should become scarcer. Mother still keeps roses in her greenhouse.

He apprised me rumor had it that when an opening occurred in France, students would quickly disappear. I was to be ready for this eventually when (not if) it occurred.

The terrible day had come.

'You are to report forthwith.'

"Amanda, I shall be leaving for France."

"Where are you now?" I asked him.

"At my flat."

The Albany was a male preserve. I didn't feel as if I could brave it.

My aunt and Becky (up early!) having a Hearty Breakfast for a Hearty Day!

"Come here, they are on their way out," I said.

"Straightway," he said.

I opened at the tap. He stepped just inside the door.

The reality was sinking in that he was really going. I could see him breathe. He was an epiphany of muscle, bone, nerve, flesh and blood. And he was going. I might never see him again, speak to him, or touch him again.

"Stay right here! There's something I want you to have!" I ran into my room, and came back with my childhood Bible and handed it into him. He turned over the cover, worn with use, opened it, and read the inscriptions-'To Amanda, on the occasion of her confirmation...'

"Are you sure you want to give this to me? He asked.

"Yes, I want you to have it with you."

"My sweet forgiveness," he said, looking into my eyes. He had unbuttoned his overcoat. He put my hand gently against his heart with a little longing sound. It was beating like a hunted animal. His fingers caressed mine which still lay against his heart with unspoken words, with a tenderness virtually unbearable.

In the distance a church bell chimed a muffled sound, reiterating the fact he must leave me.

"Will you write me every day?"

"You can count on me."

"Every day?"

"Every day, Brand."

He picked me up against him with a compress of all his desire. My arms went around his neck. When he kissed me, I felt all the long years of loneliness, the bitterness of heart which he often felt condemned him to be alone, and now—when that curse seemed to have listed....

"I'm going to drive to Dover."

He did not want to risk the train, with other volunteers, pumped up with leaving for the Front, which might well make him cry. I began to button up his coat for him as though he were a child I could protect from the elements. Every fiber of my being was reacting the way iron filings would if they were pulled off of a magnet. I could barely experience the severance physically while my mind could not comprehend it at all.

His car was at the curb. Numbly I watched him get in and start the engine. I watched him turn, wave, then disappear. No one saw him leave but me.

CHAPTER 20

Now Brand was in France. Each day was full of the stress that perhaps today was the day I would no longer hear from him. Then a letter came, filling me with indescribable happiness. Then I would slowly fade back into despair.

He wrote me about his transfer to France.

Dearest Mandra my lovely Better Impulse you were with me on my pell mell drive to Dover. I burst a tyre but I only swore minimally. Now I am seated at the dock in front of the Lord Warden Hotel. Beside me is seated the other replacement, Nick Courtenay, a 'Second Loot' who has risen up from the 'other ranks' of the Royal Engineers. As he had learned to pilot a plane before the war, as had I, he was seconded into the R.F.C. which makes him an odd duck like myself, a man of the theatre, amongst the rank and file that make up an R.F.C squadron.

If this were a play, I would have to note: 'Nick Courtenay is a man of average height, brown hair, hazel eyes, a pencil mustache, all of which brings to mind the word 'square.' His jaw is square, his shoulders are square, his frame is heavy, and he has the combative mien of a bull.

Nick is not any man's idea of a Boswell, believe me. It has never occurred to him that writing or thinking might take silence and concentration. (Here the pencil made a squiggle). He has just nudged my elbow to point out a destroyer coming into view through the mist on the Straits.

He is voluble in his regret that we are arriving in France so ignominiously with our machines knocked down into crates. I am telling him this is one of the reasons the Parliamentary Air Defense Committee was taken with the aeroplane trials in 1911; Grahame-White demonstrated how quickly our crafts could be dismantled and put into packing crates. "The point is getting the machines there in one piece," I have told him at least three times.

Now by Jove the little rotter has made a grab for my letter to see what I have written about him (and indeed the paper was bunched up at the bottom left hand corner). I suppose If I want to preserve this marvelous bit of prose intact I shall have to close my letter and mail it.'

They landed at Calais; from there, rode by tender to R.F.C. at St. Omer for assignment. *Nick had hoped we'd be assigned the same squadron, and his wish was gratified.* They were not sent over the lines immediately, but given time to acclimate. They took turns flying a biplace (two seated machines with room for pilot and observer.) They were using a Sterling wireless that weighed 70 pounds which with their own weight made them struggle to get off the ground.

We have to roll out a long wire aerial before we can transmit. The ground cannot signal back, but must make wishes known by a series of devices like one made out of what looks like large white window blinds. We must be careful to wind in the aerial completely—it is 120 feet—Brand transferred from metrics to feet for his American girl-- before coming down to land or it can become ensnared in fences, picnic tables, or wind around animate objects like stray animals or unwary staff officers.

I do miss you terribly. It rather hurts to write you as it confirms how far away you are.

CHAPTER 21

We were all following our usual routines. My aunt was out fundraising, and she had just made a successful visit to Jack Morgan at Wall Hall. The sum obtained had raised her status and the telephone was ringing more and more, and the mails were heavier. Reporters would now press her for quotes, and we noticed my aunt was wearing hats with a narrower brim without burnishments on top, which allowed her to be photographed more clearly.

As for Becky, she was still walking out with soldiers, some of whom clearly became admirers. "If I were to lose a leg," one asked her, "would you like me just the same?" The complaint he made did not work exactly as intended, for it convinced her he only saw her as 'just a flapper.' Max and I tried to go where needed, but the places were always more than we could accommodate.

It was on a basically uneventful day, if any day in that awful period could have been called uneventful; it began as a pleasant dream. I was actually gliding through the air, tipping slightly sideways, almost like a bird, uplifted by some sort of draft which flowed up from the earth itself. It must be like this when an aviator or bird forgets he is flying, I thought—in my dream.

Then, there was a sharp impact from somewhere, a shaking machine, a downward drag. A force was pulling me toward earth, turning me round and round. I was filled with fear and disoriented by vertigo. I had no control over a long plunge that was beginning to take me very fast toward the earth below. A horror came over me for my soon-to-be shattered bones along with a brief thought of myself, Amanda. My nerves struggled against a pressure which threatened to block out these, my last moments as a human being. Another part of me wanted that oblivion before the crash took me. I did not want to faint from fear.

Then I noticed something else.

I was on fire. Smoke and heat were pouring into the cockpit, pushed in with blinding intensity by the slipstream. I saw the flicker of flames burst out of the cowling in front of me. The air began to burn my lungs. My clothes were beginning to char and my skin redden. The wicker seat beneath me was beginning to crackle. I thought of jumping; I thought of the pistol in the cockpit with me.

I woke up screaming.

My aunt rushed into my room and found me sitting up in bed, trembling and bathed in sweat. She called Mr. Seddon.

"Have you been interceding for someone?"

"For my friend, Brand."

"It is rather unusual, but this is known as a pain transfer."

"I will not be able to sleep again at night," I told him. "Maybe there is something I can do. I've seen notices that groups are being formed for Zeppelin spotting. Sir Henry gave me his card at Christmas dinner."

"I forbid it!"

"Mrs. Ten Eycke, you can hardly think you are safer for being at Claridge's. The greatest safety factor of all is charting the paths these monsters are taking; Amanda would be in a position to warn you. I am sure that there will not be any impropriety in these groups; they would be under the proper aegis of military authorities. Why don't you at least speak to this Sir Henry?"

Aunt Bea had to acquiesce.

CHAPTER 22

Two days later, we drove up Pall Mall to the Admiralty Arch. My Aunt presented the card Sir Henry had given me to prove it was she who asked him for an appointment. We were Old Salts. We knew we'd have to wait. Instead, Sir Henry came bursting out of his office to greet us, which put him in more favor than Ambassador Page.

"Mrs. Ten Eycke! So charmed! One hears of your efforts everywhere! Pierrepont Morgan, the Duchess of Marlborough...."

"Tut, tut," said Aunt Bea "only the modest efforts of a woman who enjoys some good connections!" She shut her lorgnette (through which she had been quizzing his ancillary personnel).

"What may I do for you?"

"My niece," said my aunt (with her Long Suffering Look) "has some idea that the Navy Reserve is going in for Zeppelin spotting. She has some idea about joining in, but really, I am sure we shall discover it is most inappropriate for..."

"I should put her in training as a partner to another young woman who has just applied, who I think you would find, despite her rather humble background, is rather what we call a brick," he said. "I should think any man who attempted the slightest thing one might term inappropriate with Violet about, would find himself unwisely opening himself to suffering the consequences!"

He opened the door to his office. Once we were inside, several men in uniform sprang to take our coats, to seat us, and in short, to do the formalities with all the attention to spit and polish that takes 'formality' to another level. They bowed and saluted their way out, and shut the door carefully.

Lowering his voice, Sir Henry added, "Furthermore I can put her at St. Paul's. I should not tell you this, but Intelligence has it from the *most* reliable sources that the Kaiser has strictly interdicted bombing London except for the docks. I think she would be in one of the safest places next to Buckingham Palace."

He certainly knew how to work my aunt. She thought she was so discriminating, that she succumbed immediately to the intimation that information given to her, which no none else had had the perspicacity to impart to her, was her right as a member of the circle of luminaries who ran the world. Exactly how an airship pilot, miles above in darkness would have the refined capabilities to avoid hitting certain places in a crowded city was not her problem—gnostic information had been offered to her that it would be so because one of the other Personages who ran the world (even if it was the Kaiser!) had decreed it would be so!

"Allow me time to consider," said my aunt.

"Sir Henry leaned back in his chair. "Miss Twinsley will start her training Friday. I wonder if you might meet her? She is due here later. I say—why don't I get some tickets for Buchan's lecture on the war at Bechstein Hall. We could talk it over later. "

(We, by the way was quite clearly only Aunt Bea and Sir Henry).

Aunt Bea -who much preferred Take Charge Men—paused, considered and consented.

Downstairs we went, and Sir Henry rousted a Royal Navy Reserve Officer, distinguished from his more permanent counterparts by a wavy stripe on his wrist. "When is the Twinsley woman coming in?"

"She's here, Sir," was the reply.

We all sat down in another office. I peered across at Violet. We made an odd combination. I sat, spine erect, in a lace blouse with a set of mother of pearl buttons down the back which advertised the need of a maid to get one into it (never mind it was not very comfortable to lean back on a chair while wearing it!).

My hair was pulled into an elaboration Anna favored—although the tight lacing had been stopped because I put my foot down, and told her if she did not comply, I would tell my aunt, and produce doctor's orders. My boots had been wondrously fashioned with a myriad of buttons and hooks, and my skirt and jacket were a complex exercise in the tailor's art. Altogether, I was the living statement of the inordinate consumption of time and money necessary to put a young lady together for the for the shortest sortie out onto the street.

Violet's hair curled freely out from her knit cap. Her clothes were practical. Instead of my faint aura of eau de lavender, she reeked of tobacco, for her family were tobacco merchants.

"Aren't we the ducky pair!" she said with a disarming laugh, so frank about the difference in our status it effectively broke the ice.

"Now then, Mrs. Ten Eycke," said Sir Henry, (almost as though I weren't even there), "as Miss Twinsley already knows, here we are connected to all the listening posts in the country, the ones in France, in the Channel, in the Thames and Humber. When Zeppelins start a run for England, we receive an alert notice."

"How do you know it is coming for England?" my aunt asked.

"Because it will drop its code book, and when it does so, it sends a signal to Germany to indicate it has dropped it, and we can intercept the signal. Also—the Germans are going to have to navigate by radio shortly— the poor, ruddy chaps, all their dead reckoning and navigation skills in the clouds, are now useless. All that comes in here at Room 40. Unfortunately, it is a top hush-hush facility, and I cannot show it to you. However, to demonstrate to you that Mrs. Pankhurst would have reason to be pleased with the Royal Navy, let me show you our 'learned ladies' instead." These were three women mathematicians who measured stress on various parts of aeroplanes.

We passed into another room, where we met Lt. Schaffer, the officer in charge of spotting at St. Paul's. In the hallway, we heard a loud voice in the hallway. A man was striding by, with a bevy of other men at his heels. He had a decisive eye and nose, undercut by a curiously delicate mouth. The opinions that came out of that mouth, however, were far from delicate.

"Churchill wants us to issue a statement that we'll kill all our German prisoners if one Zeppelin comes over England! The man's a mad dog! Someone needs to find a muzzle for him. "

"That's Murray Sueter. I saw 'im four years ago when the Arch opened, and the Kaiser was here," Violet explained.

When we arrived at the room piloted by Lt. Schaffer, the room was filled with sketches of the Zeppelins. They were huge bags of gas held rigid by a metal structure beneath. A man in Norfolk who saw one, compared the airship to a church steeple flying sideways. In fact, although they looked impregnable, they were tremendously vulnerable, because they were filled with hydrogen, which could explode and incinerate in seconds. Rumor had them surrounded by an inert gas layer which would Prevent British Bullets from ever penetrating them, which, fortunately, proved incorrect.

Lt. Shaffer gave us each a lunar calendar. We learned that Zepplinology revolved around the phases of the moon, with most experts holding they would come on virtually moonless nights so as to be unseen, while other experts claimed they would come on full moon so they could see to bomb us. We would begin the following week.

CHAPTER 23

Now came the first night.

We wore blue jackets with wavy lines at the wrist to signify we were RNAS Reserves. Aunt Bea had arranged for a taxicab to take me to St. Paul's and another to bring me back to the hotel 'for the duration.'

The dome of St. Paul's blotted out the night sky before me the closer we came to my destination. I prepared to trot up some hundreds of stone stairs up past the Whispering Gallery to a Gallery half way up the church, where Wren's fabulous outer and inner dome started up, arching far over us...*if you seek my monument, look about you.* Here was an outer walkway around the circumference of the Cathedral, just above the row of external pillars. Here were a warren of rooms cut into the stone of the building. We were in a sanctum sanctorum, shut off by a series of blankets which one let fall before one lifted the next opened, so as not to let out a tell-tale flicker of light. The walls of the room were covered with maps. We had several telephones.

We practiced reading square maps and telephoning various batteries for the first week until Lt. Schaffer was content. The next week came passive defense.

The phone rang. Violet picked up the receiver. She put it down with the sort of smile we knew meant there had been a call from somewhere. Signals could be sent from spies on the ground, a light burning in a church tower. "Another Grasmere," Violet would say, (referring to a rumor about a Zeppelin in the Lake Country, which somehow crept out every night to observe sleeping England) after she had answered a phone call.

When I entered St. Paul's I sent a spiritual greeting to Chinese Gordon's tomb, although by now I knew enough about his life to know he was not in it, for his body had never been found. I climbed the stairs. In the dim light of our eyrie at our St. Paul's, I could make out, pinned to the opposite wall, newspaper photographs of the damage at Tyne, Lowestoft, Malden, and Heybridge, which had all been hit during the month of April, and a five hundred pound offer from Castrol to the first person to bring down a Zeppelin on English soil. Parliament had decried it as inflammatory; but at our post, sentiments ran in favor of the offer. We were on a high pitch of nerves, because information had been running about that the Kaiser had finally been persuaded to lift his interdiction of bombing London east of the Tower and the docks. Now all of London was a target.

It was not all that hard to see London; a German pilot reported that from an hour away, London could be clearly noted to his south west, by its aurora, with the Thames River a finger pointing toward it. We were, in fact, to use a tried and true Americanism, a sitting duck, except seeing, and arriving, were two different matters.

I continued my exercise of plotting out what squares covered by what batteries I would have alerted had the warning been a real one.

Next we were trained in passive defense, walking around nearby neighborhoods to see if any lights could be observed through the window shades, if street lamps were indeed painted black on their top halves, if motor vehicles had their lamps on low enough. One house obviously flouted the ban, and Violet pounded on the door. Eventually it was opened by a grey haired woman very much *dishabillé* and slightly tipsy, very much outraged and with a vocabulary which contained many words I had never heard before; however, Violet matched her word for word and threatened her with surveillance by the police until she complied. A door opened next door, and the inhabitants stepped out and urged Violet to give it to her. Finally, worn down by disapproval, she went and fully closed her blinds.

One night, I asked Violet, "Where can I get a hat like that?" The drafts had made me envy her knit cap rather than my hat.

"Ere," she said, taking hers off and adjusting it critically on me.

CHAPTER 24

'In spring, when kings take to the field,' had been written in the Old Testament.

Actually, Neuve Chapelle was a bit premature; it began in early March.

It was intended to capture the town of Neuve Chapelle, using a plan developed by Sir Douglas Haig, commander of 1st Army. If successful, it might push forward to Aubers Ridge, in front of the town of Aubers.

Bob has returned from his cruise, and in April, has returned to France, where he was ordered to Squadron 2—. —He is quite bucked to find both Salmond brothers, John and William, are both Majors in the area, although he wished he was sent to Squadron 3, under command of John Salmond, his old C.O. John —I am beginning to see why Bob admires him—who, flying as an observer, three times dropped bombs from 100 feet, which did sufficient damage to be highly successful.

Neuve Chapelle has a small stone church which survived; I visited it once. It opens into a circular ante-room leading into the church, with a bell rope hanging down in the middle, and if ever the local lads get in there without being noticed, they seemed to find it great fun to run, jump as high as possible, and swing on the bell rope, which annoyance disturbs the town and greatly adds to the joy of the lads.

I've been fobbed off to learn something about engines. Ah, the joys of being a civilian pilot with mechanics at beck and call is over, and I am now as greasy as the next man, nearly overwhelmed by fumes of castor oil and banana oil. However, I do find the rotary engine quite fascinating. The Cylinders spin around the crankshaft instead of the other way around; and speed is controlled by shutting off or turning on various numbers of cylinders.

It creates such a pull on the direction upon which it spins (torque)that more often than not one has to keep a foot on the opposite rudder pedal. Things I knew, but not the mechanics thereof.

Two chaps have left us. Trenchard of 1st Wing does not wish to display any empty seats at breakfast to depress morale.

Now, dearest, I've been sent to 1st squadron, arriving too late to gaze upon John Salmond, who left for England on April 15th. My C.O., is his brother, William.

Good enough. My new steed is a Morane Parasol, with said rotary engine.

A momentous newfangled invention has been made, Mandra. I've been told that at Neuve Chapelle, due to aerial photography, a map was produced, and were passed around to all! Fancy that! All this while we have been using Michelin maps. And as for artillery spotting a similar new device has been produced called a clock code.

Court and I (yes, he is still here with me—although he preceded me by two weeks; being an R.E., he already knew what I have been learning; we have been flying for two weeks behind the line to make us familiar with places on the ground. Court was astounded to see me using Zeiss binoculars (which are German, Mandra). I think he was about to inquisition me when I told him they belonged to my mother. When we practice in our Morane two seater, taking photographs with the 'A' camera is damn tricky—one has to hang over the side with straps around both hands so the deuced thing won't fall, get hit by the slipstream, and change glass plates—which takes a bit of doing—which will eventually be developed and turned over to our developers.

I'm sending off home for a Douhet camera. (This was a camera made in Italy).

Now here's a thing, Mandra, superstition runs riot here. Chaps have all sort of lucky items, the most flamboyant of which is a pair of ladies' knickers wrapped around the neck.

No! I am not asking you for a pair! I fancy you could embroider a silk scarf for me. (Silk is easiest on the neck when you are constantly turning your head to look around). I recall the masterpiece on the bottom of your petticoat. What do you say?

Well, of course—yes.

Odd thing about superstition. One of the chaps I've met told me of incident in John Salmond's squadron. A friend of his was looking at his bus with some distress and when asked why, said the numbers on the rudder added up to 13. The next day, a bomb escaped from being loaded on this very aircraft and blew up, killing his friend and 10 other men, and Salmond, who thought it might prove dispiriting, cleaned up the rather ghastly remains that night by himself and one Sergent. A good reason to avoid superstition.

Although it was understood via Room 40 at the Admiralty that the Kaiser had now permitted bombing in London, not just only the docks, nothing seemed to hit us while targets further north were bombed, for industrial and shipbuilding areas like Tyne promised results both in terms of material damage and agitation among the civilian populace. I received permission from our lieutenant to bring my embroidery hoop to our post, so I could embellish away at my project, which came to be watched with interest as it developed. I ripped the bottom off my old petticoat I had worn when we first met, and copied it onto the scarf—I thought he'd like that.

In the end of April Brand was able to observe the first use of chlorine gas, rolling in yellow-green clouds below him. *It is definitely some kind of unpleasant revolutionary weapon –and its only peril to the attackers is whether the wind is blowing the gas away from them, or, if the wind turns, back on their own forces. Infantry has reported finding gas masks dated 1912 and 1910, indicating Germans have been at work at this for some time preceding today.*

In succeeding days, command was engaged in a push-and pull dynamic—some commanders like John French and Douglas Haig wanting to push forward, while other commanders like General Smith-Dorrien, who commanded the 2nd Army, tried to damp their ardor.

I definitely was disinclined to dive down into the gas cloud at first, although we were told it only rises to fifteen feet—the rest supplied by my imagination— but we were issued cloth soaked in chemical to protect us. – Mandra—this may sound distasteful—please remember urine will serve the same purpose as our chemical. One never quite knows what circumstances one may find themselves in!

On our own side, the British attack was hampered by a lack of heavy artillery shells and dud shrapnel shells which had been made in America, with some actually filled with sawdust. Brand's father, usually equanimous, uttered a few harsh words about Yankee profiteers.

A dubious portrait was beginning to formulate about Sir John French, the famous 'horsekiller' of the Boer War. His form of amusements led some to ponder the possibility of leakage; secrets whispered into dainty ears to impress his pillow partner might not stay secret. Sir John did not particularly limit his predilections for female company (except for that of his wife's); he was companioned by a mistress somewhat taller than he was. His revels in London had rolled on into morning, and were not completely absent at his HQ.

However, in France there was a different story, but involving the same man, George Moore, who had bankrolled French in London. He had access to Sir John that no one else enjoyed. Moore was an able man with public relations. A bit too able: he collared journalists to complain about what came to be called 'the shell scandal.' GHQ had no check over him: he was an American civilian who was to French as Colonel House was our President: a silent partner.

CHAPTER 25

I had been reading 'The Era' from cover to cover weekly, especially as Gerald had taken 'The Lady' out on tour after a fairly successful London run. Naturally, the plays that were on tour and their casts were listed there. One day I was completely shocked to find that Lillah Compton had replaced Felicity. What could I do?

After some thought, I wrote Brand, whom I suspected would know something about this cast change. And he certainly did.

It is all a bit of a mess—I'd forgotten to write out complete instructions and the Lady had been booked to go on tour before I left. No one was about to contest the tour, Gerald just proceeded straight ahead as if everything were hunky dory. It appears that he and Lillah had put their heads together and figured this out very carefully. As nothing has been stated about it in writing, I haven't got much to prevent it at this current moment, but—there is a remedy, although one you may not care to adopt. Vessey has advised me that if I have a literary executor to act in my place while I am somewhere in France, this person could gainsay legally any further progress in this direction.

Is this something you might consider, Mandra? I am sorry, but I am really in a pinch and need someone to go-fer me. I can ask Vessey, but it would be an imposition on top of the advice he has already tendered me, and he does not understand the theatre well enough. Father does understand it enough, and you can be sure he will lend a helping hand.

Wow, thought I. I trembled at the thought of so much responsibility.

After reflecting upon the whole, however, I found myself getting angry. Gerald had indeed messed up Brand's life—even though the reading at St. Edmund's had backed the same course of action for Brand, it was for far different reasons.

The thing to do was say my prayers. I accepted.

The offices of Mr. Winship were circumspect, so quiet one felt a secret if uttered would stick there in the padding of the room. When I told him my errand, he only said he had had a letter from Brand, and that the Viscount had rung him. He showed me into a room with a table and several chairs, shut the door, and in a few moments, three clerks came in, bearing an assortment of boxes.

On the top was the will—*I, Brandon Basil George Whitefield,, being of sound mind and body, of my own free will, in this year our Lord......*I put it down as if the paper had burned my fingers.

I picked out a paper with a gaggle of figures. I put on my 'specs' and dug out the top papers, which were profit and loss sheets. Columns were set for *theatre rent, lighting, costumes, coatroom, salaries, bar* and involved assets taken in and fees paid out. I put it outside.

I dug my arms down to the bottom of the first box, and came out with a gaggle of dusty script pages, which made me sneeze. Atop them was the legend, 'The Rites of Discount.'

This is the one that made the trouble. It proved to be ten drafts deep. The first was very rough, indeed, each page a series of scraps of paper, glued together, some on top of others, to a depth of three or four sequences. The scribbles on the different pieces of paper, their rubbed, worn surfaces, and the smell of tobacco, told of being thrust into a pocket as the words or music came to him. I flipped to the end, where all the musical scores were grouped together. Brand's hand had scrawled the melody line in the treble clef on the first page. Behind it was a finished score, where an arranger had obviously filled in around the melody line.

This is the one that caused the trouble. Its lyric was a series of two-line *on dits,* one sung one line at a time, one by one diner, the other in reply to his or her dinner partner, sung by diners around a dinner table (and I recognized the table)!

For a lower discount rate

Paris still is simply great,
Liquid reserve at thirteen per
De rigueur now, my dear sir!
Edward's spending was so profligate
Burnham had him in his pocket.
Invest five per overseas
Gradual capital is the key!
Piaish dashed mercantilist premise-
Balance capital's not undone us.
Our incentives will grow lax
With this death and income tax.
If we buy more than we sell
In three years specie will be shot to hell.
Empire costs more than it makes
Oh, not that old outworn debate.
If Lord's should lose the veto
Then Lloyd George will run the show.

Now they all rise, and raise their glasses to a common toast, sung in
unison.
To the compound interest curve
We'll absorb the world's reserve!

One must give him credit—he's made the undecipherable entertaining.

Other song titles were The Philosopher's Stone, I Heard the Alchemist Say, and Tribute, which was the finale, and involved variously costumed people from all parts of the Empire coming to stack up the various forms of wealth they yielded to Britain and burned it in a funeral pyre.

I turned back to the script. It read: *The scene is set in the home of Lord and Lady Wealthy, whose vocation and avocations is the Bank and the Exchange. The house, located in Mayfair....a drama á clef.*

Next, I pulled out a batch of letters. The first was in rather youthful penmanship, but it was addressed to the Times, and dated May 14, 1902.

Sirs, Why forsee an England without the enthusiasm of a Ben Greet or Frank Benson? Why do we need a "National Theater?" As soon as you have a theatre that is national, you have theatre funded by the state. You then have art at the service of the state. Brandon Whitefield, Harrow college.

Attached to it was a page of stationery with the letterhead, "Academy of Acting, 3 Bedford St., Strand It read:

My dear young sir: Thank you for your compliment to my person. However, I am much in favor of a national theatre. I myself broached the subject to the Times some six years ago. Monies amounting to ten thousand pounds were forthcoming. But the proposed site on the Embankment was pinched by Syon House.

However your point about the state and art: I think the long run play, which will be imposed by commerce on the theatre, will be the ruin of theatre as art. Yrs. Sincerely, Philip Ben-Greet.

I moved to the most recent box, and plucked a review from an obscure artistic paper. It had been clipped and Brand had written 'interesting' on it.

Brandon Whitefield, Sir or the Hon. Or however he may style himself, has been a stimulant to the stage since his earliest productions, which were Court Theatre success des éstimes rather than commercial successes. Gradually, in the six years since he has come down from Cambridge, he has freed himself from the ironic comment on subjects so arcane that only Keynes could grasp them, which is to say, he has shed his undergraduate mentality. His is an improbable gift of wedding the melody and lyric displayed by Gilbert and Sullivan, and the true dramatist's gift of presenting the deeper forces working beneath the surfaces of the world. This unique admixture has catalyzed a rabble of an audience for him: intelligentsia; displaced balletomanes: the farouche who want their Ibsenesque slash; those interested in watching Shaw's adaptation to Arthur Symonds narrative of The Superwoman; the amorous or choleric music hall aficionados. Last night they all converged on the West End.

This play signalled the end of his apprenticeship, advanced by his dispensing of the services of Lillah Compton, whose range, however superb, is limited by the inability to hit a subtle note, or take on any contradiction to her character. And while the selection of her successor was punctuated by all the publicity a clever manager could wring, even to the inclusion of a 'mystery lady,' in the event the most interesting thing is not the advent of Miss Felicity Westcote, but the character of the Lady herself. She is a distinct advance in Mr. Whitefield's abilities in characterization, rather than caricature, in the service of his overreaching Idea.

The Lady is potentially likeable. What then? We never get to like her. It is because we see her through the eyes of her prey, Yarrell "Charlie" Harris, who, unlike Mr. Shaw's John Tanner, is slow to distance himself from her wiles, and is never tempted to compare them to a boa constrictor. We do not discover the "why" of Charlie's crying off at the end (unlike Tanner) when in the song, "Pretending that You Love me," when, in a startlingly late scene à fair, he simply reveals that their love has been made up.

Here is a man who was taken in by the Lady's ardor, which attaches itself to every new cause; he has shaped it into a passion for himself, too, and created the common fog in which they dwell together. He has bought her love for him by proclaiming her his Galatea, because, like all modern men, he has had to invent his own answer to the question, not "What do women want?" but, "what do I want from women?" And the answer is, he has been unable to invent an answer.

This takes us by surprise. We want; indeed, we are accustomed, indeed, to our playwright be a wiser and better man than we are. He should be! He has taken a stage to proclaim it! He has the advantage of having shaped the world before our eyes; like a lotus eater, he is able to create his own spell. In the past, Mr. Whitefield has pandered as nobly to the request for answers as Mr. Bernard Shaw. Now, Mr. Whitefield puts himself right in the seats with us. He, too, watches Charlie, because Charlie is one of us. Unlike a Tanqueray or a Gabler, he is able to see beyond women's own reactions to reform. His Lady will not blow her brains out, or go to social disgrace. Nor does this abdication of his role to shape her cause him despair. He must let his Galatea speak: true: she is a new creation: in her own words, just as did the midons of courtly love—the milady—except now her field is wider. She speaks: we hear the sound of her voice: we attend, as does Mr. Whitefield: and we await the world's response. Together, we seek to answer an unanswerable question. This is new dramatic territory.

That *scene à faire* would not have been there, without me.

The papers piled up before me, sheet by sheet. When the pile was completed, I suddenly put my head down on them and began to sob.

CHAPTER 26

It was early morning, May 8. I opened the door to our suite quietly. I assumed everyone was fast asleep. But all the lights were on. Becky was sitting in one chair, still decked out in evening finery. Anna was in the other, in nightgown and negligee.

"The Luisitania has been sunk," said Becky.

My aunt had been invited to a dinner at the Embassy in honor of Colonel House—President Wilson's so-called 'silent partner,' who had arrived in Europe on a 'Quest for Peace.' House was inviting all the belligerents to converse with him. However, my aunt had a prior engagement and sent Becky.

Becky was always bubbly and slightly garrulous except when she was angry. But now her words had a serious urgency and they came tumbling like an irresistible flood. "When we sat down to dinner," said Becky, "Ambassador Page told us he had messages that the ship had been sunk, but assured us that all passengers had been saved. Col. House told about his crossing on her this January. He said there had been such a terrible storm they thought they would go to the bottom. He said not to worry. So we just went ahead and ate dinner."

Anna silently handed me the morning newspaper, which Ambassador Page had sent to friends fresh off the presses. There was a front page photo of a liner with one mast fore, one mast aft, and four great stacks between them.

That was all I got to see, because Becky was still talking. "A few hours later, Ambassador Page received a message from Ireland. It said there was a rumor that the commander of the U boat had backed his submarine into

Kinsale harbor yesterday morning and warned all the fishermen to stay in port, there might be trouble that day. It made us all begin to be very uneasy.

"Word begun to come in, hour by hour. Nobody left. We all huddled together. The news came she had been sunk. Wesley Frost, at Queenstown, cabled about how many—and who—had been lost: Paul Crompton, head of Cunard, Alfred Vanderbilt and Charles Frohman. Someone said Frohman had warnings delivered to him dockside not to get on—no one knows who sent them, but it had to be somebody German. But he went anyway! Isn't that idiotic!

"Col. House told us he had a strange conversation only the day before with King George. They were speculating that sooner or later a liner would be sunk with Germany's unrestricted submarine warfare declared. The King had asked him, "Suppose they sink the Luisitania with American passengers on board?"

"I suppose now that Page and House think America will enter the war," said my aunt. "When House crossed in January, Sir John French— who is the commander of the British forces in France— asked if there had been a possible German peace offer. Well, there is bound to be a lot of chatter."

"Will you be taking calls, Ma'am?" asked Anna. My aunt had become a rather well- known spokesperson for the American community in London. To date we had maintained the protocol that questions must be submitted to her in writing.

"Yes. . . yes, I will. But I will not see anyone," said my aunt.

By evening the 'eyewash artists' had a field day with the sinking liner and a Hun gnashing his teeth in Davey Jones' locker. The telephone had been ringing and Aunt Bea had actually fielded a number of calls herself. To the others, we merely repeated what we had heard her say. As I watched my cousin, I saw she was, for once, taking things seriously without a hint of provocativeness beneath. The litany of famous American names, along with her work with her wounded soldiers, had finally made my cousin grave.

I wrote Brand, *remember it was just about a year ago Aunt Bea was herding us away from reporters like a flock of goslings!*

He replied, *Don't let the press play any stunts with you, my dearest. Stay level with your wording—don't say anything sensational.* He should know, I thought, bitterly, of Gerald. Anyway, it was too late: my aunt had already made an inflammatory statement. She told the press she would be ashamed of her country if it did not now come to the aid of the Allies.

After that the phone began ringing off the hook. For a week we were *very* popular with the British public. When Anna helped Aunt Bea step outside briefly for a breath of air, people on the street applauded. A photographer started lurking, looking for a photo or a quote. Mr. Hoover called my aunt in and urged to remember that it was he, and he alone, who made statements for anything connected to the C.R.B.

Aunt Bea's reaction was, "Men!"

CHAPTER 27

I received a note from Miss Westcote, who was now 'resting' waiting for a new part since her abrupt dismissal by Gerald.

She invited me to accompany her to a tribute for Charles Frohman, given by the theatre community, which would be held at the other St. Paul's, the site for the opening of Shaw's 'Pygmalion.' So it was that the following Sunday, Miss Westcote and I were standing on the porch, while. Miss Westcote provided me with commentary on the Passing Scene.

"Those two gentlemen together there, are Philip Ben-Greet and Frank Benson, our Big Shakespearian revivalists. The dark- haired chap with the Profile with them is Benson's cousin, Basil Rathbone. He is training as an officer somewhere—" Felicity gave a vague wave of her hand to that point of the compass, up north. C.F. brought Greet to New York to do some of the classics—'Everyman, Much Ado'- suchlike."

C.F., I discovered that afternoon, was Charles Frohman's universal nickname. This curiously misshapen Jew of German background, so crippled he walked always with a cane he referred to as 'my wife,' had never signed a contract with anyone. In a litigious profession full of strong egos, his word was his bond. Then she dropped her voice.

"Look, there is Barrie," she said. A rather short man hurried by us, with a sharp nose and a sharp chin, obviously in the grip of his emotions. "Did you hear that C.F. was said to have quoted "To die will be a really big adventure" from 'Peter Pan' at the very last?"

Barrie, a close friend of Frohman's, was choked up.

"No, I hadn't," I said.

"There is Tree!" she hissed. "Did you hear, he watched some chaps adjusting a spotlight to chase after Zepps one night and he said 'Don't waste that silly thing—shine it on me!'" And Felicity giggled into her handkerchief.

When Mrs. Patrick Campbell appeared, Felicity recounted with zest how she had thrown a pair of slippers in Tree's face during the rehearsals for Pygmalion.

We sat near the back. Many of the Personages present rose, came forward, and made Remarks. Shaw spoke of how he and Mrs. Shaw were stopping in Ireland with Lady Gregory when the news came, along with notice her nephew had been among the lost. In some haste, they got onto the channel ferry, which was loaded with the survivors of the sinking.

"They told us a fog had come up in the morning, and it dispersed about eleven, and they could actually see the coast of Ireland," he said. He restrained himself from any exercise of wit.

Barrie rose, and said "Whoever would have thought when I penned those words . . .." and could not continue. He sat down. Irene Vanbrugh spoke of C.F.'s fabled concentration at rehearsals, when he would sit on one leg, motionless, drinking in every detail of production.

Cables were read from America; familiar names, Barrymore, Drew, Maude Adams, Faversham, Shubert. There was also one from Bob Loraine, 'somewhere in France.' But I only noticed peripherally. When the service drew to a close, I saw that Murdoch had now returned to London.

Literary executrix flashed across my mind. Murdoch appeared like a specter in front of us. He glared; we walked away.

Yes, my being here with Felicity gives his lie to dismissing her for some unexplained flaw in her performance just what it was--a lie.

"I don't think I can ever forgive him."

"Why should you? Watch out for that snake."

CHAPTER 28

Suddenly we knew the night, May 31, was going to be different. The Kaiser had given permission for London to be bombed east of the Tower. Enough damage was done, that censorship of the results was imposed on newspapers. A Zepp got up as far as Gravesend anyway, and we were informed of it, yet sworn to silence. Certainly, no topography of Zepp hits would be published to let their commanders know where they had really been.

Outside, somewhere in the dark, a dog let out a series of unearthly howls. "Note it," the Lieutenant said. I wrote down the time a call had come through, and the date.

On this particular evening, listening posts had already picked up the usual signs of Zeppelin activity, but we had moved to a higher state of alert when word came it had ditched its code book. Outside, birds who should have been asleep by now, called back and forth in a strange and frenzied way. I noted the hands of the clock precisely at the hour of ten p.m. Ten minutes later we got word an airship was over Margate. Outside the dog began to howl again. I noticed that the hair had half- risen on my arms. Reports were beginning to flood in now from the Eastern mobile section. The ship had passed over the Isle of Sheppey. Then it was sighted over Shoeburyness. It was headed straight inland.

"Where the hell are the boys from Joyce Green?" muttered Lt. Schafer to himself. Wherever our night flying aeroplanes were, they were certainly not in the path of this particular airship! It took aeroplanes of that age an hour to reach several thousand feet.

Outside the very night began to rustle. Small animals and insects were mounting upward toward the house tops, which was their idea of where safety lay. Later we would learn to rely on the instincts of the animals, who seemed to sense the approach of Zeppelins in the same mysterious way they sensed hurricanes or earthquakes.

Then, the northeast began to glow. Searchlights had their covers pushed off and were beginning to comb the fleecy hair of the night sky. I began to experience an urge to run (which I fought by asking myself --to where??). Now, below, we could hear constables moving around on their bicycles, blowing whistles to warn people to seek cover. And then, in the far distance, we heard it: the unforgettable reverberation of a great sound: our first bomb.

Violet grabbed the field glasses. She had completely forgotten she was under orders, and slipped outside. "I can see some fires!" she called back to us.

The phone rang. The Zepp was over Stoke Newington, just below Harringey. She had just switched course. She had swung left ninety degrees. She was heading right for us. We could not know it was piloted by German's most famous Zeppelin commander, Heinrich Mathy, and Lt. Karl Linnarz.

Violet was watching a red glow spread, the emanation of a string of fires from Shoreditch to Whitechapel, Whitechapel to West Ham, and West Ham to Leystone. "I can hear the fire engines!" she called out to us.

"Let me know the moment you see something," Schafer called out to her, accepting the fact that, though he had not detailed her to 'spot,' she seemed to be doing very well at it.

"We have got to get its bearings for the battery!" Our Lieutenant exclaimed. Our signals stood on 'open' to the gunpost nearest to us, one set up specifically to protect the Bank of England. We held our breaths. We listened for the faintest of faint noises above us. In the searchlights, a pall of grey smoke hung below the clouds.

"He's probably letting off ballast to get above the guns," Lt. Schafer muttered. He thought the smoke from our guns had hidden her. "Come on you bugger, show yourself," he murmured.

But the battery stayed silent. After an eternity of waiting with every nerve stretched to its absolute edge, the phone rang. We all jumped.

The Zeppelin had been spotted passing Burnham on the Crouch, then Southminister. She was slipping away. She probably did not realize exactly how close she had been to a series of prime targets. Her passage back to the sea was only remarked by a salvo or two from a couple of mounted Maxim guns, and a few blasts from some of the sea-side anti-aircraft batteries.

On their way back to Germany, Linnarz dropped one of his personal cards on which he had written: 'You English! We have come and we will come again soon, kill or cure!' He put it in a message streamer: it was found in the Dunkirk dunes, and definitely stoked British passions.

When I got back to the hotel, I was surprised to find Aunt Bea, in her nightgown, crouched in an armchair, waiting for me, knuckles gripping the chair arms. "Was it close to the Bank?" she asked me.

Yes, but apparently he didn't see us."

On June 6 we were once again on high alert. But once again London escaped. Heinrich Mathy, who came to be the most highly feared Zeppelin commander), bombed Hull instead.

CHAPTER 29

Then, passive absorption of N.S.B.G. (Not so bloody good) news was interrupted dramatically! Reggie Warneford, an R.N.A.S. pilot, brought down a Zeppelin near Dunkirk! It fell on St. Elizabeth's Convent, Ghent, where earlier in the day a Corpus Christi celebration was being held, and the nuns and the children in their care had enjoyed an outdoor tea.

Later, as the nuns were assembling for chapel, they heard the great noise which was the airship exploding as the Hales bomb hit it. They looked up, and saw it falling toward them, its crew's screams audible as bits and pieces of the Zeppelin, mixed with fiery ignited hydrogen, showered down around them. They evacuated. Several nuns and children were killed (not, as later myth had it, that everyone escaped, and that one German survivor fell into one of the nun's bed).

Warneford was showered with the Victoria Cross and *Croix de guerre*, and was slated to be kept in Paris as the Royal Navy's propaganda trophy, as well as forming a liaison with a French aviatrix, the Baroness de Laroche.

Warneford had been posted to Dunkirk, and had never flown at night until then. On the night in question, he lost his two flight mates. Then he saw the LZ37; and he began shooting at it with a carbine, knees holding control stick. The Zeppelin dumped some water ballast and began to rise. Warneford could not follow in his Morane, but still, he followed, and, later, the Zep came back down the 7,000 feet, while Warneford had attained 11,000 feet, and dropped three fire bombs, which resulted in an enormous explosion. Warneford dived and desperately kept adjusting his air and gas flow until the engine stopped, and he landed in a field, where he repaired a broken fuel line, started the machine and jumped in.

Ten days later he went to Paris to receive his Legion of Honor, and was ordered to pick up a new Farman biplane at Buc. It was not completely finished and lacked seat belts and many parts of standard equipment. Once in the air, it rolled over and cast out its two passengers. A Pennsylvania free-lance reporter, Henry Needham, who had pressed him very hard for a flight, was killed with him.

The funeral would be in England, and it would be a salute to a fallen hero.

Among the gestures of public respect, a number of 'ambulatories' from Becky's hospital, she told me, wished to salute the gun carriage as it passed down Buckingham Palace Road. She asked if I would come with her.

Somehow the futility of such an end, after the tremendous outpouring, which had followed his courageous act, struck the public hard. Such public sadness called forth a response, some of which involved a sacrificial effort from those who made them.

Becky was not as confident as she appeared to be and begged me to join her.

Their group decided to get in line along the street at 7:30 in the morning, an hour early, to make sure of a place. It spoke volumes that my cousin, since the war began, was actually Up, Dressed, and Out on the street at such a Barbarically Early time! It spoke more volumes about these recovering soldiers that they were willing to stand for an hour, even if it completely debilitated them.

A large crowd lined the street, subdued, teary-eyed. We saw the procession coming down from Victoria. Despite the high emotion I had to suppress a yawn. I had indeed napped in my clothes, and felt somewhat sloppy. We made out the coffin at a distance because it was draped with a very large flag. Warneford's cap was on top of it, along with various arrangements of flowers, coming toward us on a gun carriage. Behind and beside it marched members of the Royal Navy. Behind the official procession, a number of people were falling in helter skelter. It wended its way along, like a comet with a growing tail, on its way to Brompton Cemetery.

I found that Max decided to try to lift spirits after this tragedy. A train was due at Waterloo Station carrying the wounded, and Max had wangled an invitation for us to join the entertainment organized by George Robey to welcome this train back to England. We saw faces perk up as they were carried out on stretchers and heard music; at one point, a man dressed very much like a bum came down the stairs to us. It was George Robey. He was to me the British version of Charlie Chaplin! Miss Violet Loraine was with him, and first, they launched into 'If You Were The Only Girl in The World;' Max and I sang along to one side. This was feebly but appreciatively applauded. Then Robey threw a bearskin over his suit, put on a wig and picked up a club and did some bits from his song 'Prehistoric Man,' which actually was a patter on current events; it even garnered a few laughs.

Then Max walked over to him and they engaged in a private conversation, and I saw Max hand Robey his mandolin. What could this mean? Robey threw off his tramp's overcoat, under which he had on a nice suit jacket, and was actually a rather handsome looking man.

"Miss Ten Eycke, would you accompany me?" he asked, coming over to me. I was overawed by George Robey: comedian, sportsman, violin maker and Zeppelin spotter, and now, I perceived, accomplished mandolin player. "Is there something you might like to play?" he asked, to set me more at ease.

"The one I like best," I managed to stutter, "is 'A Thing He Had Never Done Before!'" He smiled. Max smiled. Though I would hear it many times, the lines 'It went and killed our sister Ruth/when he went and told the truth/ A thing he had never done before,' always made me laugh. Perhaps the mere words written out don't seem funny; but when Robey performed it, it was very funny!

CHAPTER 30

Mandra, Something most unexpected has happened. I had not heard from 'Xiema for some four weeks which worried me—when I received her latest, I knew why.

It appears M. Desperniers died of a sudden heart attack just after her last letter.

She is quite alone rattling around in the big Paris home. The boys—those of them that are left, Robert is surviving as yet—are in the army. Her daughters are in faraway places. I decided to make a run into Paris, and asked my C.O., William of the Salmond brood, if I might borrow the squadron car for a day. Not a bloody good idea. However, one chap in the squadron brought his own motorcar with him—I should have done the same! I did not know then it was possible. He lent it to me and I made my way to Paris.

'Xiema was in shocking shape. She had become quite thin and frail, her hair has turned completely white and there are deep lines of sadness in her face—all of which are heartbreaking.

I know we were preparing for time together at leave, and although I do so look forward, I formed the idea it would be best to get her out of Paris—and to England. I petitioned my family to take her in and of course they agreed, we are vastly in their debt! I held off writing you for I fear it will be a disappointment.

He still did not know me all that well. I telegraphed, *'Of course you must bring her.'*

What do you think of this idea. I think it will be most important she can communicate when she arrives; she does not speak English. My father, I, and you speak French. What if he should ask your aunt if you might stay with us during my leave—it would be completely proper of course—my brother and I had our rooms on one floor, Maddy on another.

What an interesting idea. What could Aunt Bea say.

Of course, she will probably want to go to Mass as often as possible, and I am used to accompanying her! All that will be needed is a French translation of the Mass for her to follow—she probably knows it by heart.

This will certainly be interesting. Both the Viscountess and Mme. Desperniers knew the latter has acted more of a mother to Brand than his mother has.

His next letter told me he had pulled out all the connections he had. He had contacted a Maurice Baring at GHQ, Hotel du Rhîne, Amiens, ADC to General David Henderson. It transpired they were not completely unknown to one another; Baring had, from time to time, had a crack at playwriting.

Also, Baring converted to Catholicism several years ago—which may make him more sympathetic to my request.

It transpired that Brand, after some consideration, had decided to ask 'Xiema if she would be afraid to fly, for he felt the train or automobile ride to the coast, always interrupted and held up by essential traffic, might prove a bit too much for his old 'Xiema. She pondered this, however, and decided she would trust Brand's judgment.

He knew full well any machine taken from his squadron would be one that was needed, so, being aware that GHQ had several *avoins* at the ready in the event some *gros legume* might employ one to make a visit, he achieved permission to use one. (I was amused that Brand felt 'big vegetables' lived at GHQ). Permission granted, he would land near the coast, and then—then, his father would ask Sir Henry for a Short seaplane for the trip across the Channel!

So, Brand again borrowed the automobile from his squadron-mate, then drove to Paris. There were many things to do to aid 'Xiema. Her faithful lady's maid was terrifyingly upset. 'Xiema quieted her by assuring her she and two other servants could stay at the *maison* and take care of it.

Please pack a light suit case for her mistress; the rest could go in a truck to England God knew when; make sure to put out some warm clothing for it would be colder at altitude. Don't forget her Bible and Thérèse's autobiography. There was money in the safe in M. Despernier's *bureau* and, trusting to the thriftiest of the average French person, Madame entrusted the key to them; for there was loyalty in that day as well as robbery. Brand went to our American bank Morgan Hartjes in Paris and negotiated a contact between them and his father's wireless address in London, which might be used in case of financial necessity.

This was one event in Brand's life he planned very carefully, as he wanted it to be unflawed. The top was put up on the touring car. He would be as careful as he possibly could, for Madame was not in health; doubtless she had not slept much recently.

The drive to Amiens was predictably slow, yet on arrival, he took a quiet room for 'Xiema, as she was to take a nap! He would return to escort her to supper.

Then I had a shave and haircut and a scalp massage with eau de quinine. There are so many little vermin which share the Front with us it is marvelous to feel one's hair and scalp are truly CLEAN. I had time to visit a bookstore and found other books she would like.

He felt a good supper would set them up well for the evening and the day ahead, especially, as he wished to feed 'Xiema. Although it could be a bit raffish, he decided on Godbert's, a luxurious hotel frequented by the R.F.C.; he planned to eat a bit on the earlier side to miss the crowd.

I entered Godbert's with 'Xiema on my arm; the Patronne rocketed out her office to greet us, for 'Xiema was 100% French, with hair pulled severely back, black dress marking mourning and a well-made black hat; her gold crucifix around her neck. She seated us in a corner of one of the two rooms that make up the place, separated from one another by the hallway and clusters of archways on each side. Would 'Xiema like a small tonic before supper? Indeed she would. Obviously we could read the menu. She left us temporarily.

And of course, we had lamb with potatoes á la Santos Dumont.

At that moment, a French soldier in the uniform and kepi of colonial troops, entered and spoke with the Patronne. Apparently he was asking if he might have a plate of food that he would eat outside, but she, with typical French ingenuity, bade him wait for a moment and approached us. There was, she told us, a French soldier at the door who was a stretcher bearer and a priest. (Priests were drafted in France.) Would it be agreeable if he would join us—yes, she had observed 'Xiema's crucifix and pious air correctly. I told the Patronne I would pay for supper for all of us, as 'Xiema had taught me: always pay for a priest! As for 'Xiema, her face lit up.

I never really understood what Mr. Seddon referred to as an anointing.

However, I began to feel some strange force directing what was happening, a purposeful exactitude to it, with every motion and every word occurring without thought. At the end of the meal, 'Xiema asked the priest if he would hear her confession. There is, of course, the magnificent cathedral of Amiens, yet neither of us considered 'Xiema capable of walking so far in a weakened condition; so the priest held confession in the Patronne's office!

"Now I am ready to fly," 'Xiema said.

The following morning we proceeded to the GHQ flying field, and were given a machine noted for its stability, the BE2c. As we would be flying behind the lines, there was no foreseeable reason to need maneuverability.

This was the last missive to arrive before their arrival; he was too busy to write. He told me that at the airfield, two very nice staff officers carried 'Xiema up a ladder and gently as a mother bird put her into her nest—the observer's cockpit—and saw to it she was wrapped up like a mummy. Before they began to wrap her up, she hung her rosary around her neck. Of course she was sweltering before we took off but not a word of complaint passed her lips.

She closed her eyes when they taxied. They landed at St. Omer, where his squadron was located. They had dinner, after which, she went to sleep.

The next morning, he conferred with her—would it distress her to fly over water? If so, they could cross the Channel by boat.

"Well," she replied, "water one way or the other."

This delighted Brand, for she had always had a ready wit.

While she rested at St. Omer, she asked if he would go out and buy something, as she would be staying at the Viscount's home. He went, of course, and found *tuiles d'amiens* —-(the tiles of Amiens) fresh out of the ovens. When put artistically in a box, they appeared impressive. No proper guest would arrive without a gift. He was beginning to see flashes of her old personality appear.

CHAPTER 31

"Brandy, your chariot has arrived from Short aviation," a statement which caused him to open his eyes from his sleep at the squadron. It was Courtenay, his roommate in a bell tent.'Xiema had been taken in overnight by a civilian family of St. Omer, members of the squadron had come to know. Brand shaved, dressed and borrowed the squadron motor. He arrived to find 'Xiema being treated as an honored guest; she was being served *café au lait* with a pinch of sugar (which was beginning to grow scarce).

"I have told them I will send some coffee when we get to England." Ah yes, *de rigueur.* How will she cope with tea? Perhaps some *tilleleul?*

Once at the aerodrome, Courtenay said, "I'll spin the prop for you."

"You needn't," Brand replied.

"I may not need to, but I want to!"

So it was Court who answered, "Suck in, Switch Off," and then, after a little wait for the pressure to push the petrol up to the engine, "Contact!"

Brand presented 'Xiema to Courtenay in French. She reached out a formal hand, palm down, a gesture which meant 'kiss my hand,' in greeting, in the manner of her day. Brand spoke to her, then she shook hands.

They were off over the Channel. Brand flew through the area covered by the Dover Patrol, to be on the safer side. Below them a destroyer distributed wake, and a few trawlers were still in the Channel. Two aircraft passed them, on submarine patrol. One of them buzzed him, finding a pilot in an R.F.C. uniform with a woman in the observer's nacelle peculiar. Landing at Short aircraft factory, they found the Viscount's motorcar and chauffeur awaiting them; Brand had thought to get out of the air as quickly as possible, for the engine noise caused temporary (or at times permanent) deafness; then he threw off his Triplex goggles to give his eyes a breath of fresh air, which also cleared the nostrils of engine fumes. Once in the comfortable back seat, and in motion, 'Xiema fell asleep. And Brand, as was often the case after a flight, did so too. Only when the automobile motion definitively stopped did they wake up; his father and mother were awaiting them to alight, to greet them. 'Xiema said, with a heavy French accent, "Good day, milady," and shook the Viscountess's hand, then she shrugged her shoulders and raised her up palmed hands as if to say, "That's all I know how to do!" The Viscount kissed her hand in courtly style. Brand took his mother's hand and kissed her cheek; then he hugged his father, who was startled initially, but then returned the hug.

"Shall we go inside?" Indeed. Preparations had been made; the guest suite, with bedroom, spacious, and with a sitting room attached, had been re-wall papered with something light and airy. It had all been lightened in color, as the old dark paneling and colors had begun to change. Brand's mother did not want to add to the gloom.

"*Oh, comment c'est si belle!*" said Madame.

"She likes it," Brand translated to his mother, who was pleased, for she had tried hard to make the spot a charming one. And, being the Viscountess, when she determined to do something, it got done.

"Shall we have tea?" The great social leveler. The Viscountess's maid and the chauffeur entered the room as we left carrying her small suitcase, which would be pressed and hung up; other items were added: a lovely silk bathrobe, slippers, brush, comb, mirror, bath powder: on the dressing table, along with a vase of flowers, a case containing manicure implements the maid could use, lavender scented toilet water in an atomizer, exotic hair combs for arrangement of coiffures.

"Is everything all right, do you think? "His mother whispered to her son in English—of course—and he replied it was a bit more than all right. She smiled. One could sense the two ladies would fall back on being formal for these first days.

"Will you please ask her," his mother asked her son, "If she would like to bathe, or have something to eat, or rest, just now?"

"Could I suggest a bed tray so she can eat and rest at the same time?"

"Of course. Shall I send my maid in to prepare her for her rest?"

"Jolly good idea." He then translated to 'Xiema, who was at one and the same time, pleased, yet distressed by idea of an unknown maid, and she asked Brand, "Does she speak French?"

"Alas, no, 'Xiema, only German." Her face paled slightly.

"Would you prefer I aid you?" I asked. "I know what to do, you know, and I promise not to pull your hair!"

"*Je l'aime, merci.*"

I did my best; we removed her dress and I unlaced her corset: (she then took a deep breath which sounded like a sigh). Then I put the silk peignoir over her, and slid the corset off. *"Comme vous êtes circonspect,"* she complimented me. I was glad she found my ministrations discreet. A bed tray arrived, with an omelet (one could hardly go wrong with that!) buttered toast, kept warm with a cover, with butter dish at its right side; several croissants with jam, and a few of the candy she had so thoughtfully brought, with pieces of cheese; a cup of tilleul—linden tea—which she evidently appreciated. Of the cheese, she exclaimed, *Ah, c'est brie."* I could not tell if she were happy or sad, or both, at this reference to their former country home.

I caught up with Brand silently and caught an expression of deep sorrow he didn't want me to see as he contemplated the destruction of this family he had loved, and who loved him. "She wants me to write to Robert," he said.

"Do you know where he is?"

"He is with the 20th Corps."

"Her hair seems to stay in place by magic!"

"That's not magic, Mandra, it's a wig. She would never go out with her hair undressed."

CHAPTER 32

"Father and mother have asked us to join them for tea in mother's drawing room. It's quite small and intimate."

Indeed it was; comfortable deep leather-bound chairs, a sofa, and books overflowing onto several tables. I startled; at one end, which I deduced was the Viscountess' end, were two books in English, *Aviation Photography, and Notes on the Interpretation of Aeroplane Photography Manual*; for the Viscount, there was *L'Aviation militaire, 10th edition,* by Clément Ader, in French, who, as I noticed in a short riffle through its pages, used the word *torpilleurs* for land explosions, despite the expression torpedoes. Later Ader mentions it is torpedoes which are used naval ships; however grenades are *pour l'armament aérion.* As for 'Greek fire,' liquid incendiary (flame thrower) one hopes no one will ever have to use it," finishes our author. His wish was not granted.

At the back, complicated mathematical equations ran riot. It would take Brand's father to decipher them.

"Do you think I could borrow one of these?"

"Why?"

"Then I will understand more of what you're doing."

"Are you sure it not might not make you more anxious?"

"I'm not sure anything could make me more anxious!"

"Touché." At this moment, his parents joined us. The Viscount looked perturbed.

"Amanda, I am afraid your aunt has not yet informed me of where she has made up her mind you may lodge tonight," he told me.

"Oh, bother!" I exclaimed. "I'm too tired to deal with that." Even Brand threw me a wondering glance.

"Then," said the Viscountess, "You must simply stay here." We all turned to look at her. "This pettifogging is so tiresome. You need not worry. I shall deal with her." None of us doubted that she could. "We shall have an early diner, then I will install you comfortably in Maddy's old room."

A great weight lifted from my shoulders; I was with Brand's family. Since my Uncle Ben's death, I had been haunted a feeling of susceptibility that haunted me until that afternoon. The words 'there is a rest prepared for you to enter in to,' began to disclose their mysterious meaning; not that it was an insurance of safety, but of the peace of 'the Lord giveth and the Lord taketh away, blessed be the name of the Lord.' Brand's mother led me to their daughter Maddy's old room, where nightclothes were laid out for me but anyhow, once I sat down on the edge of the bed I was so tired I toppled over and fell asleep; subsequently, Brand took off my shoes and the two of them merely spread a blanket over me. I slept for twelve hours.

I knew, when I awakened, that some form or other of my aunt would be presenting itself that day. Interestingly, Brand's mother had disposed arrangements to the effect that Aunt Bea would have tea with me, Brand, Mme. Desperniers, and the Viscountess, who, I figured, was present of some kind of referee-cum-spare conversationalist when we three were speaking French. Then she, the Viscount, and my aunt would dine alone. Becky had been disinvited so as not to add further ammunition.

Brand's mother had said she would take care of things, and she had; she had dispatched a maid with the chauffer and car earlier that morning to ask for a case containing new clothing for the day for me. It was, of course, a seemingly churlish request to deny.

Once seated in a small drawing room, my aunt, surrounded by the Whitefield décor, my aunt felt less in command than usual, and that, too, had been calculated, and I was learning at an incredible rate. She and the Viscountess were seated and exchanged greetings, and then, Brand came in with me on one arm, Madame on the other. He introduced the latter to my aunt and I translated.

My aunt asked the Viscountess if she held a view this would be a relatively short war.

"When I was a child I was always told that Spandau had enough gold to keep the army in the field for ten months. I think they will continue as long as there is any chance to defeat France, and get ahold of an indemnity large enough to cover expenses, instead of having to pay an indemnity out."

"Do you think they can hold out despite the blockade?" asked my aunt, as I busily translated for Madame.

"I think Bismark's meat and grain tariff stimulated agriculture to the point Germany can feed her own population, although not as they are used to being fed. As long as there are enterprising merchants, foodstuffs can find their way in via Finland, Sweden or Romania, or grain from the Ukraine. And Germany has found a way to make nitrate for fertilizer. Also they have got phosphate from the slag heaps in Lorraine, and benzol from coal tar, which is adequate fuel for a motor car."

My aunt had brought a package with her, to her credit. Madame, who, it was plain to observe, was still pale, frail, thin, and beset by sorrow. Her presence made a far more sobering impression than my aunt's febrile fantasies of her imagination of me running through the house naked. She asked me to present Madame with the package, which I helped her open. Her ambitious travels had temporarily genuinely weakened her more.

"Oh! La, la!" she exclaimed, for my aunt had topped herself by presenting her with a large shawl made of alpaca. She knew very well that the British liked their homes colder than most Frenchmen were accustomed to! Should I slip this around her shoulders? "Yes, please do."

A satisfactory tea time was accomplished, and Aunt Bea rested before dinner. I went back to sleep.

It must have been quite a dinner: the Viscount had decided to impress his son's suitability to my aunt. Yes, he had his own operational trust fund;

he did make some money from his plays; although it was quite true that at one point he had become a wastrel, he was always careful with his money.

Then he touched on the change that had overcome Brand, crediting it to maturity and a long-searched for, but finally found, faith, much of which could be credited to his acquaintance with us. These changes, he added, were all a father could hope for, most definitely featuring his relationship with me. Surely she could understand that.

His wife raised a hand and he paused. "It was my fault, the problems with faith. My fault," she added. "As a result he set about embarrassing me and he succeeded. Sometimes we have been too much alike. Nevertheless, your niece caused me to change my perspective."

Then Aunt Bea uttered her 'yes, buts.' Like a warm knife cutting through butter, his mother asked, "Yet there are no formal entanglements, am I correct?"

"Nnooo," my aunt answered slowly.

"Then all she is bound by is the weight of familial opinion, am I correct?"

Apparently the high point, however, the Viscountess, when part of her husband's account had to do with the theatre, exclaimed, "Imagine having a son who could write a song about the compound interest curve!" And burst out laughing.

My aunt was driven back to the hotel, where she collapsed into an armchair!

Brand's father had a notion. The next day, he vetted it on us. "I'll wager all of you could use some peace and quiet. We could arrange to have our country home turned over to you for a visit. What do you think?"

Actually, my aunt welcomed the idea.

Becky did not. She was sent to stay with Mr. and Mrs. C.

Mme. asked Brand if there would be a place she could attend Mass. Was the house old enough to have a chapel? Yes, it was. There would be no problem to find a priest who could be found to man it while Mme. was there.

Before progressing, Mme. had to shop for clothing, and the Viscountess had a milliner bring clothing in her estimated size to the house. It was amazing how fast things could be worked out. Anna showed me how to pack my own luggage.

I had read a description of Sous Saules in one of Brand's letters, yet the flowing weeping willow trees dancing in a slight breeze, imparting momentary glimpses of parts of the house to the viewer was mysterious; this house was not fronted by an elegant driveway and an open park which disclosed the house to full view.

Brand's grandmother did not like a parade of windows open to the public stare. Motor cars entered a driveway which led up to the side of the house, more circumspect in mien, some windows with closed shutters, the ground floor limned with ivy. With such discreet chiaroscuro, it possessed a reclusive air, retired from the world outside it.

There was in fact the standard front entrance with an unused driveway and unused grand front door, but, Brand's mother had grown irritated at the continual crowd of fox hunting gatherings there, who would gallop off and leave their stablehands hours of clearing manure with shovels and wheelbarrows. On one occasion when her husband had gone grouse hunting in Scotland, she had mature trees gathered and planted. There was raging and cursing, but Brand's father, still a young man, was picking up quite some bills for the house, and he told his father, the then- Viscount, that he would inform any workmen that showed up they would not be paid.

Brand's parents did their entertaining in town and had always said if anyone wanted to open the front out again, they were free to do so after they were gone. With the advent of the death taxes, there were no volunteers. To my surprise, I found the remnant of a four in hand carriage, for Brand's father, when younger, had enjoyed driving it.

There was a brief discussion translated between Brand's mother and Madame; would she prefer a room on the ground floor so she would not have to use the stairs, or one flight up to the first story? Which would be more private? Madame asked Brand. Where would he be staying? For as alert as she had been on the drive, she was now tired and frail again.

Wherever would make her comfortable, was the answer. He was, after all, the only known person in this entirely new situation. The ground floor seemed placed to not make her a bit of a prisoner. She could walk outside whenever she wished. She did not wish to disarrange...but no, it was Brand who now was the oldest male present, assuming the role of the master of the house until he returned it to his mother.

I was deposited on the first story. Despite my noblest instincts, I did feel somewhat I had been supplanted in Brand's attention. On the second afternoon, while she was napping, he walked me outside, sitting us down on a bench.

"I'm not sure how to tell you this, Mandra," he said; terror seized me; it was over, but I did not know why! He put his hand on mine. "'Xiema has the smell of death about her."

"What!" Oh, he had been someplace I had never been. Or had he? The hospitals... Max seemed to know...

"One learns to detect it," he answered. "I think it must be her heart."

"So you brought her here."

"It would have been a very lonely death, Amanda. Mind you, I have no fears for her salvation. None of her children could be with her, so I alone am left. I say it with sorrow, but I am honored to be allowed to repay a debt...do you understand what I mean?"

"Of course. And we will have shared it."

"Indeed we shall." He kissed my hand. "And of course, she desires to become better acquainted with you."

I felt myself worried if she found she did not care for me.

Brand laughed. "That is highly unlikely, my dear, for I did not feel myself whole and sound again in this undertaking until I was here again with you. I assure you she will perceive that."

"Are you hoping..."

"Yes and no," he said with a smile. "But, yes."

He is hoping she will die while she is still here.

Three days after we had arrived at Sous Saules, after 'Xiema had completely rested, the priest arrived on his bicycle. He proposed to say Mass in her room as he understood she was in frail health; I noticed as she sat up in the chair, she wrapped the warm shawl my aunt had gifted to her, and pulled it tight. Brand sat next to her and softly translated although doubtless she followed if from memory.

"Will you come again, Father?" she asked.

"Every day if you wish, Madame." The priest was no fool. He saw how frail she was.

"Would it be convenient to hear my confession tomorrow?" she asked. "It would give me time to consider what I wish to confide."

"*Bien sûr, Madame,* that is all the little French I know!"

"Would you like me to drive you and your bicycle back to the rectory?" Brand asked.

"No, no, my son, I like my exercise."

When he had left, I asked Brand incredulously, "Do you believe in—confession?"

"Surely. Absolutely. The Anglican church practices it as well. He started to laugh. "Ah. My staunch old Dutch Reformed girl!"

"I don't think that's funny!"

"Try."

"Oooo!" I muttered.

"Come, Mandra, don't you think God has a sense of humor?"

"WHAT?"

"He must have to stay with the mess we have made out of His creation!" How can you say that!"

"Don't you lot call that total depravity?"

"Brand! You are a Whitefield! "

"Do you fear that?"

"Not until just this moment!"

"Then don't become too scrupulous. It is because 'Xiema is here. We've always had a spiritual connection. Now apparently you do, too. We'd best talk to 'Xiema."

CHAPTER 33

Aunt Bea was perusing the morning paper when Brand quickly entered, told her we were off to pick up the priest, and disappeared before she had time to collect herself to give an answer.

He insisted I ride with him although he had no need to insist! "It's a hot day to bicycle," Brand said by way of an excuse, although priests rode their bicycles in all sort of weather. We saw his figure as we drove up, standing at the end of the path to his quarters, ready for his treat.

"Good morning," he said. "This is the young lady with us at the Mass yesterday?"

Yes, father, this is Amanda Ten Eycke—my intended, when she comes to have me as her intended!"

"I see. You have my blessing, Miss Ten Eycke!" said the priest with a laugh. (Apparently he'd known Brand for some time). However, also apparently, he had not known him long enough; his bond with 'Xiema surprised him. By the time for the eucharist, it was evident Brand knew exactly what was happening, although he did not partake.

"You have known Madame for some time?" the priest asked Brand, since Madame did not speak English.

"For approximately half my life."

"I see." Apparently he did.

After Mass and confession, Madame had a nap, then lunch on a tray. Later, nonetheless, she was enough refreshed to join us outside on a chaise longue. Brand pulled up a chair next to her and I thought to do so on the other side, but he waved me over so she would not have to turn her head.

"What would you like to know?" she asked me.

What, indeed. "I am curious when Brand quoted me from your Térèse of Liseux about holy boldness, and speaking directly to God?" I asked.

She smiled. "Few of us have such a holy family to progress us so swiftly on our way!" she replied. She then told me the story of Térèse, the little flower.

Brand interjected that I had felt worry when I spit out the name 'Whitefield.'

Madame actually laughed! "Ah, yes, he led me a bit of a struggle for a few years! The theatre and what came with that."

"Oh!" She knew all about that.

"Yes, it was a trial—Brand knows—then one day, I read in my Thérèse, 'One must banish one's own tastes and personal ideas and guide souls along the special way Jesus indicates for them rather than along one's own particular way.' You know St. Paul speaks along the same lines—who is weak but I am weak and so on. It is a path of humility and understanding."

"She actually wants to hear some of my songs!"

"You're kidding!"

"*Mais non*—the fear is behind me."

"And so—where is your piano? Do you have a music room?" Madame opened out her palms expressively.

"You know I have a piano."

"Yes, but where?"

"Yes, we have a music room!" I realized they were joking with one another.

And so our last week began. As if a magic wand had been waved, we had Mass each morning then worked through Brand's *oeuvre* with its music. Madame especially, to my astonishment, liked 'The Rites of Discount': her husband had been a banker. It was as lovely farewell, for as the week progressed, we could both sense and see that Madame was slipping away from us. Two days before Brand's leave was over, she was gone.

It was decided to bury her in the family plot. There was no use trying to remove the body to Paris. Brand sat down and wrote a long letter to Robert, explaining what had happened.

And his leave was not the dud he had worried it might be: we decided to marry during it. No doubt, meeting 'Xiema had settled it for me.

What was it like to stand together with one's beloved, holding each other tightly, as the clock ticked away the minutes toward when he must leave, and we barely able to separate ourselves from each other?

After he had gone, I curled up into a very small ball, a very lonely young woman with time slipping through her fingers.

CHAPTER 34

In August we learned that the Kaiser had lifted his restrictions on bombing London, except for Buckingham Palace and historic edifices. How they were to avoid the latter was fairly dicey. On the night of the 9th, one Zepp attached the mouth of the Humber River, to the north of us. However, getting lost in a mist, the commander lost his bearings.

Also in August, Hugh Trenchard replaced David Henderson as General Officer Commanding of the Royal Flying Corps.

On the 7th of September (these dates remained very clear in my mind) we got definite reports from trawlers in the Channel that two airships were coming. Then we saw the Aeroplane Lights go on. One Zepp began dropping bombs at Cheshunt slightly north of us. I touched the coordinates of the squares for the anti -aircraft guns which covered it on my squared map. Then it got the dock area, at Deptford, and Greenwich, and Woolich. But that raid did not really get to our part of London.

Heinrich Mathy was the most well-known of the German Zepp commanders, and he paid us another visit on September 8, 1915, after a raid the night before, that accomplished nothing as far as we were concerned. He came inland over King's Lynn, and he followed waters of river and canal until at Cambridge, he could see the glow of London.

The route he came in by indicated he was steering by Regent's Park. We heard some explosions coming toward us, at Upper Bedford Place, then Queen's Square. We could hear a lot of yelling below, sirens, and a kind of rumble which turned out to be falling masonry, and lots of constables' whistles. His biggest bomb, weighing in at 660 pounds, had set off fires in the textile warehouses around Bartholemew Close, always a choice target, because the whole thing was flammable. Wood Street, Silver Street, Adle Street and Aldermanbury, within the Close, were all burning .Twenty two fire engines were there, but they were unable to save a lot of soft goods.

It seemed very hard to hold a pencil and follow the trail on the squared map on the other side of terror.

Another bomb went through Hoover's office at London Wall, but it was a dud and fell into the cellar.

More bombs at Guildhall, Liverpool Station, Finsbury Circus and Salisbury House. Then the ship dropped ballast at Edmonton, rose, and headed north toward Hage. The last bomb hit an autobus, and killed twenty passengers, blowing the driver's legs off.

"Jolly well done, Miss T-double-E," Lt. Schaffer said as we left. (This was my nickname, for the joke was that my family name began with 'T,' and had a lot of 'e's' for its size!).

The next morning, Violet and I went to view the devastation. We found that shops thought to be owned by Germans had been trashed; one store had the sign, "We are Russians."

To our amazement, taxis came down the street bearing well-dressed women brandishing lorgnettes, as if they were touring the area. It was the height of aristocratic arrogance. A Royal Navy motor came down the street, and was yelled at and even pelted with various vegetables. Realizing we were still wearing our RNVR uniforms, we beat a hasty retreat.

CHAPTER 35

Another real attack came on the 13th of October. Three Zepps got over London. The theatre district in the Strand and the Waldorf Hotel barely escaped very severe damage, but, in our world, two bombs hit the C.R.B. wooden sheds at Aldwych.

As a result, emphasis was put on developing mobile anti-aircraft guns. A sample of the auto-canon, a seventy-five m.m. canon mounted on an automobile, was brought over from Paris as a model of such an arrangement, and parked at Artillery Ground at Moorehouse Street, where Aunt Bea and I made a trip to see it.

This event mobilized efforts to re-route supplies which would have been delivered for distribution from London. Brand Whitlock, our Ambassador in Belgium, had to be notified. Aunt Bea was anxious to provide replacements if any of our warehouses got hit, and told Mr. Hoover she would like to meet with Edith Wharton in Paris on the matter. Hoover said, "Go ahead, Mrs. Ten Eycke."

My aunt took it upon herself first, to telegraph Edith Wharton in Paris, then, to pay her a visit. The French were gathering up all the influence Wharton could generate, by letting her tour in back of, and sometimes close to, the French front. Having the double of advantage of a wealthy woman and as well-known author, she was a desirable ally.

Aunt Bea made ready to cross the Channel, after visiting Sir Henry to urge him to cover CRB merchant ships en route as much as possible, a ticklish proposition, because the CRB was neutral.

"Henry told me that any interference from a belligerent nation would have serious consequences. He refused my request!" She told us. (By now, Sir Henry was simply 'Henry.')

"Well," said my cousin, who was rapidly gaining knowledge of the situation, "He would have to!"

My aunt was duly impressed by her visit to Paris, and noting all the charitable works Wharton had organized. We could tell when she returned that she felt quite put in the shade, a position which Mrs. Wharton assumed was of prime importance.

Mrs. Wharton had actually been in some trenches, which very few observers had been, handily winning the how close to the Front did you get? Competition. Touring in her own motor car, accompanied by a Mr. Berry, they often picnicked on the way.

"I doubt Mrs. Wharton will ever come back to America," said my aunt. "She is so much fêted in France, and she has been obliged to sell her house at Lenox."

I secretly had the feeling Mrs. W. had been slightly patronizing. My aunt, however, was a different entity than the American women who flocked to Paris and tried to put in an effort or two, then went home to brag about it. Aunt Bea was also from old money; there was nothing nouveau about her.

But then there was always Mrs. Wharton's writing. This was what opened the doors to French intelligentsia; a combination no one could rival.

"What about us, Ma?" asked Becky

"We shall most probably have to return to find you a husband. So many young men are being killed."

To me, my cousin confided, "I think Ma is Sir Henry's Edith Wharton."

CHAPTER 36

Meanwhile, in France, in late September, Brand was engaged in what he later would tell me, was the Battle of Loos. One of his billets was near water, from which he could hear loud frog croaks, which, of course, brought Aristophanes to mind. (This was La Gorgue). *I fly out over smoking slag heaps which hoist their fiery tops like demonic fingers reaching up from the hell below.* (Later he would show me the path of his journey from La Gorgue over La Bassee Canal, to Haisnes, then to the Vermelles-Hulluch Road, to Hulluch, and around the "Tower Bridge" at Loos).

The weather has been closing. It's hard to see as it fogs up one's goggles. Without them the rain cuts into one's eyes like razors. The scene below is shell smoke of white, black, green, and orange, while lethal clouds of gas blow by beneath my wings

Fighting is concentrated around a piece of geography which is quite distinct from the air, in the shape of a kidneys bean. The infantry is dug in, and on my right, the French are having a go at a particular local height. (This was Fosse 8 and the Hohenzollern Redoubt; and the local heights was Vimy Ridge).

There is one palatable estimanet near an old monastery in the neighborhood. At the moment, I am working with a committee developing artillery observation techniques between ourselves and our French allies.

Sir John French had raised some doubts about his abilities in handling the campaigns at Neuve Chappelle and Aubers Ridge. Able associates had produced more shells, and covered over some of the inadequate planning by journaling about a shell scandal. Now, however, he did not have these allies in his corner, and he made a fatal blunder. Situated some 25 miles behind the front lines, he had no phone lines run into his HQ at Philomel. 'A general without a phone line was to all practical purposes impotent,' one scholar wrote. He did not release reserves to Sir Douglas Haig in time. As a result, instead of advancing forward, which had seemed possible, our Tommies were driven back by enfilade fire from Auchy, and lost the Fosse, fought heavily at Bois Hugo, Pit 14 and Hill 70, but gained no ground. This sort of inadmissible planning was beginning to disgrace Sir John.

Brand photographed "Big and Little Willy" trenches over and over as the offensive wound down, hoping to see some signs of progress, but viewing none.

I just received news a theatrical colleague, Harold Chapin, who was in the Medical Corps, was killed bringing in a wounded man. He left a little boy, about four years old, as I recall. That is what saddens me the most.

The next one read, *a barrage is in progress and it rattles the windows in our farmhouse. The R.F.C. has a new Corps commander, 'Boom' Trenchard, and he has assigned all our fighting escorts to protect our reconnaissance machines.*

CHAPTER 37

"For you, Miss T.!" said Lt. Schafer, holding out the receiver. "*Vice-Admiral Sir Henry Porter*— if you please!". It was three o'clock in the morning, but Winston Churchill and Jackie Fisher had set the pattern for The Admiralty That Never Slept.

"I'm sending a motor car 'round, I wish to speak to you!" blasted Sir Henry's foghorn voice.

"Sir, I cannot come unaccompanied!" I answered.

"Then get that Twinsley woman to come with you," he barked.

"Let me ask her," I said, thinking how silly and how bold this was. I put my hand over the receiver and spoke to Violet *sotto voce*. She could come. But as I hung up, I did have an instant's regret.

There was no competition for the tub at 4 a.m. I might miss the chance to use it.

I suspected Sir Henry's order had something to do with America—I was a mere subordinate of my Aunt Bea, and I was growing a bit tired of America as a touchy subject. Americans were by now greeted with hostility, even offense, in Great Britain, even Americans *doing their bit*, like me.

"I have some things to show you." He bent over and brought up a mass of paper out of his brief case. "First, here are copies of your New York City German community newspaper, *Staats Zeitung*, which James Gerard, your Ambassador to Germany, has called a mouthpiece for the Kaiser." He threw a copy on the desk. "Next we have a peace proposal from a group who calls themselves 'Labours' National Peace Council,' but are the creation of a well-known *agent provocateur*, Franz von Rintlen." He put a copy of one of their publications into evidence. "The Austro-

Hungarian Ambassador, Mr. Dumba, was caught red-handed trying to stir up labor unrest at munitions factories in Pennsylvania, in concert with members of your Congress who are seeking to prohibit the export of munitions. Here we have a secret circular offering funds, available in Sweden, Norway, Switzerland or China, for anyone willing to destroy factories, incite labor strikes, and sabotage raw materials." Another paper fell on the desk.

Sir Henry paused. "But this is all practical stuff, "he said. "Then we come to your intellectuals, who shape ideas." He pulled out a copy of the 'New Republic.' "Here's a piece by Ralph Bourne called 'American Use if German Ideals,' which sings the praises of *kulture,* he said. "Now you see what we are up against."

"Where do you place the Dutch? "I asked him.

"If you mean have we vetted your family's sentiments, of course we have. I'm not a fool," Sir Henry snapped.

"We are not suspect," I said, throwing caution to the wind, "Like the Viscountess Stroplea?"

"You don't seriously expect me to respond to that. Our propaganda is headed up by Sir Gilbert Parker, at Somerset House," said Sir Henry. "Between us, we have a few ideas. One of them is to enlist a few citizens of your country residing in England and participating in the war effort into a broader spectrum of what you have seen while residing in England.

"You might like the idea. It is called Operation Dactylist. Neutrals could be recruited to take the place of clerking positions in the RFC to free men up for more active service. You would have a typewriter to use!" (These new instruments were in hot demand). "It's a non-combatant post, and we would set it on different legs than necessary to join up any British service in a formal way, so you would not jeopardize your citizenship. Of course, it would obligate you to some further training first, but the RFC is thinking in terms of utilizing women anyway."

"I see," I said. "How would I receive the further training of which you speak?" I asked him.

"The RFC wants me to hand them trained personnel," he said. "So it would be under Navy auspices. I think Eastchurch for the aviation and for the wireless. Then somewhere in France. Then Parker, if needs be, would extract you, and export you to America to tell of your experiences in the usual channels—newspapers, clubs, YMCA's."

"But—you know my aunt! She wouldn't think that suitable!"

"You are of age, Miss Ten Eycke. You can make your own decisions."

"May I tell the Viscount?"

"You would save us a great deal of time," said Sir Henry. "He would only move heaven and earth to find your whereabouts through his sources."

"I'll talk to my aunt," I said.

CHAPTER 38

I was just beginning to awake at 5 p.m., ready to dress eat my supper for my arrival at St. Paul's. The telephone rang, and I heard Anna answer it. "Miss Amanda!" She knocked on my door. "Some captain for you! for you!" Terrified, I ran to the telephone.

"Yes!" I gasped

I took the receiver from Anna, hand trembling. I could not speak very much.

He told me he had been patrolling, down low, near the Coast, on a quiet day, when a piece of Archie sliced his fuel line. He could see petrol pooling on the floorboards. He shut the engine off, trying to time blipping the engine back on in order to keep up his angle of glide enough so petrol and fumes would not accumulate and catch fire when he cut the engine back on, and keep the engine off as much as possible so he wouldn't catch on fire from something sparking!

"What a Scylla and Charybdis!" he said. He was still somewhat euphoric from having survived and from the hospitality offered him by a regiment after he managed to pancake down into No Man's Land amidst all sorts of shell holes, all filled with water, the land a complete and utter bog that would have sucked the undercarriage right off, and crawled ignominiously to a trench, German artillery fire all the while showering down, and his machine being hit and blown to blazes behind him in the process. But he had been well-fed, well-liquored, and—best of all!—these were a rum bunch of chaps. "They brought me to the coast to use the Navy telephones before I call my C.O.!"

"It's ruddy wonderful to hear your voice!" he bellowed for the connection was not very good from his end. "I hope it hasn't been too rotten for you! If ever I am spared, I will never leave you even for a night! Blast! The Navy wants its telephone line back, dearest!" he replied.

"Oh, it's been lovely talking!" I yelled.

"I will tell father. Goodbye for now!" Then he switched to French (so the men around him could not understand him—for there he was bellowing out a his sentiments of love amidst a crowd of Navy personnel trying to go about their business!) " *Mandra— rappelle-toi toujours que je t'aime et que mon coeur apparetiet a toi.*

Remember that I always love you. Remember my heart belongs to you.

CHAPTER 39

I was on the train to Sittingbourne, en route to the Royal Naval Air Station, Eastchurch, Isle of Sheppey, half in a state of terror, half heroic self-importance, young enough to still think what I was undertaking was of terrific significance. On my wrist was Brand's parents parting gift to me, a wrist watch designed by Cartier for the aviator Santos- Dumont. Beside me sat my Aunt Bea. She had come along to survey where I would be posted with an eye toward its suitability, and I was actually glad she was coming. I was hoping she would not spout a series of encomiums, but no, she wanted to talk about her current experiences.

"I went up north with Anna, to give talks. At first my knees were shaking! But I was surprised that people didn't seem to mind a talk given by a woman. That was pleasant! I gave a talk in Grimsby and I had fish and chips there—they were incredible."

A tall officer in blue uniform stepped up as we descended from the railway car. "Mrs.Ten Eycke, Miss Ten Eycke, Lt. Talbot." Talbot was a brown- haired, brown -eyed man, bluff in stature, florid in complexion, abrupt and efficient in his movements. He had his batman with him to attend to my luggage. We motored across the flat part of Kent, the wind cold and dank, just the sort of thing the British call bracing. I felt shy with a strange man, but Aunt Bea did not, and they chatted away.

At the sentry box, I gazed ahead at the aerodrome, the site of the Royal Aero Club, and the Short Aeroplane Works. The whole thing was set up in a square with the fourth side open to the landing field, which was spacious enough for a mile's taxi in any direction. Set improbably right in the middle of the workshops and hangars was a large Tudor house.

"Whatever is that?" I asked.

"That is Stonefitts, Frank Mc Lean's house," Talbot said. "He left his house, yacht and motor to the Navy for the duration. Also he acts as chief instructor here."

I've arrived at what almost seems to be the private estate of a man named Frank McLean, I wrote Brand.

Ah, yes, the chap who specializes in flying under bridges! He replied.

In fact, Frank Mc Lean had discovered this swathe of land so congenial to flight, and Short Brothers had bought it in 1911, and the flying rights over several hundred acres. Horace Short had designed an aeroplane for McLean as far back ago as 1908. The other Short brothers continued their work with balloons.

Between 1909 and 1914, McLean had owned sixteen different aircraft!

As he helped me down, he added, "Before the war it was quite gay out here you know. Chaps like Dare had hangars here and his sisters Phyllis and Zena came out quite a bit."

Even I had heard of these female stars of the music hall stage. Just then I heard the sound of a returning aero engine, blipping on and off in the manner which had so alarmed me at Hendon. I looked up, hands over my eyes.

"Short Biplane returning from patrol," said Talbot, with masculine superiority.

"The last machine I saw land was a Deperdussin," I said nonchalantly. I watched as the aeroplane taxied towards us, steering and slowing with its tail skid, as mechanics ran out to grab the wings, turning it, positioning it to stop. I sensed Talbot glance ever so slightly sideways at me.

"A Deperdussin *racer,*" I added.

With the engine cut, the propeller stopped revolving. The pilot staggered out, muffled in a helmet, a fur coat, huge gloves, and boots to the thigh. At this time of year a major enemy was frostbite.

"Where has he been?" I asked.

"He's just back from Felixstowe, where he guarded the tail of a flying boat making coastal observation for the Beef Run. That's the supply convoy that runs from England to the Hook of Holland and back again. I expect you find that rather mundane."

"If you'd been living with an aunt who's working with Herbert Hoover, you'd *never* find food mundane!" I exclaimed.

"Who's Hoover?" he asked, his face puzzled.

"Just an American like me," I replied heatedly.

"We'd best check in with the C.O.!" he said, sensing he was in hot water. We passed the hangar where the Short was being dragged in, the pilot gesturing to his mechanics, riggers, and armament crew. He was moving his hands parallel as if to indicate something in the wings was out of true.

"Would you like to see the hangar?" Talbot asked, carefully making peace.

"I'd love to!"

"Look in here. There's a lathe, and here…" he held it up, "is a turnbuckle, which is used to make adjustments, shortening and lengthening the wires. When you've got things where you want, you run the wire through and wind it closed," he said, demonstrating for me. "If you're over water with no air crew, it's best to know as much as possible about repairs. You can always take off again from a seaplane on floats."

We cut across the oil-stained grass to the C.O.'s office. I saluted Commander Forbes, who was seated behind a desk, with a busily ringing telephone.

"I say, I've got to put you on the role of a ship, how about the 'Galatia?'" he asked.

"Is there a Pygmalion?" I asked impulsively.

"God no! Mrs. Pankhurst and her lot would stove it in!" he said with a laugh. "I've got Annie Selfridge-Pym, the wife of one of our pilots, to show you round to quarters."

As we waited outside Forbes' office I pointed to the windsock. "I've forgotten what that is called," I said to Talbot.

"That's the effel- - " he said. "The wind sock."

"How **ripping** to have an American with us!" said a female voice in that animated British tone I often found artificial. Annie Selfridge-Pym was a rounded young woman, with ringlets she affected tossing out of her eyes every few minutes. After she tossed them, she ran the fingers on her right hand through them to hold them back.

Aunt Bea seemed to find her unexceptionable. Was she willing to walk through a light snow to our quarters? She was.

She had Sutton, her husband's batman with her, and he humped my trunk onto his back from the motor car. I set off with Annie, Aunt Bea, and Sutton lurching awkwardly along behind us like the hunchback of Notre Dame. We took a path that led diagonally back from the main compound to a bungalow.

We came to the back of the bungalow. She opened the door to a spare room, with an iron bedstead and a pitcher and washbasin on a whitewashed stand. Its window looked out over a light powder of snow which covered the stubble of hayfields stretching off towards the Channel. The curtains moved ever so slightly when the wind made the little sound which indicated it was changing direction, which I viewed with as much horror as if Genghis Khan sacked the Vatican. I asked Annie where I could Mess, thinking she and her husband would not want their privacy violated.

"Oh, right here!" she said, flinging open the door, making Pym, who was sitting smoking his pipe, stocking feet up on the fender of a stove, jump and drop his copy of 'The Wipers Times.' And so began The Door.

"I say, so you've got her, have you?" He said, standing up. The first thing I noticed was red hair. "Oh—good day, Madame!"

"I was just on point of inviting her to eat meals with us, Pym," she said, glancing at him to recall to him something they had agreed upon.

"Right, jolly fine!" he answered. "More the merrier, all that sort of thing. Ma'am, can we offer you some tea?"

"Thank you, young man, I must be on my way back to London." My aunt did not want me eating in a mess hall with a group of men. "Come Amanda, let us unpack." I didn't even realize she knew how!

I walked my aunt back to the commandant's office, where Lt. Talbot was patiently waiting on the outcome.

"I shall be returning to London," she said. "When is the next train?" It was conveniently scheduled so she reached out her arms and hugged me (and I hugged her). I walked to the auto with her, and waved as she drove away, with a wave of loneliness overcoming me, until I heard a noise behind me. It was Annie.

"Have you a beau?" she demanded.

"Yes," I said noncommittally.

"How splendid! But jolly rotten luck too, with all these dashing chaps about!" she said. "I'll wager he is in the Army." Her tone regulated these chaps to contemptibles not lucky enough to rule the skies.

"No, he's in the R.F.C.," I said.

"He flies then!"

"Yes, since 1912, "I said.

"Oh, a real *Methuselah!*" she said, brushing her ringlets back with her fingers. "I say, they have a list of **old** brevets about here somewhere, we can go down and look!"

"I don't like to look at casualty lists," I said (knowing that I would find an asterisk that meant deceased by names like Charles Rolls and Cecil Grace, courtesy some reading I had done in old flying magazines Brand had left for us).

"Oh, you are superstitious!" said Annie. "Oh, I am too. I always give Pym tea from the very same pot before he takes off."

I held out my hand to Pym. He took it. "Stunner of a wrist watch!" he said.

"Oh, did he give it to you? Annie asked, and added, "She's got a beau, Pym!"

"Now you've spoilt Annie's fun. She thought all the chaps would be over here flirting with you!" said Pym. Just then Sutton came lurching in with my impedimenta, and Pym, since the door was open, spied my violin.

"I say, do you play that? Why that's even better than Annie thought!" he exclaimed.

"We must have some songs about cowboys!" Annie breathed enthusiastically.

I went into my room. There was a key in the door. Should I lock it? Would this be considered an unfriendly act? Should I leave it open, and risk being burst in upon by both of them, or one (and I feared this more of Pym, of course, than Annie) of them when I wanted to be alone, or even more, was dressing or some other intimate act? They would knock, though—wouldn't they? I locked it when I dressed for dinner.

By evening I found a rumor had swept around the aerodrome that the American girl played the violin, and a number of officers forsook the Mess with its perpetual gramophone and came over to hear the latest novelty. After I played "Jesse James" for them they absolutely would not let me go but clamored for more and more, an entirely new reception for me. I played so long that my fingers were numb, and when I tried to fall asleep, I was prevented by the kind of euphoria musicians call 'walking on the ceiling.'

Christmas Eve was three days away. My aunt sent down a huge hamper from Fortnum and Mason, (ordered by telephone from Cleethorpes), and Annie's eyes lit up. She and Pym had been thinking how to entertain on what I gathered were straightened circumstances. I told Annie she was free to use it all. She asked a number of people to toddle round. I made a mental note to order more provisions, as I was sure they'd be offended by offering to pitch in with money. That night, I shut the door, and after all was quiet, I locked it as quietly as humanly possible.

Next day my instruction started. Talbot let me stand on a ladder looking into his biplane cockpit. "One of your biggest problems over water is compass deviation," he told me. "Your compass will only tell you what direction your nose is pointed in, not the direction you are actually headed in by taking into account the force of the wind."

"So—you don't know where you are? "I asked, astonished.

"Oh, we have some nice charts," he said. "They help you factor in your speed over ground versus your speed in the air, and the force of the wind, not to mention how much your own instruments may be off true North.

It's a jolly science, Miss Ten Eyck, especially as you must be precise, as the chaps at Felixstowe are when they search the Spider's Web."

Talbot sketched me a little diagram of a pattern over the Channel, with its center at North Hinder Light Vessel. "Here you see, the Web is cut into eight sectors, each one divided into three sections, at ten, twenty, and thirty miles."

I was beginning to see how much hinged on navigation, even if I did not understand much of what he had just told me. "Why do you fly around the Web?" I asked him.

"Because it covers the most likely paths for Hun submarines."

"Have you ever gotten lost?"

"Jove, I should say, small America!" Talbot had already coined this nickname for me, taken from one of the Glenn Curtiss's flying boats produced in New York state, and being built at Felixstowe by Commander Porte. "Last summer I had taken off in a seaplane from near the mouth of the Medway. My engine cut out. The compass had gone crazy. Engine vibration, I expect. It was now nasty weather, stage three or four, the waves were knocking me about and making the plane ride heavier and heavier. I was thinking I was for it when a trawler hove into view. I thanked my lucky stars and pointed to the cockades and the skipper took me up."

"Are you coming around to Annie's for Christmas?" I asked him.

"Annie has asked me. It all sounds frightfully jolly. "

I liked Talbot; he treated me like a Regular Person instead of a strange being from another planet no one knew quite what to do with—not that I blamed them.

"Tell me small America, is it true what Annie says, that you have a fellow?"

"Yes," I said, blushing. "It is."

"Has he got a name?"

"If I tell you would you keep it to yourself?"

"I'll keep your secret," he said.

"His name is Brandon Whitefield."

"Not the theatre chap?"

"Now you see why I want you to not tell it all around."

"Yes, by Jove!"

On Christmas day I dressed very neatly, and put on Brand's bracelet. Then I unlocked the door.

Annie had warmed up the preserved goose, and made the side dishes. It was all good, (although the goose was somewhat greasy), and if it wasn't, the wine and the company would have made it good. Pym rose at the head of the table and raised his glass.

"Gentleman—and ladies! To the defeat of Admiral Scheer!" A roar of approval went up. "Our objectives!" he continued. "Reconnoiter! Defend naval air stations! Hunt submarines! Fight enemy aircraft!" Admiral Jellicoe's litany having been recited, there was another roar of approval and a draining off of glasses.

This rather savage tone put me off a bit. I swallowed dinner dutifully, my good cheer returning. After dinner, there were carols and other music. As night came on, I excused myself.

"I have to write a letter," I said.

"Oh, journeys end in lover's meetings," said Pym. drolly, rolling his eyes, getting his laugh.

As I sat at the desk I heard a knock. I knew it had to be Annie; no one else would be so impertinent or indelicate. "Come in," I said. She stood behind me, and picked up an envelope which said 'I certify on my honour that the contents of this envelope refer to nothing but private and family matters,' which denoted it came from an officer, free of ministrations of the censor.

I stuffed my letter into an envelope addressed to 'No. 32 Squadron, R.F.C., BEF, France.'

"So he is real!" she said.

"Of course!"

"Don't get your wind up. Pym and I were just beginning to wonder," she said. Swift as a bird, she was off back to the party, quietly shutting my door. I locked it.

I picked up my pen. 'It being Christmas,' I wrote, "let me tell you why I object to your using sweetnesses, as you put it, towards me, like dearest darling girl. It's not that I'm a prig as you might think. I am simply **jealous.** I don't want you using the same terms to me you may have used with other girls—like the song 'I wonder who is kissing her now, and who will be kissing her next year, etc.'"

The admission cost me a bit of pride. But I was pretty sure he'd think it was a good present.

The next morning Talbot began telling me about the two stations that would pick up bearings on signals given off by U boats. Now I was on a bit more familiar turf, even though we were talking submarines instead of Zeppelins.

"They call us and we get a fix on it," he said. "If we're close enough, we have a go. But it's deuced hard to get a bomb off, frankly, before Jerry sees us, and switches over his engines, mans his hydroplanes and disappears."

Then he said to me like a bolt from the blue, "Small America, is your chap's father one of the pashas bruited about to be on Derby's air committee?"

"I don't really know. I know he does some kind of work negotiating for air manufacture. Why would you be concerned?"

"Because Parliament is gearing up to set in place some kind of Committee to co-ordinate air design and supply of material for the R.F.C and R.N.A.S. Some people think it is the first step in trying to merge the two services. A lot of chaps would be very upset by that."

"Good Heavens!" I said.

I kept my nose close to my paperwork all day. I was learning how to fill out a form to send an engine to the Short Works at Rochester for repair). The engine form required several trips to the shop, where Pym pointed out the ever-fascinating rotary engine, with its cylinders revolving around the crankcase. He informed me it needed cleaning every so many hours, and that it created so much torque pilots often had to fly with a foot continually on the opposite rudder pedal. He could see that was enough for one day. Women and engines, he seemed to be thinking, as he shook his head. I was thinking, after breathing in the fumes of castor oil, I ought to head for the loo.

It was tea time when I reached our common room. Now The Door had taken on another characteristic. I found myself listening hard to hear what Pym and Annie might be saying or doing, so I would not interrupt anything and also from curiosity as to what married couples did. There was silence so I opened the door.

"Be an angel friend and come talk to me!" Annie called, uncharacteristically lying in bed.

"What is it?"

"The most ghastly thing has happened. I'm afraid I'm in a family way."

"What?"

"Preggers! Going to have a baby!" she snapped impatiently.

"How do you know?"

"I didn't get the curse!" Now I comprehended the knickers thrown into a corner with forceful disgust when they failed to evidence the stain that would have saved her from her fate.

"But why is it ghastly?"

"Wives are all right if one's husband is on service in England. But not babies!" she said.

I was out of my depth and woefully uncomfortable. In my childhood world if one was summoned to mother's bedroom, there was only one person in it and all was chastely in order. Here the signs of cohabitation were slung about. Pym's and Annie's clothes were flung over the back of a chair mixed in together.

"I shall have to go home!" she wailed.

I clutched Brand's letter inside my jacket pocket for inspiration.

My own beloved. I shall immediately strike dearest and darling from my vocabulary. The latter, as it is commonplace in the theatre, the former because on the few occasions I had to take to paper with my late folly, I saluted her as 'dearest Viper.'

Thank you for that lovely gift, your letter. And for all the other goodies to eat, drink, and smoke. You will be happy to know I have never asked anyone to marry me, I hope.

You fill me with an increasingly supernatural contentment interspersed with great surges of unholy desire (i.e., lust). Perverse man that I am, I wring a decanted sweetness out of remaining true to you in these difficult times, when one lives flight to flight. In other times with no outward difficulties at all, I was a demi-libertine and had no sweetness at all fill me. Mother's legacy of blood and iron left me afraid to be tender-hearted and contaminated my wine with a lot of hardened dross. I feel softer now, marinated, if you will, in your love. I see the world even with more warmth and feel myself more vulnerable, not a bad sensibility for a temporary warrior.

Just then Sutton rapped at the door. "There is a telephone call for you at Commander Forbes' office, Miss," he said. He jumped forward as I turned ashen white. "As I understand it is from a Viscount Stropelea."

"Oh, my God!" I jumped up and ran faster than Sutton all the way to the office, my heart in my mouth.

I grabbed the receiver. Brand's father hoped he had not startled me. But he could hear that he had! He and his wife wanted to wish me Merry Christmas, and happy Boxing Day.

I asked Forbes if I could take the call somewhere else. He got up walked out and closed the door.

"Some of the chaps here seem upset about a committee Lord Derby is getting up, "I said. "Are you going to be on it?"

I could hear the Viscount's rare delightful laugh. "So they're on to that are they?" he said. "Well, I have Eastchurch on my list to visit within the next few days. You must buck up, my girl, for I shall see you, and I hope I can relieve some of the service jitters."

Annie was up and serving tea when I returned. Obviously she had told Pym about my hasty departure. They both looked awkward, not knowing if I had received bad news, and if I had how to relate to it. They looked scared, too. They could be seeing a picture of their own future.

"It's O.K!" I exclaimed. "It was just a Christmas greeting!".

"Oh!" said Annie emotionally, suddenly losing hold of the tea pot and dropping it. It shattered.

"Now see what you have gone and made me do!" she exclaimed.

I drew back.

"Come on old girl it's only a tea pot, how can it be small America's fault?" said Pym, then saw her eyes fill with tears. "Oh come on old girl," he said putting his arm around her and leading her into the bedroom. "She's off her feed today," he said. "Don't mind, America."

He evidently did not know the superstition Annie attached to her beloved pot. I peered in the door, wanting to say a word of apology or comfort, but he was bending over her in a manner too intimate to be invaded. What could I do? I had little knowledge of domestic matters; I searched until I found a rag, sopped up the tea, and collected the tea grounds onto the rag, then picked up the broken pieces of the pot. Later I had to ask Pym where to throw it all. I saved a piece of the pot for Annie, went into my room and closed the door.

Next day, Annie said darkly I should not mess about her kitchen. I said I would not.

That day, Talbot continued his cockpit lecture, showing me the Pitot tube on the wings, and then discoursing on the virtues of the air speed indicator (which had been developed here at Eastchurch) in preventing air stalls.

Behind us we heard an approaching air engine and involuntarily swung around to watch the machine land. Instead of lighting on its wheels and rolling smartly along, however, it seemed to hit, bounce, and plow in the field. "You stay here," shouted Talbot and started to run. Someone was turning over the ambulance engine. I stood rooted to the spot. I suddenly had no desire at all to see some human being all smashed up, crying out in agony. Later Pym told me the pilot had broken up his undercarriage on impact, and broken his right leg, and his heel bone, which was jammed backward by the rudder bar.

CHAPTER 40

Later when I sat down on my bed I was trembling with after shock and entertaining the second unkind sentiments I had ever had toward the Viscount. Couldn't he just have written me a letter?

When we were abruptly assembled after lunch two days later, my instinct told me this might be it, even as Talbot muttered, "Couldn't they leave off square bashing?"

We lined up and stood at attention.

I turned my head ever so slightly toward the sentry box. A motor car was picking up speed after making a stop. Sure enough, the winter light gleamed off the silver hood of the Silver Ghost.

The motor pulled up in front of us and stopped. The chauffeur got out stiffly and opened the back door. Brand's father stepped out, alone, without any entourage, immaculately dressed as ever. He wore an overcoat, a very elegant derby, and gloves. He carried an elegant walking stick. Forbes saluted him. He shook hands with our C.O. He appeared very calm. Only a faint telltale motion of his jaw would have told someone who knew him well he was finishing off one of his remedial ginger candies.

Forbes led him down the line to inspect us. The Viscount held his walking stick with its silver handle in his right hand, swinging it jauntily as he stepped.

When he saw me, he touched his hat to me without breaking stride.

I flushed. I knew all eyes were on me, even though everyone's face pointed straight ahead.

Forbes and the Viscount stopped at the end of the first row, deep in conversation. After some minutes Forbes asked all the pilots not on ready status to wait over at the Mess at Stonefitts.

"Miss Ten Eyck." I came to attention. "You will wait in my office while we inspect the premises."

"Very good sir," I said and saluted. I sat quietly in the commander's office, and no one said anything to me. At last through the window I saw them coming and jumped up. As they came in the door, Forbes said (with a slight frown), "his lordship wishes you to come across to Stonefitts with us." (I had never entered the officers' mess). Brand's father offered me his arm, which was definitely against protocol but Forbes was too ill-at-ease to reprimand it. I felt much like a baby bird sheltered beneath its mother's wing.

The pilots were lounging about, legs thrown over the sides of the armchairs, papers and tea cups everywhere. Someone rang the ship's gong. Forbes looked apoplectic. "Clear the decks!" he bellowed. Officers suddenly scurried around doing the work of navvies.

I slipped my hand out of Brand's father's elbow. His chauffeur took his hat, stick, gloves and coat.

"Please tell your men to go as they were at ease," said the Viscount. With a sigh of relief, some sat down, some lounged against the bar.

"Gentlemen." He stood, placing one hand on the back of the chair in front of him, and folding the other into his trousers pocket casually. "Rodger, Viscount Stroplea.

"I am involved in an effort by the Under Secretary of War to form a Standing Joint Naval and Military Committee chaired by Lord Derby. This is by virtue of the fact that since the outset of the war, I have been facilitating air manufacture problems between ourselves and the French. I am a sort of an understudy to Lord Montagu, who, as many of you know, has a long-standing interest in aviation. In fact, my son reminded me it was Montagu who sent out a flotilla to search for Bob Loraine when he went missing around the Needles at the Bournemouth meet in 1910. In preparation for this appointment I have tried to familiarize myself with the R.F.C manufacture facilities and aerodromes in England, and visited their aircraft depots in France. Now Montagu has urged me to acquire the same familiarity with the R.N.A.S., so as to have a better notion of the issues that this committee will be resolving. I am here to listen to what you have to say."

He turned to Forbes. "Commander, as this is an informal visit, could we open the bar?"

"Hear hear!" sounded from the back of the room. There was a flurry as drinks were handed around.

When everyone was settled again, he said, "I started my research yesterday at the Short Works. No one had told me about Horace Short." (Short had an enlarged hydrocephaloid head).

Forbes smiled thinly. "It was meningitis, milord," he said. "In his younger days in South America some cannibals captured him but were afraid to eat him."

"I should think he would make very tough digesting!" said the Viscount. Someone laughed. I could see his intention was to put them as much at ease as possible to encourage frankness, even indiscretion.

"Someone told me a charming story about a young woman he had just fired who saw him bending over to pick up his hat and kicked him in the backside," said the Viscount. "The amazing thing is he promptly hired her back again. I was told he admired her spirit!

"I had a most interesting conversation with him about an airship arrangement Churchill has christened 'the blimp,' and I had my first look at a sea plane. I solicited his opinion on whether seaplanes are as effective as needs be, given they are fairly useless when the sea is at state three or four, which is, let me see," he took out his spectacles and consulted some notes in his pocket, "50% of the time, roughly."

"Why is the R.F.C. allowed to suck off all our fast scouts?" someone yelled, anonymously, from the back of the room.

"And we don't want their offal, their Bristols and Farmans, in return for them!" Someone else yelled out.

"We don't want to fly Factory machines anyhow; they give the blueprints to piano manufacturers! "

Someone else added. 'Devil take what they say about Inspection Codes!"

"Milord—isn't this just a preliminary to merging the two air services?" This query brought a bunch of boos and negative exclamations.

The Viscount folded his specs and held them in one hand. "Let us separate out policy from manufacture, gentlemen," he said. "What would you do, for example, to supply the Army with its increasing size and needs for reconnaissance and scouting?"

"Answer the question about a merger!" came from the back of the room.

"The committee has not even begun to meet yet, gentleman. And the problems to be solved are complex and intertwined. For example, your Rumney Samson had fast scouts built so he could take off from ships in them, but I understand that is only half the problem, as they often have to be ditched upon return to ship. In the meantime, in France, we are being taxed in Parliament by a member of your service with allowing pilots to be murdered, not killed."

At this mention of Noel Pemberton- Billing, R.N.A.S., M.P., the room fell silent, as the men uncomfortably followed the Viscount's logic.

"As to scouts on shipboard, perhaps under the influence of H.G. Wells, I find the idea quite taking. In fact the other night I raided my son's library for Clement Ader, and read his description of a *porte avion*, a ship that carries airplanes. With typical precise French love for language he terms landing on ground one thing, an *atterrissage,* and landing on a ship, an *abordage.* He speaks of front wheels that will have to jam when they hit the deck. Short explained to me how you can build aircraft so as to fold the wings and store them in a hold."

"Milord," Forbes said. "Whisky?"

"Sherry if you have some," said the Viscount. I knew he'd take a sip and put it down. He needed every bit of his wits.

"Will I need a taster for this?" Brand's father asked.

"Milord, this is not Renaissance Italy!" said Forbes.

Talbot stood up suddenly. "Milord," he said, "we and the Dover barrage have not had the success of the patrols over the Spider's Web, where they can deduce where U-boats may be from the fact their top speed is sixteen knots and their underwater range sixty to eighty miles. The question is: will machines be made available to us to improve our ability? General Haig, as we hear it, has called funding for any other sort of aeroplane than he needs at the Front a luxury."

"If I may offer my observation, Lieutenant," said the Viscount. "I am a banker in the City and thus I can tell you the Committee on Food Supply has chosen to continue to import a great deal of what we eat, instead of undertaking the regulation of domestic agriculture, so as not to upset the forces of free trade in our market place. That is your trump card. Just consider what a rebellion there would be if the public could not get its sweets! Think of supply as our Front; one which the Generals are not contemplating I can assure you. But if submarines continue to sink ships, every weapon to combat them must be called into play."

"Hmmph," said Talbot, sitting back down to chew upon this answer.

"Now as to low horsepower and stability," said the Viscount. "It takes time to train a man to fly a ropey machine like a Morane or a Sopwith. Most R.F.C. recruits won't get it. Actuary reports now put an air officer's lifespan at three weeks. Stability buys us out of some write-offs at the hand of inexperience, in trade-off to its drawbacks. As far as low horsepower, the idea of the aeroplane as a platform in the sky is far more Henderson's than Trenchard's, and you will see changes which reflect Haig's thinking. In your service, with the use of airships, there is no real need for low horsepower."

"Henderson treats bombs and torpedoes like 'A Modest Proposal!" Forbes said.

"Yes, he does," said the Viscount. "One of the things I wanted to touch on this afternoon is your experience using bombsights. The issue of developing a good one is becoming an urgent matter."

He reached across to place his spectacles back in his pocket. Only I was at an angle so I could see he had slightly bent one of the earpieces from the pressure with which his hand had held them.

"What do you think of Billing's charges, Milord?"

"I personally always start with an assessment of the man before I assess his point of view. He is a Navy man; he is himself an air contractor; and he built the so called- Seven Day Bus which wouldn't fly. He is notably impulsive. He turned his business affairs over to a man he met in a boxing ring in Paris. He named his very modest company Supermarine. And last and most disturbing he carries with him a black notebook in which he claims he has proof all the leading Germans are sodomites, and lists of perverts here in England."

"Wasn't there some uproar on that head over there a while back?"

"Indeed, there was. Much of this suggests he would like to deep-six the manufacture system of the R.F.C. for personal reasons."

"He did pull off the Freidrichshaven raid," someone said defensively.

"He planned it. But I've heard you Eastchurch chaps pulled it off— isn't that so?"

Forbes handed him another sherry. Soon they were all gathered around a table, working on a formula for a bombsight, just like an industrious class at school. A delayed action fuse on a bomb would go off two seconds after it hit the water and it would explode to a depth of 50 to 80 feet... Brand's father put on his spectacles. A submarine could dive 45 feet in ninety seconds and could be destroyed by a direct hit from a bomb of only sixteen pounds . . . and so on. Pym poured me a sherry.

Talbot stood up and attempted to explain the downward trajectory of a bomb as it left a machine traveling in the same direction which the bomb would drop. It would pick up speed from the pull of gravity, and finally hit water just after the pilot passed vertically over the target. How soon one had to release the bomb from what height, got a thorough computation that afternoon.

I could see the Viscount was not just skilled in accountancy but had a firm grasp of higher math and he seemed to be enjoying this opportunity to use it.

At last, from my point of view, Brand's father pushed back his chair. He took off his specs and put away his pen, and his chauffeur brought his coat.

"Well, gentlemen, tomorrow I shall visit Marine Experimental A.D. at Grain. They are working on Lord Rayleigh's riddle that on air drag tests; the sum of the parts is greater than the whole."

"Has he tried it on a monoplane, Milord?" asked Talbot.

"Why?"

"Just a hunch. Perhaps the interplay of air between the winds of a biplane."

"An interesting thesis, young man!"

Now the interview was over. He headed towards his motorcar, accompanied by Forbes and myself.

The chauffeur opened the trunk. Inside was a case of champagne. "This is for New Year's," said the Viscount. "I expect you can arrange for it to be transported? I'd let it rest a few days."

I spotted and coveted a thick fur car rug.

Yes, sir!" said Forbes, setting off at the run.

As the Viscount and I stood facing each other he cleared his throat. I realized something portentous was in the wind.

He pulled a little box out of his pocket, gave it to me, and said, "Open it." It was a sapphire and diamond ring.

"This was my mother's," he said. "She left it for my eldest son, and Brand has asked me to give it to you."

I stood stock still in shock until finally he helped me slide it on. To both our surprises, it actually fit.

"As you can imagine," said the Viscount, clearing his throat again, "The playwright has given me some lines to say." He pulled out a rumpled telegram. "Tell Amanda she is quite free to choose another if this does not suit. Stop. In the meantime, I should like her to have this. Stop."

He handed me the telegram.

"I must say, I never imagined performing such a service for one of my sons!" said the Viscount, breaking into a smile now that he had performed his duty.

There were voices behind us. It was a couple of N.C.O.'s come for the spoils.

"I shall wire Brand tonight," said his father.

As he prepared to get into the motor, he said, "I loved my mother very much, and I am sure Brand will be glad you have his ring on your finger in amongst all these dashing chaps. Can I do anything else for you, Amanda?"

"Could you lend me your car robe? My room is dreadfully cold." Of course he could!

In no time the chauffeur had carried it over to my room.

I kept waving until he was out of sight. Talbot came up behind me and caught the flash of cut stones. "Ah, what have we here, small America—the rock of Gibraltar?" he asked.

"Not quite!" I said. It certainly would not escape notice! But I was too excited to care.

Back at the bungalow, Annie crowed, "Best of news, Amanda, I'm not in a family way after all and there shall be a party at Stonefitts for New Year's Eve!"

Annie spotted the ring. "Oh, my golly!" she exclaimed.

A bit later, she added, "I've told them you will come at midnight to play 'Auld Lang Syne,'" said Annie. "You wouldn't want the chaps to go without that!"

Someone tapped me on the shoulder. It was Sutton. He had orders for me to begin my class in Morse.

CHAPTER 41

Days went by in which my mind was sharp in the morning, terribly foggy by quitting time. I was learning how to use Morse code. Our speeds were incredibly slow even though we had memorized our Morse. My first problem was to figure out how long a dot or dash was: a dash was three times as long as a dot. Between letters was a space equal to three dots. Words were separated by seven dots from each other.

I was told I was heavy handed, and a reply to the effect that I played the violin sprang to mind, yet I restrained it from coming out of my mouth.

Our training had started once there were sufficient learners to warrant a full class, and I was the only woman in it. The atmosphere was unpleasant, as the men were of the old mentality women should leave this sort of thing to the men. Our instructor was full of himself and of the same mind as my fellow classmates. The atmosphere was hostile enough that I was so nervous, it made learning a herculean effort. Every time the instructor corrected me, I was the cynosure of all eyes.

At last, I was so very glad to walk back to the bungalow, my head clearing a bit in the cold winter air. When I saw Pym and Annie's now-familiar faces they might as well have been angels. To sit in front of the fire and feel the warmth slowly penetrating my body as I slowly relaxed was all that restored me to the resolve to try yet another day tomorrow. Pym seemed to pick up a bit on my dilemma enough to ask. "How was the ogre today?" Sometimes this jocular query almost made me cry.

I gathered my lieutenant had a reputation for being a stickler, but this was mild as heretofore all his students had been men. What could I possibly do? None of the men wanted to be the one who broke ranks to have even a little conversation. At last, I tried a female defense; I wore my engagement ring. Indeed, it received some curiosity, nonetheless, that was all.

Our instructor knew he had a captive audience, and from time to time, would pontificate on his favorite subject, himself. I cringed whenever he opened his mouth.

Today was New Year's Eve, with music. Cocktail hour—or hours— ran from *cinq á sept,* in the grand old Parisian fashion. In order not to miss anything, I brought my violin to class with me. I should have known it would draw fire. I was so used to having it with me, it almost felt like a third arm. Placing my burden under my chair, I sat up, ready to begin.

The lieutenant saw it as I tucked it under the chair. "Oho, Miss Ten Eycke, what do we have here? Music to sooth the savage beasts?"

"We've been invited to officers' mess tonight at Stonefitts, and I plan to meet my bungalow mates there."

"You can't leave that under your chair." He reached underneath me, and I heard the case banging against the chair legs. I had an immense jolt, and anger, and I stood up. "You are going to damage it," I said.

"Aren't we touchy today?" He asked, holding it level, one hand under the neck, one under the body. I looked full in his face, where I could see scorn writ large. I had been pushed so much, that any fear circulating in my brain had been replaced by adrenaline.

"Give that to me," I said. I took a step toward him. Taking a small step backward, he calculated what I was going to do, and so did I. I took another step closer, and said in a loud voice," Give that to me!" My hand flew to the handle of my case. My left hand and arm were strong from fingering the violin strings. I grabbed it, and yanked it away; he tried to grasp at it, but I was too strong.

"That could get you a court martial," he said.

"No it couldn't. I'm a civilian and I'm an American."

"Dear me! Let us have a look at this instrument. Maybe it is a Stradivarius?"

"If it was, I would not expose it to these awful weather conditions! But it's a damn good instrument! It belonged to my uncle!" I glared at him. "Knock it off!"

"And if I don't?"

"I will ring Sir Henry Porter at the Admiralty, who sponsored me to come here." This appeared to give him pause for thought. I didn't feel an ounce of guilt. Maybe the girl was growing up.

At the Mess, the airmen were gathered around for an *aperitif.* "Here," said Pym, handing me a small glass of *pastis.* They had really gone all out to imitate the French for the evening!

To my surprise, when we sat for dinner, my wireless instructor appeared. It was a jolt. "Don't fret—he's not a terribly proper chap— that's why he came late."

After dinner, I placed my violin case on my chair to repair to the lady's hastily improvised powder room. When I returned, I found Pym still seated at his place at the table next to me. "Are you still eating?" I inquired.

"No, I am on guard. Several people have lost this and that, which creates the supposition the man may be a thief. Don't worry. That chap would not even make it to the door with your violin."

I saw Talbot move over toward the ogre, and deliver a few words that were not amenable.

As I walked to class the next morning, I wondered how the night before would play out.

"Well, Miss Ten Eycke, how are we progressing?"

"Somewhat better, Sir." Knowledge that members of the Mess were behind me raised my confidence; in fact, I discovered that I was well-known due to my music. I had no idea.

I was beginning to get the hang of space between a dot and a dash, and words separated by seven dots. Once this began to happen, my musicality came to my aid, and musicality began to come to my rescue, giving me a rhythm that was called my signature.

"Send a message to me, Miss Ten Eycke." I prepared to be skewered and said a little prayer asking Jesus to come to my aid. Behind me the door opened and the lieutenant stood up and swiftly marched to what he must have considered an interloper. My curiosity was at a low ebb and I did not turn around until I heard an arrogant voice ask, "Have you never learned to salute, lieutenant?" It was Brand on his high horse.

Judging by the military code upon his shoulders, he had been promoted to major. He was clad in his British Warm overcoat, with my scarf around his neck. He had preceded a letter telling me he was coming.

The lieutenant was clearly flustered and rendered a salute, which was returned. I was in shock.

"I have come to bring Miss Ten Eycke to London for a few days."

Brand handed him an envelope which contained a letter to that effect, signed by Sir Henry. He walked over to me and with an oleaginous smile, asked, "Need a bit of a lift, old girl? Take my arm."

Now the lieutenant quickly deciding to curry a bit of favor, remarked, "Quite a lovely scarf, Major!"

"Miss Ten Eycke is adept at many things."

He helped me up from my chair. I was speechless and my legs were shaking. "Come along, we must gather up what you shall need," he said, and picked out my overcoat on a bracket on the door, which was not so extraordinary as it was the only female overcoat hanging there. He opened the door so I could come through; closing it, he placed his arm so that I realized he wished me to take it. I took it with one hand, and my violin with the other.

As we walked, me with bare hands because my gloves were in my coat pocket, he gazed at the ring on my hand and remarked, "I see father has been here!"

"Indeed he was."

"I trust he accounted himself well."

"Oh, yes. He is so gracious it is hard to take umbrage."

"He is always a gentleman."

"Shall we see the C.O.?"

"Not unless you wish to. Someone from the Arch rang him."

"Then all we need is to go to my room. I don't need much—I still have oodles at the hotel." We bifurcated the aerodrome and arrived at my room.

Entering by the side door, I began to open drawers and ransack the small closet. Annie was still present and the ruckus brought her into my room, where she was stopped by the sight of Brand.

"Oh, Annie, this is my fiancé, Brandon Whitefield." I was going to have to get used to people's reactions to him!

"Charmed," he said.

I could not say the same for Annie; charm was the least of her reactions.

She may have suspected we were eloping to Gretna Green.

"We are off to London. The Major is on leave."

"Can I help?"

It was a Mexican standoff; she wanted to hover around, he wanted her to leave. I had an inspiration.

"Yes, could you make us some sandwiches from the leftovers?"

"Oh! Of course!"

Once outside the door, we were happy to finally be in the seclusion of his motor—of course, with the top up—he had providently brought a car robe; five miles down the road he pulled over and grabbed me, and I exhibited such bad manners for a maiden I grabbed him, too. We kissed, then I broke out sobbing with emotion, and I remarked a few tears on his cheeks too. I wrapped the robe around both of us, and, slightly shivering, we held each other until we were warm.

"I passed by here last night, and I almost jumped off the train!"

I held him tighter.

CHAPTER 42

There were revelations we wished to make one to the other. He pulled into a space before the Albany building. "Come on, old girl, let's have a go at my suitcase." Officers were not supposed to carry anything, but this was a short walk. With this in one hand, and my hand on his other arm, we climbed the short entry staircase. His flat was on the second floor. Here I was at this mysterious male preserve. He fished the key out of his pocket, pushing the door open with the side of his suitcase.

The floor was the resting place of a bevy of cushy carpets, to keep the noise down. Indeed the entire flat was decorated with quiet in mind; heavy curtains, walls covered with tapestries. "What do you think?"

"It's rather like being inside a large closet," I said.

I could see that my answer delighted him, and he replied, "Yes, isn't it?

The English were not ones to show you over their dwellings, but he said, "Come along, there's the bedroom." The bedroom was relatively bare, with nothing to draws one's attention. With a grunt, he fell on his back on the bed. "I never thought I would appreciate a bed so much."

I sat down on the edge of the bed.

"Come on Mandra, come down here with me." I flopped down on my stomach so I could look at him. "We don't make a bad fit. Tell me, has anyone ever told you anything at all about the sexual side of marriage?"

"No, they haven't and I am still afraid I'll be a failure at it."

"Nonsense! Of course, you won't! I will not allow it!"

"That's kind of you."

"No lie back and think of England! We shall get a biology book and study it together."

"Whoever said that?"

"Supposedly Queen Victoria."

I was too bashful to say so, but I really did think it might be a good idea. He looked at his wrist watch. "We should get over to Fortnum's before they close."

"I just have one thing to ask."

"Ask away."

"I'd like to buy some chocolate for Violet and for Max. (For Max had been summoned before he had finished his specialist's training due to a shortage of doctors).

We crossed Piccadilly, and strolled up to the front door or Fortnum and Mason. The ground floor was rife with chocolates—the good old wartime favorite. Queen Victoria sent chocolates to the soldiers in Boer War. I bought a number of items. We moved to the purchase desk, and Brand drew out his checkbook.

"I'm sorry, sir, we do not accept checks from soldiers."

What?"

"Alas, management feels it is too chancy collecting on them."

Brand flushed. "That more or less counts us as dead meat!"

"I am afraid so, sir. I did not set the policy."

After a moment's reflection, Brand asked, "Have you a telephone I may use?"

"Sir-if you can use it quickly, before I get spotted lending it out."

Brand gave the operator a number. I heard a voice at the other end say, "Whitefield and Congreve, sir, may I help you?"

"I wish to speak to Vessey—this is his brother."

"Let me transfer you, sir!"

Then, interestingly enough, these two brothers spoke French to each other. Brand explained his situation, *á ces gens je suis deja mort*—Vessey asked him how many pounds he wanted, he replied, *cent,* one hundred and Vessey said he would bring it over shortly. "Settle yourselves and have some tea," he added.

"Decent of him, "Brand remarked. We seated ourselves in the mezzanine in back of the store, and ordered tea and tea sandwiches.

"Does your brother know about us?"

"Certainly, why do you ask?"

"I don't want him to think I'm just something the cat dragged in!" I said it with a smile. It was difficult to tell who's who when people were in uniform, and I was still in my RNVR jacket and a blue skirt. "Vanity, vanity," I remarked.

Shortly, the archetypal banker, shirt, stock, bowler, gloves, waistcoat, came through the front door. He was as neat as his father. Covert glances were thrown at him, for he was the best dressed man in the store. He had told us where to meet, and hastened to take a chair and join us.

Brand made the introductions. "Vessey, Amanda Ten Eycke— Amanda, my brother Vessey."

"Ah, from New York City, where I received my Christian name! You had been indulging in Zeppelin spotting, I hear." Had he told his brother? How?

Vessey favored his mother, having dark blond hair, the same porcelain skin as his brother, although this was their only shared similarity. His eyes were blue.

Brand and his brother were only a year apart in age, Vessey being the younger. He definitely was the fair-haired boy, having all the approved interests for a son of the family. Vessey had apprenticed for a few years at other banks. He was a quick study, and spoke English, French, German and—Spanish? As yet, however, he was uneasy about decisions.

This only had served to make him favored member of his parents, and a bit of reproach to his elder brother.

Brand said two words to him he had never used before: "Thank you."

Vessey pondered this for a moment, then replied, "You are certainly welcome." Now, the family was proud of Brand, too. Now he was creating a different sort of worry.

"How is mother?"

"She has leveled off now. I hear she wore that iron cross of hers to Christmas dinner!

"Indeed she did."

"And no doubt argued with Henry, as usual. It's a wonder Miss Ten Eycke survived her introduction to our family."

"Father and Mrs. Ten Eycke got on splendidly."

I listened, fascinated by this peak behind the scenes!

"Amanda puzzled Father when he asked her how she was and she replied *degouté, milord.* She left him puzzle out if she meant disgusted, or feeling poorly. He of course, chose feeling poorly rather than disgusted, and suggested I take her out for a breath of fresh air!"

"Fortuitous."

"Yes, of course. Will you excuse me for a moment?"

What should I do and what should I say? I asked myself.

"If a cheque will not be cashed for various reasons, the clerk may have to make good on it if it does not clear. I may look into it."

"You do not think Brand suspected any such thing?"

"I believe you heard what he said when he rang me?"

"Indeed I did, Mr. Whitefield." My eyes were swimming suspiciously.

At the hotel, I rang up to our suite. Becky answered and screamed, "Oh, my God, what are you doing here?"

"Can we come up?"

"All right!"

Once inside, I explained that Brand was on leave, and I had been granted leave at this time as well. "Can I stay here?" I asked.

"Oh, your room is not made up! Aunt Bea has stacks of pamphlets stored in there."

"Quite all right. She can come home with me."

"How could they know—"

"They know I am here already. My brother will have told them. If I may commandeer your telephone, I'll ring."

As he did so, Becky suddenly noticed The Ring. "Oh, good Lord, are you engaged?"

"Yes. We're going to purchase another ring. This one is a bit too large."

"Aunt Bea doesn't know!"

But now she would.

CHAPTER 43

The next day, we walked to a bookstore Brand knew, and which I was too embarrassed to enter. He bought a book—the book, as far as I was concerned!

We went back to the Albany. No one to disturb us. Fortunately, no one was around to give me the stare. We sat down on a sofa in Brand's office. He opened the book, and read parts of it to me; then had me look at the illustrations to make sure I knew what they were.

"How are we progressing?" he asked me.

"It's a bit hard to visualize, "I said.

"What am I to do?" There was a moment's silence. I was trying to think of something to say, but he stood up, hung his jacket over the back of a chair, sat down again and to my horror, unbuttoned his fly and removed its inhabitant.

"Look at me," commanded.

I turned. "It—certainly is red," I ventured.

"So is your face!" he said humorously. "Pay attention. Here is the scar from my circumcision."

"Oh! That's what they mean in the Bible!"

"Yes, to remove the flesh of the foreskin. Pity those poor chaps who had it done as adults. That would lay them up for several days!" He seemed to be at ease.

"Oh."

He took out his handkerchief and spread it on the sofa cover next to him. "Now, give me your hand," he commanded. I did. He placed it on his sweet spot, and shortly, out came something white. "That is called sperm," he said. "It is what fertilizes a woman's eggs."

"And then—?"

"Then they have conceived a child."

"Oh. If they do it, does it always make a child?"

"No.

"Oh."

I could tell my face still held a faint blush.

"Come over here," he said, extending an arm. Awkwardly, I slid nearer him. "There," he said, and kissed me. We lay locked in an embrace until I felt a stirring under his belt. Now I was beginning to be curious. "Can—I touch it?

"Any time, Mandra, I am all yours."

That afternoon, a momentous decision was made: shopping for my own ring. We went down to Bond Street via the Burlington Arcade, and entered a shop. The fashion of the day was platinum and diamonds which I found a trifle flashy. The clerk showed us a ring which he said was one of the best they were selling. "It requires a bit of careful handling," he said.

"Then that is not for me," I said.

It was a discreet shop and price tags were non-existent; if they had been, I probably would have fainted, for this was still the day when one pound was worth five dollars.

"Can we go walk outside?" I asked Brand.

Yes, of course." I took his arm and immediately felt closer to him after his biology lesson; I snuggled against him.

"I guess that I've grown used to a bit of color in a ring," I said. "All diamonds seem too bland."

"Did you like the sapphires in grandmother's ring?"

"I did."

"It's the stone for September, which is your birthday," he remarked. "If that is what you like, that is what we shall look for." I knew he was prepared to spend the rest of day at it, if necessary.

We went back inside; I did not see anything that appealed.

"Let's try Asprey's," he said.

Asprey's boasted a sea of rings. I moved slowly down the cases, with him standing by. He did not want to be asked any questions! This was my decision.

Finally, I came upon a case with rings that had mixes of stones, and I saw an octagonal ring I liked in diamonds and sapphires, plus, I thought it would go with my watch!

I moved away as Brand and the clerk began negotiations. As I strolled to one end of the store, I saw a small ring in gold, held together by gold shaped leaves, a foliage pattern.

"That's pretty!" I murmured, softly, so no none would hear me. Or so I thought. I was wrong. He bought it too.

"Shall we go to the Savoy Grille to celebrate?"

I knew quite well that was a spot where the theatrical elite lunched. I was shy but I knew it was time to try it out. True to what I expected, Brand was greeted by several people; I was introduced as his fiancée.

We both chose to have the turbot mousse, which was very good, indeed. When we had finished, he reached inside his jacket and pulled out a Kodak snapshot.

"This is Augustus," he said. "Informally known as Gus." It was a medium sized dog, with longish, dark wavy hair. There were two white feet, and, most sensationally, a tail that ran around in a loop, which was called, I was informed, a queue. Clearly he was one of the stray animals wandering around the battlefield areas, deprived of home and hearth by the hostilities. He was still on the thin side, but, I suspected, would not remain that way for long.

"He was so thin at first we had to feed him porridge, poor little chap! Turn it over." I did, and I began to laugh. There was a paw print on the back.

"It's jolly good to be able to do something constructive amidst chaos." Yes, this was a strange sort of being. We strove not to remember what we could not forget. I agreed with his sentiment. Brand feeding porridge to an abandoned dog surely was a change in him.

"Now that I am a Major, I shall have private quarters; myself, and your Bible, and my books. At times, Court betrays an insatiate need for attention."

"Has he been drinking?"

"Usually."

"Uncle Ben would say he is turning maudllin."

"He was jolly well right."

<h1 style="text-align:center">CHAPTER 44</h1>

How wonderful to be inside a family home again. I did not instantly fall asleep this time; I appreciated that room was ready, and a bath for a wash! It was incredibly peaceful to be under the same roof and Brand, and shortly after a thanksgiving prayer, I fell asleep.

Then I awakened to a stentorian racket. It was the ground floor telephone. I could faintly hear movements; Staines was answering. Very faintly I could hear footsteps going down the hallway toward the back of the house, and a door close.

Then the Viscount used the household intercom to ask Staines what the call had been about. "It is a Mrs. Ten Eycke, milord."

"I'll take it. This is Viscount Stroplea." He heard a torrent of distress, then spoke firmly. "Your niece is sleeping in our daughter Maddy's old room," he said. I was also wearing one of Maddy's old nightgowns. "As for anything else, it can surely wait until morning. Good evening." He hung up. He did not show any signs of being led around by the nose by Female dramatics. He went back to bed.

In the morning, we found out what had happened during the night, and I feared a gathering storm. "Brand, you and Amanda leave after breakfast, and I will deal with Mrs. Ten Eycke. I'm of a mind to take this kettle of fish up with your father myself, Amanda. In fact, it would seem to be the most diplomatic method."

Brand was not used to having his father fight his battles. "Don't you think..." he began.

"No, I don't, "said his father. We hastily departed. "You did ask me if there was anything I wished to do. What about you, Brand?"

"There is. You need not come with me if you might find it awkward. I should like to visit Calypso Valletta, Chapin's widow. I'd just as soon do it today, rather than have it hanging on my mind."

"I'll come with you."

"I appreciate it."

CHAPTER 45

In early afternoon we arrived in a suitably unfashionable section of London. The flat was up two flights of stairs and strange cooking smells breathed forth from under the door. Calypso Valetta, Mrs. Harold Chapin, opened the door to us and stood squinting at a still intact couple. I could not tell if she wished us well or ill.

"Thanks for ringing me," she said to Brand. So he'd called her! She gave me her hand. Then she called, "Vallee!" A boy of about four came out reluctantly and when he gave his hand to Brand, he also stuck out his tongue. His mother reprimanded him instantly.

"At least he's left off spitting, "she said apologetically. "He's been out of hand since Harold left."

"Tell me about the memorial performance," Brand said as we all sat down. She jumped up to get the program. She came back with Vallee dogging her steps.

"Tree was chair?" Brand was scanning it. Suddenly I remembered Felicity's story about Sir Herbert Beerbohm Tree saying to the searchlight crew, "Shine that light on me!"

"Whelan lent the theater," she added. I knew enough by now to know the theatre took care of its own with these benefit performances to raise money for whoever of its members was in need.

"And you and du Maurier played 'The Poor.'"

"Harold was always a bit upset about me being a grass widow and playing while he was away. But now I am a real widow. I guess I had some rehearsal time. My life has to go on and so does Vallee's."

"My favorite was always 'The Deaf and the Dumb,'" said Brand, speaking, I gathered, of Chapin's work, for Brand had told me that Chapin was a playwright.

"I've got some copies of it right here," she said. "Would you read some with me? Then we can have something to eat."

"Here," said Brand, giving me a copy. "You can be Emmie. No buts. I love the way he sets a scene." He read, "the fire is burning brightly behind a large three fold clothes horse covered with wet linen. . . a dresser poorly furnished with crockery but rich in undarned socks and novelettes...one can see the scene!"

Calypso launched into Mrs. Henderson, aggrieved with her daughter Emmie --I was reading her part-- who reports that Mum has mucked up her compound multiplication homework; then Emmie launches into aggrieved lament for this blow struck by her mother's incompetence. Joe comes home in the voice of Brand and informs his wife quite suddenly that his work will let him be home nights now. As Emmie I felt like sandwich stuffing in between two accomplished thespians.

Now Joe sent his wife across the road for a pitcher of beer so he and his mate Bill can celebrate. She goes for her hat and coat and...disappears. Joe goes into their bedroom to find her stretched across the bed saying prayers of thanksgiving. He is stunned.

"I ain't home forever even nah," Brand read prophetically. "I shall have to leave you again someday. Wot about vat?"

"Yes what about that!" exclaimed Calypso, departing from the script. She got up and opened a desk drawer, taking out a letter and thrusting it at Brand. "Read that!" she commanded. He read it with great care and folded it up. "Do you think he suffered?"

"Not if he was hit in the forehead."

CHAPTER 46

I received another summons from Sir Henry. Again, by train, I returned to London. The atmosphere at Claridge's was very different. My aunt was harried. Becky seemed resentful. My ring had begun a firestorm. They were taking the brunt. Not me.

When my aunt went out, I learned why Becky was especially upset. One of her walk-abouts who had gone to France had asked her to write to him, and she had been going through some of the fear and suspense I'd been in for some while: however, she produced a wrinkled copy of the Roll of Honor.

"Oh," I said, "no."

"Oh yes."

Then she hurled, "He asked me to write him!"

I was beginning to suspect some of the trouble was Becky did not know if she were special to him, or whether she was just a Lonely Stab. Here she was, a bright young thing, and I was the one who was engaged—it wasn't fair.

"Were you angry if he didn't write?"

"Yes!'

"Do you think your thoughts could have harmed him?"

"Why do you ask that?" She looked like a hunted animal.

"Annie is very superstitious, and—she has a special cup she gives Pym his tea in and—it broke, and she was nearly hysterical, she was so scared, thinking perhaps it would make something horrible happen."

"And did it?"

"No."

Aunt Bea was likewise burdened. The Admiralty, she told me, had been pressing Hoover to give them information. The Foreign Office was investigating a rice scandal and a food leakage. Apparently some former colleague of Hoover had been telling lies about him; he was in for government inquiry, and he was threatening to resign. Lord Grey, Lord Percy and Justice Rowlatt were behind the investigation. Meanwhile, in France, the C.N. was trying to undercut the C.R.B.

"It's that fellow Franqui again, "she murmured darkly.

"Do you think he would resign?"

"Everyone is taking it seriously. Even the Germans have protested through Ambassador Gerard."

CHAPTER 47

Coming up the Mall I enjoyed a few moments of bucolic musings gazing over St. James Park and pond, even though there were soldiers training on it.

By the time I arrived at the Admiralty, I was nervous. Sir Henry was as brisk as ever; he did not keep me waiting. Although I gathered from the Hoover inquiry that he and my aunt may have been at loggerheads, his position was one endemic to such relationships, and he asked cordially how she was despite any rupture.

He gave me the address of a Mr. Smith I was to meet at Whitehall.

"I'm sending you to a chap who has been a successful spy for many years. He will impart some methodology to you." He handed me a card in Whitehall.

Mr. Smith' proved to be a foreigner. He was tailored from the West End and evinced a crassly unbritish satisfaction with his appearance. From time to time he touched his jaw as though becoming refamiliar with it, from I could see that he had just shaved off a beard.

A power emanated from his physical being which was almost paralytic to me which was absolutely impartial, one that could rape and kill as well as romance. He was an eerie man. That none of this was ever turned on me, was simply a matter of expedience.

I watched his face as he read over my dossier. He had high cheekbones, and the skin descending from them was lightly pitted; he had a full mouth, the upper lip longer and thinner, moving over the lower in quick commentary, He had a long nose too full to be aquiline.

When I arrived, the man asked, amused," I'm to teach you to think like a spy? What an illusion!" Aware of my scrutiny his eyes had a strange curvature which made light coruscate on the pupils at a higher point than normal. He was aware, of course, of my scrutiny and he bore it easily.

"Haven't you any illusions, Mr. Smith?" He appeared interested in my question.

"Have I an illusion that I have no illusions?" he asked. "No, I have not. I shall tell you my illusions: it is that everything is illusion—*maya.*"

"If that is so, how can you think there is one side to another in this war?"

"I can, if I tell you why I think as I do. Thus, I do not grant reality power. I can conceive it as chimerical, malleable; thus I can change it."

"That sounds like God!"

"My dossier says I have Messianic illusions. But that is their illusion. Give a man power to take life and death as he sees it, and place him at the center of moments that shape history—is it I who have illusions, or they, who have permitted me an extraordinary human reality?"

"So they, too, have illusions?"

"Certainly."

"I think it is an illusion Brand would help his mother's country."

"Ah! The English are a sentimental lot! A man at odds with his mother is alien to their way of thinking."

"Not when it relates to Brandon and his mother."

"I see."

"You probably already knew that?"

Mr. Smith smiled. "Has Henry told you Major Whitefield has been wounded?" He asked.

"What!"

"He has been hit in the right arm by a bullet that broke the arm, went through, and cracked two ribs."

"Why—"

"Obviously Henry held the news back as he thought you would assume he would be back to Blighty for a rest, and would not go. He has given me a letter to you from your Major he wrote from hospital." He handed it to me.

"Of course he should come home!"

"Miss Ten Eycke, not if Colonel Charteris has his say. His wounds are painful, not dangerous. They are planning to curtail commanding officers in the R.F.C. from flying, they are losing too many seasoned commanding officers. Charteris wishes to keep him there."

"And—who is this—"

"General Haig's intelligence chief. There. You've had a shock. Go home and rest. We will finish tomorrow."

In a taxi on the way back to the hotel, I read the letter, written by a volunteer, to aid Brand; however at the very end he had scribbled:

And this is love of course:
You give not cause for guilt
Or for remorse.

I was back again the next morning.

"Everything of importance may be sent by wireless in scramble, and received as such. Of course there is a common R.F.C. code, but it will be understood by R.F.C. personnel; this is different, but you will have that code book. You will be able to see what has been taken down by wireless thanks to your training and will not be a threatening presence when he replies. He will use it often when communicating artillery coordinates. Wrong information can blow gas shells back on our own men. Such mistakes occur about 10% of the time, anyway. Of course, note any *en clair* transmissions, which are forbidden,—the Germans have listening posts. We do, too. You must watch for anything sent to neutral countries, like America or Switzerland."

"Switzerland?"

"An enchanting picturesque little land through which passes much of the secret monies of this world. The land of immunity. She is hostess to French bauxite, which is made into aluminium there, and used to fill orders for German submarines. The proceeds disappear Swiss banks. There are middlemen in this world, like Basil Zaharoff; he is a demi-government in himself, like Mr. Hoover. I have met him in many places."

"Hoover?"

"Even Hoover dealt through this conduit with the Germans for cyanide in 1914. The point is, certain countries are exchange points. Grain from the Ukraine."

Then 'Mr. Smith' began to show me a few things like simple cryptography with a pocket code. He showed me something like a ruler.

'This can be used in conjunction with a common book like a dictionary. Thus, a notation like '078-12 would mean page 78, twelfth word down. These notations are very small. They can be sent beneath a postage stamp. Sewed inside a collar. Watch for bits of paper. "

He fumbled in his drawer. 'Here we have the proverbial invisible inks. Heat will show up some of them." He held it against a light bulb while letters came out. "Or you can hold it against a match ever so carefully." He let me try this for myself.

"Various solutions can be used to write—the simplest is lemon juice."

The next morning I had some questions.

"Does this mean someone has a loose eye on your fiancé and family?" He replied. "Of course, in a general way. But at this moment, the R.F.C .is sending some new squadrons to a new front in France—I will not name them of course—Brand will receive one of them as its commanding officer. It will be a reconnaissance squadron which cooperates fully with the French—as you know, he has been working with them already. Because of his fluidity with French, the squadron will not need a translator. You understand this is an unusually sensitive position."

"Why would you even assume—" I began hotly.

"Miss Ten Eycke in this line of work, one must always move from the position of devil's advocate. Guilty until proven innocent. We are tightening down a bit because the Viscountess has sought permission to donate some money to internees on the Isle of Man for a burial ground. This is where the envelopes—made of gold beaters skin—are put together for our Sea Scout airships. And the White List allows open communication between father and son. Possibly a family network? I think not, but one must always take care. But to return to Brand. He will be flying a Morane a monoplane, a single seater, with a new Le Rhône engine. This means he can outstrip escorts and that he has no observer on board. He will be flying over enemy territory—well, Bob's your uncle." Q.E.D.

It was beginning to dawn on me.

"We could put you in his squadron to assist the Recording Officer."

"As a spy??"

"Wouldn't you, of all people, want to know if there is one iota of veracity to any suspicions? Ring me up when you've thought it over." He showed me out.

I fell asleep at the hotel and began to dream. I saw three women sitting inside a large pot. There we were, Aunt Bea, Becky, and I. "Pour this in," said the voice, handing me a bottle. I poured. Instantly, Aunt Bea and Becky's eyes began to glow and they thought the water was transparent rather than dirty; then they were lifted out of the pot, leaving me there alone.

"Where are you taking me?"

"To Babylon. You are on your way to Babylon."

"The evil City?"

"Choose. Will you not do the good you can do...evil is the absence of good...the absence of good...."

Behind me I heard shrill laughter; there were hags hanging in the darkening air. "Beware the fiend that lies like truth! Beware the fiend that lies like truth!"

I woke up.

I rang up.

I said that I would go.

It was only three weeks before I crossed the Channel to France. It was fortunate the time was short, for America had begun to respond with anger to the Viscount and Aunt Bea's announcements of my engagement, and threaten to come to England to sort things out.

Sir Henry spoke with Aunt Bea to the effect that when I was assigned, my whereabouts would be safe, but unknown, which was, as he pointed out, best all around. "We mustn't prevent Amanda from doing what she feels called to do," he remarked.

"We can't, "said Aunt Bea, "as you have arranged it."

Sir Henry smiled. "It'll take a load off your shoulders, Mrs. Ten Eycke!" Aunt Bea stiffened. "If your brother demands information, tell him to contact me. Rodger won't do him any good."

<h1 style="text-align:center">CHAPTER 48</h1>

It was a two storey brick house with the ubiquitous red tile roof; poles along the road carried electrical wires to the first floor, which was the only one Monsieur bothered to light. It was candles to bed. It was up to date, unlike many homes made of mud and wood beams with feed stored under the roof.

I was collected, with my baggage—including my violin—at the Amiens station by Sgt. Major Richard Wilson, the pedestal of propriety in most military units, with two assistants, in a Crossley tender.

On arrival at the house, I was introduced to Mme. Moignet, a plump woman with grey hair, dressed in the ubiquitous black for someone in the family, her hands worn, the knuckles large, her wedding ring still shining softly on her finger like love among the ruins.

But it was clear she wanted to get back into the kitchen and cook dinner. "*Ascendez,*" she commanded Sgt. Wilson, waving at a young woman who would lead them upstairs, who was, I assumed, my new roommate. Wilson had his privates carry my bags up to my bedroom on the second floor and put them on the straw mattress on the bed.

"Hello, I'm Bonnie Sue Lovat, from Edinburgh," she introduced herself after they had deposited my luggage.

"Amanda Ten Eycke."

"The Yankee, "she finished, as if this was part of my name.

After they trooped back downstairs, she said, "There is a small *armoire* in the hall to hang out some clothes."

"I'm a nurse," she continued. "Trained in Edinburgh, me Dad is a doctor and me mother was a nurse before she became our mother, so we grew up scrubbing floors! Ma is a suffragist, but she is from a good family and in her day, nurses were—not well respected so her family was glad when she 'settled,' as they call it, but no one could scarce stand in the way of me becoming a nursing sister!"

"But—what are you doing here?"

"I could have gone to Serbia with Dr. Inglis but I wanted France; I was too late when they asked for volunteers for that one. But see, there are some small family -sponsored hospitals here in France and my family knew one so they gathered up us male and female left -overs and sent us over. They sent me here to better my French while we are waiting on a small Casualty Clearing Station going up nearby. They went to see the Scottish Women's Hospital at Royaumount, and they really admired the Curé there . He went out to the border of the town every day during the German advancee—like the priest at Senlis. "

"What happened at Senlis?"

"The direction of the advance changed just before the German advance got to ite—the priest stood in the middle of the road every day. It's part of what they call the miracle of the Marne." Miss Lovat cocked her head as though my knowledge was deficient! "So they looked about for a good 'un, and he is living here until the clearing station gets finished, and meantime he visits what few locals there are."

"A priest?"

"Aye—Madame's brother. Monsieur is not too happy to have him, but he is happy for a bit of rent. She is a strict one. *Pas de entourloupette ici!*" (No hanky-panky here!)

I shook a few things out and hung them in the small armoire beside Bonnie Sue's clothing. I pushed my suitcase under the bed and discovered a chamberpot, with a lid.

When I straightened up, she was still sitting on her bed, waiting to talk.

"So, Miss Ten Eycke, how do you come by here?"

"I am part of a few people from neutral America who have volunteered to take over a position from an able-bodied man who is a ground officer. I will be a clerk at the aerodrome."

"Sounds as if you don't want to say too much about how you got here!"

"I wouldn't mind at all, but I can't."

"Aye." Miss Lovat was worldly enough to realize I had not just mysteriously appeared here.

We heard Madame calling us to table. She and Monsieur were seated. Also seated was a Catholic priest in his soutane. "This is Madame's brother, the Curé: Père Anton," volunteered Bonnie.

"Mon Père, "I said, with a little bow of the head.

"Mademoiselle! Enchanté!".

They crossed themselves and Père Anton said grace. I did neither, just closed my hands in prayer, as did Bonnie. Some kind of acrimonious tension began to evidence between the men— Monsieur addressed the priest as 'Anton.' Madame frowned. Monsieur was a very anti -clerical Frenchman, like Tiger Clemanceau.

Seeing his wife's excpression, her husband added, "He thinks I am charging too much money for foodstuffs! Imagine! I am the only good foods store out here and he doesn't think I should add money for the risk! The Germans have always declared us a dead zone for their artillery! Who knows what will happen if fighting breaks out!" (For the Somme area had been quiet for two years, occupied by German troops). "The Germans are well dug in! I have been down in one dugout 40 feet deep with beds and carpeting! I will have to change products to suit the British now!"

Now Madame cleared the table and rinsed the dishes with cold water. Bonnie picked up a bucket and went out to the village fountain. Madame shook her head and waited for her to return, boil the water, and pour it over the dishes, a sanitization technique which Madame resented, although she was told it was now necessary.

In the morning, before breakfast, they crossed themselves and Père Anton said grace. Well--why not--Brand crosses himself too. Why not be polite. A loud noise outside announced the arrival of one of the staff cars, driven by Sgt. Wilson, come to transport me to the aerodrome. I ran outside, impatient to see Brand. Madame was right behind me, and told me to stop. She handed me several loaves of fresh bread, a pot of black current preserves, and two dozen eggs, still warm from under the chickens, for the squadron kitchen.

After bumping along over the pavé, sheltering the eggs, we turned off onto a dirt sunken road, whose sides prevented seeing anything because, although the mud sides were high, there was a camouflage sheeting across the top; it was a longish road along which—as those of Picardy put it—the Good Lord did not travel often. Finally we emerged from the road and the horizon opened to our eyes—ahead lay three Bessaneau hangars, a square landing and take-off strip, a farmhouse, and its outbuildings.

It was set up as a local farm, one of the isolated farms whose names frequented the military maps of Picardy, with names like Maltzshorn, Monacu, Falfemont. Farms offered the large, square sweep of field necessary for take-offs and landings from any direction, depending on the wind. It was a farm like farms indigenous to the Santerrre; it was built in a square, with a courtyard in the middle from which, fortunately, the *midden,* or manure pile, had been removed, closed in on itself in the same impulse as plainsmen circling wagons in the evening.

Set behind it by a middling distance was a chateau, now deserted except for its occupation as quarters for the Flying Corps.

I glanced over at the farmhouse, where the squadron had their offices. Headquarters was a *fachwerk* farm building. The sun was making the red tile rooves look warm, although warm weather was rather late in the spring of 1916.

Then a fellow who had to be Captain Nicholas Courtenay ran up to me. He had to be the fellow Brand had written to me about for so long! He swept off his hat in a low bow. "Miss Ten Eycke!" he said, laughing. "Let me assist you!" He took the eggs as and I followed him over to a building with a canvas marquee spread at the front, and under it were scattered wicker chairs, several tennis rackets, and a curious dog whose nose the cook pushed away from our provisions.

Nick's accent was definitely not Oxbridge. He had hair the color of red brick, broad shoulders, and a broad, stocky figure. Although only middle-sized—raised on meat and potatoes, not delicacies—there was a push to his personality that made one feel he was not to be trifled with.

Several machines were on the landing ground, both with an observer and a pilot's cockpit --that much I knew--and both with formidable noses, one with a four bladed propellor and exhaust valves that curved up at ninety degrees past the top wing like gigantic rhinoceros' horns, the other one with ferocious piping along the cowling.

Although it was May, there was still a faint chill in the morning air. Flying officers were lounging in canvas chairs in the sun, in different types of uniform—some in the new pattern jacket, some in jackets in which they had been seconded in, one plaid cap proclaiming seconding from a Scots unit; and a few in Brand's and Court's old original maternity jackets and Sam Browne belts. One was still in his pyjamas. Most were applying themselves to cigarettes or pipes. They all, however, sported mustaches. Many pet dogs and a few cats lay scattered among them.

Three bell tents had sprung up to welcome the spring weather.

As we passed along, Nick pointed out the workshops as we skirted by them. I stared with fascination at the drills, lathes, forges, and a jumble of wings, spare parts, reels of RAF wire, chocks, sawhorses, tools and oil cans. Several of the workshops were on wheels, ready for instant movement.

We entered the small *fachwerk* farm building that was headquarters. We entered this building via a sturdy wooden door which creaked on its hinges, turning into the first room to the right, with two windows which permitted sunlight's entrance.

"Lieutenant Chambers, miss: Recoding Officer." My new boss.

Chambers was a pale young man with balding blond hair and a *pince nez*, thin, drooping, whether from affectation, debilitation, or effeteness, I did not know. His uniform was always slightly askew. He spoke with a slight stutter, and I could not tell if it really was a handicap, for such a vocal adaptation was sometimes taken up by the R.F.C, whether it was because the famous pilot Gordon Bell had stuttered, or because others did so after crashing, I could not tell.

He was far better described by Lytton Strachey than by me as 'a 'soft, spectacled, Oxford Manner with its half-effeminate diffidence.' If he was an example of the rationale of replacing ground officers into able-bodied men, he did not look the part.

Attached to our room was the former pantry and its *arrière-cuisine* into which papers were stacked in lieu of filing cabinets, with pieces of cardboard for the letters of the alphabet inserted among them. As with all the buildings of the military, holes had been made through the walls for telephone lines to pass through them.

"All right, you come with me, "Nick instructed. "Brandy is beating basics into our latest bunch of Huns." (Huns were newcomers). We went up the hallway to the C.O.'s office. The room had a white and black diamond tile pattern, there was a fireplace, a desk with telephone, scattered impedimenta. Then we turned left into a larger room.

Brand was in mid-sentence, pointing at a map hanging from the wall. "Here is where we abut the French under General Fayolle. Their front is eight miles to the south of the river," he said, pointing to Maricourt and running his swagger stick up to Malzhorn Farm. He stopped. Augustus was lying at his feet and looked up, too.

"Oh!" I began. Remember you don't know his name. "What a nice dog!"

"Indeed he is. Say hello, Augustus," he said in a silky voice, never one to leave an entrance under-utilized. Augustus got up; no longer a black and white photo, he was a medium-sized dog, with rather curly dark brown hair, some of which fell over his eyes to protect them from the sun; yet plainly he could see clearly, although no one knew quite how; two white front paws, and a queue in his tail. He came over and sniffed me, then returned to Brand and lay down again.

"Gentlemen." The new men straightened in their chairs. "Miss Amanda Ten Eycke, our new assistant Recording Officer."

One sleeve was torn open to accommodate his cast, a carelessly tied knit necktie, and slacks instead of breeches. His batman had done his best. His face had the curious dull unlit texture of a person whose energy is drawn into themselves to deal with pain. He was hardly at the height of batman's art today; in fact, he cut a rather slovenly figure in a service that prized dash. In the past I'd given no thought to his elegance, as though it were as much a part of him as his skin, but now my heart gave a proprietal tug.

I put a hand against the door jamb to steady me. Then as he finished with, "from America," and I stood up straight with a surge of pride.

"Welcome, Yank!" pronounced Courtenay, with what he called me from then on.

"Write down the location of our advanced landing fields," he finished. "Miss Ten Eycke—with me. Let's meet the Sparks." We were off to see the wireless. Augustus tagged along. I patted him.

"Yes sir, "I answered. The words rolled off my tongue with ease. If I had not fully comprehended what his responsibilities were from his letters, I surely did by now.

"By the way, "he said as we left the building, "here is your lady's latrine!" It had been tactfully attached the end of the building. I flushed. I was embarrassed by the thought of men watching me go into this little haven and close the door. For the first three weeks or so I felt every eye was on me as I entered my privy, especially at that cumbersome time of month. But after a while the parade of pilots and observers who used their outhouses, especially as the combination of nerves and smells made flying officers' stomachs skittish fellows, and jokes flew about in terms of keeping your bowels open, helped me lose most of my chagrin.

We stood side by side, absorbing and re-absorbing all the little physic links that kept us connected over distance were now connecting in one another's presence.

Yet I sensed something deeper now—a trouble -ridden man under the chipper letters most soldiers wrote—even Brand.

I had thought we ought to down play our relationship because so many men out here were far from home and those they loved. Realistically, I had yet to learn about the soldier's bonzer girls in the villages, towns, estaminets, the houses of prostitution sanctioned, even licensed by the government, and about the predicament of many an average girl with the death of the average man, which could lead a girl into behavior she might not have imagined before 1914, when 900.000 Frenchmen died before Christmas. Yet despite the chaos, many a young Frenchwoman also kept her behavior chaste. Saddest of all were the families whose family finances only depended on a daughter's prostitution.

"Come over to the field. I shall show you our stable. "He pointed out our two flights of BE2c's and one of rotary engine Bristol Scouts. Someone was throwing the propellor on one of the latter and a huge cloud of smoke blew toward us.

"Move away a bit, those are castor oil fumes!—" He said, but it was too late! I ran for the lavatory! Fortunately, I made it—it was my first acquaintance with really heavy castor oil. When he caught up with me, he was carrying a bottle of blackberry brandy.

"Here, "he said. "Drink some."

I slugged it down and it burned. My stomach felt as if it were reaching up to receive it. I sat down on the grass.

"Just let it settle. It's the pilots' antidote. I'll come back for you and we shall visit W/T."

I sat alone on a small hillside. If I were less tired, I might have panicked, but my senses were too dulled. Below me, almost like an anthill, movement was going on to what end I did not yet know. One of the machines Brand had tagged a BE2c came in for a landing, and I wondered why the pilot didn't blip the engine. I would learn it possessed a different kind of motor.

When Brand returned, he asked how my lodgings were; and I told him my roommate seemed agreeable, but our landlords less so.

"Miss Lovat and I are both Protestants."

"That could prove very interesting!" he said with a little laugh. "The priest is a good chap, though. He's grown used to ministering wherever and whoever; he goes 'round wonderfully—by donkey cart, bicycle, walking, or rowing. He won't be horrified, Amanda."

"How many people are here?" I asked.

"About two hundred. I am very fortunate in having had theatrical experience; if I cast my pilots and observers as star players, and the rest as walk-ons, as well as the personnel it takes to manage stagecraft, it gives me a paradigm."

W/T was a hut with a thirty -foot mast outside to hold the aerial. The 'Sparks' was sitting in front of the standard issue wireless with its wooden box, headphones over his ears. Our wireless was seconded to us via our 'forgotten men'-R.F.C. wireless operators assigned to different batteries nearer the front.

Brand signaled him to give me the headphones. I put them on, and at first I only hear faint babble of wireless calls. Sparks had been listening to the news from the Eiffel Tower.

"Coleman hasn't wound out his aerial yet?" Brand asked.

"No, sir."

Just then I began to hear a faint '3G,3G,3G.' I looked up at our Sparks, 2nd air mechanic Laffey. He began turning the wave length dials, now adjusting the crystals, now switching onto closed circuit. A German battery was close enough we could hear Coleman signaling his ground post. The cacophony stopped and I just heard Coleman, signaling in clock code, B to battery to ask if they were receiving him. They must have flashed back a 'yes' by Panneau signal which were white strips arranged almost like a Venetian blind. Then came Coleman's call signal again, a break, a call, and his ready to observe signal. They were over the target. Then I heard 'JJ', and Brand said, "He has a moving target."

There was a 'G' for fire for effect, and the corrections, F.2, F.2, F.2. with a break on either side to identify the sender, and then a finer correction, Z.2, Z.2, Z.2. Another salvo fired, and I heard RR, RR, RR, more to the right. The two men with me were now waiting impatiently for the KB which would signal a direct hit.

But it did not happen: the pilot turned back with a failing carburettor.

CHAPTER 49

Now it was again evening, and we were seated at the table. Once again I crossed myself. We had more of what we'd eaten yesterday, which tasted even better. I was beginning to learn the joys of *réchauffé.*

For lack of a better idea, I said, "I sent a wireless message today!"

"Did you? How?"

"By Morse code."

"Oh."

"It was a counter battery coordinate!"

Miss Lovat replied, "Good for you."

As we rose from the table, I meandered to the corner of the room, where an interesting looking document hung in a frame. I had noticed it before, but had not had opportunity to vet it more closely. I tried to read it, but the French was somewhat unfamiliar. I sensed the Curé behind me.

"Do you know what this is?" he asked.

I replied softly in French, "No, what is it?" I did not know that the Curé was an indefatigable searcher for old documents wherever he went, particularly, but not always, in old churches. He was, in fact, a more than amateur scholar.

"It is rare," he said. "It is written in Provençal middle French."

"Provençal?" I said. "That's in the south!"

"Our village takes its name from its conceit of the old broom," he said "Vetz Balai."

Monsieur rose. "Just in time for recitation of our immortal glories! *Je me couche,"* he said, and he went off, as the Curé prepared to read it to me in modern French. To my surprise, Miss Lovat came over, also interested. "I've been wondering what that was too!" She exclaimed.

Later, I translated it thus:
I'm very sad, for I am sent
Far from my lady-love, so fine
Father, to you on your estate
I send this poem as my delegate
To let you know my heart is rent;
My appetite is gone; I only dine
On my distress; and my mind's weight
'S to think on the mistake
I made to make such pliant against my fate.
Once I throve on youth and joy
And while I throve, I only thought
Anything my pen could write
Was only simple, petulant employ,
But I lament
It was the instrument
To make me of my pen repent.
My lady, you did warn me well
Not to sing what is better left a-silent
For fear my song would make my Lord suspect
More devious intent than only poetic legerdemain:
He may think I only feign my venom spent in poetry
Because I have so much, yet still complain.

I have been swept away up here
By the broom of my own making
Father, would you but give me back my own true love,
My poet's skills would be yours for the taking.

The Curé lit up with scholarly pleasure. He had to go a long way to find any interest in his discoveries! But there was one person who never tired of hearing about his studies: his sister. Miss Lovat had brought back the bucket of water and placed it on the stove; the dishes were lined up; almost automatically, when the water came to a boil, she picked it up and poured it over them, all the while listening to her brother.

"After many years, I have found out only this: the poet's name is Guillem de Mossac, and he is buried here near Guillemont, not in the town cemetery, but the one on the road to Combles, although it took a bit of digging to find his tombstone. I do not know: he came from the south, yes, but why? Perhaps his father sent him up here to make his fortune. From the fact that the poem rested up here, I suspect he never had the means to send it all the way to Provence. And from the fact he is buried here, also, that he died here, apparently without having made his fortune. It was a harsh lesson, I expect; to find all the superfluity he had enjoyed at his father's court were not easily come by."

We took a candle to mount the stairs.

"Do you want to blow out the candle while we change?" she asked.

"That's a good idea." We had both grown up when modesty was the day.

We were sleeping soundly when an eerie noise awakened me and I sat bolt upright, exclaiming," What is that?"

"Amanda!" said Miss Lovat, lunging awake. "It is the cow mooing!— Oh, well, may's well call me Bonnie." We both went back to sleep.

By morning I had also discovered that roosters get up very early.

CHAPTER 50

The next morning, Brand told me to follow him around, as he watched the new recruits. It was important, he said, if I were to be a clerk, to know what all the aerodrome terminology meant. As we began to walk, a horse-drawn mower was beginning to trim the grass on the tarmac.

"Trenchard's instructions are never to cramp our fellows from expressing themselves when they return from mission. I think you may be better at it than Chambers. He has a terrible habit of looking bored. Perhaps it is his way of making their accounts shorter so he will have less work."

"Do you expect the men will talk to me?"

"I expect you will listen to them, and there is nothing that encourages a speaker more than a charming woman." We were, I was instructed, off for the target butts. I was not terribly enamored of firearms but I could see I would have to get over it. As we drew closer I could hear the sounds of machine gun fire, and the smell of gun powder. Augustus sat down here; the noise, to animal ears, with far better hearing than ours, was too loud.

The pit was located in the lowest part of a small dip in the land, so there was the least opportunity of being hit by stray bullets. In the middle of the pit was what looked a bit like a wooden replica toy, with a wooden seat and a wooden hump with the machine gun on top of it. The seat was mounted on what looked like a slanted platform which could rock back and forth, which, Brand told me, was a hawker special, invented by Major Lanöe Hawker, C.O. of 24 Squadron, based nearby at Bertangles.

Like most war- time pilots, I noticed, Brand's face had its nose sharpened, his cheekbones more sharply delineated, his eyes sunken, and fixed in the stare which was then called an eye for the country.

The Armor Sergeant had a new recruit in the seat with the gun, which was almost a silhouette, because, as Brand explained, "We strip the stock to make it lighter," in front of him.

"Fire off a few rounds," ordered the Sergeant.

In a minute or two, the gun jammed.

"Now what is wrong? You want to fix it as quickly as possible or you will undefended."

"Magazine latch, perhaps, sir." The recruit was nervous. He carefully pointed the magazine again, making sure the ammunition drum was pointed arrow forward. He riffled with the cocking handle, which had three positions, to see if anything had slipped. The Sergeant ripped the drum off, and pointed it toward the student.

"Look at this edge," the Sergeant commanded. "It has a worn rim. I save this drum to make this point to chaps who are starting out, like you. Always check your drums before you start out. Don't count on your ack- emmas to do it."

Brand picked it off its post and held the one side of the drum toward the student. "You see here?" he asked. "The bullet is misshapen. It makes it the wrong size to fit into your ammunition drum."

"But whatever can you do to predict that, sir?"

"You can do what an old friend of mine did when he learned the machine gun in South Africa. Check beforehand whether each bullet will fit into the drum."

"Phew! Jolly lot of work, sir!"

"It's your life, "said Brand.

CHAPTER 51

In the afternoon, Brand and Court were standing on the edge of the field, watching a recruit take off with a trained observer in the nacelle.

"Oh, Christ!" cried Court. "Never turn home to mother!" Thinking something sounded wrong with the engine, the recruit, forgetting his training not to do so, tried to turn back to the aerodrome, and crashed. Court ran off to call the squadron ambulance.

I had just seen my first fatality. Like many in the R.F.C., it had happened in the training phase, for these young 'huns' were not fit yet to fly over the line.

In an unseeing way, I walked away from the scene, afraid to see more; I had brought both men a cup of tea, and now I unwittingly hung onto the teacups. Seeing me drag along in a daze, Chambers grabbed my arm, and said "Come with me, we've a load of paperwork to do."

So today I learned the ritual of how to cope with loss.

I also learned the value of ritual and routine.

"Pull out their records, will you?" he commanded, pointing toward the enormous bread box we used as a filing cabinet. I riffled through the names and pulled out 'Anderson' and 'Lubboch.'

"Read it off to me, "he said inexorably. I began the litany of next of kin...religious preference...

But there was much more. More than I could imagine.

There was a Report on Casualties to Personnel and Machines, in duplicate, which would go via Wing and Brigade to GHQ at St. Andre aux Bois where General Trenchard and his aide Maurice Baring would find them stacked, and telegram to send replacements, for 'Boom 'had the policy there should be no empty chairs at meals. Then there were reports from the Medical Orderly and the Equipment Officer.

"If it's a write off, we can send it to G.S.O. 1—or maybe even have a bonfire!" said Chambers. "If not, off it goes to 2 A.D. and they will try to fix it."

At the bottom of each document was a space for Brand's signature.

"You'll have to take these in to him, "said Chambers. "Here. Take their mess bills, too."

"What do we do with them?"

"The C. O. pays them. He doesn't like to dun dead men's families. He'll send men to go through their effects." Chambers went off to talk with our Equipment Officer (E.O.) as he wanted to finish off out 'bumpfs' for prices for military sources. He told me he was going to prepare a list of Mess expenses to pin up later.

The bodies were laid out on sawhorses in a hangar, and life went on as normally as it could with two dead bodies, except—there was one other thing to learn.

Nick had imbibed his usual ration reserved for such events, the he went into the office, and I saw people leaving. What was happening? Soon enough, we heard Court bellowing "Damn it, Brandy, you are bending over backward too much for these recruits at the expense of your veterans!"

"That man ought to be court martialed," Chambers muttered.

"I don't like to see these babies buy the farm any more than you do but you're getting off balance. It's not your fault they send us chaps not yet properly trained! "Brand replied, in a slightly louder voice than usual. First they have to learn to **fly!** And I hate to just throw them on the end of a flight and hope for the best!"

Finally their voices dropped to a normal pitch. I learned that this was the way they dealt with crashes.

When it was time for me to leave, Brand told Sgt. Wilson he would drive into the village with us. "I want to talk to the priest," he said.

I discovered that our squadron had no Padre. In the breech, Brand and the Curé had worked out something appropriate.

"What are the religious affiliations of the deceased?" asked Père Anton.

"Anglican," Brand replied. "Please bring your violin."

"Yes, sir," I replied.

The Curé asked if someone should read a verse from the Apocrypha often used by the Catholics; he had an English translation. Brand took the book and surprised us by asking Bonnie to read the passage.

'But the souls of the just are in God's hand and no torment shall touch them. In the eyes of foolish men they seemed to be dead; their departure was reckoned as a defeat and their going from us a disaster. But they are at peace...'

Bonnie's soft lowland burr would, I heard, be different than Brand's reading it yet again from the prayer book.

Permission had been secured to use the village cemetery by wiring back to the Mayor, who had fled further back behind the village. The members of the squadron were there at the cemetery, brought in by limber, along with the ambulance. They lifted the wooden coffins down –made by the squadron carpenters— with Brand in front of the procession. He held back slightly to save me from the scent of blood and sawdust. I was, truth told, shaky. To my surprise, although I was holding my violin in one hand, Bonnie took my arm. After all, she was a nurse.

At the last moment, we saw Madame, standing at the cemetery gate.

The service went by. Bonnie read from the Apocrypha, and I could see this was moving for some of the men who recognized her familiar accent. I was so caught up wondering what to play only paid half attention.

"Holy God, "murmured Madame. A woman, reading from the Bible! Only priest did that! Bad enough when the Major did it, but—a woman!! She began to say her rosary.

One man rends, another mends.

Chambers handed Brand the Anglican burial service and he read it. Then, it appeared he had something to say.

"We have," he began, "the sad task today of rendering last honor to a flying comrade. We all recall his story. It is an all-to-familiar one. He arrived a week ago, fresh from flight school, full of enthusiasm and impetus dash, ready to have at the Boche.

"It is always the plight of C.O.'s like myself to have to try to hold such fellows back. One knows one can only succeed in dampening their ardor into the dull work of completing their training.

"His sacrifice--however untimely some of us may consider it--is the ultimate one, and we should salute him, for he made it willingly, in the spirit of the Gospel, laying down his life with all the good cheer and pluck that characterizes so many men of our nation.

"We have already commended his soul to God. Let us also pray for ourselves, who have to watch the perpetual deaths of such young men, a process which can harden into indifference to defend sanity. Let us pray we have the stamina to welcome more young chaps like this among us."

Finally the dreaded moment came. I rosined my bow and it took forever, or so it seemed; all was silent but for the usual noises of nature in the Silent Land. Playing for a bit of time, I bowed 'God Saved the Queen, while from the fog Uncle Ben's advice came to me: use Watts or Wesley. 'O God, Our Help in Ages Past.'

When I finished, Brand asked, "Is that all you wish to play?"

"I—have something, but it is written by an American," I replied.

There was not a breath of wind. They appeared to welcome more, for, as the Curé said, this was *un enterrement de premiere classe en musique*—a first class funeral with music. I did not realize the real luxury of this funeral, in a time when many men's bodies were never found at all, or if they were, were unidentifiable, known to God alone; or were put into graves never located again, or thrown together in mass burials: in the trenches; remains were even planted under duckboards or stuffed into sandbags.

"Can you sing it?"

"I don't know if you could hear me!"

"Close up ranks." They gathered closely around me close enough I wondered if I could really breathe and fill my lungs! I had learned the technique of playing and singing at the same time from my uncle, with the violin against my shoulder, as I had played songs with Max—who was a hopeless singer.

"'Once to every man and nation, Comes the moment to decide, In the strife of truth with falsehood For the good or evil side, Some great cause, God's new messiah, Offering each the bloom or blight, And the choice goes by forever, Twixt that darkness and that light.....Though the cause of evil prosper, Yet 'tis truth alone is strong, Though her portion be the scaffold, And upon the throne be wrong, Yet that scaffold sways the future, And behind the dim unknown, Standeth God within the shadow, Keeping watch above his own.'"

When I finished, I heard Brand give a slow whistle of exclamation through his front teeth.

Court whispered, "Sing that for me, Yank, when I go West."

As men began to trickle out of the cemetery, I had a moment to ask Brand, private moment, I asked, "Is it OK for Court to yell at you that way, Brand?"

A short laugh, then he replied, "It is our ritual for really rotten days like yesterday. Some chaps wonder why I don't send him down. I mentioned it to him once. Putting his revolver to his head, he said, and I quote, 'You can take me out of here in a blanket, Brandy, but you can't break my fucking heart.'"

"What does that mean?"

"It means rather than leave the squadron he would shoot himself."

Why? There was no time to ask him.

Sgt. Wilson returned us to the Moignets; Brand and Madame rode with us. Mme. asked Brand if he would like to stay for supper. He had already tasted her cooking and gladly accepted. M. Moignet swiftly evidencing a keen sense of military protocol, lifted two plates, one for himself, one for Sergeant Wilson, and went outside.

Madame first served us a hearty glass of homemade *cassis*. She made sure Brand had a substantial enough glass to banish the cares of the day.

As we sat down, Bonnie demonstrated an appreciation of need before I even perceived there was one; she helped Brand slide his chair in, and, before she sat down, inquired, "Shall I cut your dinner for you, Major?" She had things to teach me

As for me, I suddenly had an eerie feeling: I wondered how many Germans had been seated at this very table to have dinner?

How was it we sat in this little circle of civilization? I had passed by many houses whose residents had fled, homes flattened to the ground or torn open to the stare of passersbys, the intimacies of bedrooms, kitchens, dining rooms, parlors, hanging pendulously, ready to collapse on signal, as if a curtain had been torn away to reveal their insides.

The men were served coffee and brandy; there was cheese and a peach tart.

The next morning, I awoke, stretched my hands over my head, bent at the elbow, and said, "What a fine night. I slept so well I must have missed the rooster."

"You didn't miss him. We ate him last night," said Bonnie.

CHAPTER 52

It was night on the Somme River

Bonnie and I were seated hip to hip on a board across the Curé's *coronet de barque,* the flat bottomed, punt-like boat used upon the shallow river to move through the market gardens growing here in peat bogs.

Occasionally a ripple would swirl on the surface as a fish fin touched the ceiling of its watery home. Far off explosions filled the air with stabs of light which flickered across the water, but the strange contours of Picardy muted the sound. The Fourth Army was filtering in to our part of the Front and the stillness was broken by the muffled sound of men marching.

The Curé pushed his stick into the water until it hit the dirt bottom, twirled it loose from the mud, lifted it out of the water, only to thrust again; thus propelled, we moved along in phases past a wall of willow leaves trailing in the water, until we came to the fencing around a garden, when he halted and tied the *barque* up momentarily. Then we heard the squish of his booted feet moving through the garden, distilling vegetables into his canvas basket, murmuring, *"Poussez, mes 'tits, poussez!"* Yes. Grow, my little ones! Bonnie was humming *Sur le pont d'Avignon.*

The good Curé had felt a little diversion would be nice after the funeral. And it was peaceful tied up there, with just the very gentle waves of the river rocking us.

That day, I was passed to the photographic section with Lieutenant Spenser. He was working up a contour map, placing elevation lines up one side and down another of the terrain. My eye, however, was first drawn to photographs of the trench line. I was surprised that they did not go straight, but in a saw tooth fashion, and seemed to be outlined in white.

"That's the chalk soil. It turns white when it is dried by the sun. The trenches are cut into bays so no one can jump in one end of a trench and get off fifteen rounds rapid at some chap a quarter of a mile away!"

"Oh." I gazed at the contour maps. "How can you tell how high things are?"

"Look here." Here was a conglomeration of photos of objects in our sector, which showed the shadows that they threw. The hour of the day was marked on each photograph. "We calculate the height from the shadow and time of day. Here's the ruins of a brick factory...and one of a sugar beet refinery. He gave me a 'simple example.' It was of an aeroplane dropping a flare over a target which formed a right triangle with the ground from which a battery commander using a cotangent could determine his angle of fire. Needless to say, I could not follow his explanation.

In the corner some modelling was going on; a landscape; one could see how the land declined down to Maricout,went upwards to Montaubon, and fell, again, the rose toward the not-too-lofty heights of Guillemont and the ridge that ran from it toward Pozières, through Mametz forest.

"Here's what we've used," Spenser continued, picking up a mahogany box bound in brass with leather handles. "This is an A camera. The observer can hold it over the side and snap photos. Some would cut a hole in the floor and take photos through it, but now we have a C camera that bolts on the fuselage. The Major has one of them for his Morane."

Then Brand came in to ask me to write something out for him.

'To the officer commanding Third Wing, R.F.C., from our Squadron in the Field: Sir, I have the honor to report, as per orders received yesterday, I will dispatch Captain Courtenay tomorrow's date, as commander of a flight to designated point SWS Albert, to join Brigade practice of contact patrolling for Fourth Army and et cetera.' P.S. Tell Ludlow-Hewitt I owe him a dinner.'

(This to go by air drop—safer than telephone or wireless).

As we returned from the river garden, Père Anton ducked low as he pushed us under a piece of canvas upheld by four wooden poles, and Bonnie went forward to the front of the *barque,* jumping ashore as quickly as the prow hit land, tying a rope, looping it around a pole. We lifted the two full canvas bags, bulging with early vegetables out; the Curé took one, and Bonnie and I each took a handle of the other one and we walked along. Through the night we heard the ever- present rustle of troops moving in under cover of darkness.

Madame was waiting by the door. Her eyebrows were drawn together in a deep frown that looked like gathering thunder. She began to berate her brother in the *patois,* heavy with 'ch' sounds.

"What is going on? "I asked Bonnie.

"Oh, she is giving it to him for taking us with him—apparently we are underage."

"Under age?"

"Yes, apparently priests are only supposed to go places with women over a certain age. Maybe if she added the two of us together we would be proper."

"Oh."

"Oh, she is one of those bossy women who probably wanted to be a priest herself."

Bonnie did not particularly care for Madame.

"Really?"

Meanwhile, instead of answering tartly—as we expected—the Curé dropped his bag at his sister's feet, drew himself up with dignity, and said, "Cancel my rent." Then he turned and walked away; he had a bicycle nearby, and as his sister suddenly realized she had insulted him, he rode by on it, *soutaine* blowing behind him, on his way to the small chapel at the center of what once had been the village.

She started to run behind him, sobbing, calling his name; but he did not turn to look back.

Meanwhile, her husband, roused by the tumult, burst out the door, crying, "Now look what you have done, you accursed woman and her brother! He has canceled his rent!"

I think he might have hit her except that we were still standing by, open mouthed. "Go inside!" he commanded. What happened there, we did not witness.

CHAPTER 53

"Ah, here comes a new 'un from St. Omer," said Court, with a certain resignation. The B.E.2c came in uncertainly; it made a bumpy landing. Here he was to fill the spot of an aircrew we had buried yesterday.

The pilot threw his seat belt over the side. He carefully fitted the toe of a shiny new boot of a shiny new pilot's kit into the port foot stirrup. He jumped down with ungainly nonchalance. The observer got down shakily. Only then did we notice that that a lower port wire from the port elevator horn was several inches away from the tail plane.

"Bally thing snapped on me in the air, sir. They've got women working on these crates now." Then, noticing me standing next to Court, a member of the just-castigated sex, he flushed.

"You'd better be glad there are," said Court. "They sew better."

"And—sir—" the pilot continued, "I rather fancied my altimeter was not too accurate as I was descending."

"They aren't always," Nick replied. "You shouldn't have your eyes glued to it when you are making your landing. Didn't they tell you that? Didn't they try to train your eyes?"

"Yes, sir," mumbled our new member.

"You might have your ack emmas check the mounting. The C.O.'s inside."

"Oh!" The new pilot's face registered relief that this roughshod person was not his commanding officer, and embarrassment that he had not read Court's pips correctly.

He flew better than Courtenay had expected, but he was nineteen years old.

Brand buzzed Chambers and asked him to tell me to come to his office. What could this mean? I wondered.

"Miss Ten Eycke," he said, "The lads took notice of you fiddle-playing at the funeral. I used to play piano for them so they could sing, which is a jolly good thing for morale. They are wondering if it would be feasible for you to come and play some songs at the Mess."

"I...don't know!"

"I fancy I could play a bass line on the piano," he added.

"I suppose we wouldn't know unless we tried it," I replied. The Mess! That had been the forbidden zone for me!

"Shall we try it then?"

"—Yes."

"No time like the present. Get me Courtenay!" He yelled enough for Chamers to hear.

"I have to get my violin."

"We'll pass by Madame's."

Madame did not, of course, think our plans to be proper, but for me, to be alone with Brand I probably would have risked any impropriety.

The chateau was unoccupied, its residents had long ago fled to southern France It was a bit damaged but generally whole. In front was a wild mass of weeds, flowers, trees and even a fountain with no water in it, which had, prior to the war, been a lovely set of formal gardens. Court pulled up and we entered through the main door where I gawked just as busily as any tourist. As we moved further in, remains scattered here and there advertised that this space was occupied by airmen; caps, books, neckties, and other detritus were scattered throughout, growing heavier as we moved to the grand salon, which had been transformed into a Mess, with a battered piano in one corner.

"All right, old boy, come back for us in two hours."

Court smiled.

Brand walked over to the piano, flipped back the lid with his left hand, and fingered a chord—of course the instrument was slightly out of tune.

"Oh dear," I said.

"Don't worry. It won't matter. It will be too noisy for subtlety."

"Have you any sheet music?"

"Scores. In the corner. For those there is no sheet music we have a gramophone. I've picked a few songs off while listening to it."

"I'm off," said Court. As soon as he disappeared I slid onto the piano bench on Brand's left side. He put his arm around me. "What a time to be incapacitated," he murmured. We were silent for a moment, wondering how to begin.

"You know, when I heard you were coming, I was terrified and ecstatic," he said.

"So was I. I didn't want to create any trouble for you."

"I was content that you fitted in quite adequately," he said, "and that we both managed faking the fact we only slightly knew each other! I am presuming that it will become obvious to the lads that gradually they will develop the notion we are sweet on each other. You are a better actress than you suppose,"

"Yes!" I breathed. "That will be nice."

His face darkened. "But there is one thing you must promise me. In the case the Germans make a breakthrough, and you are at the aerodrome, jump in to one of our automobiles; if you are near Madame's, find Père Anton. He knows of some old tunnels dug by the Huguenots. Don't be stubborn. You are a woman and if we are ever overwhelmed by Germans… I can't bear to think of it."

"But Brand—" I said and stopped.

"Whatever?"

"If something like that happens and we are caught—well—I might as well say it—what makes you think I'd want to live the rest of my life without you?"

"Have pity, Amanda. I can't bear to think about not protecting you."

"I think—" I said, haltingly, "we could say a prayer that God will keep us together."

He sighed. "On condition Mandra, if it is not granted, you will do as I have told you."

I knew that I would terribly burden him if I were to refuse. I also knew that I could have faith that whatever happened was meant to be. I reached back for his hand on my shoulder. We sat that way for a little while. Then I said, "I guess we ought to practice."

Out came the pile of sheet music, and out came my specs. Atop the pile was a song title *Keep the Home Fires Burning,* by Ivor Novello. "How did you get this?" I asked.

"I asked Boosie's to send me the latest," he replied. "Ivor has a real winner with this one!"

I stood at his left side, and, as he was only playing the bass keys. He was able to turn halfway toward me and begin to sing the words. He had a nice, easy-going voice, definitely not a show-stopper; but then, that was why he hired people who were!

We attempted "Pack Up Your Troubles." At first—as one would have expected—we had trouble establishing the same rhythms, but gradually he decided that if he just played chords rather than attempting the bass melody line, it would make more noise. I tried putting my violin at my shoulder and trying to sing along, but all that happened was that I started to learn some lyrics. There was one about a dying young aviator, and when we got to the last line of the last verse, "Take the crankshaft out of my kidney and assemble and assemble the engine again," I was upset.

"Sit down," he said. I obeyed and sat beside him. "Understand, Mandra, it is cathartic for the chaps to mock death."

"Oh."

He had one arm in a sling and I was holding my violin in one hand; gently he reached for it and put it atop the piano. His one arm went around me and both mine went around him. With my breasts pressed against him, he knew I was aroused. I touched him while his tongue was in my mouth. We were both trembling slightly. Yes—his indoctrination plan had worked.

I was suddenly very tired. We had been working for about two hours. "Come on," he said. "We have a guest room where you can lie down."

Up the grand staircase—which was shaped into one flight of stairs until a landing, when it bifurcated into two flights—and down a hallway to a *chambre á coucher*, where he promptly left me to rest. Since I had nothing with me but the clothes on my back, I simply lay down and went to sleep. When I awoke, I could hear the clamor of people around and about in the chateau and surmised that the officers were gathering for dinner.

There was a knock at my door so I opened it and found Court there, with a tray with my dinner on it. "Apologies from the master," he said. "Best if you eat up here." So I did. Then I sat down at a dressing table and combed my hair.

About a half hour later, Brand came to get me. "All right, I've got the lads to understand that their better behavior is required this evening," he said, with a smile. I was surprised to be greeted with enthusiasm by men who knew my name. I gathered that since their C.O. had his arm in a sling, singing had been somewhat abbreviated, and they missed it. When we burst into song, I wasn't sure if they heard the instruments or not! But the fact they were there, and could be heard underpinning the racket they were making, obviously kept things together somehow. Never before nor since have I ever heard such rousing voices. After another two hour stint, I was definitely exhausted, but happy; now I could understand how much it raised their spirits.

CHAPTER 54

It was a busy day: Spenser called to me, "Miss! We need some help! We've got a Froggie here!"

Stepping into the photographic section, heavy with the odor of metho, I could sum up what stood before me: an Englishman and a Frenchman, face to face, and frustrated.

I had on one side a Frenchman who considered John Bull a rather dull and unimaginative fellow, whose lovemaking habits with women were the laughingstock of the continent, and, perhaps, a practitioner of the love that dare not speak its name.

Meanwhile, Spenser would view this Frenchman as incomprehensibly volatile and full of overblown rhetoric, vain about his amatory prowess, and apt to combine the two into such conceits as the hands of a flier are the hands of a lover. Spenser assumed these chaps could easily become *mackerels* (gigolos).

They began, in unison. And in their own language, addressing a stream of remarks to me. I had to ask them to speak one at a time.

After a second's pause, the Frenchman proclaimed he would defer, and, in tribute to the sacred Allied unity, let Spenser begin. He accompanied this verbal bouquet with an eloquent gesture.

Spenser received his secession as right and proper.

In practical and straightforward manner, he began to proceed to illuminate his visitor. He pointed to a photograph of what we took for a newly discovered German battery.

"Mais, c'est une fausee, c'est trés eveident!" exclaimed the Frenchman, putting a hand to his hip in self-assurance.

"He says it's a dummy, "I translated.

"A dummy, he says! How does he think that?"

The Frenchman tapped the photo with his finger. "*Pas des herbes roties. pas des traces assez profoundes.*"

"No burnt grass, no tyre tracks deep enough," I translated.

They stared at each other. The Frenchman did not back down, Spenser did. It had been chauvinistic of him to assume the superiority of British know-how in the face of the French pioneering the art of photographic reconnaissance. They were also the race which had perfected *trompe d'oeil*, familiarly known as camouflage.

Now, while the atmosphere was not exactly the arm-in-arm with which General Joffre referred to our forces, for certain nationalistic attitudes remained, Spenser tried enact the laconic Britisher, the Frenchman, a practitioner of *élan*.

After we finished, I asked our visitor if he would like a cup of tea.

"*Une peu de la chaleur aujourd'hui, Mademsoiselle, n'est pas?*"

By heat he was not referring to the weather.

As he walked toward his aircraft, he said, "*Á bientôt, Mademoiselle, je vous porterai des fleurs, la prochaine fois!*"

Court may not have understood the words, but he understood the sentiment. He muttered to his retreating back, "This is your country, old man! Find yourself your own woman!"

The last event was the most august. We heard a plane approaching; Court raised his binoculars. "It's a DH2," he said. "Call Brand. It may be Hawker." Lanöe Hawker was a nearly legendary figure: holder of the V.C., inventor, strategist; a fighter who embodied his later instructions, able to show his pilots how to get their DH2's out of a spin. Now the DH2's lower speed, which was accompanied by greater maneuverability, made it a fine escort for reconnaissance aircraft. For his high -spirited squadron mates, he had designed a curtained bottom for the mess tent so officers with too much of a skin full to walk, could just roll out.

"Let's see what he's got this time, "said Court, who, like Hawker, was a Royal Engineer. With an aura of displeasure, Court noted, "He wanted to mount two guns, but Splash nixed it.—I've heard he may have made a double drum for manufacture."

Down came the DH2 straight as an arrow, with a beautiful three-point landing. Brand was now on the tarmac, and walked over as the machine came to a stop. There were evident warm greetings; Hawker was still wearing the thigh high boots he had invented. The conversation was private: they stayed beside Hawker's machine.

When he took off again, Brand walked over. "Lovely chap. He always says we do the most dangerous flying. And he's right, of course."

CHAPTER 55

After dinner, Bonnie said, "Be careful, Monsieur does not wish any tales to be told. You must remember, the Germans have been here for two years and they have been good customers and he doesn't want the wife scaring them off. You've seen that big Bouvier he has tied up outside?"

"Yes, of course."

"He'll load him up with goodies and send him across."

"Good Lord."

"Food has no boundaries!" she said with a laugh.

"Doesn't it bother you Germans may have been eating supper downstairs?"

"I suppose I should. Don't worry, when our casualties start coming in, I will."

"I have a friend who is with the Royal Army Medical Corps," I ventured.

"You've had a letter from him since we've been here, am I right?" No use trying to hide an envelope.

"Yes. He thinks he may be posted up here."

"Has he got a specialty?" asked my nurse.

"He was doing studies to be an alienist," I said.

"He'll get plenty of practice here."

"Max is also a third order Franciscan," I added. "We used to play music together in hospitals."

"That is the violin, then?"

"Yes. "

"Somehow I feel you knew the Major before you came here."

"Yes, "I said. "Our families are both in banking so his family looked us up when we came to London. I think they felt I'd be safer with someone who'd look after me. I am an experiment! The R.F.C. wants to know if it could use women to replace some of their ground personnel. It's even better that I am a neutral of course—I can write home about what is happening."

"You know that is what you are doing?"

"Bonnie, people like me never know what the upper levels of the government are thinking."

"You seem very much involved."

"We are. My aunt, my cousin and I have been here since the beginning."

CHAPTER 56

Bonnie held that Madame would relent of injuring her brother, and would enlist us to come with her. Bonnie had been right. After five days, Madame came to me to ask if I—or if we—would accompany her to see her brother.

"Why does she need both of us?" I asked.

"One each side to protect her from the fofus!"

"What are they?"

"Wandering souls."

"Oh."

"Yes, the old people still believe in werewolves, men who change into werewolves in foggy weather, and so on. Scotland is just as bad."

In the evening after supper we set out. Despite the sounds of artillery rising and lowering, we heard the birds starting to quiet down. The imminent sense of an unknown horror was moving closer. It was hard to realize that soon Bonnie would be leaving us to move over to the Casualty Clearing Station, which was just now beginning its set-up. The only thing to counter everything was the smell of chicken stew Madame carried for extra incentive.

It was a very small stone church, built in far simpler times; it possessed an attitude of having been thrown together. There was a bell to ring. Père Anton answered our summons, and did not seem surprised to see us.

"Come in, come in."

"Anton—*mon père*—" Madame was unsure how to address him in his official capacity. Unable to stand the pressure any more, she burst out, "I have come to ask your forgiveness! I behaved ab—ab"—-

—"ominably!" said her brother, finishing the word for her.

"I am very sorry. PLEASE come back to our home!"

"It isn't the same without you, "added Bonnie—which certainly was true.

"I've brought you some strew!" cried Madame.

"Quel pot-du-vin," said her brother with a smile. "What bribery, indeed! I know you are nervous because soon the offensive will start."

"My husband will still be selling goodies to the Germans, I am sure," she replied.

"*Il sera un vrad funambule,*" said the Curé calmly. He will be a true tightrope walker. Apparently he did appreciate his brother-in-law's business skills. It would be a tricky business and his sister was not happy at the idea. Yes, he would come back; it would be a delicate balance to maintain. The three of us heaved sighs of relief.

It was early one morning after his return –Monsieur was not oblivious to the fact his presence gave an element of neutrality—that, early one morning, the Curé was sitting alone in the garden. I asked if I might sit down with him, and he nodded, "*Bien sûr.*" I had not been sleeping well during the last week, as Sir Henry's mission was bothering my mind.

I noticed his worn shoes poking out from beneath his *soutaine* and something about his presence seemed to be encouraging me to talk to him, as if he'd appeared from some unknown summons.

"My friend Max told me there was some prophecy that France would have to suffer?" I asked.

"Ah, yes!" he laughed. "If she does not mend her ways, stop cursing, go to Mass—instead we have Tiger Clemenceau!"

"Is prophecy commonplace in France?

"Not commonplace, but understood to happen—of course!"

"How do we know if one is true?"

"Alas, only by its fruits—there is one that a queen would destroy France, and then France would be delivered by a virgin from an oak grove, which is La Pucelle—our Joan."

"I have always been fascinated by that business of another Moses and another Elijah," I remarked. Then I took the plunge. "What if there were another Guillem de Mossac?" I asked.

"What if 'that which has been is now, and that which is now to be has already been?' And if you displace Guillem from the past to the present, then there must be another domna—another lady—who would try to warn him," he replied.

"Yes," I said, squirming uncomfortably.

"Perhaps if she is warning him, she might come under a cloud as well, is this not true?"

"The politics of how to warn someone isn't altogether simple, "I said.

"So she, too, has a drama."

"I suppose she could not be perfectly sure of what he'll think about her warnings—perhaps it is better not to...?"

"Not tell him? To live in an unspoken truth is a form of a lie. I do not have to tell you whose language that is. There is a dark veil across this for you?"

"Yes."

"Such darkness is not unknown in the spiritual life. Then we can only follow what we are told."

We went inside for breakfast. When my ride came, as I got up, he made the sign of the Cross over me.

At the aerodrome, I hurried over to Brand's office and crashed in. Court was there, talking with him, but when he saw the expression on my face, he vacated immediately. I began to talk in a low voice so we would not be overheard; he got up and shut the door. Then he sat down again; there were dark shadows under his eyes which gave them a haunted, sorrowful look.

"What is it?"

"Do you know that people with German relatives are sometimes observed by British intelligence.?"

"I have no doubt Henry has a tail on mother."

"Not just your mother!"

"Am I being watched, too?"

"Yes."

"And by who?"

"Me."

"Dear God!"

"Are you angry?"

"I am furious, Amanda!!" His eyes were fierce. "What did they tell you to make you keep that QUIET?""

"That I would be the most likely person to be interested in the outcome. That you would kill me if you were who they think you might be."

"And you believed THAT?"

"What I believed is that if you really were a spy, I'd rather be dead."

"Someone else could have made a false report. Sometimes you are too honest for your own good! How were you to find this out?"

"I have the top secret code."

"I don't believe I've even used it since you have been here!"

"No, you haven't. It was something else that convinced me you are in the clear."

"Which is...?"

"They were only thinking of England. When I saw you and 'Xiema together, it struck me you would never betray France. That's all."

"Give me some time to calm down and think. When you bring me the bumfs to sign we'll talk further?"

There were, as usual, a pile of papers to sign; and to give us more time, he signed them himself with his now-recognizable left hand scrawl.

He commenced in a very low tone; I had to bend down to hear him. "What I do think is that they may be after father, and are ready to use every tiny bit of leverage."

"Why?"

"He has become quite involved in air matters and his view that that the two services should combine is most unpopular, especially with the Navy, as they have the private contractors in their pocket. But in the immediate there is this damn Bailhache committee, with Pemberton-Billings shooting off his mouth."

"Yes, I heard them discussing him when I was at Eastchurch."

"Now this Billings chap says our BE2's are so inferior our pilots are being murdered, not killed. What a jolly thing it is to tell our pilots!"

"Isn't that awful in the middle of a war!"

"It's business or politics as usual to a lot of chaps, may they rot in hell." His face turned savage.

Suddenly, his look changed to one of satisfaction.

"Mandra, I think we can leverage this in our favor! They are examining the BE2's—and we have two whole flights of them. It would be a reasonable request for father to come see them in the field."

"Do you think so?"

"A refusal would only cause more bad blood."

"But how can we reach him?"

"Telegraph from Amiens. I'll send it."

CHAPTER 58

'Arriving Hôtel du Rhin tomorrow.'

So we set out on the Route Nationale, the *pavè* rumbling under our tyres. We passed La Houssoye, Harvey-Kelly's Squadron 3, with their Moranes, to the Route Nationale below Albert. Amiens was sixteen miles behind the Front so it did At that point Amiens not receive barrages; on the other hand, Albert was completely deserted.

We passed the sentry at Querrieux, the one curve in the long road, a chateau which housed the headquarters of Fourth Army. The park was filled with linden trees, and vaguely as they moved one could see a large brick chateau beyond, where General Rawlinson sat in the front room, sitting on a wooden chair, with maps spread out on a wooden table. The rest of the small room was taken up by bookcases.

There was Brand's father, immaculate as ever. Smoking a cigar and reading the newspaper, it looked as if the slightest piece of dust would be mysteriously prevented from landing on him. He was shooing away a large goose which kept trying to peck at him in a quest for something to eat.

I was quite different from the young lady he had met before. My skin, which had never been exposed to the sun before, was slightly tan, and my once smart outfit worn, especially a side seam in my once-smart boots; my hair had bleached to light blonde and was braided into one pigtail which Bonnie helped me make every morning.

Seeing us, the Viscount waved down the head waiter, a man with a distinctively forked beard, who, behind his back, was called von Tirpitz after the admiral of the German navy who sported a similar beard.

"Service *au grossiot!*" Service for the big shot, he told one of his subluminaries. The Viscount discarded his cigar, which was promptly pecked at by the goose until deciding it was not his meat.

"He appears not to have your taste in tobacco," Brand observed to his father, with a smile.

"Is this BE thing what this is really about?" his father asked.

"No," said Brand.

"Shall we go up to the room?" his father asked.

"It would probably be the most private spot, even if it is right across from Intelligence. We can watch the red tabs coming and going."

His father smiled. "I agree. It certainly has the virtue of impudence!"

We entered a shaky elevator and each said a silent prayer it would not fall apart while we were *en voyage*.

The Viscount's room was rather ornate, in the style of the time, with heavy, fancy curtains and a heavily mattressed bed. As we entered, he sniffed appreciatively, for the scent of thyme still hung in the air. The French still used it as an insecticide.

"Now then, what's this all about?" Brand's father asked, as we were seated.

I told him about Operation Dactylist and my injunction to watch his son.

"Amanda told me Henry said if your aunt did not have an answer she would not rest until I got one. That is true. I knew you were in France. Was there more to this interchange?" asked Brand's father.

"Oh, yes, that when I returned from France I would go to America and give talks on the war," I said dismissively.

"Ah! There you have it!" said the Viscount. "They are using every bit of pull they can manage to get America into the war—which of course you would know from his approaches to your aunt. Had he asked you to simply go and come back with your impressions and make a tour, of course, you would have said no. He had to bait the hook with something better. Believe me, they will use whatever comes to hand."

"And—if anything happened to her—" Brand managed.

"It would be immaterial, my boy. Henry could use her for a martyr."

"Bugger. Perhaps she should—"

"No," I said. "Or he will understand the cat is out of the bag." Then I added, "I guess I was naive?"

"Not really, my dear. They built up a presentation sufficient to alarm you that Brand may have been in danger."

"Henry did this so he could use it somehow?"

"I don't know what the 'somehow' is, but believe me, there is one. Fortunately, he has also provided us with an example of low ball politics."

"It's a Mexican standoff, then?" I asked. They both smiled at my idiom.

"Shall we move to the aerodrome?"

"Indeed." The Viscount's man, Johnstone, appeared, handing his employer a small bag containing necessities like a razor, hair-brush pyjamas and a toothbrush.

Once in the squadron motor, we began to inch our way through the crowd of men milling in and out of bookstores, barber shops, oyster shops, and establishments which sold *tuiles d'Amiens* macaroons, and wine. More than one man was *un peu étoile*, starry-eyes drunk, and in no mood to grant us right of way. Several times Brand had to get out and remonstrate with someone or other to move. Sometimes it took the recalcitrant time to realize he was outranked; sometimes, he received a humorous rendition of a salute.

As he regained our motor, he turned back for a good look at the cathedral, which was several streets to our left of the hotel. Perhaps his glance even wondered to the street parallel to *l'Amiral Courbet,* on which stood the *Palais de Justice,* which housed the worst invalided cases of the war. It was a fate every soldier dreaded so much it was mainly unspoken.

But before we left, I asked, "Do you want to ride by the theatre again?"

Amiens had the oldest theatre built in France, so, of course, he was attached to it!

I drove him by 59 Rue des Trois-Cailloux so Brand could point it out, graceful building that it was, with its three large -arched windows with doors set beneath them to his father.

Then we turned around and faced ahead, and let civilization slip away behind us once more.

The ruins of wheat, barley and potatoes began to appear on both sides of the road. To our right, more and more appurtenances of the coming offensive were springing up, and we saw some earth-colored camouflage Red Cross tents. Ahead was the Hanging Virgin at 'Bert.'

"We must keep up the Bailhache bit," his father noted; and apparently the news had already spread, for as we turned into the aerodrome, we saw several motors parked by the farmhouse.

"Brass from *Les Alençons,*" said Brand.

"Bigger fish, my boy," said his father, nodding toward a middle-aged balding man standing in the midst of General 'Splash' Ashmore's emissaries, his hat beneath his arm. However, they did not notice us. Brand had, as would be natural, left Courtenay in charge, and the upturned eyes were watching him perform what Lanöe Hawker called 'the BE2's party trick,' a tail slide. Court had contacted Harvey-Kelly at La Houssoye when we passed. Court got into the air.

He was beginning to level off, but the nose was still up; he was still climbing vertically. Then the switch would be thrown to idle and the upward thrust stopped. He hung, neutralized for seconds, between heaven and earth, stripped of all force save gravity. His tail began to slip down toward us. A murmur from the crowd. He flipped the nose over, and something tipped his lateral balance for a moment but he corrected it without even a glance at his bubble. He plunged down and came out level, once again in the embrace of CP, CG, and angle of incidence.

"Bully show, old boy, "murmured Brand.

The watchers, who had been standing stock-still, began to move and look around them. When we got down, the balding man replaced his hat, came over to us, and rendered a salute, which Brand returned with his left hand.

"Trenchard sends his compliments," said Maurice Baring.

How charming!" said Brand's father, with a faint smile. Trenchard's scorn for committees was well-known.

I was sent to the transport line, to send transport for Johnstone to the chateau.

To my amazement, when I returned, having been tactfully removed from introductions, I found the group huddled together planning a dinner! They were smiling as if the universe was just as pleased by their notion as they were, as if this ceremony should elicit the admiration of the gods.

"Will you be giving us a bit of verse, Maurice?" Brand was asking.

"Ah, Shaw's beat me to *arma virumque cano*," replied Baring. "Or even *omnia Gallia divisa est.*"

"All the better, it leaves you plenty of room for inspiration."

"I trust you will enjoy your visit to Samarobrivia," Baring said to Brand's father. Fearing from his reference to Amiens of Gallic days that Baring was about to launch into Latin, the Viscount replied, "There are those of us who do not use our Latin as often as you communicants of the church of Rome."

Then there were introductions all around, hand shaking and saluting. Top brass staff was here, but not the top top brass; no one wanted to steal the Viscount's thunder. They would, however, make an appearance later.

I was dispatched with the Viscount to show him the way to Monsieur's store; we turned down a dirt road flanked by elderberry bushes readying to send forth white blossoms. The store's windows had been shattered long since, and Monsieur had replaced the glass with paper for the duration.

As we walked along, Brand's father said, "I want to show these boys some appreciation. Here they are stuck with flying a machine which has been malignantly maligned. It's bloody awful."

Stooping slightly to avoid hitting his hat on the top of the door, Brand's father stepped inside, running his eyes over the rows of preserves, the Gaulloise cigarettes, the tinned goods of paté, meat, and the rarer vegetables. Monsieur came in, wiping his hands on his apron. He smiled to see me, then stopped, caught unaware by the viscount's resplendence.

"This is the Major's father, "I said.

"Ah," he said. "The English milord." He extended his hand. Brand's father wore gloves, whether to finish his appearance or to avoid contact with anything unhygienic: in either case, he likewise extended his hand. He had the fated look of a man who expected to be overcharged.

He sketched out his needs succinctly: hors d'oeuvres, soup, fish, meat, potatoes, vegetable, cheese and dessert. If Monsieur had any local specialties to suggest, he was open to suggestion.

"There is wild duck, coot, heron, pork, rabbit; eels, too, although he thought they were *hors le gout anglaise* of this particular slice of society; paté of course, fruit with *lait bouilli.*"

"What have you got for fish?"

Monsieur had the French version of Dover sole. And a few local fish.

"Look at the bruises on the, man!"

"I have only one old man with a *barque* and a French aviator who drops bombs on the river, and the *èclat* kills the fish," said Monsieur apologetically.

"*Poisson obu—shellfish,* the Viscount murmured softly to himself with a slight smile. "I suspect there is an enjoyable sauce to cover the bruises?"

"*D'accord.*"

They settled on a hypothetical menu and the Viscount asked him to quote him a price. Monsieur scribbled figures on the brown paper he used to wrap parcels. Then he announced the result, while the Viscount reached inside his suit coat for the francs on which wartime France ran. Cash on the barrelhead. Devil take cheques or promissory notes.

"I take it you enjoy a monopoly." He said this as acidly as a man could who believes he has his finger on the fluctuating pulse of commodities from New York to Shanghai.

"It may sound inflated," replied the storekeeper, "but, milord it is *au prix òu est le beurre,* which your son can ascertain to you. (Yes, it was the price butter was at). "No matter how much I would like to overcharge you, custom prevents me, your son has been a guest at our house, likewise the mademoiselle. One does not violate such personal connections."

"*J'ai peur que je fisse une bêtise.*" The Viscount was afraid he had made a gaffe.

"No, no, *vous ne êtes pas un äus.*" No, his customer was not a shilly shally shopper; he'd come straight to the bargain without any of the small talk, which might be intended to soften a merchant up.

"Let me see," said Brand's father. "What about plates and glassware?" He hadn't seen the Mess hall yet, but he knew it was in a chateau.

"I have the stock from the chateau safely hidden," said monsieur slowly, with a certain delight.

"If we set an assurance fee against possible breakage?"

"Better than that *francfileur* deserves!" This was said with all the scorn of a royalist sympathizer for a local noble who had fled his chateau.

"Let's say—" said Brand's father, and mentioned a more than generous fee. We all knew something would get broken!

"Now, as to wine—"

The Viscount sighed. "I'm afraid these young bloods think only of one thing, and that's champagne. Ah well. *Mieux que la gnole.*" Better than the French white lightning of his youth.

He and Monsieur sighed together, as if seeing glasses for Madeira, Claret, Bordeaux, Burgundy from famous vintages and for the Rhine whites, disappearing from the properly set tables they still held in mind.

"These poor lads haven't had the leisure for the *finesse* of bygone days."

"*Dommage, ils ne sauront rien.*" Monsieur was not commenting on a public school education, but a generations' deprivation of gustatory knowledge.

Like a commander deploying his forces into the field, Monsieur continued to write. He might be a bourgeois, but as a merchant, he had knowledge of the finer things by his exposure to the tastes of his unbidden guests. "All will be ready tomorrow night," he pronounced. Clearly he had developed a backup personnel.

Back at the aerodrome, Brand remarked to his father that his mother must have ceased to be ammunition for Henry any more, as he understood that she rarely left the house.

"I'm afraid that isn't so. She's become interested in ameliorating the conditions of some detainees on the Isle of Man. Part of the process for constructing envelopes for Navy airships is done there, at Douglas town; I'm sure Henry has an eye for that."

"And you allow it?"

"In the same manner I allowed 'The Rites of Discount.'"

"Aren't you walking a thin line, father?"

"I am. But I've friends who will warn me if there is any talk of internment. I've moved funds to Switzerland. There is a little village near the mountains. We've already been living quite differently than before the war."

That is why Vessey is essential.

Then it was time for Brand to go over to the farmhouse and assign the day's afternoon patrols, —and time for him to wonder which of them would be back again.

"Shall I be permitted to watch the afternoon take-off?" his father asked his son.

"You can see whatever you like. You have permission to be here. Let Amanda take you around. Chambers be rotted. He can handle all the work for one day."

At the edge of the tarmac, Court asked our distinguished visitor if he would like to watch the patrol figure for the needed petrol against the anemometer. Their machines had half an hour before take-off get engines were tested and ready.

"What is your formula, Captain?"

"Mean average twenty miles per hour for the wind, put against our hourly readings for each day on the anemometer. When the force of the wind is with you, going over, you will need less petrol, but, coming back, the west wind is against you, and you will need more. You add or subtract from the mean average. Fuel consumption is about 7 ½ liters an hour, 6 ½ if we fly lower." Court added, "The artillery observation must also provide batteries with force of wind and wind temperature where they are."

"The force of the wind today is?"

"Thirty miles per hour."

Nick had a pencil and paper, but before he had figured things out, on paper, Brand's father had figured it in his head. Nick stopped in mid-calculation. The Viscount waved a hand. "No, go and check against me Captain, one should never run a column only once on something this important."

Then Court showed Brand's father how he had adjusted his dihedral to make maneuvering in his BE. easier. After this, he was running a short lecture to our newbies. Beneath his ladder to the cockpit stood an Ack-Emma holding a baragraph. He was demonstrating how to check the accuracy of altimeters. This is involved showing new recruits how to set up the recording cylinder, how to equip the stylus with ink, and how to engage the gear which brought the pen against the paper-wrapped cylinder at the push of a lynch pin.

The veterans glanced away, lit cigarettes, pushed toes of boots into the grass, waiting for the schoolmastering to be over. They knew the discourse would move on to the rev-counter check for worn springs against the air speed indicator, and finally, the compass. A pile of small boards and screw magnets were on the grass for making any corrections in deviations, along with an alidade to facilitate checking compass points on the ground with its sight and straight edge.

Earlier that day, I had walked over to Court's BE fuselage. The joy stick was tied down; a short wind whistled against the wings and wires, electing an occasion a soft squeak from its pulleys and turnbuckles. I saw a line of small linen squares near the trailing edge of the top planes and smelled the dope which had been used to put them on. A little closer and a little lower and the bullets would have hit the pilot. I stepped into the shade of her dihedral and patted her on the lacings. I could faintly sniff the smell of gun powder.

He would tick off his crew for not having blown out the Pitot tube to his satisfaction; he would eat a very small lunch, he would lie down his batman would shake him, and he'd be up again for an afternoon patrol.

"I expect this came about as you are a Royal Engineer!" Said Brand's father, who paused and added, "Captain, have you written this down somewhere?"

"No, it's all in my head."

"Could you write it down for me? I purpose to show it to a few people."

Now the patrol began to suit up. Brand's father stood next to Court's machine watching the pre-ignition procedure as the mechanic twirled the machine for the suck in of fuel, as well as using a priming gun. Court motioned him to step back before he threw the switch for Contact. The roar of engines blotted out all other noise: Court's pennons whipped in the slipstream. The flight would rendez-vous at a fixed point in the air.

He raised his fist and the group began to taxi. Off they went, and we watched until they were out of sight.

Then I took him over to the hangars. Here a BE2c had been unlaced, much like a lady getting out of her corset. It revealed her longerons and the jointure of her two sections of fuselage. Since German tactics were always to shoot the pilot, Sergeant Wilson always checked this connecting point right below the pilot's cockpit with the greatest of care.

They discussed the observer's downward view from "Stability Jane." The Royal Aircraft Factory had already set the bottom wing back several feet; this stagger adjustment had minimally improved things, although its purpose had been aerodynamic rather than for visibility's sake. Now, the Factory was at work yet again, decreasing the size of the bottom wing and increasing surface area of the top wing. A Jane so modified was designated a BETUCI become a BETUF on our squadron forms for the Aircraft Depots.

Now, I bid Brand and his father a good night, as they were going to Mess at the chateau.

At our dinner, Madame asked Bonnie and I if we could help preparing the dinner for the officers in the chateau kitchen. She had three women to help her, *bien sûr,* but this was an elegant menu.

"I will ask the Major," I replied. (The Major was agreeable to letting me off early, in mid-afternoon).

CHAPTER 59

Bonnie Sue was waiting for me on what had once been a lawn with plantings in front of the chateau, and the waterless fountain.

"Follow me!" she said. She had come to take me to the chateau kitchen which was partially underground. It covered a vast amount of space, had a gigantic open fireplace for roasting, various tables upon which do various chores, and scores of copper pots and pans hanging from the walls. The table closest to us had people skinning the fish prior to soaking them in milk.

"We're assigned to vegetables," said my roommate.

She led me to a table piled with potatoes, peas in their shells, and asparagus. I stopped at the table with no idea what to do. Madame darted over and told me to first peel the potatoes.

"How do I do that?" I asked humbly.

"*Regardez!*" She picked up a small tool and the peels began to fly off the potatoes. "You have never peeled a potato?" she inquired incredulously

No, I never had. In fact I had never really cooked anything. I began to peel at an abysmally slow speed. Bonnie watched for a few moments then said, "Let me take that over. You can shell the peas. That is easier."

I realized that my inexperience had made me a slight handicap, and was tremendously embarrassed. Bonnie could even talk as she peeled!

"Is that true, you never have peeled a potato?"

"I'm afraid it is." In some societies this would have made my status clear, but here it only made me a nuisance. I was all thumbs.

"*Faites attention!*" She cried over to the fish table. She pointed to a cat which was slinking under the table.

"We need something to focus on so this won't be so boring," she added. I noticed that at one table the workers were singing softly.

Meanwhile it was slowly sinking in just how much work went into feeding a family like ours day in and out. Clearly now I realized how above average our meals were. I thought of Violet. How she loved a fresh piece of cake! Slowly my thumbs were beginning to ache from opening so many pea pods. And after this would come a formidable washing up.

I was overcome by a feeling of shame; I looked down so no one would notice the few tears this revelation was occasioned by. No one did but Bonnie, of course: and she asked what was the matter.

"I feel so useless, "I said softly.

"It's not your fault the way you were raised, "she remarked.

"I know it isn't, but how can I go on like that if I live through this war?"

"It seems to me you can live any way you want," said Bonnie. "Though I don't guess many people would be upset by not having to do chores!"

"How did these things get done in your family?"

"Oh, the cook had a night off once a week and mother cooked and got us to help her. And of course, being a nurse, we learned to scrub everything! That had to be done correctly—better than a housemaid would do it."

She said with a smile, "Tell me, how did you get here, anyway? You're from a neutral country."

"My Uncle Benjamen died, and his wife—my Aunt Bea—decided to travel a bit to help her with her mourning, so she brought her daughter, my cousin Becky, with her, and I came along to keep Becky company."

"And how did that work out?"

"At first it was –trying, because my aunt seemed to feel she was the only one that had a right to feel sad. But when the war began that began to change."

"How?"

"She began to belong to this religious group and she got more sympathetic to people's problems, starting with some refugees, and then working with Herbert Hoover, who is also from America; he started the

Committee for the Relief of Belgium, which feeds people who would otherwise probably be starving, and it changed her a lot. It changed us, too. I joined a folklore group that played the sort of music I learned from my uncle, and I met a Franciscan named Max—the one my letter just came from--and we started to play at hospitals together. And then I had nightmares so I had to stay up at night and I joined a Zeppelin tracing group, then a Naval chap suggested I learn Morse code, so I did that, then I came here."

"What do your people back home think of all that?"

"Oh, they are not too happy, but then they don't know the whole of it, either."

"What are your people like?"

"We are of Dutch descent, and we are Dutch Reformed, and we live in New York City, and the family has been in banking for several generations.

"We live close to each other, and my uncle and aunt lived on the same street, and my uncle was very dedicated to the folklore movement in America, and collected all sorts of songs, and taught them to me, and we played together, and I was always practicing, I don't think my parents were too happy about that, but they didn't want to start a fuss, so I just kept going over to my aunt and uncle's and kept learning new songs. Sometimes I could even go with my uncle to some of the gatherings. "

"Did you go to school?"

"No, we had tutors."

"It sounds a bit—grim!"

"Oh well we are a very religious family so we don't do many things other people in New York do—that's the way it is."

"This is very different than all of that, isn't it?"

"Yes, it has made a lot of changes for me."

"Are they going to marry you off?"

"They have always had someone—the same boy—in mind for me, but I don't think I want to marry him."

"Did you meet someone?"

"Yes, I met someone."

"And who is that, pray tell?"

"I can't really say."

"You don't have to. It's the Major, isn't it?"

"We've tried very hard not to let on. Is it obvious?"

"Not really—it's just that I know you better than anyone else here!"

"He's very busy now."

"I'd say so!"

"No one really knows if either one of us or both will survive the war, of course."

"That must be awful."

"So many people are in the same situation. There is a path that seems guide us. It comes from the music my uncle taught me."

Suddenly, I thought of my uncle. Tears sprung into my eyes; I had never had my own chance to mourn him, we were all so busy minding to my aunt. Soon the tears were running down my cheeks.

"What's the matter?"

"I just thought of my uncle. If it hadn't been for him, I would simply be another Dutch girl living in New York City." I wiped my face with my sleeve.

"How did you get here? You left that out."

"No one knows exactly where I am, not even my aunt."

"It's a secret, is it?"

"Yes," I said. "Yes, it's a secret."

"A secret that lets you be with him."

"Yes, it does, and I take some comfort from believing that if everything here gets mucked up chances are both of us might be killed."

"Yes, "said Bonnie. "All of us who are up so close to whatever is going to happen have considered that."

"A few days ago, Brand told me to go and find the Curé if there is a breakthrough. I promised that I would so he wouldn't worry."

"Would you?"

"I don't know. How can you know what you would do in a situation like that?"

"He may be thinking what a horde of violent men might do if they caught hold of you, "she said realistically.

I was silent. We all had heard stories of German atrocities. I sighed and kept on shucking. Bonnie's pile of potatoes which she was now cutting into shape for *pommes* frites was also growing.

"The thing is when you are forced up against all this, a lot just drops away and doesn't have much meaning," I said finally.

'Yes, "said Bonnie. "That's a state of being that I like. When my casualties come in and I am tending to them, little else does indeed matter. All that matters will be the present moment."

"What about you, Bonnie?"

"I will stay with my patients."

"How do you know that?"

"Oh, in emergencies I have become so exhausted and so involved that one hardly has any sense of reality except the one you are in. It's a kind of gift."

"But what about your family?"

"They would understand. They understand the demands of medicine."

"That must be very strengthening."

"Yes, it is. You have no regrets."

"That's amazing."

"It gives you a freedom to live your life."

"Are you Presbyterians?"

"Of course!" She replied with a laugh.

"Does that allow you not to fear death?"

"Only when I think about it. You'd be a fool not to worry where you might end up!"

"At times I wonder whether I am being selfish not to want to go on living for years and years with Brand gone," I said.

Madame came to us to inform us her brother was coming to give dinner his blessing.

"That's good for a last supper!" said Bonnie.

She had just given a name to what was about to happen.

CHAPTER 60

It was raining in Picardy. The hand of fate, in the guise of bad weather, had overturned some of the best-laid plans in military history.

Scores of wells had been dug, six and eight inch water pipes laid, miles of railway tracks put down, tons of guns brought up, more tons of shells stockpiled in depots, and forward dumps stocked with military supplies for advancing soldiers. The plan of attack was the brainchild of General Rawlinson, our commander of Fourth Army, and approved by General Haig; it was not a new plan; it was one used the spring of 1915, an intensive artillery barrage preceding an infantry attack. Theoretically, our guns would flatten the German defenses and cut their barbed wire. Then our infantry would just walk over and take the German lines.

General Haig and General Trenchard moved up to forward headquarters, Haig to Chateau Val Vion, Beauquesne, Trenchard to Chateau Auchy aux Bois, Fienvillers. This was General Haig's first full command, and it was not at the time or place he wanted to attack; the tactics were not the ones he would have used, nor were any forward trenches dug to get his men closer to enemy trenches.

The attack was scheduled for the end of June, but on the 23rd, there was a freak thunderstorm, which blew snow into our fliers' faces, hit observation balloons with lightening, and turned the topsoil into a quagmire. In front of us, the eighteenth and thirtieth divisions, the latter of men from Liverpool and Manchester, hugged tightly to the French on their right side. Behind the two divisions were reserve forces. To the north, General Allenby was to make a feint at Gommecourt which fooled no one. The three divisions in our center were backed up by cavalry in reserve, in case a breakthrough could be made after the infantry had quelled the opposition.

On the 24th, artillery was scheduled to begin intensified fire, but clouds and rain hampered spotting, reducing us to intermittent flying. The next day, the weather cleared enough at 3:30 that, as pre-arranged, all guns stopped fire for an hour, and reconnaissance flights sped out for a good look around. Briefs from Fienvillers told us five of Jerry's observation balloons had been shot down. This may have granted us a brief spirit of optimism, which was rapidly eroded in the next four days, when the weather grew worse.

Almost hourly, Brand had to decide whether or not to order men up; day and night, he was inundated with telephone calls whose level of frustration implied any calculations about margins of safety verged on cowardice. He stopped eating anything but soft -boiled eggs and drinking warm milk because his stomach was made even more raw by tea or liquor.

Our connection with the men on the ground, which made escort pilots refer to reconnaissance fliers as the Lice Patrol—made us touchy about our inability to perform our duty for Tommy Atkins, who was counting on us for the success or failure.

Royal Artillery was using its 18 pounder guns to cut the barbed wire for this task, the most important one of the offensive. If there were not enough holes in the wire, men could easily be enfiladed and killed by machine gun fire. Artillery had not chosen to use shrapnel; they were overruled by Headquarters.

Eighteen pounder shells had time fuses. The fuse had to be properly set which was an art in itself. The nose of an 18 pounder shell was loaded with shrapnel which had been embedded in rosin. The pellets had to be exploded out of the shell at a certain height and certain distance from the wire to cut it on the graze.

If a shell did not explode correctly, with the shell dropping off as the pellets exploded, shell and shrapnel would fall into the mud together. The impact would often explode the casing, and splinters would fly about, giving the illusion of a scatter of shot; but the swathe of the shrapnel would have been completely absorbed by the tumble into the wet earth. Such a fall into wet earth was termed a point of impact, and difficult to tell from a point of explosion. The puff of smoke given off by the fuse was small, and shifted quickly with the wind. For this reason, Phillips would not let his men use field glasses, for they would lose track of a point of impact or explosion trying to focus on them.

Phillips was worried over the 18 pounders, but most of his mind was on the 15 inch howitzers, the largest guns on our front. There were only six of them. Their trajectory was 11,000 yards. and thus they were outside the sights of ground observers, and set in soundproof dugouts. Of all the guns they were most dependent on the eyes in the skies, especially since there was substantial potential for aiming error.

"You should see the path of one of these babies," said Phillips. "The shells weigh 1400 pounds, with 200 pounds of explosive. It bends the trees as if there were a hurricane and blows tiles off the roofs."

The next day, he had a demand.

"Look here, skipper, we've had a call from a 15 inch howitzer. They know there is an ammunition dump about 6 miles back; our trajectory can just reach it. Battery is sending over a map. It's in a hollow in a woods and without aerial observation they cannot hit it. He'd like us to salvo the two points of high ground on either side, so they can get the coordinates for their line of fire with the distance between the two units of measure."

Brand grunted. "We shall think about it when the weather lifts a bit more."

A few moments later, I saw Phillips cross from the farmhouse to the supply hut, his shoulders hunched against the rain. Any airplane that flew in heavy rain needed a replacement for its prop, but somehow I thought nothing of it.

I did wonder why he rang someone up while both Chambers and I were out of the room, and I came back, and surprised him.

Then, we saw him on the tarmac, struggling to get off the wet ground in a bad wind in his BE2C. Brand began pacing up and down. "I hope the blighter gets back. It will be hard to replace him as captain of our art obs flight."

He was tired and he was frustrated, still with one arm in a sling, a useless bird, even though the R.F.C. had ordered that commanding officers not fly. I couldn't think of anything to say that might be helpful so I didn't say anything.

An hour later, the phone rang. It was news from the 15 inch battery.

It was Phillips. Whether he'd gone lower than he intended, whether his altimeter misfunctioned, whether the battery commander did not calculate aright, whether he'd turned too soon in his traverse, or did not have the safeguard of clear weather in which to see the big shells coming end over end, we never knew. But the battery commander's voice was shaking on the wire. Nothing remained of someone you saw only an hour ago and his machine.

I was aware of the tremor in Brand's cheek. "I must ask Fienvillers for a replacement," he said. His hand shook as he picked up the telephone receiver.

"Would you want Captain Courtenay to try to photograph the area, sir?" asked Chambers.

"No, "said Brand. "I don't want to chance losing two flight commanders."

Around us, the landscape was magically appearing again, as the weather cleared into what John Buchan called 'A translucent blue summer evening.'

Soon enough, General Trenchard motored up in his Rolls, received salutes, and sitting on his shooting stick in our mess hall, gave our flying personnel a briefing from the Summary of Intelligence. The offensive would begin in the morning. Maurice Baring stood silently at his side. Brand thought that he was praying. General Haig, who was also a religious man, called Baring 'Nicodemeus'.

There was little sleep anywhere that night. In the hangars and workshops, our crews were working all night.

At Madame's, by three o'clock, all of us, save for Bonnie, who had left a few days earlier to go to her post, were in the kitchen.

Madame decided she would make fried eggs—*oeufs sur le plat*—and kept sprinkling water every few seconds to test whether the fat was hot enough. Finally Père Anton said, "Asperges me!" as if the pan were speaking. The increase in the barrage told us we were near the final hour. The ground was vibrating.

Suddenly I could wait no longer. I asked Monsieur if I could borrow his bicycle. He agreed. As I pedaled along, I was amazed to hear myself singing, "And the rockets' red glare, The bombs bursting in air..."

Ahead of me was a strange darkness, whose penumbra, made by the touch on the horizon of the rising sun, was heavy with smoke. The darkness was leached piebald by flashes of exploding guns and star shells. There was a light rain which would stop shortly. It was going to be a hot day. Already mists were rising into a ground haze which hung heaviest over the river and its bogs and marshes. The air was dense with dampness as though the earth was sweating off the moisture the rain had dropped on it over the last hundred and forty- four hours. One pilot said the mist was like a lake that had stones thrown into it which would represent artillery fire. For a short while it obscured the ground.

One flight of our squadron was up in anticipation of the final acceleration of the barrage at 6:30. General Rawlinson was already watching through binoculars. Sometime before this bedlam ceased seven mines which had been laid by sappers who'd tunneled for months underneath the ground, would be set off. They would send tons of earth heavenward. The last, and biggest, Kasino Mine, went off a bit late. The shock waves that passed through the earth were heard and felt on the other side of the English Chanel.

Then, there would be silence—a silence as dread and as anticipatory as the half hour in the Book of Revelation—and the barrage would stop.

The infantry would jump off and go over.

Then the guns would begin again. Batteries would re-sight and move ahead of the infantrymen in a pre-arranged series of lifts.

Contact patrol came back. Court reported that they had seen the 18th and 30th Divisions moving well ahead. He'd seen our men in the German front line trenches, and inching up the slope toward Montauban on Montauban Alley. When Montauban was taken, the only living thing there was a fox.

But they'd had none of the pre-arranged signals from the ground troops, some of whom had pieces of metal on their backs to throw off signal light.

"I suppose they think flashes will bring down German battery fire," said Court.

The barrage was lifting much too far ahead of the troops. There was no way to call it back to focus on German traversing machine gun fire.

However, Court could now fly over Monauban to pass over Trônes Wood, which lay between Guillemont on its right, and Bernafay Wood on its left. Our men had cleared Trônes Wood, and Generals Maxse and Congreve wanted permission to move in and consolidate the Wood, in conjunction with the French. They did not receive permission. The Germans were able to funnel back into Trônes Wood. Pushing on after a success was not utilized.

Of course, Brand was far too busy to give thought to me. I was wrong. One night he gave me a copy of Walton's 'Lives', with its sketch of John Donne. A little poem was laboriously written with his left hand on the fly leaf.

That vigorous intellect
Crowns a head already crowned
With an incongruous ringlet
Soft as feather's down
The same mix
Is in her gaze
It melts and it convicts
As though she were my end of days:
And when I look into her eyes

Love by love's then multiplied.

CHAPTER 61

Courteney was busy photographing the progress of the infantry. He had lost one member of his flight, and another had come to take his place.

The left side of the Fourth Army was in such bad shape Haig had broken it off, re-named it the Fifth Army, and put General Gough in command, who had orders just to keep it stable.

To Gough' s right, the Third Army lay still and broken. Its casualties were heavy, caused by having to cross Mash and Sausage valleys. It did not bode well for the center of the plan—the most important part.

Our part of the Front was doing well. The successful right of General Rawlinson's army pushed on this morning beyond the four- thousand -yard objective set for it, because this was the maximum effective range of the barrage. There were reserves behind them provided a breakthrough became possible.

The Germans had fallen back to their second line beween Pozières and Longueval the night before, and were counterattacking this morning. Our center had Pozières as an objective but failed to take it. To our right, the French were moving into Hardecourt aux Bois, moving nicely, bolstered by the XX Corp, the 'Iron Corps,' which was touching ours. They were nibbling toward Maltzhorn Farm, which they would take the following Sunday.

Meanwhile, their Fourth Army counterparts resisted a German counter-thrust and worked at pushing out toward Fricourt, Contalmaison, La Boiselle, and Ovillers, and all the various woods from which villagers exercised communal right to cut their wood. Court ranged over the ruined homes of Picardy, the old dwellings of Huguenot weavers and dyers who had used their pastel or woad plant to make their famous blue; over stumps of trees, ruined houses and holes in the ground.

Then he passed Lonely Copse, with bisecting German trenches, one which ran north and south into Fricourt, the other, east and west over Fricourt Farm.

After throwing back a German counter attack on Montauban, our troops were moving in to Caterpillar and Bernafay Woods.

July 2 brought heavy rain.

We had a new art/obs flight Commander, Captain Smith-Hawkins.

On July 3rd, we had a visit from Boom Trenchard and Maurice Baring. The C.O. at Vert Galant, Ferdy Waldron, was missing. Then Trenchard and Baring stood at Squadron until after dark, hoping to hear a returning Morane engine. Waldron was one of the pioneers who had first come to Fance with General Henderson.

Trenchard lowered his legendary voice to ask, "Father still mucking about with Curzon and that lot? Still going after the B.E?"

As far as the inquiry, "said Brand, "Father thinks O'Gorman will have to go."

"Um, "said Trenchard, at this mention of the head of the Royal Aircraft Factory. He leaned back to light a cigar, leaving Baring to continue the conversation. Baring was a far better interpreter of the General than the General himself. Behind him, a B.E. was having mud and oil taken off its undercarriage, with soap and water.

Now we were carrying bombs. They were the only way to reach beyond the range of our artillery into the German second and third line trenches, and the guns on reverse slopes. The German Generals had forbidden any voluntary evacuation of these trenches.

July 4th and 5th produced rain and thunderstorms. Somewhere out in front of us, the 13th Corps took Bernafay and Caterpillar Woods. On the 6th, the sky cleared. Court skimmed over Montauban and the Brickfields as below him the 30th Division was skirmishing with the ever-counterattacking Germans. He picked up Willow Stream,—which branched off the Ancre River just above Méaulte—and followed it to the north tip of Bernafay Wood.

He followed the ground as it rose to almost 160 meters near Pozières. There was a hail of ground fire. He turned back over the French section, and came to Maricourt, and what was left of its sleepy streets and a church with a statue of the Maid in a full suit of white armor.

On the 8th, the 13 Corps struggled into Trônes Wood. Their only safe passage was a lone trench named Trônes Alley. They fought every inch of the way under the protection of General Fayolle's French guns on the right flank.

On July 11th, we would be spotting for the 18th Division. They were using a new creeping barrage which had been such a success it was emulated across the Front. A creeping barrage was like a curtain moving just ahead of the men, forcing the enemy to keep down until our infantry were on top of them.

Our air activities were performed largely uncontested. Hawker's command to his squadron was:

ATTACK EVERYTHING

And they did.

July 12 was a busy day, but showers closed us down in early evening. Chambers put an inquiring head into Brand's office. Would we come to the Mess to see a play? When we were all seated, someone ceremoniously lit the biscuit tin and candle footlights.

Brand had been asked to perform some theatre, and he produced several skits. It now appeared that during the period of rain, members of the squadron had written and rehearsed something. Apparently the men had plucked up courage to try it out themselves!

A figure stepped out in front of the curtain. It was robed and wreathed like the Attic muse, in ribboned sandals. A red sash ran diagonally across its bosom in the fashion of Brittania.

It was Lieutenant Chambers!

He held up a hand for silence from the dress circle to the balconies in a Keansian manner.

"Come not hither in the instance
You seek song, or dance, or jest—
For tonight, it is our stance
To present you with Significance!
We intend you be offended
To the limit of your wits;
Then we'll take you to be mended
By some music and a bit
Of commentary which entrances—
And makes one feel wiser than his circumstances
That's the stuff to make a hit!

Brand had prepared to be bored, but the rest of the audience whistled and clapped and someone even threw a bouquet.

But then another figure shimmied out from the wings. He kept sideways to us until he was front and center. He turned around. He was labeled 'Mr. Henrick Ibsen'

Brand groaned. He realized what was coming.

Ibsen said, "By arrangement with His Majesty
I've let out one specific play
Can't you guess what these lads plan?
It's a spoof of my drama 'Brand.'

There were cheers from the floor. The curtain parted; there stood Agnes, Einar, and Brand. Einar was sporting some converted cowboy hat. I suspected maybe he was supposed to be a cowboy. I suddenly noticed Chambers was also playing Agnes. I was wondering how much of a roman à clef this was meant to be!

Einar is going about his role, introducing Agnes to Brand.

Lo, Agnes, here's a solitary self
Gloomy from his childhood days

See if with some woman's stealth,
You can chase the clouds away.

Just then another figure emerged. He was labeled, 'Plot.'
"Pardon me, chaps," he said to Einar and Brand. He pulled across a curtain of blue ridges across the stage, ,saying,"This is the fjord scene." Then he disappeared.

"Very well," said Einar, turning toward Agnes:
'Agnes, my beautiful butterfly
Let us go on, you and I,
And revel down the summer nights.
For I am too proud to fight!"

The audience let loose with a host of catcalls and remarks about Woodrow Wilson!

The stage Brand—who was in khaki—came up to Agnes:

Will you come with me, my dear,
To a place that's swell,
To the very seat of fear,
The very door of hell?

Someone called, "He's talking about the estaminet at Flixecourt!" The audience burst out laughing.

'Brand' continued,
Will you help me with the job
Of burying this old world's God
The world shall be our new stage
Where you and I will write a page
About this debacle-cum-war:

For those who wonder what they're fighting for!'

Agnes looked back and forth, at Einar, and then at "Brand', wringing her hands in the best melodramatic indecision. Finally she declaims:

Einar, I regret to leave you
And my native soil,
But I must follow the true
And manly scent of castor oil!
(Cheers burst out)!

Agnes then burst out:
You can use your talents to make sense
Of lives that are one large immense
Towering mountains of offense!
Who drink, and curse and then get laid
And don't go to church parade!
If you can master the West End,
You should be able to send
Some chap West with a real soliloquy
One that doesn't have to gild the lily.

Suddenly, outside the klaxon blew. We did not realize the rain had stopped. We were in for an unusual nocturnal visit from a German bomber. In the dugout we all pressed together, except for one man who ran to turn off the electric lights. The underground chamber with sandbags for a roof was full of smells of infrequent baths, castor oil, and sweat trapped in heavy military uniforms. Smith-Hawkins, Phillip's replacement, was on one side of me, embarrassed at being squished together and leaning sideways in a posture which reminded me of a stork.

There was an explosion at one end of the tarmac. Our ersatz anti-aircraft machine gun began firing wildly. Since they were using ammunition which included incendiary bullets, Brand jumped up and shouted, "Don't fire tracers! They will pin point us!"

Suddenly the aircraft veered off. Shovels were broken out with many a joke. The bombing holes were filled in. Our nocturnal visit was part of a German counterattack against one we had launched on Trônes Woods. But our Tommies held on, and we kept the right foothold of the base of General Haig's plan.

This sort of barrage was going to be used for the 13th Corps, who were going to sneak out into No Mans' Land in the dark of July 14th for a night attack. This was Rawlinson's idea, and Haig and Fayolle did not support it, although Fayolle promised artillery cover. In fact, one British General pledged to a French colleague, to eat his hat, if it did not succeed. The men had white strips to hang onto to guide them in the dark. In daylight, Court saw them lying on the ground like covering from unwrapped mummies. The General did not have to eat his hat.

Haig, after its success, called it "the highest tribute that could be paid to the quality of our troops."

The next day, the Germans were observed bringing trains up with troops milked from the line and Lens and Lille. They were stiffening. But our attack pushed through Longueval; then into Delville Wood behind it, with the aid of South African troops.

Meanwhile, the 13th and 15th Corps wanted to take High Woods back. The 13th wanted to use the new rushing tactics they had learned from the French. The 15th Corps wanted a cavalry charge. Unfortunately the horse soldiers were all the way back at Morlancourt.

We had a visit from the French art/obs officer, who wanted to meet Phillip's replacement. Like General Foch, he thought the British artillery had spread their targets of fire over too many targets. He said he expected pockets of resistance at Longueval. He was right. Meanwhile, as the cavalry horses picked their way along, work parties of the infantry were filling in holes and placing planks over bridges to help the horses. The Germans made their way back into High Wood. Court reported he had seen the Decclan Indian Cavalry, readily spotted by their turbans.

"By God," said Court, "they are still carrying lances! I though pig sticking had gone out of style."

Some of German troops crossed a road and plunged into a field high with corn; it sloped up toward High Wood. Our men were firing at the corn from Delville Wood, but, due to the shelter of the corn, men were having a hard time to spot the enemy until a pilot from 3 Squadron flew his Morane low, his observer firing tracer bullets into the corn and the Switch line, which revealed the whereabouts of the hidden enemy. When the horses arrived at 7p.m., they were beaten back from all but the edge of the wood under heavy fire. All forces retreated the next day, July15.

The Germans re-took High Woods.

CHAPTER 62

Now it was time for the M.O. to strip off Brand's cast. It had been eight weeks.

Photographs showed that Jerry was milking his line for more troops; in fact, by the end of the month the Germans would have more than twice the number of battalions on the Somme than they'd had on July 1.

Smith-Hawkins flight was taking its time becoming used to their new flight commander. The members of the flight would demonstrate their lack of nerves by putting down a hand of bridge and joining the flight's preparations for take-off, only to return and pick up a hand again. He finally made his way into their favor when rumor had it Mr. Churchill had called this offensive 'fruitless.'

"What the hell does he call Sulva Bay?" he had exclaimed.

Headquarters sent a request for a long reconnaissance which would demonstrate how many new German forces were being filtered in to the battle. Brand was the one generally assigned to this sort of mission—he was good at it, and despite the general orders that commanding officers should not fly, Hawker flew, and was not reprimanded. There was no direct order, but there was an assumption.

Brand had his Morane taken out of its hangar, the motor removed and given a tune up, and the rest of the machine gone over with a fine-tooth comb.

She was a small, speedy and dangerous machine. She had been flown against a captured Fokker at St. Omer and judged superior to it. She stood a bit over seven feet off the ground, gazing up at the B.E.'s as a pony would at a less diminutive horse. Her single wing jutted out from the fuselage just below the cockpit. She had sluggish rudder and aileron control, and such a quick elevator that the slightest forward slick of the stick would set her on her nose.

There she sat in the morning air, a lady impervious to her many critics, who claimed she was nothing but a fast ticket West. Her mitered fuselage, which fed into a conical cowling which gave her a nicely streamlined nose which was painted red to distinguish it from a Fokker, gave her the sobriquet of Bullet. Her mien was ferocious, with a two-bladed propellor thrust through her spinner, which looked vaguely like the bone through the lip of an African warrior. The stubby shape of the propellor had the incidental virtue of helping keep the petrol pressure up on her rotary engine.

Like any real lady, she feigned indifference to all her rivals, and to rumors she might be supplanted by a newer model, a Type AC.

We both knew it had to be done, but I was having strong impulses such as going AWOL together,—Switzerland? I couldn't sleep and I couldn't pray.

Morning came too early, but I was awake anyway.

There was the Morane on the tarmac.

Brand came walking toward me on the way to his machine. He stopped beside me and said in a low voice, "Always remember that I love you."

"And I you."

Then he put everything out of his mind save for the mission he was supposed to accomplish.

My legs wouldn't work; they were too shaky. I stood and watched.

Court came up to speak to Brand, and said, "You can't take this mission, Brandy. You don't know how the Front looks now, and you can't even straighten out your arm."

Brand began to reply when Court cold cocked him. He sprawled on the grass. There was a collective gasp.

"Get a Bristol out." Court told his air crew. "Get a stretcher for the Major." As Brand was out cold, Courtney was commanding officer for the interim. His crew obeyed him.

It was a court martial offense to strike an officer.

The Medical Officer and an assistant came with a stretcher and rolled Brand onto it. I followed behind, my back to the tarmac, my ears picking up all the signs of a take off. Court disappeared into the distance.

Brand was coming around, but still woozy. "Where am I?" was his first question. Slowly he came around and got up.

"He hit you, sir," said the M.O.

"Don't think I don't know it," Brand replied, touching his jaw.

"What are you going to do?"

"Bloody well wait until he returns." He proceeded to walk around the aerodrome so everyone would know he had recovered.

The day wore on into night, and still there was no sign of Court. Brand ordered bonfires to be built on the tarmac, laid out in an L shape. My ride had forgotten me in the events of the day. I was just as glad; I stood waiting with the rest.

Finally Brand said to Chambers, "Mark him down missing."

It struck me that Brand would try to complete the mission tomorrow, with a horror that held me paralyzed to the spot. I just managed to get into the car which drove me to Madame's. I couldn't sleep, so I got down on my knees and prayed.

The next morning they told me he had left shortly before dawn, to take advantage of the darkness. I tried and failed to operate normally; I filled out a report that Chambers told me was all wrong. It was a long reconnaissance; the wait would be correspondingly long.

Hours later, we heard the sound of a rotary engine and all rushed outside. Those of us on the field became aware the Morane's progress toward us was unusual, unsteady. It would have a rough landing. After Brand cut the engine and his crew ran out to grasp the wings, and the Morane rolled to a stop, he did not get down. Chambers called for a ladder. The M.O. climbed up to the cockpit; he gestured for assistance.

They lowered him down as gently as possible and placed him on a stretcher. My feet began to work again. As I came up, they were easing him out of his flying coat, and the bottom of his shirt and necktie were bloody. On the faces around me I read the grim news that they were coming to grips with losing their commanding officer.

He had been shot in the abdomen and the M.O. put on a dressing to stop the bleeding. Brand spoke very haltingly to Chambers, telling him what he had seen as best he could. Brand reached sideways and grasped my hand in an iron grip which only tightened. Outwardly he gave no sign of pain. Spenser drew up with a regular tender with a mattress in the back; regular ambulances were supposed to give way to military traffic, and a tender was military traffic. I knew where he was headed; the nearest Casualty Clearing station sheltered Bonnie.

Since he was still holding my hand I stepped up as they lifted him, and sat on the floor of the tender beside him. It was better sitting down for now I was trembling with shock. I would have given anything to have someone who could tell me how to interpret the blood which slowly stained the dressing, and if it signaled Brand's last moments. Now we were no more an active part of the war, but part of its detritus. Over and over I just prayed, "O Lord make speed to save us, O Lord make haste to help us."

He made one utterance which informed me he had left everything—not just the literary effects—to me. This was not especially reassuring. He was chilly to the touch and labored to breathe, and I tensed as I listened.

Finally, I stretched out beside him. It comforted me.

In the heat of the day, his skin felt chilly to my touch as I clutched his hand.

Spenser was trying to make the best time he could and cursing volubly at each delay. At last, we pulled into the reception area of the Casualty Station. Orderlies lifted Brand down and into the seriously wounded section.

Then, as if in an ironic comment on all our moral niceties, they cut the clothes off him. It was the first time I had seen him naked. An orderly wiped him with a hot sponge. Another orderly went through Brand's pockets and handed me the contents, telling me to be careful they weren't stolen. He was being covered with hot water bottles and blankets to build up his strength should they decide to operate.

Then the doctor appeared who was in charge of triaging. Was he too badly injured to be saved? Bonnie appeared at my side, asking what had happened. This lent a positive element. The doctor put back the blankets and contemplated his stomach. The personnel awaited on the decision of the god of this place.

He said, "Laparotomy. Get him ready."

Then he paused and took Brand's pulse and frowned. He cast a Draconian eye on Spenser. "This chap could do with a transfusion; would you oblige me?"

I glanced at Spenser for the first time since they had taken Brand's clothes off, and saw him already unbuttoning his blouse. It was before the time they could check blood types; if they did not match, the patient got the cold sweats.

They started rolling him toward the operating theatre. His eyes were glued on me as I scurried beside him. For an instant I saw terror in them, and seized his hand, telling him I would be waiting, bending as low as I could while still watching where I was going. Spenser clung to his other side like a leech. Bonnie was in front of him, and at the door they all proceeded through to the operating room except for me. Bonnie pulled the white mask up over her face. The party went through the doors into the glare of the acetylene lamps of the operating room and the door closed.

I did not think as much as simply reacted. Hope alternated with despair.

At long last—long after I had turned sideways to lean up against the wall, trying to preserve what little strength I had left, they brought him out again, smelling of chloroform and looking frighteningly still. Spenser was right behind him, looking very exhausted, but with a hand on Brand's stretcher.

Brand was taken into the ward. Bonnie put a screen around him, which was usually done only for the dying, so I could sit with him separate from the routines going on around us. I was forever grateful. Spenser sat down beside me without a word.

Bonnie bustled in. She told us he'd had a transfusion and that they debrided away the tissue from the wound to prevent gas gangrene. She said he had been hit in the abdomen by a bullet. He must, I thought, have been standing up trying to fix something.

"Will he be all right?"

"If any waste falls into the cavity we may have peritonitis. Look here at these drains. There were two of them." —She moved his blanket back carefully.

"This drain is for irrigation. We've just stopped using saline and are now using sodium hypochlorite." She moved a post near him. "I can hook the solution here and it will drain into him. The other one is for discharge. We must watch it for puss. It's general practice to keep abdominals for ten days. Then we send them to a base hospital, then across to Blighty."

"What will happen if he develops peritonitis?" asked Spenser.

"It is often fatal. We must wait and watch the drains. "

I waited, seated at the end of what had formerly been a dormitory building for girls learning the fabric trades. Beds were crushed together and there were the smells of blood and puss and sphagnum moss, dilute of garlic and saline solution.

The doctor appeared behind the screen. He was a surreal figure in his whites decorated with blood. His manner was as artificially cheerful as a man is who has had to be cheerful when there is nothing to be cheerful about.

"Here's the bullet I took out of the Major," he said, handing it to me. I closed my hand around it without looking at it.

"He must have been down near the ground because it is a rifle bullet, probably from the infantry, lucky, if it were a machine gun would, there would have been more than one bullet in him."

The doctor left.

I was given the status of a relative of the wounded, and I was very grateful. I could not have left him. Spenser was of the same mind, but two hours of sitting in the anxiety and succeeding in numbing boredom of a hospital made him decide to return to the aerodrome.

Bonnie stopped briefly to tell me I could sleep in the tent assigned her. She said Brand would have only fluids, and that we would feel his abdomen to see if it was hardening, listen for bowel sounds, and taking his temperature, as well as changing the dressings. Since some of the doctors at the Station were homeopathic, they'd try aconite drops. I had moments of awe watching Bonnie.

"Hey, sister," said the man in the next bed when she emerged. from behind the screen. You haven't got any fags, do you?"

Then began a period of Brand falling into a troubled sort of sleep, or, a demi-awakeness, all dimmed by morphine. Sometimes he would recognize me. At other times he would talk to me half-incoherently about people and things of which I knew not. At other times, he seemed to see Courtenay. If he would look that way, or start to talk to him, I grew frightened and called him and called him until I interrupted his communion with the dead. He seemed to have forgotten the recent present completely.

I would creep out to Bonnie's tent and lie down with my clothes on, then start awake, and in the night, stumble back to the ward on the duckboards which would guide my feet. He was still there, lying still, remote from me, empty of all magnetism which flowed between us, a bundle of stilled energies concentrated purely on its own survival.

One day, the Curé came in a donkey and cart with provisions from Madame, and I was so moved, I hugged the bread close to me.

Bonnie appeared. She had something to ask of the Curé. "If men die without the last rites, will it harm them?"

Père Anton laughed. "God can deal with men's souls. Haven't you heard the story of the man who was dying crying out, 'Yes! it is the good God on the telephone!' It certainly beats the ritual 'God, I give my life freely for my country.'"

The gramophone had been playing 'It's a Long, Long Trail a 'Winding'; it was switched off in deference to the clergy. The Curé took the seat beside Brand's bed, greeted him as if he could hear him, and announced he would read from his breviary. 'My soul waiteth for the Lord more than they that watch for morning," he read. Brand was still, as if he were listening.

Before he left, he handed Bonnie a bottle with some liquid in it. "Madame has made some sweated beef. It is very restorative."

I went back to him and put my head on the pillow next to him. "Entreat me not to leave you," I implored in the words of Ruth. "Where thou diest, I will die, and be buried beside you."

I kept looking at the drains, half hoping, half fearing.

The next morning, Brand opened his eyes and recognized me. If I tried to leave, he would seize my hand.

Bonnie took me aside." Do not become completely optimistic," she said. "They often rally before the end." However, the next day he motioned me to bend over so I could hear what he wanted to say. "Have I babbled of green fields?" he said (one of the disputed wordings in Shakespeare.) From then on, he continued to improve slowly, and there was talk of transporting him to the railhead at Vecquement, then evacuating him to Rouen.

I went outside to rest. Nearby was a little devastated village, but with a rivulet of water still controlled by a stone wall which passed to the town fountain. Feeling oddly alone, I gazed about me. I heard a creaking noise; a woman was coming, pushing a wooden wheelbarrow. She wore a black dress with a protective apron over it.

She was one of the women one saw everywhere, guiding a plow, leading a team of horses, binding and stacking corn in the fields, running wheat or oats through a threshing machine. Something told me she was a young widow.

On the dashboard of the wheelbarrow a large yellow cat was perched, waving his tail majestically to keep his balance. Behind him stood two wooden slatted buckets held together with metal bands, containing laundry. When she stopped, he jumped down and began rubbing against her legs as she lifted the buckets and put them against the wall, and removed her sabots. When she began washing the first bucket, he jumped onto the load in the second one, lazily contemplating his world.

In the middle of licking his paw, he noticed me. He deigned to get up, stretch, then jump down, coming over to extend his feline greetings and perhaps get his ears scratched.

Startled, she gazed about her, sensing he was gone.

He jumped into my lap, and I scratched his ears; when I saw that she missed him, I got up with him in my arms and returned him to her.

'Where have you gone, oh men that I love, where have you gone, my company.'

For her, all the faces coalesced into one, lost, beloved face.

CHAPTER 63

Several days after Brand had gotten back onto solid food, Spenser arrived to take me to Madame's to collect some of my belongings. I was to meet an ambulance with Brand in it at Vequemont late that afternoon, and go on with him to a base hospital at Rouen. I could take this train because I had telegraphed Sir Henry, and he had recalled me.

"Mandra," he had said weakly, "Ask the new C.O. if anyone got a photo of Court's wreck. Get my money and my papers and Augustus"... he trailed off.

At the last, I glanced back at the straight backed figure in her long skirt and red cross, returning resolutely to her duty." Just a minute," I said to Spenser. I ran after Bonnie. I said goodbye and thanked her.

Now, when the aerodrome came into sight; it would be the last time I ever saw it. Every familiar vestige of it would press in on me with an intensity which was borne on the desire to remember. It had become my country and my home. It had become my home and my country in a way that my native country and home would ever be.

Captain Yarrow met me at the door. "Howja do, Miss Ten Eycke," he said with a little bow. He was a younger man than Brand—not surprisingly. "We have the Major's kit all put together. How is he? I hear it was rather touch and go for him."

"It was pretty awful."

"Rotten show for you. I've been whipping things into shape—new boy in town, that sort of thing...I got rid of that Morane—deathly little beast. When a sergeant showed me the copper wire he wrapped around the air screw in case the deflector pates did not function perfectly, I'll tell you, it made me go completely goosey! Wherever did he get ahold of these Le Prieur rockets?"

"I hope you gave it to Hawker."

"As a matter of fact, I did. He rang me about it. He told me to also send the Le Prieurs , which he pronounced Le Prayers.

Then I remembered I had a mission. "Captain Yarrow," I said, "I realize this is an odd request...one of the Major's friends was killed in mid-July. He crashed near Trônes Woods... could anyone snap a photo..."

I thought he might think I was morbid or deluded, but he treated it as a perfectly normal request.

"Why don't you leave it with me," he said.

Sgt. Wilson was waiting for me. In his hands were Brand's flying scarf, the bottom brittle with dried blood. Suddenly, I was desperately anxious to get to the rail head and make sure he was all right.

"Tell him I shall write the news," said that good man. "Where shall I send it to?"

I had nothing to write with. There was nothing for it but to ask Lt. Chambers for a pencil. He granted me request without really seeing me as if I were a ghost.

At the house, Madame suddenly embraced me, and began to cry. She felt me evaporating from her grip.

We made the run to Querrieux in silence, then swung south through at Bussy-les-Daours. We stopped at Vequemont on the north side of the Somme.

There was the railway platform station. Sweating stretcher bearers were unloading ambulances which pulled up with relentless regularity, discharging their contents two from the bottom, two from the top. Several women canteen workers in snappy uniforms walked up and down the rows, bending low or sitting down on the platform, lighting cigarettes, writing out service postcards, giving drinks and dispensing sweets.

"Where are you from?" I asked.

"Why, we are the Smith Unit!" She replied.

"You stay here with the luggage and I'll look for him," said Spenser. I watched his figure intensely. He did not seem to find Brand and I grew apprehensive, remembering my uncle telling me sometimes drivers of ambulances would just throw out the body of a man who had died. I watched every incoming ambulance like a vulture.

"Here he is!" Spenser yelled. I ran over. How thin and pale and fragile he looked in the full sunlight.

"Hadn't you best been getting back?" Brand asked Spenser. He was no longer Spenser's C.O. so he didn't want to make trouble for him. Spenser hung on for a few more minutes, holding his place in his old squadron for a moment before starting off to find his place in his new one.

The grey train with red crosses on it rumbled into the station. Brand was only thinking about things dreamily, without the concern of a well man; he was a sick man, and like a child, he was happier to have his own way than a well man could have imagined he could be.

The loading process began and it was clear it would take some time, while we were at the back of the aggregation; there was nothing to do but wait. With his fingers laced through mine and the sun on my back, I was suddenly very glad to be alive and with my love.

At last we were on the train, with me seated on a supply box across from the holders in which Brand's stretcher had been placed; the crowding, the heat, and the smell suppurating wounds made me remember the Clearing Station. We crept along through the long French twilight; the roll of the hills grew steeper as we moved toward the Channel. The train moved slowly, stopping inexplicably from time to time as more than once we were shunted off onto a siding while a military transport passed us. Nursing sisters and orderlies were up and down the aisles beside the stretchers, which had been arranged eight to a carriage, occasionally aided by several of the walking wounded.

As the darkness slowly embraced us, I slide over next to him and crouched on the floor out of the way, my hand on his arm. A sense of slothful passive dreaminess had captured me as we rocked along, a cortege of helpless men being borne where fate would toss them.

Brand began to be restless. He whispered my name. Untold thoughts and wisps of anxiety were assaulting his pain-dulled brain. Suddenly, he whispered, "Would you mind terribly if we don't have children straightaway? I feel too knocked about to be a father."

"No. I don't mind." As far as I was concerned, reality was only the two of us.

I sat nodding beside his stretcher, in a position my muscles would regret the next morning. Brand concentrated on absorbing the pain of the joltings of the train; morphine was only given as an absolute necessity.

Shortly after dawn we reached Rouen. The unloading began. Ambulances pulled up to take the men off to General Hospital No.2, and the newer facility at the racecourse. Brand was tagged for a Hospital Auxilaire.

I'd assumed I'd be taken up with him, but there were no orders to cover me.

Dizzy with fatigue, I asked what to do.

"You can find a taxi in the station!"

After about a twenty minute walk, I found a horse-drawn taxi. I explained my situation. He asked if he should take me to a nearby hotel. I agreed. I asked if he could drive me back to the station for my extra luggage. There, I learned that all the luggage had been stored.

With a hole in the sole of my shoe and hair tied back with a ribbon, I hardly looked like a person seeking a good hotel. I had never booked a room, paid a bill, or ordered a meal. It was frankly seedy-looking and recalled all Madame's lectures about lice. I signed the register and a young boy wrestled my baggage upstairs. I kept ahold of my traveling valise with documents and money, letters of credit for Credit Lyonnais and Comptoire d'Escompte ; I had also hung on to my violin.

An orderly opened the door to Brand's cell—small, but amazingly, after all this time—a private room!

The nurse told me the doctor wished to see me in the empyrean of the hospital. "Hurry up!" she instructed.

The doctor was brief but clarifying. "He has had no major organs hit, and his sexual organs are functioning," he said, emphasizing the last as if it were something I would want to know. "The trouble is the doctor at the clearing station took a little nip out of his intestine, then sewed it up, so we will have to find out what he can eat without difficulty."

"Have you told him yet?"

"Go back down and visit with him. I'll stop by later and then we can tell him."

When I got back to his room, however, I found the doorway blocked up with hospital personnel who had crowded around the figure whose back I could only see.

Robert Loraine had come to visit Brand.

He had brought one flight of his squadron to France at the beginning of August, and called around to find his friend. On the first dud day, he'd flown his F.E.8 to Candas and begged a motor for Rouen. The weather was not the best, but he had pioneered flying in bad weather.

Now a group of V.A.D.'s and Sisters were hovering in the doorway, eyes gazing raptly at the physiognomy New York critics had called, "New York's most beautiful man."

The Matron came and shooed them all away. She was not immune; with a sly smile, she asked him for an autograph. He obliged with a flourish. His voice, in this small room, was circumscribed, like a horse under strict rein, for his tones were born to reach the last row of a theatre.

Brand presented me.

"I'm told they thought you might be scuppered! They thought that of me, too, old boy, but here I am again."

"Last I knew, you were at Gosport."

"Righto, I was working up Squadron 40, which was originally slated for reconnaissance; but then we were assigned escort duty with bombers. It was dicey—men kept flowing into training and out to the Front—so many, that I and one lieutenant were the only originals left."

"What are you flying?"

"FE8's. They didn't come through right away so we trained on DH 2's. But I flew both prototypes in Squadron 5.

"You are based where?"

"At Treizennes, near Aire; only Flight A has arrived. B and C will be along later. How do you read this order on C.O.'s not to fly?"

"It's a bit emasculating. But at least I had a broken arm to cover."

"I rather dread it."

"Well, old boy, you've already done a good share. How' the lung?"

"It makes me a s bit short winded above a certain altitude."

"I shouldn't wonder!"

I was the cynosure of all feminine eyes as I showed him to the door. He touched his mustache ruminatively, then polished his eye glass. "War's hard on chaps of sensitive conscience," he said, bade me farewell, and I watched him striding down the street.

A few days after Loraine's visit, we were on a hospital ship bound for Blighty. Brand's stretcher had been laid on deck, for the ship was crowded to every corner. I sat beside him and watched waves skip by on the Channel. Overhead, the seagulls shrieked shrilly to each other in their ancient language, as, miniature BE2c's, Fokkers, and Moranes, they glided over us, oblivious to our human tragedies.

Now the white cliffs on the English side wavered into view through the sea mist. There was a minute's silence on the boat. Then a babble of emotions broke out at the first sighting of home.

After a long sweat of lifting and banging around corners and setting stretchers in holders we were on a train bound for the vast recesses of Victoria Station.

I was sure his father was somewhere outside when we got to London, but there was the usual crowd to watch soldiers being taken away in ambulances. When I finally reached street level, I saw a line of taxis, with the hood of the Silver Ghost among them, and I ran down the street, as I knew where they were taking him.

"Shall we go to the hospital?"

"Yes, certainly!" To my surprise, when I got into his motor, I found the Viscountess seated there. Its opulence seemed almost obscene after a Crossley.

His parents were prepared not to be shocked by his appearance but they were, of course. After greetings he asked, "Father, have you got things set up?"

"I have the rector from St. Edmund's. Amanda's aunt has let the banns be said. She said if there were complications, we could simply say things will be delayed. Amanda's aunt is waiting for her."

It sounded like a death knell; my heart sank. They agreed to come with me.

My aunt greeted me with a stiff kiss. "Sir Henry visited and told me where and why he sent you, and that you had done well," she said firmly. "After all, Churchill has forwarded the opinion nothing will gain our cause for American sympathy so much as American bloodshed in the field. You could have been an American Edith Cavell, if someone had been so obliging as to have killed you!"

She was obviously angry.

Brand's mother, always the first one to be frank, said," We are blessed that neither of them has been killed, Mrs. Ten Eycke."

"I told my brother-in-law that although I am not keen on their marriage, it is the best solution to what has been a compromising situation. He agreed."

"Would you prefer we take Amanda to our home?"

Aunt Bea made an effort to master herself.

"No," she said.

CHAPTER 64

I awakened to the smell of tea somewhere nearby. Opening my eyes, I saw my cousin at my bedside. "I was beginning to think you would sleep forever," she said in her best, beautiful, indifferent flapper tone. I sat up. She handed me the cup.

For a moment I thought I was in a dream in which I was floating in a well-ordered, immaculate world, where everything was clean, where the sheets were luxuriously soft, and my nightgown was silk.

"You can have your hair cut at eleven," she said.

"I've got to see Brand first."

"He'll be happier if he sees you with a trim!"

But she had no idea of the state I was in that would not relax until I saw him again. I jumped out of bed and ran into the tiled bathroom, pulled a warmed towel off the rack and washed off as quickly as I would have done at Madame's. Becky stared in disbelief as I threw the clothes I had come in on, and was ready to go out in twenty minutes.

"Do they think he will be all right?"

"Perhaps he will have some problems with digestion."

"How disagreeable." She made a face. I scurried off by taxi to another splendid hospital on splendid Park Lane, owned by Mrs. Freddie Guest. A butler showed me in and to the lift that had been installed to handle patients and hospital equipment. It wasn't until I got to the first story that the place smelled a hospital smell. On the ground floor the air had been heavy with the scent of fresh flowers.

A nurse pointed to Brand's door. I had forgotten precisely where he was since yesterday. I knocked, and at his voice, opened the door on a charming scene. Brand's gentlemanly aplomb had been perfectly restored by a shave and a tog-out in glorious mauve silk pajamas. He was drinking tea made from unchlorinated water in a properly-flowered English teacup. The smell of scones and poached eggs assaulted my ravaged senses, grown dead on hospital stewed beef and chlorinated tea.

A Sister in the room with the breakfast tray looked slyly at me as if I were something the cat had dragged in. Maybe Becky had been right.

"Have you had breakfast?" he asked.

"No—"

"Here. Have one of my scones." He was dunking them in his tea to soften them up. "I've been able to toddle around a bit this morning. They've made a chapel at the end of the hall. We could be married there, unless you want something more elaborate. They say they will let me go in a week."

"I'd rather not wait any longer. I'm just wondering what we should do after you are released." Brand had let his flat at the Albany and put his possessions in storage, in preparation for making a full break with the past.

"There's a hotel, and the gate house at Sous Saules."

"That sounds good to me."

"Good. Then I shall make the hotel reservation." He was quickly coming back into a bit of his old self. "Slip down and see the chapel for yourself. Make sure you like it."

I suddenly felt a tremor over the idea of taking care of Brand myself. But I didn't let on. I stepped past the rustling well-tailored skirts of one of the nurses and the coattails of a footman bearing a glass of claret to one of the patients.

For the barest instant, I tried to imagine Bonnie working here.

The chapel was dark and quiet. It had a bevy of crests, names and scenes on the stained glass windows, obviously taken from other buildings. The large front window bore a copy of the Beatitudes. Someone had tried to make it nondenominational by using plain altar clothes and adding a small crucifix in one corner, but had only succeeded in eradicating the chapel's personal quality to the extent that disinfectant covers an original smell until its pungency dissipates.

Back in Brand's room, I said it was OK. "All I have to do is find a dress and someone to give me away," I reported.

"I'll ask Vessey for my groom's man."

Aunt Bea had insisted I visit a dressmaker for a gown. It was practical, anyway, as I, too, had lost weight. I clutched the dressmaker's address in my hand; my aunt was at the door tapping her foot, fingers snapping her watch case open and shut every other moment. I hastily slipped out of my worn garments and stood still while the basted gown was lifted over my head by a slender woman with wire rim glasses. I could smell a whiff of lavender from a sachet pinned somewhere inside her bosom. I stood stock still as she moved around me, for any movement was punctuated by a jab with a straight pin. My aunt tugged at the side to indicate it should be slimmer. She didn't want any intimations this might be a marriage of necessity as well as haste.

"When can we have the dress delivered?" my aunt demanded. The dressmaker's reply was unintelligible, for her mouth was full of pins. My aunt restlessly to a table and rooted around for her cheque book. She must have dealt with this woman for a while or I could not imagine her giving payment before the dress was delivered.

"I'll send it around tomorrow," said the dressmaker as she plucked the pins out of her mouth. "Best wishes, Miss."

"Thank you."

"The Viscount rang to invite us to dinner."

"I'm going to visit Brand."

"Someone ought to go."

"Why don't you?"

She acquiesced. After Anna had helped her on with her evening cloak, I rang, only to find out Major Whitefield had eaten dinner and fallen asleep. Becky came in.

"I'm glad I missed that kind of evening. Let's send down for a tray of cocktails. Anna! Would you ring downstairs and..."

"I most certainly will not, Miss!"

"Oh you really are an old bore." Becky picked up the receiver.

"I have to call Violet," I said after she hung up.

"Must you?" She did not like my 'East End' friend.

"Righto, of course I'll come," said Violet. "I'll see you then."

A tray with a pitcher and two glasses appeared. Becky poured each glass full. Distilled hospital anesthetic: that was my first impression of a drink made with gin. Becky would finish the rest of the pitcher. Then she applied new lip rouge. "Anna!" she called. "Be a good sort! I want to put on something comfortable."

Becky extended a languid arm. Anna braced her foot against a chair and pulled her up. I sat contemplating the little clusters of silver framed photographs which had sprung up around the room. Pictures of Aunt Bea with Herbert Hoover, Nancy Waldorf-Astor, Margot Asquith. I picked up a picture of Aunt Bea with Lord Curzon and Walter Hines Page, and contemplated Aunt Bea's hat. Again, it was a sparer model of millinery which fit closer to the head, allowing less shade to fall onto her face when someone took a photograph.

Becky re-appeared in a diaphanous gown trailing behind her like a tipsy Lady McBeth, hugging the outside of the room with her hand to steady her passage until she collapsed into an armchair.

"Oh, God, I'm tight, I'm going to be sick." She ran in a wobbly way toward the bathroom, with me following her afraid she would fall, until she got her head over the toilet bowl and vomited several times, then got the dry heaves. Finally she slid over on her side, curled up around the toilet bowl, then rolled over on her back.

"Oh God, I hope I'm not getting to be a dipso," she said.

However, all was not really ready: the rector was upset at the chapel instead of his parish. So we asked Mr. Seddon. He agreed.

"I suppose I shall have to give you away," said my aunt.

"No," I said. "Neither you or my family really wish me well; there's no need to try to make nice." I left for the hospital. If she had been cordial I would have agreed.

The morning of the wedding, Anna awakened me with a breakfast tray. She unpinned the curtains and pulled them back to let the light fog of an overcast London day caress with windowpanes.

However, a little miracle had occurred: Max was on leave and in London. A perfect antidote to a grey day! He would be the one to give me away.

Brand and Vessey had maneuvered to allow him to wear his uniform. Vessey engineered most of it; Brand was now used having to be helped by other people.

Aunt Bea was now beginning to soften in her irritation enough to perceive this would be viewed somewhat oddly as reported in the paper; she began to pitch in more willingly, and plan how we would enter the hospital without Brand seeing my dress. She wrapped her evening cloak around me. When we arrived, she huddled with a little group who were embarrassed as no music had been planned. Brand settled this problem by sitting down at the chapel piano and playing "Jesu Joy of Man's Desiring." I doubt anyone thought to recognize it as German except his mother. Max was very pleased. He stood up and moved toward Vessey and Mr. Seddon. Max and I approached as Brand played and we all converged while he took my hand. As we turned to face Mr. Seddon, I heard the rustle of my skirt in the deep stillness. I stirred a bit uneasily as he proceeded in the litany to "Marriage...was ordained for the procreation of children," as I vaguely remembered our conversation on the train.

Then Brand took me as his wedded wife and I took him as my husband. Vessey handed him the ring and he put it on my left hand, American style. Mr. Seddon pronounced, "Whom God has joined together let no man put asunder."

Then, as arranged, he had two chairs brought so Brand could sit down instead of kneeling, and Mr. Seddon went through the rest of the service quickly with no sermon and ended with communion.

At the back of the chapel, Vessey handed each of us a glass of champagne for a toast. "Any port in a storm, what?" said Becky, tossing her curls to indicate she was up on the latest slang. Brand's mother was still a very erect figure, but she'd adopted the habit of leaning on her husband's arm. It gave her an air of fragility and I wondered for a moment if there was something we did not know about her health. Brand's father was beaming happily and looked as though nothing would complete his happiness as much as lighting up a good cigar. Violet came at the end of the line so we would have a chance to talk. Vessey handed her a glass from a distance which indicated she might well be infected with some slum disease.

Vessey tapped his cigarette case against his glass for our attention while he made a toast. He raised his glass.

"Make us glad according to the days wherein Thou hast afflicted us and the years in which we have seen evil," he quoted. We all raised our glasses. By now Brand was done in, and Vessey wheeled him back to his room. I walked down back the hall behind them.

Brand stretched out on top of the bedsheet. The doctor was sitting beside him in a straight backed chair, looking over his charts. "What do you say if I give you your husband tonight?" he asked.

"Tonight?" I said. I had no idea they'd be releasing him so soon.

"He's rather set on it. The hotel is around the corner in easy call. I've given him his regimen. Bring him for a checkover tomorrow. Make sure he doesn't try to do too much." I looked at Brand; he smiled sunnily. The doctor glanced at his watch. His time was not time that should be wasted.

"They're going to let him out, "I said to his father, as he just appeared in the door.

"Really?" said his father, looking like an unemployed ministering angel whose telephone had just rung. He arranged for his chauffer to pick us up in an hour; he and my aunt deployed Anna and Johnstone to put things away in our hotel room.

"Do you want me to help you with your gown?" Anna asked, but I wanted nothing so much as to be left alone. I said no and finally they left us; Brand was asleep in a chair shook his arm gently.

"—Are you anywhere as near tired as I am?" he asked.

"Exhausted." I took off my shoes. He took off his tie and shoes. We lay down together and he put a blanket over us. In several minutes we were both asleep.

I awoke and it was night. I sat up quietly. I went into the bathroom, shut the door and turned on the taps for the lure of sinking into a hot bath was more than I could resist after months of bathing from a pitcher. While the tub was filling, I struggled out of my dress.

With a sigh of delight I slipped up into the chin in hot water. The steam was wonderful...my head slipped down...I snapped up...it fell again...

"Come out before you drown," he said. He took my hand and helped me out of the tub. I stood up, suddenly aware I was stark naked.

"I'm too formally dressed," he said, wiggling out of his clothing. He was still very thin. The red scar on his stomach stood out angrily. But he also responded normally to being alone with a naked lady.

"I don't know how you are—I don't know what we can do." He took a bath sheet from the towel rack and put it around us. "The good doctor said I was not to let you play ride a cock horse to Banbury Cross with me, but that a moderate approach would be consistent with my recovery. Here, let me find you a nightgown—I don 't want you catching cold." He lay down.

"Do you want your pajamas?"

"It's ever so nice to be free of Ectoplast," he said. "No, I'm not cold, and I'm not modest either. But I don't want my casual exhibition of myself to offend you." He nodded toward his upright member.

"It does make a point."

"We both have wedding night nerves. I've never been married either."

I recalled our biological manual—it claimed losing one's virginity might be painful.

"I wish we could just get it over with," I said.

"Mandra, you are going to have to help me. It's a –bother that the first thing I am going to do may hurt you."

"Can you just—make it natural, rather the way you usually do?"

"Don't say it is you don't mean it. I'm awfully vulnerable that way—awfully, awfully."

There was a moment's silence. Then I answered, "I do mean it."

"You recall I told you?"

"Yes, about preventing pregnancy," I said.

He reached into a drawer for a rubber sheath that were sold in garages. I was a bit appalled at this unromantic side to things. "All right," he said, "I shall make it as easy as I can."

"O.K."

I could feel him release an ardor he'd held in check before. He held me close to him, but gently. When he felt passion had made me as ready as I could be, and him as eager as he could possibly stand to be, he half straddled me, and I watched him enter me with a detachment born of curiosity and knowledge this event might hurt me.

"Shall we have it over now?"

"Yes!"

He gave a hard thrust. I gave a yelp. He gave a groan of long deferred satisfaction.

Finally we were 100% man and wife.

An hour later, Brand called down for some supper and a bottle of champagne. We ate slowly, savoring what was not quite yet wartime food. Brand poured us each a glass of champagne then another.

"Are you giddy yet?" he asked.

"Ummmm..."

"Best you are, at these outrageous prices!!"

CHAPTER 65

One morning, when he had improved, his car was brought around. My trunk and his were loaded on to the luggage rack. The Viscount's chauffeur Perkins turned the crank for me, then climbed into the back seat. I nosed out hesitantly into the morning traffic. Brakes screeched. A horn blared. I jammed on the brakes and stalled right in the path of an oncoming lorry. Brand took in a breath. The lorry stopped inches from my door. The driver climbed down, casting an eye over our fast and fancy touring car with a woman in the driver's seat.

These were the days, when as C.G. Grey put it, "Driving a fast car was a man's job."

Brand got down. The driver took in the cut of his jib: although the driver may have been a prime specimen of British beef, he was only a white feathered shirker to the man in front of him who had been shooting down Jerrys in the skies of France. However, he didn't really seem to care.

"Are you sure you want me to drive?"

"Don't be a twit."

After two hours, we arrived at the gatehouse of Sous Saules. At the station, Perkins reminded me to watch out for my petrol license; it was a hot item on the black market.

It was here Brand made a full recovery. As for me, I slowly began to realize I, too, owned a past of this house: 'with all my worldly goods I thee do endow.' We had to visit a local doctor to be updated toward reclassification, which we dreaded. On these journeys Brand always wanted to take the wheel, and like most young men of his generation, he drove as though driving slowly were one of the seven deadly sins.

This was a period of strong emotions for me. What would happen when he recovered? Would he be sent back to the front? I knew that with this increased intimacy it would be all the harder for me if something happened to him. On the other hand, forget the future—*carpe diem.*

"Don't worry, I am owed a spot of home duty," he would assure me.

When that day came, however, we were in for a surprise.

Brand was appointed to a committee gathering information on his old familiar process of working out artillery shoots between the British and French. He was posted to Paris in January, 1917.

"Why don't you think they didn't order you back to the Front?" I asked.

"I honestly don't know. But Haig always says war is a young man's game, especially as it applies to the Flying Corps. I am thirty-one—and most of the members of my squadron are ten years or more younger."

"Do you think it may have to do with your father?"

"Only if someone other than he is thinking about it."

I had a surprise; Brand had written to all 'Xiema's children still living and Robert, when he heard we would be moving to Paris, set it up for us to live at the family *hôtel particular.* 'Xiema's two women were still there, and they had cleaned up the house as best they could. Of course there were things like cleaning the chimneys they needed a man to do. They had found a man too old to be drafted but not old enough that he could not still do domestic chores. Enlistments were supposed to be limited to age 38—but many 38- year -olds looked a bit more ancient.

I knew Brand could be arrogant and braced myself to absorb it, yet on our own, this side of his personality rarely exercised itself; with nothing at home to rile him up, he was more even tempered, although I could count on him to be obnoxious if the occasion warranted. We did not really argue but would have occasional heated discussions. He would now and then say it was a surprise—a good one—to have a wife that feared the Lord. We both were used to having time alone, and we would do so in Paris. I would go to an unoccupied room of the house and practice, and he would sit at a desk and write. It always a joy to see each other again!

My husband was a practiced lover, which did not particularly surprise me! On the other hand, it took some time for me to even appear comfortable being naked with him when we were not in bed.

Paris had grey, misty mornings and the streets were almost devoid of motor cars or horses, as most of them had been requisitioned. All the doctors and dentists were at the Front, so the children were largely untreated for illnesses; between mortality at the Front and pediatric mortality in city and country, there were fears for the continuance of the French population and French teeth.

Flowers were still bedecking the statue representing Strasbourg, which had been under German control for 40 years since the Franco-Prussian war. The atmosphere was always tense, and the nearer German troops came to it, the level of fear rose close to panic. Refugee children with no adults to accompany them wandered about. All street lights were turned off or burned under blue-wash shades. One American woman described the atmosphere as similar to living in a house with a person who was terminally ill.

Almost immediately, events took a dangerous turn; the Germans declared unrestricted submarine warfare. Lord Balfour went to Washinton to meet with President Wilson to suggest America build more ships.

When the Germans began bombarding Paris which began punctually every night at 9:30, I thought, ironically, that while in England I had seen the results of bombing from high up, now, I was seeing it from the ground low down. One thing remained the same, however; the fear of bombing was greatest on high moonlight nights. Foggy nights were welcomed. When the *alerte* was sounded, I raced to turn off lights and pull the curtains.

Brand's father asked him if he would prefer him to write about social events, or what was going on the government and Brand replied 'the latter.'

Lord Northcliffe has replaced Balfour in America. Diplomacy has hit a bit of a log jam. A new young Englishman, Sir William Wise, seems to have the ear of Col. House, who has the ear of the President. This young man undoubtedly has a keener perception of what the war on the ground is like, for I understand he was gassed in Flanders while serving with Duke of Cornwall's Light Infantry. There also is a rumor he is MI6.

Good that someone has a direct line as I also understand both our ambassadors--Spring-Rice in Washinton and Page here--are not in Wilson's good graces.

The staff at the Desperniers were eager to have dwellers in the house who they knew and to be able to fall back into the old routines and who could make decisions. They were rather pleased their Master Whitefield was bringing his new bride to live with her with them. They pointed out to us the nearest *abri* –air raid shelter. There was, as always, a new bed to get used to, so it was several days before we slept soundly.

It was strange but interesting to be an American in Paris as Americans began to filter in. First came the medical services so badly needed, provided by the Red Cross, seven months before American soldiers began to appear.

The committee to which Brand had been assigned was composed of three staff officers with no real experience at the Front; Brand and his compatriot, Geoffrey Mandeville, who also spoke fluent French, were there to interject reality into planning.

When a cooperative offense was planned, he and Geoffrey were to read over plans, then go to check how art/obs was progressing with the ground batteries and the air spotting of batteries, then, lastly, OK-ing the joint plans with the French. Apart from their own mission, they did not have any broader insight into the overall plan of things.

At first, he and Geoffrey did not pull together. Mandeville was somewhat imbued with the superiority of fighter aircraft and their pilots. After becoming exasperated with him, Brand acquired a list of casualties for the last sixth months, and how they were killed: nearly three-quarters of them were from artillery fire. Geoffrey was completely startled.

The first English-French attack in 1917 in which a committee participated, was a disaster. David Lloyd George was now Prime Minister, and he had succumbed to the boasting of a French general, Robert Nivelle, who claimed he could launch an offense that would end the war.

He did not seem to care who knew his plans. He had had some successes at Verdun, but on a smaller scale.

Although it was April, the British, who began the offensive, were pelted with snow and wind so badly pilots and observers had to be treated for sea sickness during Easter. A hundred horses froze. The weather was brutal. As the British moved toward Arras, the Canadians, who had practiced maneuvers all winter, were readying to join the assault.

It seems finally that the unrestricted warfare, plus something called the Zimmerman telegram, has bestirred America to declare war on April 6. From what I hear, the British offensive is not doing well, and that the French are demoralized.

Demoralized was putting it gently--the French army had begun to mutiny. When the French turn came, it developed that many of the pilots and aircraft were missing, having been sent back to ferry new machines up to the Front. The French infantry refused to leave their trenches. Other French generals attempted to cover for a brother in arms, but one had the courage to report of Nivelle, *il n'a pas été la hauteur de la tâche qu'il assumé* —he was not equal to the task.' General Nivelle was replaced by General Pétain, who began trying to raise French morale. He treated troops as if they were his sons.

This was the period named Bloody April, in which several squadrons lost 100% or more of its members, which had to be completely replaced. It was the heyday of the von Richthofen Circus.

Living as we were amongst fear, anxiety, and uncertainty, the only moments of peace we enjoyed were quiet moments when with lights turned out except for moonlight shining through the darkened window, we sat on a small sofa which just fit us both upright with me turned at the waist enabling me to drop my legs perpendicularly over his, leaning against him with my head on his shoulder, letting what silence there was wash across us, holding each other tenderly, closely, somewhat erotically, until the noise stopped and all feeling drained from us until we were one entity.

It quickly became obvious that an American army would take at least a year before it took to the field; however, our Navy, under the command of Admiral Sims, immediately began working on a convoy system, with the U.S. sending destroyers to the effort semi-monthly.

Aunt Bea wrote from London a very upset letter to tell us Hoover had returned to Washington to become Food Administrator, and her fears things would fall apart without him.

Why hadn't the British Navy planned to defend against the submarine? Winston Churchill had proclaimed the Navy was able to handle them. The U.S. Navy had a specialist in submarine warfare, Captain Frank Schofield. They were ready for the challenge.

To our surprise, one night, an arrival was announced; it was Spenser, and, miraculously, Gus. Spenser had a bag of Court's old belongings he thought Brand might like to see, and Gus hurtled into Brand's arms. Among Court's things, Brand found a Royal Engineer's badge, with its motto, *Ubique*. Brand sorted through things slowly, pausing at each one. Gus kept pushing his nose under the papers seeking attention. Brand was reading so I would take him out for a walk. Taking care of him had me walking him several times a day, and I always rather felt that the elegant French Parisian dogs found him *declasse*. At first, he would even sleep beside my bed; gradually he wormed his way up from the floor and slept on Brand's side of the bed while he was gone. Generally this was fine, unless he began to dream. I was glad of his company often when I left the house. He was a big enough dog I felt quite safe.

Brand's friend Loraine was now a Lt. Colonel, and his Wing 14, which was composed of four squadrons, were left to keep connection with the French while the rest of the British forces moved northward. One of the Wing's squadrons was equipped the new, successful Sopwith Pups. In July, Loraine was marked down as beginning to suffer from neurasthenia.

British forces were now occupying Arras. Pleased soldiers commented on its neatness; one soldier declared it was almost as clean as a civilized city. Arras sat on quarries, with much underground space which the British, aided by New Zealand troops and a unique digging machine imported from New Zealand, extended with tunnels and even turned it into an underground city like Verdun, with light gauge railroads, hospitals, and decent quarters. Their digging resulted in troops being able to get up close to the German lines before they could be spotted. The beginning of the battle was a great success which deteriorated as the battle went on, marked by General Byng and the Canadian forces taking Vimy Ridge.

The British move north continued into the battle of Messines: the objective was the ridge, measuring 260 feet above sea level, the perfect observation post. This was a very notable battle, for British sappers had tunneled under the German lines, using one false trench, and a real trench below it, into which they put a million pounds of explosives. The false trench fooled the Germans, and twenty- two mines were put in place, nineteen of which exploded, making the loudest man-made noise to date: it was heard all the way to Dublin. The ground felt like an earthquake. The flames went up in pillars toward the sky. German losses were heavy that day. British losses were light.

On the ground above, counter battery was the most important factor in preparation; however, Geoffrey and Brand were continually frustrated by the French, who were still mutinying and deserting. The British exchanged artillery units so as not to inform the Germans how many artillery pieces we actually possessed.

At this time, Brand and I were felled by the first and weakest, attack of the flu, and spent a month recovering. Later attacks of it would prove more lethal.

Quite a snafu in America with J.P. Morgan, who claim--unsubstantiated--that they were promised by Balfour the Treasury would pay their overdraft. Result: all loans to Britain were suspended by several tortuous days. It had developed that Sir William Wiseman has House's ear.

British scouting had become more sophisticated, with all information sent to the Army Control post, through which the information was centralized and distributed; as a result of all this, the first day of the offensive moved ahead by a remarkable two and half miles, through "White Sheets' and Messines to nearer the Ypres canal.

I asked Brand, "Do you think these heavy barrages could change the weather patterns? They make the air shake!"

"Your guess is as good as mine."

In Paris, in June, there was still rain and chilly fog.

While he was away, I would sit in the kitchen many an evening, at first shy, watching how cooking was done, and afraid Madame's maids had to tolerate my being there. But they gave me a job rooting among the dried herbs and bringing forth the ones they would require to cook a particular dish. Although I would still sit in a corner to be as invisible as possible, gradually, I became used to being there, and they, to have this uninvited visitor. Naturally it was more usual for them to have Gus in the kitchen, for many dogs in France could sit at the dining room table.

While he was in this area, Brand managed to visit Toc H (Talbot House), the creation of Padre Tubby Clayton. Visitors left rank at the door and intermixed. Clayton was dead set against pessimists; to enter one had to be cheerful. Brand made his way up the narrow staircase to the Upper Room, where he found a portable organ and a hymn book, so he started to play for himself, but soon groups of men collected around him and sang along. *It was some of the most awful singing I have ever heard, as some chaps were tone deaf. But the Holy Spirit listened anyway.*

The high-spirited side of Brand's personality had gone into eclipse some time ago. As one war poet put it, 'laughing hearts are dumb.' There was also a saddened kind of darkness from time to time, when, I realized he was brooding about Courtenay. He was wrestling with the fact his friend had sacrificed himself for him. I remained silent until he came out of it, until one night I said, "Greater love has no man than to lay down his life for his friends."

"I know. I will carry that with me to the end of my life."

The United States is growing frustrated by all the various British financial people pushed into the United States. There is a request for one 'big man' instead of a herd of functionaries. I heard that Wiseman had to tell Bonar Law to watch his tone dealing with the U.S.--it was the sort of arrogance that had caused the Boston Tea Party!

The next offensive Brand worked on was Passchendaele -Staden Ridge, Belgium. This area had traditionally been dry as it was reclaimed marshland, but, beginning in August, as it had been receiving torrents of rain since June, the rain and the shelling, which had plugged the drains, began to stir the earth into a quagmire of mud so dense a soldier could drown in it.

It now seems assured that the 'big man' we will send the U.S. Is Lord Chief Justice Reading. The whole month of August appears to be taken up by preparing for this mission. It's said that Reading has been sent not only to clear out the financial problems, but to advance the tactics of the Easterners. I've heard that this would include taking Austria and Turkey.

Passiondale--as it was sometimes spelled-- was a horrible situation. It was an open plain with no real cover, hosting a large -scale offensive rather than a limited one like Messines. It was so muddy they could not bring heavy artillery with them and had to settle for just using eighteen pounders. Rifles became inoperative when covered with mud. Even some of Haig's subordinate commanders urged him to call it off, but he persisted, lending sufficient ammunition to the opinion he was relentlessly wasting British, Canadian, and Australian troops. It was the nadir of British generalship.

However, Second Lt. Woodbridge, an observer, brought down Manfred von Richthofen, who was wounded in the head by a bullet.

Now it appears a Supreme War Council has been formed to which House and his party have been invited, but mainly to listen. There are no military representatives on this council. How frustrating it must be for Haig and his Generals to fight two wars, one on the Front, the other on the home front. Lloyd George had just returned from a conference at Rapollo, Italy, and will proceed after this another in Paris. Building unity is like trying to clean the Augean stables.

After Passchendaele, Haig tried to press forward to Cambrai. Brand had been nervous in the days before the Cambrai offensive, but I knew enough not to ask why. The plan was to use no preliminary barrage and no spotting. What spotting there was, was done by binocular, or low voltage registration of a battery caught by microphone. On Nov. 20 tanks moved forward, with Infantry following close behind and flattened the defenses; it did not continue to achieve success.

The first day was such a great success bells were rung in England.

After that memorable first day, however, the German lines began thickening with troops from Russia, which had been taken out of the war by the Russian revolution. They, too used a new tactic, using low-flying aircraft ahead of the infantry to clear the way. Air forces were reinforced by the von Richthofen Circus.

Lloyd George ordered two divisions south to bolster the Italian Army after its defeat at Caporetto. The Italian Army was superbly disorganized because there was no national language, only dialects—it was nearly impossible to convey orders.

A week has passed before the move to the Paris conference for which we appear to have made no arrangements, leaving the Americans to set up their own interviews with members of our government. I think that the Americans have formed an opinion on some of our lack of efficiency. I have a rumor that Wiseman really is MI6.

By this time, opinion was growing against the wastage of men on the Western Front. Churchill wrote: 'Let them traipse across the crater fields. Let them rejoice in the occasional capture of placeless names and sterile ridges." Some politicians, Lloyd-George and Churchill among them, were still in favor of attacking on a different front in the East, instead of the continual battering backed by the westerners. However nonsensical, Churchill and Lloyd George had not lost their designs on the Eastern Front. After Gallipoli, Churchill lost office and spent an entire year trying to legally prove the defeat was not his fault. It turned out he had only looked at a map of Gallipoli, not at the actual terrain. Kitchner took one look at the territory and had withdrawn the troops.

Haig concluded action on December 7. He and others of his stripe felt the war would continue on the Western Front.

In Paris, I have heard, the main bone of contention is a unified opinion of how to treat Russia after their revolution. Other than that, the main-- perhaps only--issue was shipping. The Americans, I hear, have set up a ship building entity at Hog Island outside Philadelphia--word has it they have even figured out a way to make ships out of concrete!

By this time, I had also found something to do: teaching embroidery at an *oeuvre,* which was by definition was a place to make work for women otherwise impoverished. I began to think of how they might make extra money for Christmas. I thought of setting my class to making Rin-tin-tin and Nanette emblems, these being the hypothetical boy and girl who sent the German army in the wrong direction, as it might be an item popular enough to make some Christmas sales. Perhaps it would be enough of a success that women could buy little gifts.Gus was with me and rejoiced in being patted to death.

In the end, the plan succeeded.

The issue of the moment appears to be Russia. Groups have been organized to present Allied issues to the Russia. I hear one group will be headed by the author Somerset Maugham. Their main objective, of course, is to try to keep Russia in the war, and to thwart the Bolsheviks.

We stayed in Paris for Christmas. The hiatus allowed communications of a more personal type.

I have been hesitant to write about your mother in the event of not creating worry. Her doctor had told her that the distress of these times has weakened her heart, and that she must not continue at her present rate of activities. This led me to dread I might become her jailer. I suggested she pursue her daily reading of the newspapers in bed, and, it seems she has adapted, is even enjoying, this arrangement, perhaps because it was I who suggested it. She has always presented her analysis of the news to me verbally, but, as per another plan of mine, has started to write out said analysis in bed. As usual, she is pithy and I have collected what she writes in a folio.

She has kept on accompanying me to church and asked me to read the Bible to her in the evening. As with almost all things she undertakes she is very serious about it.

"I was wondering if she were unwell at our wedding," I told Brand.

Shortly after the New Year, Brand said, "I've heard the Crillon is about to furnish an American breakfast. Enough Yanks are staying there who can't make do with croissants and coffee. Shall I make a reservation?"

"Yes!—Oh, I don't think I have anything proper to wear."

"There is a rather more up-to-date modiste on rue Cambon. Let's take a look."

He always knew where he was going; he had spent summers and some holidays with the Desperniers. I often marveled secretly at how sophisticated he was, never realizing it would be reversed when we finally visited New York. We ended up near the Ritz.

We arrived at Chanel. I was always very quick at deciding what I liked or didn't like; which was why I sometimes designed and sewed something myself. It was a suit: the jacket was plain colored light tan jersey cloth, with a flowered pattern at the lapels and cuffs and at the bottom hem.

"Would you buy something because I like it?" he asked. It was a bit more daring than I was used to, but we bought it. OK, I decided, I will get a new haircut; and I was sold lip rouge and powder. I wore it to an after New Year's dance. (There was little dancing in Paris during the war.)

"Gee, it's awfully crowded," I observed.

"Good," he responded. It meant he could hold me closer.

After several dances, I asked him, "Do you think I dress like a prude?"

I heard a low laugh. "I shan't allow you out and about in that frock unless I am with you," he replied.

We had been hearing from Aunt Bea, who appeared contented working with her prayer group, but was worried by Becky's casual approach to the flu and safety regimens pertaining to it, and shortly after New Year's we received her news. *My dear, sweet Amanda, I have some terrible news. Becky has died of the flu. I did not write sooner as I did not want you to try to cross for the funeral and be among a mass of people. People at home are terribly upset, but this disease is stalking through them, too.*

"Now someone has died for me," I said to Brand. "If she hadn't marched us down to the theatre I would never have met you. "

Now we each had our own example of the atonemement.

The year 1918 brought renewed military activity. The War Council did not believe the Germans would attack on the Western Front. Haig's forces got whittled down by leaders who were sick of the degree of attrition under the Field Marshall.

Talk is about a Fourteen Point proposal having been made up by President Wilson. I cannot help but think that the idea of making up points was suggested to him by Pope Benedict's eight points, made by Benedict in August and circulated to all governments. Indeed some of President Wilson's 14 Points seem closely related to the peace note the Pope composed.

The Easterners were wrong. On March 9, German Gotha bombers hit Paris. On the 23rd, the Paris gun started firing. March 21 brought a German breakthrough, marked by the use of Bruchmüller's artillery; poison gas shells mixed with explosives, and troops massed in a line instead of spread out over the Front. The Germans used infiltration, small groups piercing the British line, until the British learned how to cope with this: they fell back before their attackers until the German advance stopped. It was a curious psychological fact that an advance could only run so far before it would peter out.

In artillery movement after March 21, planes were in the air sending coordinates to batteries, but the batteries were moving about so much they either neglected, or did not have time, to raise their masts. Aeroplanes had been busy spotting for days before that.

General Gough had predicted the attack on his Fifth Army, but didn't have enough troops to halt the Germans. He handled it so well so he was fired. The public was led to believe it was because he botched it up, and were encouraged by his departure.

There now is an underlying fear we may lose the war. American troops are beginning to arrive, and the Allies proclaim that their use should be integration, called amalgamation, into the British and French troops-- however, Wilson and General Pershing appear to object.

On April 1, our two rival air forces were united under the rubric The Royal Air Force. John Salmond was in command of the R.F.C./R.A.F., while Hugh Trenchard was slipped sideways to command something called the Independent Air Force, which consisted of Hadley-Page bombers, (4000 Pounds unloaded) head quartered at Áutigny- la- Bois. There had been a long discussion about who should command it, but the British finally fixed it so Trenchard took orders only from the Air Board, leaving Salmond and Haig out of the picture, making Trenchard the pet child, yet one who would have to gather equipment from the French.

This is something I was party to--Trenchard offered his resignation to Lord Rothmere (Air Minister) as he was unable to see his request for more squadrons accepted. This was accomplished in March, although Trenchard was asked not to publicize it until April. As a result, there was widespread conviction Trenchard had pulled out during a crisis, and heavy criticism of him. Trenchard was sitting on a park bench when he heard two strolling soldiers castigating him. He had not realized that delaying his announcement until April would create widespread antipathy towards him.

The German Army drove the Allies back toward the Somme, but were stopped nine miles from Amiens. Ludendorff finally gave up on Amiens and attacked back on the river Lys, trying to separate Calais from Dover, while the rest of the German Army fought with the French in the south. On April 9, the Germans unleashed Operation Georgette, which was so unsettling it evoked Haig's letter of April 11:

"There is no course open to us but to fight it out. Every position must be held to the last man, here must be no retirement. With our backs to the wall and believing in the justice of our cause, each one of us might fight until the end."

The advance was so threatening that the Smith Unit had to leave its position near Amiens with only the clothes on their backs, helping the infirm and the elderly to evacuate with them.

We have imposed conscription on Ireland.

American soldiers had begun arriving in France; American divisions were almost twice as large as European divisions. These men were young, fresh, and vigorous; they all had white teeth. The French were not enthusiastic users of toothbrushes. There was tension between the French military and General Pershing, who did not want his troops dispersed between French units; he kept them together and trained them together, which the French interpreted as being held back. An appeal to President Wilson had caused some American troops to be released into Allied armies, but General Pershing insisted on retaining his main force as purely American, although he finally did approve of some troops being sent to help the French. Wilson was in favor of it too, as he wanted an independent seat at the peace negotiations.

The sympathy between French and Americans seemed far more convivial that our relations with the British; American views on segregation prevented colored troops being used with American forces, however, the French were more than happy to welcome them.

A tremendous flap over amalgamation and transport. The British and the French both wish to disperse American troops among their armies; General Pershing, however, has remain adamantine to these proposals which is creating a public rancor. He is against transporting brigades rather than divisions.

On April 20, either Capt. Roy Brown or Australian ground troops shot down Manfred von Richthofen. His wound had not completely healed. A small piece of his skull could still be seen on the side of his head. He was buried at Bertangles.

Fighting was back and forth at the end of April: on the 24th, the Germans took Villers Bretonneux; the next day, the British took it back. On the 30th, an offensive had no success against the British and French; the offensive was shut down. May was marked by attacks from German Gothas on London, until the Germans called it off. They were trying for a few brownie points if they lost the war.

The French had been driven back from Chemin des Dames, and from between Soissons and Reims; four French and four British divisions were also overcome, but at Cantigny, an American division was victorious. We also held the line at Chateau Thierry, forty-five miles from Paris, and had suffered the fiasco of the Lost Battalion.

At Dunkirk, Brand's friend Loraine was commanding Sqn 211, former Royal Navy machines. Haig called the squadron indispensable. "Salmond still wants to use him," Brand told me, "even if he is on morphine for neurasthenia. Poor chap is stuck with DH9's."

On June 30, the French attacked using the German tactic of a strong offense on a part of the line successfully. In July, Theodore Roosevelt's son Quentin, who, like Kipling's son John, was very short sighted—so much so he was once reported to have hooked onto a German squadron instead of his own—was shot down at Camery. The Germans recognized him as the son of a former President, and gave him a military funeral.

Vigorous, too, was the addition of women as clerks, chauffeuses, and Hello Girls; I was glad they were there, as it would make me less of an oddity. In Paris, in June, the weather had remained rainy with chilly fog.

August came with another offensive planned by Haig.

One tactic was to bomb out the bridges that crossed the Somme, which did not succeed very well. After the first day, the Germans started sending in reinforcements. R.A.F. assigned fighting scouts to cover our bombers, but this was unfortunate, as they kept losing the bombers they were supposed to be protecting. However, the German air force, which had always practiced the economy of leaving a fight that was not going their way, was forced, now, to fight it out.

One by one, names of villages familiar to us were re-conquered: Thiepval, Mametz Wood, Delville Wood. On the 29th, Ludendorff evacuated Flanders.

Ludendorff kept his front line further forward than necessary, to be in a stronger position when the armistice they were calling for might happen. Above all, he wished to avoid a surrender. Implacably, the Allied forces kept pushing them back: battles at Albert, Hindenburg position, Selle, Sambre. On August 8th, a defining moment came: German General Ludendorff called it the black day of the German Army.

Now it appears discussion has begun on the issues over a peace.

American troops had begun filtering in in sufficient numbers. Of course, American fliers as well as ground troops were in action now; the ebullient Elliott White Springs' opinion was succinct: the Germans could fly, but they couldn't shoot. Other Americans agreed. Wannabes who claimed they had been part of the Lafayette Escadrille began to emerge at home.

At last an end has come. Whether a stay of arms is as successful as a surrender would have been, only time will tell.

An Armistice was signed at 5a.m. on the morning of November 11 in a railroad car, a success for the Germans, who did not want a peace treaty. They even pestered Wilson on its behalf—for an armistice was just a stay of arms, not a peace treaty.

The people of north France interpreted it, not as an end to the war, but a pause, while Germany prepared for another invasion.

General Pershing informed his troops that the Armistice would begin until eleven o'clock—but not what to do until then. A number of American sub-commanders kept the war going, needlessly, until that time; while people at home in America were celebrating, American soldiers were still dying. The British made a symbolic attack on Mons and conquered it.

Celebration was mixed with somber reflection.

Before we left France, we decided to visit back to the spot we had served in together. It was sentimental, of course: a useless expedition. The war of 1918 had covered the ground with shell holes, course grass, stumps of trees, and devastated buildings, and a few squatters here and there. The only people around were generally groups looking for those whom they had lost. Later would come sight seekers.

I sat down and cried.

All of it had dissipated like a dream.

Two months later, I was standing at the front rail of a gigantic ocean liner.

The sun was just beginning to lift over the horizon. Mists were rising over the ocean waves. Occasionally the bow of the ship plunged into a wave, and sprayed my face with salted mist.

I was straining my eyes into the vast expanse before me, looking, looking for something. Then, suddenly, in the very furthest distance, I saw her. Miss Liberty holding up her torch to me.

I ran down to our cabin to awaken Brand.